THE NEVER NOT YES

A DYSTOPIA

BY

JONATHAN EPPS

MESS HALL PRESS
2025
CHARLOTTE, NC

Acknowledgments ~ Thank you to Amy Soderstrum for her editorial work through the years and her constant support. Copy and line edits by ebooklaunch.com. On page 394, Mina quotes from Toni Morrison's novel *A Mercy*.

Publisher's Note:

The Never Not Yes

All are fallen . . .

PART ONE

DECLINE

PRELUDE

Energy stopped that summer. It was on and off, at first. A few minutes here or there. Then hours. Whole days. Couple weeks. We sweat like rigged-up field horses. The electricity came on once again for forty-eight consecutive hours, and we thought we were saved. But then it stopped. For good. Connection to the Internet was like some futuristic thing. Police station and public library had it spotty, I guess, but no one else. At least in our neck. That's when Gordon Pickford grabbed his shotgun, went out back to his toolshed, and blew his brains out all over the chicken coop. Some people thought it was dramatic or cowardly. They said the season would soon change and the temperature drop. That he should have held out. What with the two years of lockdowns from the virus and now the power trouble, it didn't surprise me.

Gordon wasn't wrong in what he'd said lay ahead, just wrong to go out like that and leave his family all alone. He knew what most people had brushed off, them saying we'd done it before. The human race had done it, made do without electricity, I mean, but none of *us* had. That might as well have been ancient history.

It was going to be tough. And not only was it tougher, but it was brutal. Gordon Pickford knew that.

And those were just the early days . . .

CHAPTER ONE

Three Miles Outside Hot Springs, North Carolina—Six months into decline

His kin had called him Ant, short for Antonio, because he was much stronger than he had appeared in childhood and he'd kept the name, though resenting everyone at first for noticing his slighter stature. He'd since grown into a robust young man, slightly taller than average, which was like a small miracle for how long it had seemed to take for him to get there.

The Hobbes family went back generations in this quieter part of the country, of mostly African descent but met with the shock of European blood when the two civilizations clashed, perhaps merged, in the slave trade. The Hobbes name being given rather than adopted, the original patriarch had kept it once he'd become literate as a symbol of the admixture of ancestors whose lives it took to get him to the point of literacy and hope for a future in this English republic. The Hobbes bloodline had withstood all the travails of American history to become a well-off farming clan, the most recent patriarch of which had a take-no-prisoners style, especially when it came to dragging everyone to church.

Ant had never minded. His grandfather did his damnedest to be a good man and a better example, sharing his knowledge, his know-how, and his wisdom, even if his love came through the instruction of those things that, with his passing and in the middle of a national disaster, were much more lasting expressions of love than the occasional hug. Those, his grandmother had provided in abundance. "Hugs 'n cookies," she'd say. "That's what *I'm* here for." Though she'd undersell her influence in deference to the man, more for love and for show than what in reality was the case. Equally weighted in all the family's lives, they organized and managed their kin as if heads of some bucolic state untainted by envy but motivated by joy for life and love of the Lord.

Ant's parents had worked the farm, too, but were more aloof to the boy's daily care, not from neglect but from preoccupation with daily toil and his grandfather's need to be centrally involved with everything. They had lived, mostly unprovoked, by the old man's favorite phrase, "Everybody's happier when they do it *my* way," though his wife would improvise a comic note each time she heard it. But, to Ant's grandfather's mind, the world was too precarious, the popular culture too seductive, the tawdry influences too available to let his legacy of effort and prosperity fall to those cheaper forces.

Expected to read a passage from the King James Bible every Saturday and Sunday morning, Ant better understood the Christian spirit, its dedication to making good sense of suffering, than most of his white counterparts. Formerly embarrassed by his religious upbringing, he now cherished it, however carefully he would manage the expression of his belief around others. A Christian man, whatever his race, was once a figure worthy of imitation; now, the same type of man, even a black man, was vilified as equivalent to a white supremacist.

Ant walked with his head down along the country road, the first of a few muddied roads before the highway, where cars were rarely observed like endangered species. A federal bill to phase out gas-powered vehicles completely—thence to favor the coal-burning ruse of electric power—had made driving the fossil fuel-reliant engines a misdemeanor, liable to a large fine, but more importantly a social taboo, liable to ruination.

A weathered cowboy hat shielded his face from the bake of the sun. His grandfather had called them "rancher caps," despising the word "cowboy" as it illustrated to his memory a shiftless rider, more often law-troubled than industrious—men he'd known in his early days, the rare ones of whom disregarded basic differences in appearance. His grandfather's voice was a constant murmur among Ant's thoughts, and one scene kept replaying in his mind as he continued the journey on foot, leading his bull to the house of a stranger in the hope of finding a heifer to mate it to, one day for food and right now for luck. The murmur returned that moody memory to his thoughts, set on the kind of evening that quiets all passions and resolves one's soul within the body, and it occurred sometime near the beginning of the power troubles.

Electricity could be unreliable in the countryside in good times, especially in the wake of severe storms, but the constant in and out of the power was not yet the daily norm. Everyone had had their theories about the flickers once a pattern had been discerned, as countryfolk did and do, where they find themselves, but managed on with life as if it were the least of their concerns. Strife was just one parcel in their total package.

Ant had been summoned to the reading room. Walking toward it, he'd heard the old man bickering with himself.

"*Goddamned* light," he said, like an ancient schoolmaster disgruntled at a problem that never went away. A faint rattling of metal filled the hall. Ant stood at the entrance to the reading room and watched as his grandfather choked a lamp like a goose.

"What're *you* laughin' at?" he asked his grandson, both from humor and annoyance at his predicament.

"Nothing, sir."

The old man released his hand from the ceramic base. "This thing won't stop blinking."

"Have you checked the lightbulb?"

"Have I checked the lightbulb?" he asked the air, bewildered. "Course I have." The old man reached under the lamp's shade and gripped the loose bulb, twisting it tighter. He turned the switch again, and instantly it shone, illuminating his creased and disgruntled face. "Come, sit," he said, giving Ant an eyeful, directing his grandson to the chair facing his. "Do you know why I've asked you here?"

"No, sir."

"Have you talked to your mother today?"

"A little."

"She say anything particular?"

"No."

His right hand stroked his grizzled mouth and chin, as he stalled to find the words. The tension in the man unnerved the boy. "Your mother, son—" He fought back tears. "She's not doin' well at present." Ant shuffled in his seat. "You seen her go to her room a lot?"

"Yes."

"Well, she's got a sickness. She's got a cancer in her."

Ant's eyes widened at the news, his stomach tightening at the way it had been phrased.

"Don't get scared, now. Don't get weak on me. I need you. I need you to be as strong as I used to be." Ant nodded, fighting it back. "Your father—" He paused again, then looked directly into his grandson's eyes. "You're a man now. Been one for a while. I'll say this to you once. Your father—he ain't worth shit." Ant nodded some, more reluctantly this time. "You best know that from me." He leaned forward. "I don't know how long I have for this world either, and your mother is going to get sicker. She's seein' the doctor in town, and we're gonna try and do all that we can, but you need to brace yourself for the worst of it, you hear?" Ant nodded more forcefully. "And with these power outages and this strange stuff happenin' in this world today, you better do more than nod at that. I'm counting on *you*." His pointed finger tapped the young man's chest, near his heart. The landline rang.

"*Hel*-lo." A neighborly expression removed the sadness from his face. "Uh-huh. I'll be right over." He returned the receiver to its base and stood. "You come with me now. Gordon Pickford's locked himself in his room again an' won't come out."

5

* * *

Before Ant set out and down the road, he rummaged through an old box in the front hall closet—the morning hour was sadder than his memories—looking for anything that might be handy to have on the journey, or anything he might want to look at for strength: an overlooked tool, family photos, some kind of memento—anything to give him a reason to continue valuing his life. He picked out his grandfather's old handheld radio and checked the underside, which was missing its cover, but two AA batteries were secured in their slots. Surprisingly, it switched on, and he turned the dial until the static resolved into a clearer sound. A grave-sounding voice droned from the box like an aging man flattering an impetuous child:

"Now, I want to be very clear—" Soft applause from a previous statement fell into silence. *"Too much of what's happening in our country today is not normal. I know this. You know this. We know this . . ."*

Ant caught himself nodding with the opening sentiment, but shook free of it, remembering his distrust of the man, of all of government. The monotonous rambling, like a mesmeric spell, continued in the background of Ant's spiritual defiance.

". . . our problems . . . change so that we may reemerge a monarch and fly on into the future . . ."

Then came the aggression, the offensive posture held for any countryman who might question the will of his superiors.

". . . the Other Party today is dominated, driven, and intimidated . . . former president and the Bleed Red cohort . . . threat to this country. They lie . . . everything is doomed. This is a lie. We have never been stronger, nor more united. The economy is back. Jobs are everywhere . . ."

Ant didn't have to reflect much to remember the countless hungry souls he knew who'd turned to drugs because their education was inadequate, and the jobs had fled the country to some other place.

"*. . . threaten the very foundations of this republic. They promote authoritarian leaders, and they fan the flames of political violence that are a threat to our personal rights, to the pursuit of justice, to the rule of law, to the very soul of this nation.*"

The scuff marks on the old radio box came off easily with a little spit and thumbing. Ant's hands could busy themselves, but his higher senses were distracted out the window toward the family gravesite; he shook his head at the hypocrisies of day, the tyrants his grandfather would have confronted without hesitation—the world gone totally mad with lies and the kind of fraud that hid behind unimpeachable language. Language to nod at, a heresy to reject or to deny.

That night, he couldn't sleep, too focused on the threat he felt embedded in the President's speech. He had wanted to sign up to Bleed Red after hearing one of them speak at the paint-stripped recreation center in town. Now, the government called anyone affiliated with them terrorists. Ant was a young black man. There were other black men from his community at the same talk. The reps from Bleed Red were all different colors, but the main speaker was a brown-skinned Hispanic of some kind. Ant couldn't help but bristle to think his forefathers had been ostracized for their color once before and now for their politics. Now, they were white supremacists too. It was almost uncanny, but he clung to himself as surely as ever. No one would ever tell him what or who he was.

The journey was a country eight-hour walk for the thirty-odd miles, making room for the time needed to locate the woman's homestead and the slower pace for being tethered to the large beast, which would pull the harness to every puddle that passed under its nose.

The animal stopped. Ant tugged at the rope, not looking back, as it pushed its front hooves into the mud, making the man a raft to a barge. It either needed to shit or to defy the enforced activity from natural instinct. Ant stared into its eyes, which stared dumbly back. It shook and jerked its massive head backward, whipping the rope, pulling the man to the ground as it grunted. The leather sheath strapped to Ant's back had loosened in the fall. He pulled the strings at his front to keep the scabbard from chafing his shoulder blades, then pushed away the bull's head now hovering over his own.

On one knee, he sighed into the distance of the open road, exasperated with the slowness of the animal. It groaned as globs of shit dropped from its backside, splatting onto the moist earth in a pile. The scent filled the space around them, moving downwind as Ant swatted the air, pulling the rope line, jerking the bull's head generally southeast toward their destination.

Boldly, the woman had given him her cell number and the address, but he'd have to find it on foot. The satellites used for public GPS had been quickly restricted to military access, but that was no matter. The now-dead phone in his pocket couldn't have been of use anyway, but he'd brought it in case this woman still had access to some power. His response to her post from the message board a month and a half before his family fell apart said he'd be open to breeding his bull to her heifer for a fee, wanting to contribute more directly to the finances his grandfather had been struggling to keep on balance. Her response hadn't come within the time his interest in the opportunity matched his attention to it, so he'd forgotten, cast it off as one of many empty hopes. When she did respond, the only Internet Ant could have accessed was the library's own sketchy satellite, and that was a good five miles from the farmstead, so her message went unanswered.

Just before GPS was disabled, his grandfather died. Ant paired the two because his mother was struggling at the height of her illness when his grandfather passed, and then his father fled in the midst of these troubles in a personal panic. Losing his grandfather, mother, father, and the GPS combined in his mind as an unwelcome promise of his fate to be alone and lose his way.

Once the grander man and patriarch was gone, Ant's father's reawakened lusts triggered long-dormant dreams of a different life, but in his will to freedom was a mental angst for lost time. He and Ant's mother argued about his plans to get to the big city, a fool's errand in its own right for the danger, but he was convinced things would be better there. He'd pulled one of the sharper machetes on his son during the young man's final plea for him to remain sane and stay with the family; its high sheen reflected a wicked slash of the sun into Ant's desperate eyes. It was then, watching his crazed, middle-aged father trip across the furrows of the ploughed field as he ran, fallow before the planting season, that Ant had realized he had inherited not only his grandfather's position but his reason, his will, and his determination to be in control of his life. Finding the better way would have to work out by the application of his particular motives and no one else's.

At this convergence of events, his mother, Mabel, lay sweaty and dying on a cracked leather sofa in the parlor, the thin edges of which cracks cut into her sides, the only pain to distract from the cancer for its difference in kind. There was no relief. She died as if she had lived like a nineteenth-century country woman in the unattended agonies of death.

"I see you," she whispered. Ant knew she wasn't speaking to him. Her eyes unseeing, her soul spoke out. "*Coming. I am* coming. My people. My family," she said, staring into the greater beyond. "My love."

Every evening and into the night before she passed, Ant would do his best to console her body, patting a cool washcloth on her fiery head and wet, heaving chest. Unable to remain still, she writhed against the malignancy of the hateful mass plotting within her; like a black hole extinguishing all sources of light, the tumor extended its wrath to encompass as much space inside of her fragile body as possible before its villainy could no longer grow darker inside the whole of her kindlier self.

Finally, one early morning, she had settled, seeming to sleep: Relief overwhelmed her body and his mind—all giving in to exhaustion. At some point, fighting had become death's ally in pain. Securing her mind to fate and the expanding love of God, she'd drifted peacefully, slowly; and then silently, she breathed her last breath.

Ant stood and moved to the kitchen as she appeared to sleep, thankful she rested, thinking nothing more, before hearing a sudden and loud gulp of air trailed by a rattling coo, startling him. He ran back into the room and gently pulled her lifeless body to his, shedding tears above her quieted form, a rousing in himself, surprisingly deep, he'd had no power to suppress. He cried for her absence, for her pain, for the knowledge that he was now totally alone as the last in the distinguished line of the farm's progenitors, the only man of the Hobbes clan left standing, and his longing for her return was subsumed by the silence.

The grave lay parallel to his grandfather's. Ant wrapped her frail body in the cleanest of the remaining sheets and eased it into place. Holding the family Bible, he improvised a prayer, a plea to preserve the souls of those who had loved him and whom he still loved, praising the day he would come to join them. Many subsequent mornings, he would stare at her plot, watching as the bright brown dirt regained its modest kinship with the dull earth, and the past shuffled down its winding coil to revisit upon a wearied mind the losses and remembrances he alone would maintain. Once the image of her grave lost its distinction in time, he made the trek to the library, where a signal, however weak, revealed the woman's answer. The certainties of the recent past had transformed themselves into mystery.

His father had freed the horses on the morning he'd abandoned the family, suddenly incensed by the symbolism of their captivity, so Ant had to walk with the bull. Tossing off the heavy thought and indecision of his memories, he quickened the pace once the ornery bull, plodding down the sorrow-filled road with its master, had again adapted to the consistent motion of the walk.

As he strove forward, Ant's heart proved incapable of abandoning the past, his mind revealing another ghastly sight, the first he had seen in the happier, more comfortable days, just at the cusp of trouble: Gordon Pickford's morbid body contorted on its side. His brains were sprayed upward against the wooden siding of the weathered shed. That was the omen of doom, but no one had appreciated its eager message, except for his grandfather, who'd brought the younger Ant to help care for the body so the man's wife and children did not have to see it. The only other image from that barren, pale morning that Ant had kept in his mind was his grandfather's face, not shocked nor disgusted but understanding, serious, and, for the first time, afraid.

CHAPTER TWO

Suburbs: Marietta, Georgia—The Beginning

"I'm nervous."

She laughed at him.

"*What?*" He chuckled. "I am. I hate parties. I'm no good at small talk."

"Yeah, yeah—you and everyone else," she said.

"Put me on a battlefield, I'm fine. A fancy dinner party? I'm toast."

"No, you're not. Calm down." She searched for a quick line to pacify his fragility. "You're the caviar *on* the toast—" she teased. "You're handsome and amazing and wonderful and never stop talking once you start—" He hadn't gotten the joke.

"I just gotta get comfortable. That's the part I hate." He pointed to the space in front of him as they walked.

"Everyone does. Relax, please. They're nice," she said. "And you get weird when you're nervous."

"I know," he said sheepishly. "What does he do, again?"

"Real estate."

He rolled his eyes. "And she?"

"Stays home, I think. I don't know. I think she has some online business thing."

"Of course, she does."

"Look, you don't like it, you can excuse yourself and walk back home. No big deal."

They hurried, and as they approached the walkway leading to one of the bigger houses in the development, the felicity of a

Super Bowl office party well underway met the more silent conditions of the chilly night air. The peak days of winter's chill kept the outside frozen quiet. But a mass of people was gathered in the great foyer of the colonial manse; a slender woman peered through the glass in the door and out at them, then opened it.

"Jenna, you made it!" The couple smiled in unison, eliminating their truer feelings. "And you must be Jeremy." She reached out her hand to shake his. He'd almost saluted her from nerves but caught Jenna's encouraging eye and gently took his host's hand, hesitating, wondering whether he should kiss it. "Come in—it's freezing out here!" she said, continuing the exclamatory assault.

Inside, the house was alive with vibrant light—the whole house afire—making every available corner of the extensive floor plan visible to guests. It was a mixed party, attended by both neighborhood folks and businesspeople: employees, clients, executives—most of whom were acquainted with the inclusive hospitalities of their hosts: the gregarious charms of the wife and the kingly generosity of the husband.

Pru escorted the newly arrived and least known couple into the dining room where a makeshift bar had been placed for the evening. "We have just about every kind of liquor, wine, or beer you could want," she explained.

"Are all of these people from our side of the hood?" Jenna asked with only partial irony as her eyes toured the room, estimating the revelers and their associations by degree and type of their finery. Most of the men wore sports coats, few had on ties. The women had donned flirty cocktail dresses or pants with structured tops: the latter more likely to be corporate climbers, the former more likely to be wives or wives-to-be.

"It's just us, babe. Nelson and I, and you two. Everyone else is either Nelson's client—past or present—their significant other, or one from his small army of agents. There's a smattering of neighborhood peeps, but they're from the west side," she said.

"We're keepin' it real on the east side," she continued, making what she imagined was a gang sign with her right hand's fingers, but looking more like an arthritic grandma pointing at some irrelevant thing pestering her clouded vision. Jenna tried not to laugh in her face. Jeremy shut his eyes in pain of the tortured humiliations to which some white people would stoop to seem cool by adopting something, they knew not what, the depth, pain, danger and belonging to which, they couldn't possibly understand.

All around the house, the lights began to flicker and then went out. The music stopped. A rush of exclamation infused the space above their heads, traveling up and down the stairs and into the many bedrooms and closets, filling the house with drunken innuendo. It remained dark, as the thrill adopted a conspiratorial whisper, a kind of fearful fretting that the party was over just at its peak, and that they'd have no choice but to stop what they were doing, discontinue their conversations, abandon new friendships, and leave without the satisfaction of a proper ending. The nervous excitement had passed beyond the point of titillation and now persisted for too long.

"*Who's* being silly?" Pru questioned playfully, hands on her bony hips. After the chattering settled into mumbling, she asked, *"What's going on?"* more seriously, as if someone in her service would have an answer. The power suddenly restored, electric music reanimated the air, and the party continued as if ever uninterrupted.

In the distraction, Jeremy had broken from the women's company and ordered a beer.

"That was weird, right?" He threw the question like a comment as opposed to a more personal greeting. "You from around here?" he asked the young man back at work, shaking an icy drink he had silenced in the outage.

"Nah, from up north a bit. I do these gigs, when I can, for college expenses." The extra information seemed like an excuse.

"Pizza and beer?"

"What else, right?"

"I'm in school myself," Jeremy announced, trying to develop the conversation, trying to relax. He leaned his elbow on the bar's edge, but it slipped off the glossy, imitation wood. The younger man observed him more closely as if he was too old to admit the fact, knowing he was being used as a test subject for more important figures floating in the sea of drunken revelers. Jeremy smiled and looked away, tucking his other hand under the mistaken elbow, propping it up as he drank.

"*Nice*," the bartender said with an enthusiasm he'd used to ironize disinterest. Jeremy pivoted and relaxed the supporting arm, placed his beer on the bar.

"I was in the military my whole career. Just got out. Decided to get my degree, make good on all that free money," he said, beginning the speech he'd planned earlier in the shower, then looked around the room. "Maybe get into logistics, or hell—even real estate with these folks right here." Jeremy gripped the beer and gestured toward the buzzing crowd. The bartender just nodded at the speaker and took an order from another guest keen to get a round of drinks. Still not comfortable with how he might present himself, Jeremy crossed the room and entered another where he could stand back and observe the crowd. Inevitably, if he talked to strangers he was trying to impress, he would ramble.

Touring the perimeter of the spacious den, packed with clusters of murmuring professionals, he edged closer to a trio of two men and one woman who looked like the kind of people he wanted to be around, maybe emulate: neither too serious nor too flamboyant. Well-dressed but not to impress, and their eye movements, assessing the crowd, seemed to match his own skepticism. Their unselfconscious coolness magnetized his attention.

"I wonder how many people *here* do?" he heard the woman ask.

"Who knows? It's like a mind virus."

"Seriously."

"I had to go to some mandatory HR training—well, they didn't call it *mandatory*, but the way they presented it, it sure sounded like a threat not to miss it." The two men murmured in sympathy. The woman shook her head, as if to rid herself of disbelief. "Anyway, it was about pronouns and how to use them and *who* is using them and *how* to announce them in meetings. It was crazy what they were saying. I wasn't even sure I understood what it all meant."

"Don't forget the 'whiteness' crap," the first man said.

"What do you mean *whiteness*?" she asked, astounded.

"You haven't heard that one yet?" The others listened more carefully. "You know, the whole privilege thing—if you're white, you're automatically granted certain privileges in society, et cetera. You haven't had to work for anything—you just have everything, somehow." They nodded but didn't respond. "And being on time and doing your job efficiently, expecting others to be efficient and on time—it's—it's hard to figure why they're doing this."

"One of the pronoun sets was, like, zeer or zer or something? What the hell even *is* that?" the woman asked, not expecting an answer.

"No clue," said the first man.

Jeremy disengaged, intuiting an awkwardness if he spoke, given the subject, and tried casually to walk off for another beer as if he hadn't heard a word. He'd had strained experiences with other kinds of people, especially tourists to his native Hawaii, where a conflict between rich mainlanders (who had been acquiring, then fencing off ancestral lands) and real-born Hawaiians grew uglier by the season. But Jeremy harbored no hate; it was more like a kind of wariness until character could be proved, and once proved, never doubted, a trait his time in the military had helped to distinguish within him. A man of good character only had to wait for time to catch up with the ignorant surmising of greedy minds.

Jenna had apparently spied her wandering husband before he had a chance to see her, startling him when she spoke from behind his shoulder.

"A penny for your thoughts," she said quietly, like her grandma used to say.

"Not even worth that much," he replied, avoiding her request.

"Having fun?"

He didn't respond, just looked at her like she knew well enough to know he'd rather be at home with their new puppy, making a sad face.

"I know, but he'll be fine in the crate for at least another hour."

"An hour?"

"Thirty minutes, minimum. We can't just walk in here, say hello, have a drink, and walk out. Pru said this was sort of a welcome to the neighborhood for us. We can't be ungrateful."

"Fine."

Smiling at his frown, she said, "You should go and find Nelson. Introduce yourself. Actually—*there* he is." She pointed in the direction of a prosperous voice. "I'll go with you."

Their other host stood before a large flat-screen unit that played highlights of the playoff games from weeks before, holding court over his newly recruited agents. Jenna found the right moment and introduced herself, then Jeremy. Nelson obliged the interruption with a cursory handshake, then resumed his extemporaneous routine.

The program was suddenly interrupted. A voice-over proclaimed a special announcement. Some of the guests quieted; some still chatted. One man said, "I know what this is. There's a virus. In the Far East. It's spreading."

"I read about that last week," an eager new hire added.

"What?" a few people asked, and then the chatter increased.

Pru gripped the wood siding of the threshold and drunkenly stepped her high-heeled shoes down into the sunken room one at a time. "What's going *on* in here?" she asked absently.

Nelson turned up the volume. "Everyone quiet down!"

"This is an NBC News special report." The next image was the President of the United States broadcasting live from the Oval Office:

"My fellow Americans, tonight I want to speak with you about our nation's unprecedented response to a viral outbreak, originating in southeast Asian swamplands, now spreading throughout the world.

"Today, the World Health Organization officially announced that this is a global pandemic. We have been in frequent contact with our allies, and we are marshaling the full power of the federal government and the private sector to protect the American people.

"This is the most aggressive and comprehensive effort to confront a foreign virus in modern history. I am confident that by continuing to take these tough measures, we will significantly reduce the threat to our citizens, and we will ultimately and expeditiously prevail over this deadly virus."

Pru's delicate, bejeweled hand covered her open mouth. A simple dread spread slowly across her face. "*Oh my god.*"

* * *

Two years later—

Jenna paused in the small hallway between the bedroom and master bath listening to Jeremy's gentle snores. The husky sibilance of his snoring eased the urgency of her otherwise hectic day. He had calmed her, not just in this moment, but fundamentally. Almost two years since they'd moved into this first new house, the excitement for renewed life and a first marriage—a future family— had brightened what was becoming a personal gloom—forever single workaholic had not been a goal per se, but it certainly had been her trajectory, pre-Jeremy. Advancement was an unarticulated expectation she'd held since childhood. But that had dissipated, as all things do, and she contented herself with possibilities previously tossed outside the scope of her pursuits. Children ranked among the top in this new era of her womanhood, and, rather than a shock, it was revelatory to imagine herself doing the work of raising children with a loving and devoted husband.

Jenna peered deeper into the darkened bedroom. The early sun peeked around the gaps of the shades, making the room look warmer. Jeremy's body, large and protective, heaved up and down in deep sleep. The ancestral kakau he'd had hammered into his flesh moved as if narrating a silent story with each undulating breath, rolling like the waves on the crest of a foaming sea. Quietly, she closed the door and went downstairs to make a decisive start to the relentless distractions of the workday which lay before her.

As a newly minted Executive Director of Marketing for a startup health foods firm, she had learned that meetings had become a way of doing work. Over the past two years—the pandemics, and their corresponding lockdowns—they were virtual, and the practice had carried over into the reawakened world. No one had gone into an office building since it began; special events, held a few times per quarter, were conducted at resorts, restaurants, or private homes: a time for executives to mingle, show off, glad-hand, or act inappropriately. She'd hated having to go.

Above her pajama bottoms, she wore a blouse and a single string of pearls her grandmother had given her upon graduating from college. Light makeup highlighted her more delicate features, and her hair, she'd twisted back into a knot, pinning it to the crown of her head. Twenty minutes before the call, she went to pour a generous cup of coffee to sit and collect her thoughts.

Grabbing the pot with her left hand, reaching for the mug with her right, she pulled it off too easily from its base. It was empty.

"What the heck?"

Looking more closely, she saw that the machine was off. There was no light behind the function screen. She leaned down to see the plug still inserted into the outlet. The stove's digital clock was blank, not even blinking from a remedied overnight loss. Just black.

"*Fuck*," she whispered.

Her laptop was still plugged into the wall. Flipped open, the screen illuminated, but the battery was at 20 percent—way too low for the newfangled holographic projection marketing had insisted they start using. Her phone on the countertop read 25 percent. This was too important a day for delays.

The power company's line just kept ringing. The Wi-Fi was down, but the weak regional signal was enough to search PGI's website for a customer service number. The outage map gradually populated with little red flags, which slowly and eventually covered a majority of the service area except for a fine vertical line running through it, where the cell towers stood.

"Power's out," she said flatly to the unlit kitchen, as if it were a joke for someone else. Two-year-old Mullet looked up when she spoke and began panting, which caused her to look around, finally noticing the lack of air-conditioning, wondering at how it had made everything look a little heavier. Helpless, but used to taking action, she swiped her keys from the rack and went out to buy some coffee, denying the futility of the reflex, hoping the local coffee chain would have a fresh pot.

The eager dog hopped onto the front seat, sniffing at the vents, anxious to feel the cool draft to which he'd become accustomed. As they began to blow, he stopped sniffing and gently shifted his head side to side, his furry snout hair fluttering wildly in the false wind. Jenna plugged the phone into its charge and called her director.

Another line that kept ringing. Not even voicemail picked up the call.

"This is weird," she said toward the windshield, scanning the empty road ahead.

During lockdown, the wait at any drive-through had become an everyday ritual, but this one was empty. Not a coffee fiend in sight. A sign was taped to the inside of the window that read: No Power/No Coffee. A figure darted across the background beyond the glare on the glass. She honked. A young man approached the window and slid it open.

"Yes, ma'am?"

"Sorry—I just—want some coffee."

"There is none."

"Really? None?"

He stared at her dumbly and nodded.

"Why are *you* here then?"

"Had to move the ice outside." He gestured to the side of the building. "So it don't melt nowhere inside." He gestured behind him.

She nodded, pushing Mullet's sniffing nose away from her face, staring at the ice but through it too.

"And now I'm fixin' to leave." His face was blank. "Have a blessed day," he said as he smacked the window into place and hitched the latch.

She remained in the drive as if mesmerized by some parallel, subconscious state. She thought of another store nearby before accepting what she'd seen earlier on the map, how widespread the outage actually was.

Her phone lit up with a voicemail. She hadn't even heard it vibrate when the call came in. An automated voice began:

"Hello, this is an automated message from the Portland home office. You are employed in one of Fresh Farm's southeastern territories. Due to the outage in four regional states, business as usual is cancelled until energy is restored. Thank you."

"*Jesus* Christ," she said. "Four states?"

She scrolled the news, most of which she'd usually ignore, and sat there reading all the headlines about the loss of power. It wasn't just the Southeast, but major outages across the Mid and

Southwest too. Intermixed among the headlines, links, and threads were the inevitable social consequences: videos and images of the violence and looting that always accompanies a stark failure of the system. Then her phone lost its connection completely.

* * *

"Apparently, it's out all over the place. Can you believe this shit?" she asked, throwing her keys onto the granite countertop. Jeremy was more distracted by the mismatched pajama bottoms and silk blouse.

"Where'd you go all gussied up like that?" He laughed.

"To look for coffee."

He nodded. "You look like a crazy person."

"Right now, I feel crazy."

"Why, because the power went out? This is, like, the third time this month."

"Really?" She was incredulous.

"Yeah. Paying attention to the world around you much?"

"I'm always in my head, you know that."

"I do. Today more than ever." He pointed to her outfit. "Plus, crude is, like, a zillion dollars a barrel, so let's not take trips that have no plunder, okay? Here—" He plated her breakfast. "Have some eggs. At least the gas in the stove still works."

"And I almost said no to that," she said into the stuffy air.

"That's right. You fought me on that—and if you had won, would you be eating my delicious, frothy scrambled eggs right now?"

She shook her head like a schoolgirl as she tore off a chunk of bread from a soft and chewy breakfast roll that he had handed to her.

"I love your frothy scrambled eggs," she said, her mouth stuffed with the bread.

"That's why I make them." He bent down to kiss her forehead, but noticed a sudden, faraway look in her eyes. "Hey—" He tried to assure her. "Everything's fine. It's a power outage. It happens. No big deal," he said, wiping beads of sweat from his forehead.

"I know, I know. I don't know why, but it really freaked me out this time. Like it's just going to keep happening until it all shuts down, and we have to fend for ourselves in a zombie-land apocalypse."

"That's right. That seems sane. Keeping thinking that," he teased and playfully nodded like at an asylum patient.

The low hum of the AC unit interrupted the pause in the dialogue between them as it pushed out cooler air. The digital clock on the stove began to blink; Jenna's laptop dinged alive, and the couple exchanged a quiet expression—a kind of relief unspoiled by uncertainty. The easy modernity of their lives, the disruption of which was once unthinkable, had already unmoored itself from permanence, but they remained ensconced in the views of a prior decade. Jeremy swiped at the television menu from an app projected by his phone in parallel to the television that then projected the image above him, selecting the morning news show in the middle of an emergency segment.

"—so, I really think these massive outages, however shocking, are not the result of any incompetence in public service or the power companies themselves," the expert said, "but a large population which relies too heavily on their homes being entirely air-conditioned at all times. It's these first-world indulgences that have caused the failures."

"And the too-large population who refuses to sacrifice," another quickly added. "And some populations are better equipped for the heat than others and therefore do less damage. I would also like to include, with some urgency, that climate change is no small part of this. Every state in the nation should follow California's example and ban all gas-powered vehicles, confiscate the ones whose owners will not comply, and implement a window for tax breaks on the purchase of any new EV transportation."

"I'd like to add," the host interjected, "that every homeowner should get a tax break for covering their roof with solar panels."

"Hear, hear."

"Agreed. This should have been done twenty, thirty years ago."

The co-host negotiated the final point: "The bottom line is this: We have a climate change problem that is beginning to do its work; we have an energy shortage because of it; and we must implement major social justice reforms required to make all of it right again. It's all linked."

Jeremy and Jenna, shaking theirs, watched as each of the nodding five heads concluded the segment glaring into their respective cameras. Jeremy swiped at the air and shut it off.

"You heard from Nelson or Pru lately?" he asked, suddenly curious.

"Not since I went over there, however long ago that was now."

"And they were all weird, right?"

"Yeah. Both double-masked, eyes like hostages. Backed away when I walked up the steps to hand them the dish."

"Crazy."

* * *

Suburbs: Miami, Florida—Three months into decline

"Did you want, like, three or four apples, or what?"

Charlie's partner didn't respond like most people, those who would be quick to observe and seem to want to please this strikingly handsome man with a jawline chiseled from marble, an intensely lusty brow, dreamy blue eyes, and a megawatt, movie star smile. But Roland was usually content to ignore him.

"Roland, how many do you want?" Charlie sharpened his tone, then brushed aside the question and threw four of the shiny pink orbs into the flimsy plastic bag. "You know, you never have a problem ignoring people when they're talking *to you*, but God *forbid* anyone does it to *you* when *you're* trying to talk to them. The hypocrisy is quite impressive."

"Be quiet," Roland finally whispered.

"What?"

"I'm trying to listen to these women," Roland said between clenched teeth. Charlie quieted and listened with him.

"What am I supposed to do?" one of the women asked. "Just throw out all the food in my fridge and come back here to spend another couple hundred to replace it—if they even *have* it? These outages have to stop. They go on for days!" She was on the verge of tears. The other woman agreed, empathizing with the stranger confiding in her, these mutual frustrations. "How do they think we are going to afford this? The only good thing is my kids have been playing outside more often." She tried to laugh through the worry. "But I just can't afford to keep coming here when the power's on, driving around to find an open, unaffected restaurant when it's off at my house, waiting for hours, and hoping there's food left when we sit. Coming back here to replace spoiled food. It's too much."

Overhead, select fluorescent bulbs blinked in sections around the ceiling; the vegetables against the wall seemed to shift beneath the fluctuations of light and dark; the misty veil showering them spurted on and off.

"Oh, *god*," Charlie exclaimed, exasperated. The woman looked over at him, teary-eyed and desperate, as if he was to blame.

"When does this stop?" she implored him.

Surprised by the directness of her address, he shrugged. "How could I know?" he asked, looking away. Then, everything went dark, and the woman broke down. The acquaintance moved to guide her new sister toward the exit. The only light shone through the windows at the front entrance, growing dimmer toward the darkest back of the store.

"Let's go," Roland ordered. "And bring the basket with you."

"How are we going to pay for it?"

"*Cash.*"

On their way out, Roland slammed a hundred-dollar bill into the open hand of a cashier. Around them, others grabbed as much food as they could carry and ran out.

* * *

Roland Woolf, tall and slim with beady eyes like a venomous spider's, hunched before the decorative Venetian mirror of his master bathroom; his hands gripped the edge of the marble slab beneath it, supporting his wearied frame. He was remembering this episode at the grocery store, which seemed like a decade in the past, but one that had happened only a few weeks before. That was when the outages had begun to last more than a day or two but four or five. The disdain he'd felt for anyone at the time who'd expressed unquiet concern had triggered the memory, believing the calamity a necessary endurance to transform from an economy run by fossil fuels to one that was sustained by clean energy. The disdain lingered as contempt, like the stink of a rankling mold as the guilt it had unreasonably acquired spread like a virally infected fungus. Thereby, guilt and shame were transmuted into rage and back again.

Roland pawed at his wrinkled face, trying to measure what life he had left.

Deep, sustained sleep was a luxury in recent years. At fifty-five, Roland's brain was abnormally active in quieting itself of intrusive thoughts—too much of life had usurped any hope for contentment. Only his peace pills, as he called all painkillers—two of which currently sat on the countertop—could tame the thundering squall of his mind so that his worn-out body might steal an undisturbed six-hour rest from responsibility. But the pills made him groggy and weak, and weakness was another enemy to his mind. He had forgotten to take his life-saving meds, the important ones, the night before, a once-a-day pill he could not miss, every day, until the end. When he would forget, it was the first thing he had to do immediately the following morning. That pill, dwarfing the other two, was already cupped in his hand.

The fourteen-inch television installed flush to the wall at his left was set to IBBC News. Nothing if not prepared, he'd purchased a generator to supply the juice of the house's electronics in case of outages. Even if the world lost power, he would not. Most of the fairly wealthy had acquired one in the early days, and the poor were priced out for the demand. As he cleaned his teeth, he gave an ear to the updates on the global turmoil which had upset the supply chain for all types of manufacturing, construction, and distribution. His was a family-owned steel-scraping business that depended on all three sectors. The news segment described how the shipping industry was being particularly hard-hit. He switched the station.

"—has been lost. Officials blame, *quote*, right-wing terror, as Portland struggles to resume cell service. All metropolitan towers have failed, some of which, it has been confirmed, have indeed been vandalized. Most troubling is the news straight from Central District that, except for small portions of Seattle, all of Washington state is without power for the foreseeable future. Experts on our own program warned of this in early March when parts of western Washington had reported days-long brownouts."

"Fucking fascists," Roland mumbled.

Popping the pill into his mouth, he slugged some fusty, overnight water to push it down.

The power had come back early that morning after five straight days. Shirtless, he stood under the largest vent in the master bedroom's foyer, allowing the cool air to cascade down his half-naked body. Charlie, his partner eight years younger, walked past him to pee.

"You're up early," Roland said.

"I slept like shit. Drank too much," Charlie replied.

"Smoke-a-thon too, huh? I saw butts all over the patio."

Charlie coughed up some phlegm and laughed. "I had an ashtray—somewhere."

"Clean it up, will you?"

"As you wish, Lord *Over.*"

"Very funny. It's disgusting."

"I know. I'm sorry. It's gross. I need to stop," Charlie said, repeating his line on the recurrent subject as he focused his aim into the bowl.

"You've been saying that for probably ten years."

"And you keep saying you're going back to the gym, but all I see is that gut getting bigger."

"You mean my prosperity?" Roland rubbed his slightly protruding middle, diverting to humor for a change.

"Yes, fat boy." Charlie flipped up his briefs and gave Roland a sweet kiss on the cheek, then rubbed his best friend's belly. "Ugh—thank God the air is back on. I was about to go full Jack Torrance on you," he said, developing darker levity as he walked down the hall toward the other side of the house.

"Don't forget the will's suspicious circumstances clause!" Roland yelled, teasingly.

Charlie's obligatory, laughing complement to Roland's final threat concluded the tired bit as the sound traveled back down the passageway to please the ears of his keeper; one of Charlie's strengths in mastering such a master was his ability to read the notes of the composition and to sing on cue those needed to maintain the harmony.

Roland stayed under the cool air, also tired of their scripted humor, and closed his eyes. His worry had redoubled since the last outage. A premonition in the form of a feeling drowned his innermost sense. Without detailing a list, he knew that what he wouldn't do to survive in a time of great calamity would be far overshadowed by the heft of what he *would* do. He gazed through the half-fogged glass of the French doors before him and into the peace of his private backyard, thinking no more about himself but knowing everything that might occur could steal it all away, and the ultimate nature of his fate could prove the hurricane he'd constantly fled: However privileged his life while living, his death was going to be difficult.

That afternoon, he'd had an appointment at the hospital to extract blood, a routine as regular as a mortgage payment. It was unusual to meet the physician's assistant at the hospital, but Gary was a friend at this point, and he was picking up shifts at Holy Cross to help with the chaos the staff shortages had triggered.

The exterior of the hospital appeared both abandoned and overcrowded. People streamed in and out of all entrances and exits, but the windows were dull with the absence of their faces. A wetness like water leaked from the majority of the sills to the next level down, staining the concrete as it traveled, until whatever it was dripped onto the pavement below. Roland stood beneath the strongest of the streams to observe the drip and could see its color, a bluish-gray sort of liquid tinted by an accumulation of dirt and debris from the neglected façade of the building, blocky and brutalist in its design and its vibe.

Observing the commotion at the hospital's entrance, his mind expanded beyond the preconceptions he'd held for life as it should have been, and he absorbed the preternatural contours of the decaying and disorganized scene: Among other strange sights was a woman on the ground, moaning in a language he couldn't decipher. An old man with a walker, blood streaming down his head, alone and unattended, passed by his right side. Two small children bellowed at their father, who held their hands but stared dumbly at a brick wall. This same hospital, only months before, efficient and well-regarded, had been altered by the gradual misapplication of the sensitivities in human nature, now set conspicuously on the brink: Trivial social concerns had superseded the fundamental interests of the institution. Not a man easily surprised, Roland's eyes widened with each new sight, as he was forced to note how oblivious he'd been to the unanticipated fluctuations in the social collective's psyche. There was madness in the air. A preoccupation with phantoms unaffiliated with the present moment. Rather than succumb to the shock, posturing like a madman yelling, *What the hell is going on here?* he pushed aside the distorting effects to his soul and continued into the pathetic building for the appointment.

Security lines, a routine inconvenience in practically every public place, including gyms and grocery stores added a year prior, and one time especially at pharmacies when they were crammed with people desperate to fill prescriptions—a news report had suggested a collapse in pill manufacturing—had all been deconstructed, given up for urgency, for the need to keep it moving. Society was not so much organized anymore but a sort of *managed chaos*, a phrase overused by politicians at the waning days of civilization's peak in the first two thousand years of the Common Era. This new millennium had begun to reveal a darker promise.

Big Government had installed various security apparatuses to inhibit mass shooters initially, and looters latterly, but those killers and thieves had become so abundant during the food shortages and power outages of recent days that rather than blockade entrances with security scanners, fully armed police officers were stationed in these positions instead, an expense paid for by property taxes. Schools had been shuttered the greater part of two years, so those funds were redirected to lethal enforcements. Officers had been trained to kill at the slightest waving of a gun, a program which had caused some controversy among the deniers of present realities, their insistent activism a sorry pretense of the lost era. But the days of moral seething and political preening were over. There was too much discomfort in daily life to give any time to it. Mistakes and accidents surely occurred, but they were as inevitable as death itself.

Drops of dark, muddy blood stained the margins of the lobby floors, leading to the elevators, surely remnants of assaults, murders, rampages that at one time shocked the nation but appeared now as stains on the more innocent past. Violent crime was as regular as the day going into night. Formerly, in the Old

World, just a simple population of pathological types would dare to do such things, but now, here, today, in this age—anyone harbored the explosive potential to do vicious things, our animal nature no longer inhibited by the many shimmering rewards and dangling hopes and possibilities keeping it in check. Individuals who might have been lauded in the past for humanitarian careers were now thoughtless to any impulse to rape or pillage what they needed, or worse, what they wanted. However, Roland assumed the custodial staff was as short as the others, or there were bigger messes with which to contend, still refusing, himself, to see the world, as it was, coming to an end.

Patients, terminal or mentally deranged, and whatever family or spouse (or whoever accompanied the sick) far outnumbered those in hospital attire. Ranked among them were even more security guards than nurses, doctors, or administrators. All told, Roland figured the number of individuals who occupied a position in the medical hierarchy was probably a tenth of the lobby's total population. But it was even unusual to see any of them there—a further sign of the shortages. Those accompanying the sick all seemed to complain, to each other or yelling toward the ceiling, about the insufficiency of the care their loved one was receiving. Roland didn't count them as much as assign relative numbers to groups and take an average. Though appalled at the dried swaths of bloodstains and overall mess of the floors, littered with tissue paper and all assortment of strewn debris, he marveled at the juxtaposition between the disarray on the floor and the grandiosity of the soaring twentieth-century architecture of the lobby itself. A mural loomed behind him, both of a town and a nation unified by a single vision, a distinctly American town at the dawn of its imperial century— abundant farmlands cascading down and past the perspective of the artist's eye; women and children reaching toward the sweep of a prominent wind, soaring upward, blending corn with grain, to a kind of cathedral point, nominating the formerly robust civilization to the grace of heaven's most sacred rewards.

Roland texted Gary since the check-in line was not only overwhelmed with visitors of all kinds and needs but disorganized and poorly run by two overworked young women: one who looked on the verge of tears, and one who looked on the verge of murder.

Where do I go?

He waited roughly thirty minutes before an answer came back:

Third floor, second elevator on the left, second corridor, walking south. Room 341. If you walk up the north wing, you'll find room 341 but I won't be in it. Hurry.

Hurry? Roland thought. "I would've been there thirty minutes ago," he mumbled. *If it weren't for all these losers in the lobby.*

The compass inlaid at the center of the lobby floor revealed which wing went south, but still he got turned around in the labyrinthine repetition of what seemed like an endless extension of hallways, one branching from another like a many-tentacled leviathan, each room like a suction cup already suffocating a victim.

On the third floor, he at first sensed, then could smell the sour musk of death and dead bodies.

"Roland—over here," Gary called from a room down the hall. Corpses of the recently deceased, mostly on gurneys, a few on the floor, slumped over onto themselves—all covered in white or light blue sheets—were positioned like leftover hospital wares yet to be tossed out, and Roland wondered just how long they had been left there, ignored for the living: How long before they would begin to rot and fall apart? Gary read his face but said nothing.

"Have a seat and roll up your sleeve, please."

"Busy day?" Roland deadpanned. "It's like a morgue up here."

Gary mimed disbelief. "Tell me about it," he said almost lacking sarcasm, widening his eyes as he prepared the needle to extract blood from Roland's arm. He spoke while focusing on his work. "Five straight days without power *and* our generators are out of diesel because the idiots who are supposed to keep them ready haven't done their jobs, and people who need machines to live then die. And they will die quickly. Thus, the pileup."

Roland simply nodded, taking the information reluctantly as the shocking subtlety of ignored but obvious truths moved him further from disbelief and closer to accepting the demoralized state of public life. "Most people have no idea how dependent we are. How fucked we are—"

"They live in the matrix of unreality," Roland interrupted with the kind of bluntness he used to reserve for friends in private. Suddenly, he had the answers, seeing everything as it was, as if never in denial himself. It wasn't finally the permission to speak boldly, exactly, but a power play that one could no longer deny anything.

"Seems insane, but it's true. They are totally disconnected from what is right in front of them. Some will probably try to sue the hospital." Gary shook his head. "Pointless."

"I'll admit to being surprised at the disorder here," Roland said, trying to regain a moment's control. "I haven't left my house in a while." This, he indicated, was a final word in a discussion he did not care to continue. Gary noted the resistance and didn't push it further, labeling the vials of blood, trying not to comment under his breath about Roland's obvious struggle with denialism. The lights began to flicker and then went out; a deep hum sounded throughout the massive building like a galactic spaceship powering down, and the men were hushed while machines were noisily trying to start.

"Please let them work," Gary whispered.

The hallway bulbs began to flash like a strobe.

"You'd better go," Gary said. "It'll be chaos if the generators don't kick on. Last time, only one worked in the north wing, and everyone tried to cram their way into it."

Roland nodded. "Are you gonna be all right?" he asked more from pleasantry than from care.

"Yes. Go."

Back home, Charlie was in the office on a virtual call with his sales team. Roland observed the man with whom he'd spent the last twenty-three years, watching the familiar gestures and expressions he had sometimes resented, not from anger or animus, but habituation: Sameness tended toward redundancy and could provoke his urge to break out and into something, not just new, but wholly different. He turned away, imagining a life diametrically opposed to this, maybe one that might have included a wife and many children—how might that have changed him—when Charlie came into the room.

"That was a quick one," Roland said, exiting the daydream.

"The COO's camera went out. We were all just sitting there looking at each other, so we ended it."

"I heard this morning that Seattle was having some issues," Roland offered as he moved to his armchair.

"This shit has got to stop." Charlie stood before the television and swiped it on, repeating what had become for him a constant evaluation of the latest events of decline.

"—for that quick look at weather," the anchor said, then paused and pressed his hand against his earpiece. "They're telling me now that Chicago's O'Hare is experiencing total power loss. Backup systems have failed as the upper Midwest grid is down. Riot police have been dispatched across the region. Ticketed passengers for upcoming flights are advised *not* to go to this airport. All arriving flights are being diverted to Denver, Dallas, or Atlanta." He paused, listening. "All departing flights are cancelled. Please call the 800 number at the bottom of your screen or, if possible, visit your carrier's website for information about specific flights."

"If someone can't get online, then they're not able to watch this program either, jackass," Charlie said, shooting Roland an angry and urgent look, trying to get him to see the unfolding catastrophe that was the state of the world. Roland met the expression as if subdued by denial and set his eyes on the screen in his lap.

"It'll all come back and be fine. Stop complaining so much."

Charlie clenched his teeth, flexing his muscular jawline, pausing to discipline an emotional surge, trying not to yell, but instead, he exploded. "You're a goddamned fool! You always think everything will be fine. You and I are not seeing things the same way anymore. Look around you! What the hell do you think is happening? This isn't some *random* glitch, and we aren't going back to normal. Wake *up*!" He snatched the superfluous remote control and flung it at his partner, who flinched, defending himself against the projectile.

As Charlie left the room, Roland sensed the trap of the very characteristics that had used to serve him: stubbornness, resiliency, defiance, and a fear, not new, but threatening to overwhelm his notoriously ironclad reserve. If things really did collapse—if society as they had known it ceased to function— then all supplies and services, not at all limited to but certainly including medical assistance and availability of medication, would cease as well. That would cause some problems for him. Calmly, he swiped the television back on and resumed his work.

* * *

Two Miles East of Weaverville, NC—Four months into decline

Mina Galani lowered the volume of the iPad, a once out-of-date model now like a luxury appliance, that sat next to her easel and switched from an outdated news-pod to an outdated arts-pod, the episodes for which she'd downloaded a year before, programs, at this point, she'd listened to a thousand times. The old news was too bleak to support the joyous feel of the peonies she had been painting for nearly two weeks. The last time she'd cared to listen to a live broadcast, she'd noted how straight-forward the coverage had become, no longer making excuses for "central power" as the political far right had begun to call the federal government, who in turn had quickly labeled them "enemies of the state."

The "Red State" governors had long ceased taking orders from the federal executive and the DC power bloc at large; and Texas—at the vanguard of the opposition, a state with its own power grid, which had been modernized after notorious brownouts a good ten years before the rest of the country, ever the rugged separatists—finally hearing the cold whisper of its history, was becoming the independent nation it had once promised itself to become.

A war raged but in pockets; it was sectarian and regional. American versus American or mostly unaffiliated, undocumented individuals versus whoever, as was the history of the territorial wars of the nation (the first civil war the only possible exception), some imported for this specific conflict to further confuse sides as cover for the most corrupted minority in American history. All soldiers fought through their divisions to the point of blood—to the death, instant or extended.

In her small and quiet corner of the South, it had yet to materialize as relentless war. Certainly, it was as potentially dangerous a region as any: Thieves, murderers, and miscreants of all kinds roamed like nineteenth-century highwaymen—road agents, as they had been called—but this was almost a Southern tradition. Crime had begun to spiral, even before the initial signs of energy insecurity, resulting from the political prohibition on punishing criminals, mostly marginalized men and a handful of women who apparently had no choice but to commit violent crimes. A deeper look into their lives would certainly catalyze this understanding; they were, in fact, impossibly far from acquiring the attributes of a decent life and would not tolerate the poverty consigned to them. Excuses endlessly promoted the crimes.

On any given morning, however, Mina could enjoy the tranquility of nature—her sighs, songs, and sounds: a mellifluous gush of a motherly tune—as if war were an artless fantasy of historical men. But Mina knew what was happening, and it pained her, unable to express the angst, the blue-black angst that colored womanly disgust for the rough-hewn needs in men, except by nurturing the bounty of life around her. Painting had become her sole personal recreation, a distraction from the destruction, a way to mirror Mother Nature and to find peace.

The power was on one day, off the next, but her Wi-Fi had totally gone out, so she'd continued to rely on satellite Internet— a temperamental technology, depending on the wind and the weather—connecting to stations when she could, replaying programming from better days.

At fifty, Mina was retired from the world and increasingly reclusive—no longer a member of the many organizations she'd previously patronized, not that they much existed anymore. Years before, already the creative arts had devolved into an uncritical, insipid mediocrity, her tolerance for which had died far before the community had imploded. She could only wonder at the decrepitude of its current critical state, or if artistic productions of any kind were anything measurable to merit. The overproduction of bad art was as old as culture. That's not what bothered her; it was the recent idealization of it, the narcissism of its makers, the limitless investment in egotistical fare whose only interest was the reciprocity of praise, however false: The more servile the praise, the more value had been given to the piece. The three-year-old coverage on the program she was replaying discussed a contemporary exhibition and sale of an obscure artist in Holland whose piece on "the blankness of genius" had sold for an offensively high price.

"Piece of shit, more like," she grumbled as she lightly stroked a fine pink highlight onto the edges of the principal flower on her canvas.

About two decades she'd spent in Massachusetts, near Cambridge in Boston, but once the cell towers had failed for the avenue of New England-proper, off of which Boston had fed its need for juice, she'd had to travel south, first in a carpool, then by bus, traveling through regions that hadn't restricted interstate transportation. Some of the trip she'd made by foot in the exodus of electricity refugees—most of whom stopped in the New York City or Washington, D.C. metro areas because New York attracted like-minded metropolitan types, both high and low (many of whom had been eager to exploit the new vulnerabilities of the wealthy who had refused to leave the city for prejudice toward the rest of the country). And in D.C., the power had yet to even flicker, a perennially privileged bubble doing well to maintain the belief that not much had changed since 1998. Avoiding predatory police seeking to fine or even to arrest those migrating to more secure territory had been a pitfall she'd managed to evade with feminine sleights of hand: masterly feints of helplessness or endless compliments on the bravery of their mission and rather *large* muscular frames.

Mina had followed the fallout from the failing cell towers in the Pacific Northwest and the subsequent violence that had been the first scaled confrontation in the country, as well as the first sign of the rest of the nation's contiguity to total collapse. This provoked the immediate if slightly rash migration of those in other parts of the country where oppressive government dictates seemed to suggest an approaching and similar fate. In the months after that first infrastructural failure, those who could move from areas where similar trends could be discerned did so.

Too much of life had been transferred to phones, immobilizing the very idea of self-reliance in most of the citizens but instigating its resurgence in some others. There were those who believed social collapse was a combination of terrorism and bureaucratic incompetence, in both government and private sectors, but they were the minority. The two sides mostly believed one and vilified the other. Once it came to a head in the streets, those regional hot wars had begun and were still being waged with lives.

The elegant, if understated, North Carolina cottage home her family had owned for close to fifty years had been purchased by her intrepid grandfather, the stoic Greek American and often critical man who had raised her. Ever-prepared with secondary and tertiary plans for the possibilities of the nuclear-armed world, he had purchased the four acres after a clandestine promotion to the newly coordinated Central Intelligence Agency, an evolution of foreign intelligence-gathering as old as the Revolutionary period. Its preceding incarnation as the Office of Strategic Services was made on the heels of the colossal victories of World War II. The nation had then entered its imperial phase, however tentatively. It was to be the patriarch's off-the-grid hideout, installing the latest in DIY technologies he could acquire, being one of the first with satellite television in 1980. It was a well-rigged joint, however decrepit and expired most of the technology had become.

When she wasn't painting, Mina nursed her garden, which by necessity had become exclusively devoted to sustenance: hardy vegetables, herbs (ryegrass for the cow and goats), and what fruits the Carolina climate would support. There was a pear tree, an apple tree, and a plum tree that the old Greek had planted in a cluster of three like the triune of a loving God, dropping their fruit to His children. A religious man from another era, seemingly a parallel world that had cultivated prosperity by faith, this North American primogenitor had made the effort to include the symbols of his gratitude for divine grace wherever he could.

Beyond the rows of roughage, she'd kept three hens and a rooster, a single heifer, who was ready to breed (but Mina had no bull) and two goats which did breed occasionally to some success. She had traded one of the recent kids to a local young couple who'd also determined to live independent of civilization. Between the two homesteads, they'd taught each other how to trade and barter appropriate to their needs by fairly measured, reciprocal offerings.

With the foresight instilled by her family's example, Mina had purchased ten solar panels before the supply chain for nonessential goods had broken its essential links. Some were installed like rooftop gables on the ground facing east and west, and some lay flat facing heaven—all to catch the most direct rays of nuclear fire dawn, doom, and dusk. Since the panels were five years old, she'd had to learn to arrange and maintain them without guidance from a more seasoned user so they might last.

All of the work required of a farmer had reformed Mina's once slightly chubby midsection. Now, she had never been fitter, having to take in the waists of many pants. Gazing into the full-length mirror of the guest bedroom, where all her sewing needs were achieved, she pulled at the roots of her once raven-black hair, using her fingers to comb through the dominant gray and white layered among the remaining black. Dark eyes and olive skin decided her Greek appearance, while her intellect could match that ancient country's legacy for inspired thought.

It had been six weeks since the power grid was largely operational, coming off and on the past two, but in preparation, she'd already begun to live as off-grid as she could since first arriving at the cottage. Ultimately, the gas-powered generators would be a vital crutch (for which she had one thirty-gallon vat of fuel remaining), and she had three large battery packs to charge the few computer products she'd acquired during last days that would someday match their expiry. She'd only use this auxiliary energy when absolutely necessary during a blackout; otherwise, she'd wait until power was restored, not knowing when or if it would go out forever.

These days, the words of an American commonsense philosopher, Reginald Sowes, from an interview she'd watched a dozen times, floated through her thoughts like a native melody: "Every man thinks talk of total breakdown is foolish—if not downright *lunatic*—until it comes, and then, with a sudden shift, everything fails, the pillars of the holy temple collapse, and a new dark age, born of moral desolation, begins."

Ten pounds of freshly cut ryegrass began to limp and lose its hydration in the late-summer sun while she fetched buckets for distribution to the cow and goats. In the side yard, she'd grown the over-seeded ryegrass and kept it fully lush, except for older patches which would eventually die off in the coldest part of winter. She clipped it with a manual reel mower, collecting the grass in piles before feeding the livestock. Nearer to the corn, on an elevated mound of earth that drained and dried out the fastest, she'd grown oats, almost twelve weeks from the plot's last grazing, and they were ready to harvest again.

Keeping this makeshift farm was her new workaday way. Life before had been so different; she'd never dreamed she'd work her own private farm to survive, and as Sowes had suggested, no one could have imagined this would come to pass. And yet, it worked. Never had the sense of security been like the feeling of working the methods of one's very survival. Never stronger, nor healthier, the strict determination to live had enlivened her spirit, reestablished her faith, and returned her mind to its inquisitive nature.

The American Brown Swiss, Sally Baby, shuffled over to the fence. Her large, moist nose grazed Mina's sweaty chin as it swiped the air, then it nuzzled at her side where the bucket appeared, into which the animal's head vanished. Mina was desperate to find a bull. Milk would be nice; cheese, even better. If she failed at breeding the young cow, she'd have to slaughter it for the meat; otherwise, Sally Baby was just a time-consuming, labor-intensive pet.

The goats were reproducing, providing their sweet, grassy milk, though one of the two latest kids had been snatched in the middle of the night, yet by what was still a question that continued to trouble her. The kid that remained was healthy and very securely sheltered inside a little shed each night with its parents.

Whenever the power was on, Mina would spend precious time searching the regional community apps to see if any local farmer had a bull but no heifer or would accept some sort of trade for a breeding session if they had both. Mina didn't have much to barter but fruit and vegetables, a painting if they desired, but she would offer what she could, even her labor: time teaching children, picking fruit and nuts or whatever needed harvesting. She hadn't been a farmer long enough to be accustomed to the desperation of spilling the blood of her keep to survive.

Out of the two rows of corn she grew, a third of it was feed. Five husks shucked earlier that morning were left in the hot sun, so the shaved kernels off the cob were a little drier, making it easier to toss to the chickens. "Before you shuck the cob, it's called an ear," she said out loud as she worked the corn bare, imagining a gathering of farmer's children at her feet. "The cob is the fibrous pole. The husk is the case of protective leaves." She spoke to herself or to the animals like a teacher or a midwife of the land, doing all her own husbandry. It kept her sane, though it wouldn't appear so. Culling all the bits of chopped kernels, she swept the cutting board, and they filed into a stainless steel bowl, throwing it out to the fowl in handfuls, then retreating for a tall glass of water.

Mina used the public water from the faucets to clean farming tools and wares, never to drink. She didn't trust it. There had been a polio outbreak in the Charlotte metro area, and though she'd been vaccinated, it had been many decades since those shots, and it was a certainty that disease festered in the neglected municipal pipes. It was perhaps less likely out in the country, she'd guessed, but this particular risk could be avoided.

For when it rained, she'd maintained a system, the original structure of which was left over from her grandfather's tenure, a simple system to collect the house's runoff into a vat of activated charcoal—coals burnt red hot to become more porous and filter-effective—underneath which was a layer of aquarium filter sponge, and beneath that collected the more purified water.

If it had stormed for more than a few hours, a flowing creek, large enough to wade through in parts, effusive when it had rained for days, collected in clear pools from which the animals usually drank. Any water used for cooking or drinking had to come from the six barrels stationed around the house's perimeter.

Mina rarely thought about her fate but obsessed over the weather. Mostly the rain. Forecasts were hard to find, not just because of the outages, but broadcasters had almost entirely stopped posting them for the interruptions and the near impossibility of accuracy. The disruptions in time had inhibited the service, so when the power was on, finding one could take hours and too much digging online. And the more she dug into the search, the less reliable the source would be. There had been an amateur meteorologist who'd had a page. It was broad enough to make room for the gaps but didn't stray far from the region's annual patterns that were already assumed. So, she carried on with this life, virtually alone and surprisingly contented. To her mind and upbringing, acceptance of one's circumstances was a sister to success.

* * *

Two months later—

On what felt like a Sunday, Mina twirled soft yarn around her fingers and wrist, winding and unwinding the fuzzy rope, remembering her brother, who had passed from the suggestive effects of the pandemic that had taken root in his soiled mind during the second and much more socially disruptive lockdown. He hadn't caught the illness but had started to drink, not having been much of a drinker prior to. Dennis, whom she'd called Denny, had been twelve years her senior, unmarried, with no children. He'd been caretaker of the cottage—keeping the animals alive—but chose to live in a rented trailer two miles east of the property. Once, she had found him collapsed in his home and then started making regular visits to comfort him. But it wasn't enough, and finally, she'd found him one gray afternoon under thick, oppressive clouds, hanging from a tree by a rope. He'd left no note, nor explanation, just wanting out.

While she mused on the sadness in Dennis's life, though feeling his presence and a peace his memory had brought with him, seeming to prefer the other side, the power suddenly came on, and her phone made its synchronistic ding, a sound she hadn't heard in months. It was more of an intrusion, startling her from the emotional mixture of her memories. She dabbed her wet eyes dry and checked the screen. There was a text from a young man farther west toward Hampsburg, deeper country with fewer people, a man with whom she'd had one exchange two months prior. He had a bull, but he'd had "other things to tend to," he'd said. Over the course of their chat, she'd told him the name of her town and some of the local markers for finding the residence, informing him that she was armed and not alone, just in case. Finally, she sent her address, knowing the risk and prepared to defend her life, but growing desperate beyond caution for life to become something more than enduring apocalyptic solitude.

The text she'd received said that he had lost everything, was prepared to risk what was left, and would be walking the animal her way by morning.

CHAPTER THREE

Weaverville, North Carolina—Six months into decline

Mina shielded her eyes from the noon sun as she examined the black beyond the deepening blue of the sky, wondering how long before another storm and how far into space these realities might extend before transmuting into a thing so different as to be virtually nonexistent.

Her water supply was running low. The aspect of the leaves—slightly withered, beginning to dry, some already rusted brown—evoked September harvests, fuller moons, and foggy nights. The recent two-week drought—she had counted the days to sixteen—had depleted half the water reserves, so the romanticized cornucopia of a late summer's take was too stark a reminder of the difficulty she faced.

The sun moved past its peak at hot summer noon, and her thoughts turned to the bull, more than to the man. That morning, she'd loaded the small handgun in the front bureau, shot it a few times into an old stump for comfort, reloaded it, and slid the infernal thing into her deep front pants' pocket, folding an apron in half, tying it around her waist to help hide the bulk of the firearm. If necessary, she would kill the man to keep the bull, although she hadn't quite premeditated this point, only made herself ready for anything. Intuition alone would tell her of his intent. Impulsivity was not her preferred mode of deciding important movements through life, but these circumstances required more than civil patience could afford.

45

The last message was marked Yesterday 4:50 AM: "Leaving before dawn. Prob 8-hour trek. Slow-moving. Near you early afternoon I reckon. No connection between here and there. Be on lookout." *Did that mean this morning?* she wondered; or did he leave before dawn yesterday, and he was somewhere nearby searching for her at this moment?

Reading the message for the hundredth time, the uncertainty grew more threatening. Squeezing the phone, she eased her hands into the wide front pocket of the apron and with the one not gripping the gun clutched the small pruning shears she used to trim her potted plants, scissoring the sharp metal repeatedly, nervously staring down the driveway that led up to her home.

* * *

He had tried sending her a picture of himself and the bull in the days leading up to his decision to seek her out, but it never went through. The library's Internet connection had been too erratic for media. Hope hobbled along. The apprehensions of meeting a stranger in the before-world might have precluded the encounter, but now anyone whose interest in survival—in sharing, in working together—was worth leaving home for. He was a loner on the road, looking for something to give his young life to, but he worried. Any bad decision could tip the scales toward despair—a state of mind more concerning than death.

When he finally arrived at the general location, he scanned the highway shoulder for mile markers and the northbound ramp she'd told him about. It was Exit 16 going east if the signs and markers hadn't been overrun by nature or knocked down by angry hordes of teenaged boys, she'd said. He chuckled at that remark, realizing she must have thought he was older. Instinct told him she was at least middle-aged, if not elderly. Her tone was too direct and all-knowing to be his contemporary.

The bull had been walking steadily for the last hour, making up for time spent grazing and moaning. It was thirsty. Between

Hot Springs and Weaverville, the ground had dried up; the change from sloppy mud to wispy dust occurred within a mile. Here, the grass was as overgrown as everywhere but yellowing or wilting. Any chance he'd had of staying with her, if the vibe was good, would evaporate if water was scarcer. Would she want to go back to his farm? It was an uncertain proposition, as the main house was falling apart, all the animals were either dead or had run away, and the farming land had gone bad since the fertilizer had run out.

A gentle, thicker breeze pushed against his body, and both he and the bull stopped, raised their heads, and lifted their faces into its pressure. With eyes closed, he perceived a whispering of strange voices, but it was just nature and the hum of God throbbing with life all around him. A wariness grew within his mind, however, as if he was being watched by something, not just looking nor simply seeing. A healthy bull would have a high bounty to the right person, and he worried about the possibility of thieves. He opened his eyes at this shift in intuition, reached behind his back, and momentarily gripped the handle of the farm's second-best machete, then tugged at the strings on his front to tighten its sheath and trudged on.

Before he saw them, his gut clenched at having sensed them. Three dark forms, all arms and legs, rushed from a mass of taller grasses.

His weapon came easily out of its place as he thrust it high into the air. A chain was instantly latched to the bull's harness. The large beast groaned, resisting the force of the highwaymen's assault.

"Nice-lookin' bull you got there, son," the point man said, holding a bat with nails protruding from its cap like a makeshift mace. Ant eyed the spikes. The point man smiled, his teeth a brownish mess, bringing the bat to his dominant side.

Ant looked back, checking the position of the other two who smirked at him, seeming to watch, having secured the bull. Both opponents stood their ground, weapons up. Ant fell forward, pushed from behind. The point man swung, striking him atop his scalp, grazing but notching out a small piece of soft flesh; again, quickly the bat lodged into his thigh. The young man roared and, in a swipe, lodged his blade into the man's crown. The face went blank from shock. Ant wiggled the weapon out from where it was stuck. The second blow almost took the head from its neck. The body teetered, then collapsed. The third blow removed the head completely. Ant turned back.

The one who'd pushed him froze in shock, disbelieving what he saw. The other, Ant could see jogging away to a safer distance, howling for the other to follow.

"*Run*, you *dim*wit!"

Blood dripped down Ant's face and onto his heaving chest as he glared at the loiterer, who stepped back slowly, gulped but had no spit, then tripped away, choking on the thickness of the air. The bull bellowed into the wind.

* * *

The sign for Exit 16 was fully intact. The shirt he'd tied against the gash in his head, he tightened, and limped toward the ramp due north. The bull followed, obedient to its master's step, without needing the lead of the rope.

* * *

A chill had descended with the slowing of the wind, and Mina smiled, observing the gathering darkness in the clouds. It was a quarter past 4 p.m., and she wondered when he'd show. The power hadn't come back, but she switched on the generator every hour on the hour to check for messages. Conserving that power was a strictly enforced priority, but this bull was one of a few things she'd allow herself to waste it on.

The encroaching night pushed off the last of the day. Dusk was usually a comfort, but this evening, it made her anxious. Having full view of him was a necessity. She paced the porch, trying not to wring her hands, when she saw a shadow moving within the remnant light, the silhouette of a hunched man and his beast; and the closer he got, the more the reflective paint of the white house illuminated his form. He limped, was injured. She resisted the impulse to run to his aid, gripped the porch railing with one hand, the gun in her pocket with the other, leaving the spur un-cocked.

"You all right?" she called, trying not to sound nervous. He was short of breath, speaking through his exhaustion.

"I'm—I'm *hurt*," he forced out.

She continued to eye him.

"Dizzy—" he mumbled. "*Please* help—" He dropped the lead to the bull and fell to the ground. His tone too earnest to doubt, she ran to him.

"Careful," she said, pulling him up, resting his arm atop her shoulders. He was younger than she had expected. He set his tired eyes on hers. The motherly instinct relieved the strategizing other as she helped him up the stairs, easing his worn body onto a couch placed outside on the porch under a row of windows running the length of the living room. The bull walked to the base of the house and grazed on the yellowing grasses there.

* * *

Suburbs: Marietta, GA—Eight months into decline

Jeremy's eyes opened by themselves, that is to say, consciousness had not revived prior to his waking; they shot open like from an instinct to danger. That nebulous state between sleep and wakefulness did not ease him into the day before he found himself staring at the wall, alerted to something—at the ready. Many years in the United States Marine Corps could do that to a man. His father had had wild flashbacks in his dreams, jumping from the bed, pulling off its mattress—and his wife with it—to raise a barrier against incoming at Fallujah, screaming for backup, cupping his hand as if holding a walkie-talkie and spitting fiery words into it. Another time, he'd sleepwalked both fists and arms clean through a glass window. Jeremy had forgotten these childhood disturbances until recently, as the son becomes the father and the son, now the father, remembers his.

In the more recent war provoked by an expectedly swift Chinese invasion of Taiwan, at the Battle of Taipei, Jeremy had endured the stresses of rigorous battle and its greed for life. But this didn't concern that. This was something far more familiar and far more ruinous. Its darkness was a memory not to be remembered, but his subconscious had hoarded its leftovers, and it was time for him to review the trickiest part of his past. Sweat slipped off his nose as he flipped back the damp top of the sheet.

In the backyard, where he kept a small space for training, he fixed the bulbous leather gloves to his hands, pulling into place the Velcro straps with his teeth. A heavy bag hung from a sturdy branch of a Southern live oak. Jeremy stepped to the cylindrical mass and leaned his forehead against its rough skin as if praying. His two young children, half a world away in Europe, appeared from memory, animated by enthusiasm for his return home someday in what felt like a lifetime past.

He began to beat the sides of the bag slowly, then with a drop of mercy, then faster like a drum while tears and sweat flew from him. The force of each blow rippled down his arm and up the stem of his spine; the images of each babe flashed inside his shut eyes, as if by flashes of lightning. The chain rattled and swayed; the sturdy bough of the tree bobbed as his face twisted more tightly. Destroying the mass before him, a final image of his first and still reviled wife descended into the frame, and his arm shot out like an unholy wrath. The whiplash in the chain broke it free from its place on the bough, and the bag fell as a dumb lump to the ground, bending in half and keeling onto its side, slumped as if defeated. Jeremy's body mimicked its collapse, falling to his knees, finally unmoved as all emotion was exhausted by the exertion.

* * *

This was a regular event Jenna had gotten used to seeing, however much the frenzy of the activity had bothered her at first— knowing nothing about the children, not even of their existence—thinking nothing about the intensity of Jeremy's emotional display, not much liking questions about her own, but feeling interrupted by it somehow, like an uninvited schism in the fabric of a reality she'd attempted to define and control for them both. She had never asked him questions about those passions, which to another viewer might have looked like unresolved but inexplicable rage, and assumed it was an exercise of the same extremity of feeling she also had to manage.

Exiting the house near the kitchen, she lugged a pot of fouled water to boil off its contamination for the day's use. Every drop they took from the tap they put to the flames to avoid sickness of any kind. Any sort of weakness now could spell doom for the long-term chances of their survival.

Jeremy cocked his head, moved his eyes sideways to see if she was watching, but she had moved to the farthest corner of the yard to collect wood for the outdoor hearth they'd constructed from leftover pavers, the final pieces of which they'd taken from the front walk, which had been initially designated for their use. The mound of splinted chop that she'd arranged—something like a marriage between a log cabin and a teepee—seemed to mock the tiny lighter she had filled with an ounce of fluid.

"We need to go easy on that stuff," Jeremy said, toweling his wet skin dry in the crisp morning air; vaporized sweat rose from his body like smoke. She paused but didn't look up, aggravated in an instant. "Just sayin'—I mean, I was a Scout and a Marine but never could manage to make fire by rubbing wood. Hated that part of Scouts," he said into the drift of their emotional exchange.

"What *did* you learn how to do then?" she deadpanned, easing herself into the victory of a pyre alive with flame.

"Kill things," he said casually and shrugged.

"In *Boy* Scouts?" She hid her smile with the clean side of her hand.

"Yeah. Before the nonbinary, gender, whatever-they-were took over."

"Uh-huh—"

This topic she brushed off, not wanting to reweave the whole of the chaotic tapestry that had defined the country's politics and preceded its fall. If she gave him a single word on the matter, he'd fly into an unproductive, useless rant, leaving them tangled in unanswerable questions. She always thought best to leave the integrity of people's struggles to themselves.

"We need more wood," she said, like an order.

"Roger that," he replied, removing the other towel around his waist to clothe himself.

"Can you wait?" She put up her hands, wanting to laugh but feeling stuck between humor and agitation. Sometimes, in her eyes, his sexiness seemed to have an ill-timed flagrancy, and he didn't care, nor even notice. The simple and unencumbered activities of a man, alone in nature, freed of civil pressures, were enough to provoke her basic needs, wishing to rip off her own clothes and jump his bones. But she could not. She must not. Not now. And this might have been the root of her agitation.

He froze in position, his underwear stuffed in his hands, confused. "Why, what does it matter? Never looked at me naked or something?" He laughed like a devil, bouncing his junk around to be funny.

Her smile soured as her mouth tightened, opposing the interruption, more in tune with the consequences of his desires than he was.

"I'm trying to get this ready for breakfast," she simply pleaded. "And it's just weird. I don't know. It's annoying."

"What is?"

"Never mind."

"What's the matter? We do this all the time."

"I know. I just—I just don't want to see *anyone's* private parts right now." She blushed saying the words. "It makes me—" The pressure to say the truth inhibited her ability to say much of anything.

"What?" His hands, palms up, were thrown to his sides like a clueless boyfriend. His briefs dropped to the ground. She couldn't help but lose a reflexive burst of laughter but regained herself.

"It just bothers me right now, all right?" Her hands, palms down, were thrown to her sides like a referee.

"All right, all right. I'll go around the house," he said and kissed her on the forehead on his way, still completely naked.

Her mind had grown unresolved, partially from unsourced guilt, partially from incessant worry, and when he joked or became too playful, it distracted them from all the practical concerns, and she didn't like it. The only thing they had time for was to secure their safety and survival. Children were out of the question so sex was out of the question.

The remaining lighter fluid measured half a pint, she guessed, then studied the worn furrow that ran the length of the wood she'd previously used to try rubbing a flame to life. Doubt increased her worries. She could always get it to smoke but never to light. They needed fire to boil the water more than anything, and they were running out of the fluid, but she had used it again anyway, warming her palms above the flame.

There were some neighbors left in the development, but one was a disturbed shut-in of a man; an old couple who had decided to die together at home and might already have been gone; and Nelson and Pru, peers who had spent an occasional evening with them to touch base when they all had needed the company. Lately, however, Jenna's mind played too spasmodically with her thoughts to socialize.

Jeremy returned, fully dressed in the same dirty clothes, and embraced her from behind. She froze, wishing she could melt into the warmth of his hulking body.

"I love you," he said, knowing she wouldn't respond. "We're going to figure this out." Then he went inside. Intimacy between them had been reduced to him hugging her stiff body. Desperate to return the affection, she couldn't. Not now. Not for a while. Not for so long that she could no longer imagine when. She couldn't repeat this to herself enough: The absolute worst thing she could have to deal with in this situation was a pregnancy.

The fire burned evenly at its core, and she watched as the stronger flames attached themselves to the blocks of wood, the bulkiest of which she readjusted, pulling and pushing them with her fingertips to put the logs closer to the more active center.

Kneeling in the dirt, with Mullet trotting all around her, wagging his tail, sniffing at her concerns, she stared at the orange flame, drawing her eye deeper into its preternatural dance—her eyes blind to their perceptions, lulling her mind to leave her body and travel into the past.

Her father stood across the way, younger than he would have been, and she wondered if they all were still alive. The cell service in their area hadn't worked well in weeks. Sometimes, there was a signal, enough to bring up a website, but it would fail immediately, dashing hope against pain. Calls would go through and then drop. When she'd last spoken to her parents she couldn't exactly remember, but it felt like months. Jeremy's family was far away in Texas and never much called anyway.

The logs on top of the heap had fallen into the center as coals, so she prodded them into a glowing mound and laid another, heftier log crosswise above the orange inferno when a shadow darkened her view of the flames.

"Would you go grab the eggs?" she asked without looking up.

Among a shy group of vigilante looters, they had ransacked the local grocery store some weeks prior, doling out fair shares of everything left worth taking. There were subsequent trips back to what was now a simple warehouse with stores of both rotting and select viable foods, only not as efficiently carried out. Jeremy had

had to muscle his way into and out of the hoard those final couple of times. It was the end of the easily available food. Current circumstances were decidedly not how either of them would have imagined experiencing married life. The last time they'd left a somewhat viable grocery store, older women, generally empowered by collapse, charged younger men with the heftier tasks as they hauled as much of the nonperishables as a human man could shoulder. From then on, those buildings became infested with rats and mice of all kinds, vermin of all sorts: flies, roaches, maggots—feeding on the remaining, festering foodstuffs.

After that first trip to what they'd quickly christened the doomed depot, Jeremy had dug a six-foot hole in the ground and threw in as much of the ice as they had carried away, once stored deep in the company's coldest freezers. The eggs and whatever meats that weren't spoiled they'd kept down there. Mullet was routinely scolded for sniffing at its perimeter.

"Babe?" she asked, looking up, focusing on the grisly figure before her. Mullet, returning from his morning tour of the back woods, stooping his head low, stared at the man, beginning to growl and displaying his canine wrath. She fell backward, caught off guard, losing her breath.

The man looked weathered beyond his years. His beard was dirty and wild; his stare was extinguished of its spark; his hands trembled and were stained with blood.

"Jenna?" he said roughly, when she realized who it was.

"Nelson? *Mullet*—no. *Sit*. What the hell happened, Nelson? Are you all right?"

* * *

Jeremy eased out of the house, cautiously observing his neighborhood buddy, as Nelson and Pru had been acquaintances more than good friends. Jeremy had perceived a codependence in them both, a complaint Jenna had disliked, preferring to leave those kinds of judgments alone. But Jeremy's military training had refined his eye to spot psychological weakness in other soldiers in order to strengthen them. It seemed the lockdown on top of lockdown and the subsequent social decline had wreaked havoc on both Nelson's and Pru's psyches and better sense; and finally, the continuous failures of the power grid seemed to Jeremy to have further developed their difficulties into madness.

* * *

Jenna rose to her feet, struck with a sudden feeling about Pru, alarmed for her safety in an instant. Nelson stood, staring at the ground where Jenna had been squatting. Walking behind him, Jenna mouthed the words "Blood. On his hands," and pointed to the top of one of her own. Jeremy looked at the blood-rusted fingers and nodded back as she jogged away from the yard.

Nausea weakened her pace as she ran, making it difficult to breathe deeply and run faster. Fear inhibited action: Nelson's already loose switch had flipped. She stumbled, repeating, "Oh my god, Pru. Be alive. *Be alive, Pru.*" Jenna practically flew up the entry stairs to their home and started banging on the door, but there was nothing. In the backyard, she yelled more loudly, calling Pru's name. She banged on the glass door there—but no sign of the woman. Through the glass, she could see what looked like a ransacked family room, adding depth to the effect of the couple's mental fragility. Her heart pulsed at the center of her throat. Back in front, she finally saw Pru like a drugged-up sprite searching aimlessly around the yard.

"Pru!" Jenna sobbed. "Thank god, you're all right."

"I'm *fine*," she said as if trapped in a distant cloud.

Jenna approached, tears on her face. "I thought—I thought—" she said, stopping herself from saying what would just add more mania to the already tortured circumstances of their lives.

"What's wrong?" Pru asked, her eyes red and dry. Her lips cracked from thirst, she leaned toward Jenna and pulled her to her chest. A foul iron stench on Pru's body revived Jenna's concern.

"Pru? What's wrong. Something's happened, I—"

"There's been an accident," she said, nodding like a child.

"An accident?"

Pru looked toward the ground but gestured to her womb.

"Oh, god. Let's go inside."

Pru's unnatural calm was an obvious mode to cover shock, shocks to her traumatized system that had built, one by one, since the first of the lockdowns. The more Jenna observed Pru, the more she perceived the depth of her dissociation, a similar look she could see in Nelson, though exporting none of the information that now sprang from his wife. Jenna carefully pulled back the long, knitted shawl Pru had wrapped to her front and saw the tragic mess of the undergarments.

"Do you have clean water?" Jenna asked softly. Pru simply shook her head, eyes fixed to the floor like a lost little girl. "Let's go back to my house. Nelson is there. We should all be together right now."

Pru nodded sweetly, coming around to a more present version of herself.

* * *

Jeremy stood over Nelson, who was seated on an old stump, tipping a cup into the dazed man's half-opened mouth. Water spurt from its sides as he drank. When he saw his wife, Nelson reanimated and dropped to his knees, sobbing her name, lamenting his failure to save their child.

"Oh *shit*," Jeremy exclaimed to Jenna specifically. "I didn't know."

She shook her head to shut him up, telling Pru to go inside.

"I'll be right there," Jenna said.

The silence which followed didn't need to be filled with explanation. Carefully, she transferred the purified water from the barrel to a bucket, grabbed some ripped cloth towels from behind the hearth, and went to tend to Pru.

"Take Mullet in too," Jeremy urged before she closed the door.

Inside, the woman lay on the floor, virtually passed out.

"Stay with me, Pru," Jenna insisted as she cupped a mug full of the water and brought it to her patient's lips. Pru's eyes began to brighten as she took the liquid down and its chemical properties revitalized her aspect. Jenna propped the ravaged woman against the wall and then ran up the stairs, rifled through a medicine cabinet for hydrogen peroxide, grabbed some pillows and a blanket from off the bed in the spare room, and hurried back.

"Do you mind if I—"

Pru smiled and grew weepy, softly saying, "*No.*" Her wet eyes dropped a tear from each duct. Nelson's moans resounded through the walls of the house. Pru shut her eyes tightly as if not wanting to hear him.

"You're both going to be fine," Jenna said, holding back sorrow while she cared for the remains of the miscarriage. Most of the exterior blood had dried and cracked, indicating a length of time dangerous to the mother, making her vulnerable to infection. The final piece of clothing revealed the tiny, lifeless boy, between three and four months old and about the size of an apple. Jenna had to summon the fullest might of self-control to repress the grief it inevitably provoked, touching the deepest points of her hardy spirit.

Her own miscarriage had happened before she and Jeremy had married—at the time, she'd known an ambiguity, both a sadness and a relief, accepting the misfortune as the natural frailty of life but wrangling with a wretched kind of failure. Moving on somewhat easily from that experience seemed callous to her in this moment of profound reflection.

Jenna cupped the child in her hands and placed its body into a cloth and gently wrapped him up, handing back the covered babe to his mother, who held the stiff mound in her delicate palms.

"He tried—" Pru said, holding the baby but looking at Jenna. "He tried to help, but he couldn't. Once he saw—" She wept, looking down at the parcel and pulling it to her chest.

"I know, I know. I understand." Jenna dabbed a cloth wet with peroxide around Pru's thighs and privates, cleaning the mess. Pru sucked at the air between her teeth, then sniffled up the wetness the sharp pain had produced in her nose. Jenna dunked another cloth in the purified water and wiped Pru's nose, mouth, and face, trying to tidy her distress.

"Thank you. You're so kind. Thank you for being so kind," she said.

Jenna nodded and wanted to break down, but feared she'd not regain herself if she gave in to this particular sorrow—the one on top of the many that could push even her to the brink. She had to look away.

"Can we bury him here? Please?" Pru asked. "And can we stay? I can't go back to that house. Nelson needs Jeremy, and I—"

"Absolutely," Jenna replied. "You can stay with us. We need you too, but right now, I need to go check on Nelson—"

Pru thanked her again, and Jenna rushed away to the men, to make sure Nelson had gotten his feet beneath him, to dig the grave, looking back once more at the bereaved mother gently cooing to her lost beloved.

* * *

They waited until she came out. Jeremy had talked Nelson back from the edge of his ineptitude. Shook sense into the man, while emphasizing their need to accept things as they are, not as they should be, and set to digging the grave, barely a foot deep into the moist and mushy earth, dug deeper at Jeremy's insistence. *From womb to tomb all people go*, Jeremy thought.

Later, the impression of this truth silenced any need to speak while they moved within death's ritual mime, circling the meager depth of the spot, bowing their heads while Pru laid the babe to rest. Jeremy took the shovel from Nelson's hand, thrusting his heel onto its step and into the mound of muddy earth.

"No—wait," Nelson said. "Can you give us a minute?"

"Of course," Jenna said, taking the shovel from Jeremy's hands, pulling him away from the site. The reduction of their lives to their certainties intensified an instinct to ceremony. No other distraction was possible, nor more important than this. Jenna clasped Jeremy's waist; her head fell against his sturdy frame; he rubbed her shoulder and stroked her fair hair.

Nelson and Pru held both hands over their son's grave and wept. Nelson spoke inaudibly to Pru, who nodded and wept harder. They knelt on the ground and together gently covered their son with earth.

* * *

Jeremy looked up and saw a pair of strange eyes glowering from a dirt-blackened face, leaning behind the thick trunk of the southern oak. Then another set appeared at the opposite yard side. Another body behind that one. A hectic dog on a leash jumped wildly at its side. Two others appeared at the far corner of the house. They were surrounded. Jeremy backed up farther toward the back door.

He whispered to Jenna, "Go get the shot gun." She leaped inside. The movement provoked the gang to move closer, tightening the circle of the threat.

"*Nelson*! Get over here!" Jeremy howled.

Nelson pulled an almost lifeless Pru toward the back of the house. Jeremy grabbed two baseball bats leaning against an old grill, threw one to Nelson, who missed the catch.

"Get her inside! And pick up that *goddamned bat*!" Jeremy yelled as he rushed the closest vagrant, swinging the bat at his head and missing, then connecting with his stomach, knocking him to the ground. Pru screamed from inside. Mullet barked uncontrollably beside her. Nelson stood with the bat in his hands, nervously eyeing an ever-closer vagrant.

"Be ready to kill!" Jeremy ordered.

"*Jesus*!" Nelson exclaimed.

The dog was unleashed.

The horde closed in.

Jenna stepped outside, and Mullet burst through the door behind her.

PART TWO

COLLAPSE

The birthing light on the new day made its own appeal to quietude, as if gods of the ancient past had commanded full revision to history and the complete works of man.

All was still.

Birdsong was silent. Wind had yet to blow. Clouds unseen above. Words unheard among the living, just the sun's softest glow crept across the orchard of all creation.

CHAPTER ONE

Weaverville, NC

Ant had slept clear through the night on the outdoor couch for the past five or six weeks, preferring to gain her trust with distance, and as he lay under the duvet undisturbed, the chill of each night dispersed, and the warmth of each day rose about him. She watched the regularity of his breathing from the threshold of the front door. *He's a good kid*, she thought, feeling blessed to have companionship with someone whose values and views matched pretty well to her own, knowing the dismal lows to which American manners, culture, and society had devolved. If you so much as tilted your head wrong toward someone, they wanted to kill you dead and then some. The old Wild West had returned to claim its right as the natural law among men contending for power without order.

Eggs recently snatched from the hens were beginning to simmer in goat butter on the woodburning stove built into the backyard kitchenette her brother had devised. Bread that she had irregularly supplied by the young farming couple, she sliced and set on the cast-iron plate to brown. Ant appeared and began to pick a handful of the remaining mint leaves from a bush near the patio.

"Soon be out of that," she said.

"Yup."

"What I wouldn't do for a cup of coffee—"

"Never drank it," he said.

He ushered the mint to the cutting board, slicing it to release the flavor and sprinkling the julienned leaves into their glasses, pouring water over them, which served in the place of a more vivifying morning drink. Ant handed her a glass, and they clinked them together.

"To another day on the lam," he said as they pulled the beverages to their lips.

"If only there was somewhere to run away *to*," she said.

He nodded, smirking. "This is about the best place I could imagine for the time being."

"And what next?" She goaded the odds of something else, better than this. He shrugged, pulled the eggs off the stove, and plated them.

"Isn't it getting a little cold at night to sleep out on the porch? It's almost Halloween," she implored for the hundredth time.

"Couple more weeks before it'll be too much, but I like it for now. Don't harm me none."

She acquiesced, having tried many times to get him to take the guest bedroom. They sat to their eggs. Watching her eat, he thanked God in heaven for an honest companion. The prospect of a nothing-world had at once shattered all his young dreams— any and all self-stylized versions of a life—and though none of those dreams had revived, having no ostensible chance to emerge at the cusp of possibility, he could at least content himself with someone who'd treated the moment like they still might.

"You'd mentioned your dad running off, and your grandpa being your real father. I had the same, though my dad didn't run off as much as be carted off."

"Broke the law?" Ant asked between bites. He tore off a corner of the bread with his teeth.

"It was unclear exactly what he'd done," she said. "He was in the family business, you might say." Ant looked at her for more, like she was going to tell the story, but she'd been so used to keeping silent about her family's employment at the CIA that she muzzled herself even now. The innocence of his curiosity, however, was enough to snap her out of the oldest of her childhood spells. "He was posted in Eastern Europe, in the early eighties, right after I was born." She hoped that was enough and tried to let the rest of it drift toward the dusty shimmers of the morning sun. He said nothing but gave her his full attention, so she continued. "And, in that line of work, things sometimes happen. Unexplained things that you have to live with."

"Was he a spy?" he asked.

She nodded. "I suppose."

"If that isn't the most far-fetched thing I ever heard," he said. They laughed for different reasons.

"I can understand that, but it's true. My grandfather who raised me was C. I. A." She enunciated each letter like a dirty secret finally brought to light. "All the way. My father had worked under him for a time, came over for a cocktail party one night and met my mother."

"That's another world to me. Might as well not be real. My people weren't college folks like yours, but my grandfather was a smart man. Industrious. My mother read a lot of books but didn't much talk about them. I know I'm smart, but being out in farm country, helping my grandfather with operations, more or less kept me from school."

"Well, the schools had turned into such a mess of disinformation and incompetence anyway—" she added.

"Correct," he said, as if capping an angry point. Again, she nodded knowingly. "And it's not like us country black folks ever had our moment. The power pigs, as I like to call them, only ever started worshipping our skin color once they decided to use us as a totem for their backwardness."

"Ain't that the damned truth," she said.

"You say *ain't*?" he asked suddenly.

"Not usually."

"I figured." He paused, looking at her like the devil might be amusing. "Just don't do it to try to relate to me. That's what *they* do." His finger pointed northward.

"I understand. Meant no harm. Can't say anything anymore without it being suspect, I guess."

"Now that's the *real* damned truth," he said, shifting his finger to heaven.

"Should we give it another go with the bull and Sally?" she asked after an affectionate symbiosis reformed in conclusion to the talk.

He nodded. "Just let me go wash up."

* * *

In the corral, the bull sniffed at the vigorous urination shooting from Sally Baby's backside, sticking its tongue out and into the stream.

"Yuck," Mina said, confused at the behavior.

Ant walked toward her, tucking in the front part of his shirt, cocking his hat back. The bull began to moan, almost to growl, curling its lip up into the air toward the heifer.

"That's what we want," he said. "I'd wondered about her estrous last time we tried it, but now we can be assured." The bull got louder, raised its head higher, curled its lip for longer. "There we go, buddy," Ant said, praising the beast.

"What's he doing?"

"Flehmen response. When they sniff or drink the urine to see if she's in heat. He can smell it in the air too, like any male would. That curling lip action signals his interest. Our timing's on point today."

"I see," Mina said, understanding but not used to the primal habits of such large animals. The goats obviously mated, but she never saw it, nor studied their behaviors leading to the act. Ant opened the gate to the corral and gestured his arm to give way to Mina. "Part of me wants to sit this one out," she said.

"Nah, it'll be fun. We've done it once before and 'specially cause we know she's ready this time."

"He was kind enough to show us."

"Won't have to do much but keep her nearby. We're here to help ya, big guy," he said finally to the bull, which snorted as he patted its flank. Ant closed the gate. "See, he knows!"

Mina laughed. "Yeah, but the other time, it didn't work and was over quickly."

Ant ignored the attempt at an excuse. "Now—you just stand at Sally's head and talk to her, like before."

Mina touched the soft, flat side of the cow's jaw and stroked the bridge of its snout.

"There, there, sweet cow. My sweet Sally Baby."

Ant pulled the bull's harness toward Sally's hind, and the bull instantly rose to its back legs; its skinny pizzle shot out of its hold and became fully rigid. "Keep her steady now."

Mina braced herself for the force as the bull mounted the heifer.

"Real easy. All good."

"Is he doing it?" she asked, steadying her weight against the heft of its thrusts.

"Yep. He's in there!"

"You're doing great, girl," Mina whispered to Sally.

After a half-dozen or so pushes, the bull fell off Sally's back. In the light, the bald spot from Ant's head wound showed its scar and reminded Mina of the many nights in the first days when he grew comfortable with her tenderness as she'd helped him to heal.

"And he's got 'er done!" Ant pushed the bull away toward the farther side of the corral. Mina winced at the expression but understood its import.

"Let's put her in with the goats for now," he said. "That way, he won't bully her more."

* * *

I-95—Outside Jacksonville, FL

"Charlie!" Roland commanded from behind. "Hold up! Slow down—" His breath was shallow, interrupting the exhortation; his once strong voice had weakened. "I can't go any farther right now. I need to rest." Charlie took the weight of Roland's heavy side against the strength of his body and walked his companion into the shade of a large tree along the barren highway where they sat among tall grasses. Roland pointed to the large cooler they'd taken turns lugging individually down the road and then sharing the load by the handles. "Pull it into the shade," he ordered.

Charlie obeyed, then opened the lid to feel the coolness of the ice packs, which had warmed, removed two bottles of the medication, shook out a single pill from each, and handed them to Roland, who swigged a mouthful from the last full water bottle, swallowing the pills.

"You all right, bug?" Charlie entreated.

"I'm fine," Roland answered with his "leave-me-alone" sternness.

"No, you're not. I can tell," Charlie said.

Roland sneered at the obvious. "I'm still pissed off about having to leave the Audi."

"If it makes you feel better, you can still see it." Charlie hopped up to point it out in its place along a jagged line of abandoned cars down the road. "And there's an abandoned Porsche three cars down from it." Charlie sounded proud to have located a comparison.

"Ninety grand just to park it on I-95 in Two-Fucksville, Florida."

"At least we got pretty high up the state."

Roland turned to his side and groaned in pain.

"You all right?" Charlie's question wasn't answered.

"Observation isn't enough for you?" Roland quipped.

"What do you mean?"

"Nothing."

Charlie flicked the piece of grass he had been ripping in half. "Any idea where we are?"

Roland looked over at his longtime closest mate, partner, companion, never-husband—whatever the hell they were—and wanted to mock him mercilessly.

"I mean, I'd guess we're just outside Jacksonville," Charlie said.

"You'd guess right—" Roland couldn't suppress his sarcasm.

"Wonder how crazy it got there. Or how crazy it *still* is."

Roland shaded his eyes to look up the road. "Who knows," he said. "Seems pretty quiet here." He laid his head back onto a thicker patch of the grass. "I honestly couldn't give two shits what happens at this point. It's all over."

"It is. Has been for a minute," Charlie said, reviewing Roland's tall, gawky body, his right leg twitching, his breath shallow, his gaunt but still handsome face and thick brows which formed distinct points at their centers when he raised them. Charlie was the fairer both in color and character, ever inclined to defer to Roland's more assertive nature, a weakness he'd grown accustomed to accepting. But the world for which their relational dynamic had evolved was now ended, and he wondered how they might fare from this moment to the ends of their fates. They both knew Roland was facing a soon and certain end, but would it be months—a few years?

A figure moved toward them, far enough away for them to avoid detection if they moved deeper into the woods but exhaustion and resignation had overcome their mutually protective instinct. As the figure resolved, it revealed the bandanna on his head, baggy, loose pants, and a large handgun roosted in its holster. Charlie had begun to regret his decision to stay put by the road. The figure had finally seen them and approached.

"Eh-yo!" he called. Charlie became rigid. Roland looked up from his rest and squinted at the man who sauntered toward them. "You got any food?" he asked.

"No," Roland answered coldly.

"What's in that cooler then?" he demanded, moving his holstered hip in their direction, and glared at them as if self-satisfied.

"AIDS medications," Roland said flatly.

The man's face dropped, becoming repentant. "Man, I'm sorry," he said with surprising humanity. "You got AIDS?"

"Not yet." The man looked confused. "I've got HIV," Roland explained reluctantly. "My medication is in the cooler to keep it from going bad, but it will likely soon spoil from the heat and become ineffective, and then I will develop what is called full-blown AIDS."

The man said the last part with Roland in unison, suddenly understanding the situation. "My ma always talked about two uncles who died of that when she was a kid," he said. "That's some rough shit. She'd always say they were corpses before they were dead." His eyes had remained wide.

"I will be, yes."

Charlie's deepest and long-mitigated sympathies for his partner's condition almost burst out of his eyes, but the shock of Roland's unreserved candidness kept it back. He never spoke a word of the virus, hardly told a soul, but here and now voiced the facts of his fate without fear, nor shame, but stark acceptance.

"I thought that was over 'n shit?"

"It was never over, just hidden, managed by the drugs."

"Damn. That means—"

"Yes. There will be many people who will soon suffer the old death."

"Fuck me. Be like the walkin' dead up in here!"

"Already is," Charlie said calmly.

All three men reflected on the statement, wondering at the insecurity of the present conditions and the myriad possibilities which might befall any one of them.

"I escaped from that gang culture just north of here. No way of knowing what's next for me, but I got away from all that. So, if you goin' up that way, just watch out, especially with you two being homos and all. Sorry, but you know what I mean. They'll fuck you up. Like a prison war: white gangs, black gangs, Latino gangs—all that shit but, like, on steroids—like, literally. They runnin' things up there. Just be careful with yourselves."

"Thanks for the advice."

"We just might decide to sit here and die as we are right now, anyway," Roland declared.

The man nodded, not knowing what to say to that kind of submission to circumstance, being more of a fighter. "Well, ah—" He sniffled and wiped his nose. "If you do head on up that way, and you're looking to get something, I'll tell y'all this: Don't do business with nobody but Rathausen."

"Rat-who?" Charlie asked.

"Rathausen."

"And who is that?" Roland asked.

"Self-proclaimed King of the Oil Slick. That's what they call the trail that trades the government stockpiles from Bayou Choctaw, West Hackberry—" He used his dirty fingers to count out how many. "Big Hill and Bryan Mound over in Texas. Guess it's illegal an' all, but I don't really know what's legal or illegal no more."

"I see," said Roland. "We have no need for oil."

Charlie almost spoke when Roland pinched the fat on the back of his thigh. "Ouch!"

Roland sat up, crossing his arms around his knees. "*Shut the fuck up*," he muttered to Charlie, who understood not to mention the Audi.

The man creased his brow at them. "You both queers, then? I mean, shit, I ain't judge nobody or nothin', but—"

"Yeah, we're gay. We know. We need to be careful about it. So—where does this rat house guy stay?"

The man smiled and started walking off. "Headquartered in Jacksonville. Ask around, and you'll find him. He moves around a lot. He's got a good rep for being fair is all. That's why I mention it. But, you know, be careful and don't be too gay." They watched as he bid them good luck and moved farther down the road. "I'm off to Texas!" he yelled back, finally.

"You're going the wrong way," Roland mumbled.

"That was weird," Charlie said after a moment processing the exchange.

"Expect everything; be surprised at nothing, love-bug," Roland declared before lying back down, rolling to his side, and falling into a deep sleep.

* * *

Halloween was close, perhaps a week away. Mina had wanted Ant, urged him if not begged him, to move inside and take up the guest bedroom as his. But he'd had some doubts about the benefits of officially making a home with such an older woman and a white one at that. His fingers squeezed at his temples at the thought of rejecting her and her kindnesses, a seemingly racist one that guilted his conscience. He didn't want to imagine a mixed-race man of many generations and multiple American legacies could possibly indulge that kind of thought, but he'd had it. He gave it room to the more argumentative side of his mind, allowing it to prevail: She was white, and he didn't want that, no matter how beneficial the match.

The duvet made him too hot even if the temperature kept dropping lower by nightfall. He lay on the couch under the roof of the porch, staring through a crack of sky between the ledge and the canopy of the old American sycamore that sheltered most of the house. He searched for meaning in the twinkling orbs above, though discerning nothing but their subtle beauties. *It is all firelight*, he thought, the enchantments of the gods, illuminating their minds by cerebral lightning, flares, and fulminations, giving meaning to our silly-seeming existence.

It was time to leave.

At the next midday, Ant packed a small lunch of bread, cold scrambled eggs, and some goat butter, filled a liter canaster full of the drinkable water, and headed out.

"Goin' roamin'," he said, casually sliding the machete back into its sheath and strapping that to his back. Neither sure if he would be back by sunset nor if he'd be gone forever, he'd only packed a single day's portion of food to prevent alarm and not to take too much from her. Resourcefulness was not a doubt he had about himself.

"What for?" she asked, bewildered at the suddenness of his departure and inexplicably worried.

He looked back in response, and the hard but loving doubt in his face reminded her of their indeterminate relation.

"I'm not trying to stop you from doing anything," she said. "I'm just curious. I haven't, what should I say, *cohabitated* with someone in a while and thought it would be a small courtesy to let me know. That's all." Sudden nervousness grew around her speech, threatening something.

His wariness grew wise. "Just going to check out the local scene, if there is one, see who's about, what the talk is. Or see what's up for trade. See if there's a trading post or something like it—" The reassurance he aimed to provide and the sensibility of his explanations appeared to have cooled the instantaneousness of her concern.

"All right," she said, nodding. "That sounds good. You'd probably be more likely than not to find something like that west of here. Just be careful. Bunch of maniacs out there."

"Always am," he said as he grabbed his hat and sprang off the porch. An abundance of youthful energies had reached capacity in his vibrant frame; his aura practically shone with the likes of it that his deference to her security and sudden neediness could only be understood as satisfying mutual respect. Any further debate on his leaving might have provoked a supernova of wild determination. He needed to explore.

* * *

For the first time in weeks, Mina was left alone. Even though she'd been entirely on her own for months, this suddenly, inexplicably made her nervous. No one was more self-reliant, no one more emotionally independent. So why had her emotions collapsed inside her small body? Since lockdown, the energy upheavals, and her brother's suicide, perspectives on the unpredictability of others had threatened to destabilize the possibility of longer-term relations. Trading with the homesteading neighbors was one thing; living with another person in cooperation but no further definable reason was another—a bond had formed, more for her, she guessed.

Once Ant had disappeared behind the trees on the street, she'd wondered who he was, why he was there with her, and what he might be looking for now. Suspicion subordinated her goodwill but vanquished the troll of emotional betrayal to buttress the necessity of her continued survival. Suspicion had proved a great stabilizing mental state to inhabit. She stared long after his disappearance behind the line of trees, wondering if he'd ever come back.

* * *

On the road, there were some other walkers, day-trippers and longer-term travelers in various states of thirst and hunger. Ant nosed around a few paths newly trampled into the grass to feel for promise, but nothing jumped to his senses. Eventually, one or two stragglers he'd passed had become a dozen bodies, maybe more, walking in a kind of single-file line. As they all moved closer to one another, some kept their eyes permanently aimed at the ground, saying nothing, regarding no one as if traumatized by some unspeakable act, just following the flow. Others became chatty, discussing their successes and minor failures.

"Where must we all be going?" one of them said, as a kind of elbow to the side, an inside joke that hung in the air like a slur, almost offensive even to hint at the existence of the marketplace, not wanting to attract the wrong kinds. Ant observed the man who had said it, reviewed and judged him as he became irritated by the indifferent reaction to his networking style. A woman with her teenaged son moved to the other side of the tall, strong boy,

76

demonstrating an aversion to all men but him. Another man, dressed to hike a thousand miles, strode ahead with unnecessary speed, thrusting a sleek walking stick like a futuristic ski pole into the earth before him. All seemed to announce who and what they were. The path narrowed, and it was clear why the man had wanted to pass everyone who suddenly and inadvertently formed into a cluster of traffic. It was slow-moving, a bottleneck, but it led to an opening that Ant could see, a clearing like a private sports field where a makeshift trading outpost had sprung up.

Within ten miles, he had found what he had been looking for: information, goods, trade. People numbered in the many dozens, and he maneuvered among them to estimate their potential value to him, their intelligence, their openness, before he approached. There were barrels of apples, red and green; mounds of squash and piles of pecans. A boy of ten sat on a stool next to the harvest with a shotgun slack across his lap. His younger brother ran in circles around him.

"Quit it!" he yelled at the little maniac, trying to knock the kid down with the heel of the rifle's butt. "Keep your damn self still, Ro*by*!" It was slightly jarring to see such a young boy speak and act like a grown man.

A tower of pillows—some yellowed, some florescent white —leaned against mattresses stacked twelve high with no guard. There was silverware, dishes—all manner of household items— boxes of books with a sign that read "good for kindling." Then there was the fuel: gasoline, lighter fluid, a dozen bags of charcoal overseen by three heavily armed guards watching Ant's every move while he perused the goods and wares.

An elderly lady stood smiling but mute over the gallons of cider and towers of donuts she was trading for yarn to knit the kind of winter shawl she was wearing. It was a brilliant, psychedelic mixture of color, like haphazardly pieced together. She clocked the puzzled awe in Ant's face.

"Got to use whatever you've got on hand," she said and winked. He understood and nodded knowingly before passing.

As quickly as he could easily snarf a dozen donuts and down a gallon of cider, he had to conserve his appetites to spare whatever he might trade for something more important.

From behind what looked like a nineteenth-century pioneer's wagon, the inside resembling a small apartment, cracking and grinding sounds filled Ant's ears seconds before the earthy, sweet smell of ground coffee floated under his nose. Two women—one with large and beefy hands; one with slender, strong ones—worked at a station selling many pounds of beans their husbands had pirated from caravans coming up from Florida. Over a mortar the size of a large vase and holding a pestle the size of a small bat, the beefy-fingered woman cracked and ground the bean pellets into a rough chop like a home cook, while the slender-fingered woman refined the product in a smaller bowl. The muscles flexing in her overused hands revealed a life of working with them.

"What do you want for a pound of that?" Ant asked them both. The slender-fingered one refused to look up, while the beefy-fingered one estimated his worth and then spoke.

"A pound? Don't have near enough supply to dole out that much a time." She stared at him while the slender-figured one scooped another bowl of beans into the larger mortar.

"I see."

"Don't look like you got much to bargain with, neither."

"That's true. All I've got is some cold egg sandwiches and a sharp machete. Neither of which are on market."

"You'd expect a freebie then?" she asked, slamming the pestle into the mortar, sending bits flying out beyond its rim. The hostility was hardly a sign of a willingness to negotiate. An older gentleman waddled over, trying not to use his cane.

"See here, young man, if I may interrupt now—" Ant regarded him with a neutrality he'd perfected around a type of people he did not always trust. Sometimes, it was like dealing with blood; other times too sneaky. "These two here are angling for a few cords of white ash I trade behind that old school bus, but I don't drink coffee. Nor my wife. But I got the best firewood around, thanks to a secret tree farm I tend to and ain't *no one* knows about it. White ash. Burns the hottest." Ant nodded plainly, wondering where this would go. "But I've got a problem at the moment. Got a tracker stuck in the mud couple miles south a here. Need a strong young buck as yourself, if you'll pardon the expression, to help me free it up. You loan me your labor; I'll trade them my wood for your coffee." Ant again simply nodded but said nothing. The old man thought it'd be a sure thing, but Ant regarded him with the best damn poker face he'd ever seen. "You go on and think about it. I'll be here till dusk creeps up." The women observed Ant eagerly. Suddenly he had something they wanted badly.

Ant thanked the old man and walked away to give it some thought, not wanting to appear too easily dealt with, and to scope out the rest of the hillbilly bazaar. Within three feet, he caught the boy with the rifle making a wrenched-up face at him, staring at him for what seemed like one hateful reason. These were not his people and not even like his townsfolk. It amazed him how quickly a people's character could change when too far away from home, especially now that everything was up shit's creek. The boy's mother stood at her son's side with the same wrenched-up expression, which had the contours of a smile but none of its pleasantries.

Instead of backtracking, Ant walked the full perimeter before locating the school bus and approaching the old man, two fine horses grazing at his sides, who straightaway traded two cords of the prized wood for a pound of ground coffee, giving it to his wife to hold until payment was due. Ant's confidence in the man was secured. The horses were attached to a newly constructed wagon, whose enormous wheel the man smacked out of sheer joy to finally secure some assistance.

"Not quite as good as the olden days, but she works." His wife climbed into the front, slightly modified from an old sedan's car seat. "Accommodations by Hyundai," he joked, now smacking the seat top, and she chuckled. Ant climbed onto the couch of a backseat row. "Yours is from a minivan. Not sure the model. Found it at the clearing." He continued speaking, telling wild stories about their first few weeks in the newly broken world, as the horses pulled them beyond the marketplace. "You been to it before?"

"Nah. Didn't even know it existed. Was looking for something like it, however," Ant replied graciously.

"And where do you stay? 'Round these parts?"

"I'd say about three miles north." Ant lied to keep all the safer locations a secret for now.

"With your family?" the wife asked.

"With a friend," Ant said.

"Not too many a those these days, are there?"

"Almost none."

"We keep to ourselves mostly. Been preparin' for this apocalypse a while. Bible says as much. And it's a life that suits us just fine." He gestured to his wife who turned to face Ant and nodded pointedly. "Kinda like the Amish 'cept without those costumes and rit-chals!" His belly bounced like his chuckle could shake the whole of the world. "I got nothin' but time for all this," he finished, seeming to refer to the catastrophic collapse of society with the kind of levity only the truly wise can convey. His wife smiled and permitted his silliness, looking off her side of the vehicle toward some memory as they moved.

The wagon approached a tractor that was more than ankle-deep in a muddy puddle. The back right wheel was a foot deep in muck.

"It's why some a my wood went wet today, dammit." Again, he gestured to his wife like to a business partner.

"We don't want wet wood," she affirmed.

"Lucinda, here, she drove the wagon behind me. Usually use it to bring down the cords, but I wanted to get some fuel for this little beast, so I took it down too. Then the sumbitch got stuck."

"Because you got cocky, Albert," Lucinda said, correcting the record.

Ant took off the sheath and laid it and his backpack on his seat in the wagon. "I'm wonderin' if I shouldn't take my boots off," he said out loud.

"Probably best to," Lucinda answered. Ant acted on the advice. "Wet shoes ain't no good for walkin' and no good when they dry, neither," she added.

"Tractor's only a forty-six-inch front blade, but I'm too old, for my back." Albert gestured his left thumb toward his lower back and winced in pretend pain.

Ant stepped his bare feet into the cool sludge, and Lucinda cringed for the slimy feeling.

"Careful there's nothing sharp down there, now," she said.

Locating some stable footing against what felt like a brick, Ant placed his hands on the bumper. "Ready?" he asked expectantly. The old man leaned over the seat and turned the ignition, then stepped back, using a stick to push the gas with one hand and the other on the wheel to guide the motion. When the stick touched the gas, there was a great lunge forward. Ant slipped and would have gone under the vehicle as it came sliding back if he hadn't, like a crab, hopped instantly backward.

"Shit, son. Careful," Albert said.

Annoyed, Ant instructed him how to best and more slowly ease pressure onto the gas. They rocked the tractor back and forth at first.

"Now—let's rock it again and then on the third forward push, you press down on that pedal. Won't need much," Ant warned. "Ready?" he yelled over the reignited engine. "One. Two. *Three!*" The tractor bolted out of the hole; the old man fell onto his side, and Ant fell facedown into the mud. The tractor bounced off, looking like a derelict trying to escape from work. Lucinda observed the men with that grateful kind of Christian pity.

Businesslike, Albert said, "Let's go home and get you cleaned up."

* * *

In the dark, firelight bounced around his face. Its heat warmed his skin and enlivened his eyes. The shadowy effects dancing in unison had made a mask of his features. He rubbed his colder hands and shot warm breath into the gap cupped against his mouth. Lucinda roved behind them, lighting candles and placing the wax rods into lanterns around the room; then she removed the empty bowl of the broth she'd served him and returned to the kitchen, doing nothing to disturb her guest's peace. Ant faced his reflection in the window and, looking through it—the firelight had produced an unfamiliarity in the image—peered into the nebulous dark, imagining Mina's concern. He hadn't actually intended to stay away a whole night, but fate had figured his plans for him.

"Was the soup to your liking?" Albert asked, sitting by the fire in a large armchair, taking apart a rifle across his lap to clean it.

"It was good—thank you."

"The bread I got special yesterday," Lucinda added, standing between the men. "Did you see that sweet little lady with the donuts and cider?"

"Yes, ma'am. I did."

"She's, well, her *kin*, anyway, they're the flour producers and make bread for the trade. She makes the most pretty shawls. So dainty and sweet." Lucinda held her arms tight against her chest, imagining the item.

"It was very good bread."

A silence, not an escort of discomfort but a wave of restfulness settled among them, the kind of silence that is strange just for being strangers but a comfort nonetheless, while the firelight continued to make shadows on their faces. Staring through window, Ant leaned forward into the night, straining to see its dark play and what it might tell him of the future, still wondering if Mina was all right.

"Have you got a proper weapon?" Albert asked.

Ant threw his hand toward the machete in its sheath under the windowsill. "Just that."

Albert measured its length from his seat. "Looks like it could be a use, but I mean a real weapon, like this rifle here." He lifted it like a gesture of a gift.

"No, sir."

"Call me Berti, if ya please. No need for sir."

"Okay, Berti."

"I don't have none to spare, but I know where you can get one, and a good couple hot meals too. A beer if they have it. Afraid I don't have much work for you with my sons livin' so close, but I know a place." The information proved an antidote to the young stranger's seeming disinterested or distracted soul.

"How far from here?" Ant asked.

"Some miles, not exactly known. It's hidden, hard to spot. A hundred acres but well disguised and well patrolled at that." Albert sat forward in his seat, nodding at the point to convey the danger. "You stay with us the night, and I'll take you there in the wagon come morning." He eased himself into the full depth of his chair, distracted curiously into the darkness outside to see what foul thing attracted the interest of his guest. Ant couldn't help but gaze into the void, his light brown eyes doleful and full of thoughts. "I know nothin' about the world but the doings of my farm and the whereabouts around it. I know every actor and player within a fifty-mile radius, but beyond that, it's a scene on a stage I ain't never read, nor will ever read. But I'm smart enough to know its reach and power and to fear it and to prepare myself against its lust for domain over all living things under God, even me, Lucinda, and our little space here on Earth. We've been blessed, but it is rapacious of a beast, a great free-flowing vibe like a music machine in the looming air all around us, pushing the limits of our interests, always been there but never been this hungry in our times. We must be on watch. We must be on guard. And, if we must, we must die against it."

* * *

Mina lay in the dark, grown more accustomed to it than she might have anticipated in a world where electric current was never not in use, above and to the side, beneath and across the way, even while we slept: a matter as ubiquitous as air. But she did worry. About him. About his safety and whereabouts, far more intensely than expected. The missing company was felt as a kind of abandonment, a loss of security, comfort, and companionship, the strength of which, the sadness it had provoked, only a woman could know and only an older woman should resist and not keep too long in the realm of those phantom feelings. His presence in the home had provided such a degree of consolation that she'd slept through the night and soundly after the first few days proved his trustworthiness and his merits, and since then until tonight, she could feel the roundness of the loss. Now she was sleepless, walking into the bathroom. The light off the moon shone mineral white, lending ghostly shadows to any movement around her.

The backyard was lit by the bright paleness of the moon's glow, a shade of light that keeps its crevices, like on a stage half a second before its actors appear and a spotlight enunciates the soundlessness of that serenity. This scene seemed out-of-time, spooky, and frozen of life. A fat, dark mass stole her comfort and her attention as it moved deeper among the surrounding woods, circling the gaps and splinters of the trees, then darting out from behind a thing that had enlarged its figure, reducing that mass to a harmless tree trunk.

A large canine stepped into one of these spot-lit gaps and sniffed at the air as a prologue to drama. Startled, Mina pawed at the countertop for her eyeglasses to resolve the image. She'd never seen the animal before, and it was prowling, wolf-like.

"You little *fucker*," she mumbled, suddenly realizing it as the likeliest culprit in the earlier disappearance of one of the goats' kids. The animal patrolled the perimeter of the corral, sniffing at the ground on a mission; the bull lifted its head to the moon and groaned at the intruder, which growled and showed its sharp teeth. The bull stomped and pulled at the dirt beneath it, lunging once at the dog, which had moved off, vanishing into the woods. Approvingly, Mina softly nodded and went back to the warmth that was now a cold spot in her bed.

He remained still as her image left the frame of the window, staring up at the now lifeless space inside. Behind him, the dog, whose eyes sparkled like diamonds by moonlight, turned its head away from its master, its panting floodlit by the cold. Instinctively, he went to the back door and tried the knob, but it was locked, so he stared through the single glass square at its center and into the house, assessing its contents and spatial relations.

Alarmed by the creaking of the deck, Mina hurried into the bathroom, ducking beneath the sill in time to peer above its edge and, squinting, to see what looked vaguely like a man walking back into the woods.

* * *

In early morning, Albert presented the one-pound bag of pulverized coffee beans while Ant gathered himself from jumping off the wagon.

"I don't know where your road's goin', son," Albert said. "But I know it's somewheres good." Ant took the bag. "The entrance to the farm is down this field yonder toward where it drops off into a crick. You'll likely run inta someone with a big ole gun. Just put your bag down, raise your arms up high, and say Berti sent ya."

"Thank you, sir." He hesitated. "Albert."

The old man's face lit by the revelation. "Sir Albert!" He chuckled. "Now *that* I *could* get to likin'!" He slapped the reins against the horses' hind and rode off, lifting his hat and waving it behind him.

Shielding his eyes from the rising sun, Ant spotted the way toward a decline in the field and began walking, resisting overactive nerves, steeling himself against the armed confrontation he was expecting to face, hoping his color wouldn't interfere with their reason or their hearing.

As soon as a single foot had stepped onto the farther bank of the creek, he'd heard a bullhorn honking five times in short, emergency bursts that had receded, growing fainter by the second. Breathing deeply to wrangle the excesses of his heart, Ant braced himself, calming inner warnings. The sound of stomping hooves of many horses settled atop the mound of earth rising before him. He took the sheath from his back and laid it on the ground, but secured the backpack to seem normal, unafraid, innocent like a hiker. First a dark brown horse's head appeared above the rim of the hill, then a tan one, a white one—then a rancher hat, two, three above those horses' heads.

They'd confiscated the machete, but he was accepted for work once he'd named Albert as his referral and they'd discerned that he was at least mixed. A gruff-speaking man with a handlebar mustache, thick, gray, and white opened the splintered wooden door to the shed where Ant was to spend his nights.

"There's two cots left a here. Pick whichever one you want. It's apples today. Beets tomorrow. And persimmons on Thursday." The man stepped outside the shed back into the daylight. "You shit in that small shed by the stump in the ground. The other is for a lady, if any happen through here." He turned back, finally looking Ant in his unflinching eyes. "For your labor of three days, you'll get a firearm and a box of bullets for your journey away. Two meals a day, breakfast and supper. And if yer caught eating anything of the product, you'll be banned for life, and lord knows what else. Whatever you come with is yours but guard it. We don't play lawyers for nobody but ourselves, tending to e-judicate by a hot pellet to the head."

His stale breath hit Ant's nose as the rancher pointed to his chest, barely touching the shirt above his flesh. Ant's face fell slack and calm, staring back as if at a judge, repentant for being there as a pretense for succeeding there.

"If you show any signs of bad temper, mental illness, er any kinda flaw in your manly composures, you don't get nothin', and you'd best to watch yer back on your way out. You hear all that?"

Ant conceded. "Yes sir, course." His country voice asserted itself as he could still feel the ghost of the man's finger on his chest, wanting to rub it away.

"Put yer things on the cot you want and set to waitin' by the shit shed for the flatback to bring ya to the field." Ant understood, and the man climbed onto his horse, seemingly exasperated by everything. "Final word: Keep yer hands off the women who work here. Better not be a meddlin' type."

There was no one around once the rancher had left, and Ant tried to whistle to soothe his heart, but his tongue flopped forward from the heat of the growing day. Only a few belongings were scattered among the cots, which totaled a dozen. For ten other men, there wasn't much to show of it. The pound of coffee was his most valuable possession, so he'd hidden it in a rotten old tree stump behind the shed and went to the appointed location for the flatback, which he assumed would be the only transportation around the fields. Soon enough, it arrived, looking like the tractor and cart for the haunted hayrides of better days. The driver tipped his hat, and Ant hopped onto the back, seating himself on a bale of hay, improving his view of the hilly land.

By process, the leaves were in the final stages of swapping summer green for the rich autumn colors like peach, apple, and strawberry-rhubarb for the eyes to eat. The noise from the tractor's engine smothered all other sound, isolating Ant's point of view. Enabled by the deafness produced from the noise, he observed the scene like a tourist and not like a worker. Three days he would stay at this plantation to get his reward and carry on back to Mina. But when the tractor crested the hilltop, a feeling, more like a wariness than a trauma, invaded his wandering soul. Rows and rows of men in fields, orchards, and groves toiling for next to nothing for some larger purpose: the same context; the same people; the same nation; the same region even, but a different story to be told.

"Apples for you, I'm told," the driver shouted over his shoulder as he switched off the ignition. "That's the second orchard down bout half a mile on the left. Can almost see it from here." He shifted in his seat, extending his arm to point it out. "See that one tall oak in the middle there? Just beyond that." Ant thanked him for the service and hopped out of the tractor. "See ya at the mess tonight," the driver said, quickly restarting the strident engine and carting the flatbed away.

* * *

While Ant picked apples out of shady trees among sullen, taciturn men, Mina searched the woods for any sign of the man she thought she'd seen the night before. Paranoia had worked on her in the past, especially after Denny's suicide. Shadows fooled her for a man more often when she feared or felt haunted. Knives, shears, scissors and other deadly objects she hid in a box that she'd pushed under her bed. She'd leaned a golfing nine-iron against the window frame, tucking it behind the curtain. The chamber of her handgun was full and resting in her front-right pocket at all times.

Tracing the grounds of her property, she observed nothing that would suggest a stranger had been stalking them, not that there would have been explicit signs, but she had to feel the space with her senses, matching what she'd thought she'd seen to her intuition, which had since heightened to the apprehension of a threat. There was a newly hardened pile of dog excrement near the entrance to the corral, but the animal she had seen clearly with her glasses.

"I'm fully armed!" she announced into the air. "And I've killed a man before!" Stillness dwelt in all that surrounded her as her words broke apart, impotent on the crispy air. Nothing moved nor made a noise. She scanned the woods, like for a ghost one perceived by chills up the spine but couldn't see. Silence and stillness. She cocked her head to the sky and screamed like an Irish banshee.

A tenth of a mile away, he lifted his head at the sound of her indistinct yelling and pulled his crusty lips across his teeth to smile.

* * *

Barrels against barrels of red and pink apples, dull and shiny, lined the tractor-stamped grass as men dumped each one into industrial-deep, steel cartons the size of shipping crates, groaning with each lift; moaning with each tilt setting probabilities among them, figuring who would be likeliest to spill the fruity globes onto the grass and not dump into the crate. But Ant had developed a keener style. Instead of hoisting the barrel, threatening to sprain or break the back of the man who toiled with its weight, he bent at his knees and sprang up, lobbing the barrel into the air, twisting his torso in the motion so the apples would spray out of their respective barrels and file into the carton as if by the precision of a factory line. The men nearest him regarded the ingenuity as a kind of performance and resented the newest one among them for his hubris, but while Ant was preoccupied with his work, some attempted to mimic the maneuver to poorer effect. Apples began to cascade down the side of the container, bouncing off its edges and pelting the men's heads and shoulders. Some laughed; some were irritated. Ant offered to demonstrate, and two accepted the instruction. A third spit on the ground and walked back to the barrels, hoisting and dumping them just as he had before.

"Somethin' too feline bout you, son," he said before turning back to the work line. Ant dismissed it with a cheeky smirk, knowing the natural production of enemies was something only to make note of. Once necessity proved the need for action, he might pounce but now he just smirked.

"Ignore him," said one of the two impressed by Ant's style and who had tried the maneuver, now wanting to perfect it.

"I did," Ant replied flatly.

"I mean no intrusion." He paused to wonder at Ant's continued disregard for friendliness. "I'm Henny. Hendricks in full, but I used to drink a lot of brandy." It was his introductory joke to someone he liked. But Ant either hadn't heard him or hadn't cared. A robust man with thick fingers and a heavy, dark beard, Henny laughed for himself.

"Fine by me," Ant said, thinking any kind of response would be sufficient. "I don't busy myself with other men's habits."

"I don't drink that shit anymore," Henny said, punishing the point like a reflex to soften the blow of Ant's disinterest. "Gave it up for Lent once and haven't sipped a drop of it since." Ant remained aloof but finished picking up the fallen apples and throwing them upward into the cargo dump. "So—ah—where you headin'?"

Ant resigned himself to Henny's attempt at an even chat. "Nowhere particular. Just here and there, wherever I can work, find some resources."

"I hear that. I'm from up north, originally. Been down here long enough to start sounding like them, though. Troubled days we got. Even more trouble ahead."

"Doesn't seem like it could get any worse than this."

"Bro, this farm is a rarity around here. Why you think they patrol it so hard? I'm headin' to Texas. Hear it's rebuilding better than anywhere and making quick work of exiting people who aren't for law and order." Ant looked up. "Seems like as solid a bet as any. This farm is good for a temporary stay, but you don't want to hang here too long. They've got a strict hierarchy and don't take well to outsiders trying to get in."

"Definitely got an intensity about it."

"You're sizing it correct. You remember when they first told you about steppin' out of line? They mean that shit. They will fuck you up and throw you out. Can't come back, either." Ant nodded as they continued to walk between the line of barrels and the slow-moving tractor; the one doing his maneuver, the other standing on his toes and dumping the barrel overhead. "Anyway, man. Texas. Think about it."

"I'm not going with you."

Henny laughed. "I know, man. No worries. Just lettin' you know about it. You seem like a good dude." Ant cut his eyes at Henny. "I'm not hitting on you, don't you worry. Just lettin' you know is all. I only talk about Texas to people I'd want to live near."

"I hear ya."

A whistle blew loudly but distant.

"Time's up."

"Can't be five yet, can it?" Ant asked.

"Sure is. Look at the sun. They're real prompt. That's one of the good things. When work is done, it's done. They don't want anyone overworked, and they do want people to come back for the work, if not to stay too long."

"What do we do now?"

"We leave the barrels here for the next crew to pick up tomorrow." Ant stood still as Henny walked off, turning around to wave him on to follow. "Well, come on now. Follow me to the mess for eats."

* * *

The setting vermillion sun enflamed her cheeks to a rosy hue, and Mina squinted after its distance, wondering how the night would go. All morning, she'd hunted him as deep into the property as she'd felt the courage to probe. But he'd had his eye on her at a greater distance and sooner. The wolf-dog was tethered to a leash, which he held. It was one that never barked but growled, though he listened to the panting beast for that guttural resonance, sometimes provoked by being leashed. The tension between being hidden and being revealed aroused his deepest pleasure. Binoculars gave him a closer view, but he would walk backward as she advanced, searching the woods for the threat, and he mocked the terror in her face in his thoughts, exciting his nerve to attack her that evening.

* * *

Shadows of quickly moving things swept her periphery, but when she would turn to face the apparition, it was a gently swaying sapling or a couple of squirrels, one chasing the other around a thick and wrinkled trunk; even a white-tailed deer hopping to safety: never the demon-man she anticipated. But she knew he was out there, having seen him walking into her woods, no matter how blurry the image was without her glasses; her instinct knew it just as well, could sense it in the ether. If she had been blind, she still would have known. Every sense and its corresponding spirit, even the ones that rise higher into unspeakable realms, had been triggered by the essence of an evildoer mixing among them.

Inside, she locked all the windows and both doors, barricading the front one with a bookcase, though she'd strained her back pulling it into place. Most of that day, she spent loading and reloading the gun, assuaging the building anxiety with confidence, watching the backyard all the while, almost hoping he would come so she could blow off his head once and for all. But she knew he would be the type to approach in the night. At dinner, she took some goat cheese from the cellar and made a sandwich with stale bread, barely finishing the meal.

* * *

The mess hall was loud with boisterous talk, the clanging of dishes, the calls for more drink, and a whistling match for the women's attentions. They were the servers—mostly women, young and old—milling about the floor, answering the men's requests and questions, keeping any foul talk in strict abeyance if not completely suppressed. There were five of the farm's perimeter soldiers with automatic rifles at the sides and corners of the massive dining hall, eyeing the room for indecency against the business of the women.

Ant claimed his seat next to Henny, who'd pointed to their table near the food line.

"It's good grub, but if ya don't get in there fast, it's gets a little—I don't know. It's not as good after a while in those serving trays, ya know?"

Ant said nothing, just assumed Henny knew what he was talking about.

The food was served with ice-cream scoops. Brown and green lumps of some concoction inhabited his tray. A slab of meat which could have been a pork chop but was colored more like beef steamed in the cooler air. They sat to eat.

"You'd think," Henny said with his mouth full of the softer green stuff. "You'd think this being a farm, they'd have better food." Ant nodded and listened. "It's not that it's bad. Like I said, it's grub. But you'd think—"

Ant looked around their table and then more widely into the room to estimate the number of men in the mess. An unusually white smile caught his eye; then eyes locked into his as if waiting to be seen.

Skin like faintly toasted bread, not quite caramel, not quite brown. Thick but well-managed hair pulled off her face by a headband. Eyes like a leopard. Dressed like all the other servers but altered, meant to be noticed. Ant looked down and away, not expecting to find someone like her in this place.

Henny bent his thick neck around to see. "She's still lookin' at ya," he said, chuckling. "Damn pretty. Don't think I ever seen her."

"Stop," Ant said.

Henny heard the command in the sound of the word more than the word itself. "I gotchu."

"I don't need any of that kind of trouble here."

"No doubt. I've seen 'em hustle one or two of us straight outta here for it."

Ant looked up and then down again. "Shit, she's coming over here. Jus—talk about something else—"

"A'right—so, uh, tell me about that special move you do with the apple barrels." Ant almost rolled his eyes but started laughing, rousing Henny.

"What's got you two all in stiches?" she asked.

Ant took sudden control of himself. "Aw, you know," he said in a cavalier way, "you know how men can be—"

"Sure do," she answered, not hesitating. "Is there anything I can get for either of you?"

"I'd love some milk if there's any left," Henny said.

She nodded. "And you?"

"I seem to be all right."

"Great." Smiling, she walked back into the kitchen.

"Don't seem so bad."

"No. Not at all." Ant seemed surprised. "Seems normal."

"I guess she looks like she wants the attention more than she acts like it."

"Maybe. But she's also bait," Ant said, eyeing the armed soldiers eyeing them. "She's probably been told to flirt with us to see who responds."

They went back to eating, though Ant's disposition had changed from guarded to more curious now that he'd imagined it might be a setup. Her openness, her coolness had transformed his prejudice into attraction. But he had to remain in control.

"Whatd'ya say we hit the bar after?" Henny asked. "All they serve is watered-down beer, but it's all right. You'll get a buzz after your fourth one."

"There's a bar here?"

"Yes, sir, but like I said, no one is getting too drunk, least not us. Costs money, though—another way they can take back what they're giving us. You here on the wage or the trade track?"

"Trade." Henny looked surprised. "I don't have a proper weapon, just an old machete. I need a gun."

"I understand," Henny said and then winked. "Beer's on me then. Money wages probably only good for something here anyhow."

* * *

It was getting dark. Like an old invalid, Mina had spent more hours of the afternoon than she'd wanted in a chair she'd placed in her bedroom that both faced the door and had a view of the backyard. But she had dozed off and, of a sudden shock, like hearing some preternatural noise in the distance of her mind, she jolted awake, searching frantically through blurry eyes and a groggy memory, desperate to confirm the security of her position. There was nothing. The room, the house, the yard—all was calm and quiet. Another setting sun framed within the window of the far side still illuminated the room. Her silhouette fit perfectly within the boundary of the casement and darkened what fell behind her. All seemed well and undisturbed, though it was not.

Two oil-burning lanterns she'd found in the cellar, filled earlier, she now lit, watching as the flames burst to life. She placed glass hurricanes over the tops, which tamed the fire and regulated the light they gave like a portable furnace, hanging one on a hook by the chain of the stairwell's missing chandelier, carrying the other upstairs to the room. The gun she gripped in her hand, searching the house for the intruder again, checking the locks one last time before settling back into her bedroom for the night.

A hinged window running along the porch where Ant had slept had not been locked, a window she'd never much used but figured Ant had opened to provide airflow across his face. Locking it, she proceeded to recheck every closet and corner on the first floor, even venturing outside and into the storage basement, which she'd locked, unlocked, then locked again a third time to make sure, and went back inside. An eeriness haunted the house and her mind; even the smell of it seemed to have changed, the air like wet mud, mocking the careless way fear muddies one's perception of what's around them. At the base of the stairs, she sniffed at something rank, however faint, hanging nearby.

* * *

He watched as her nose wrinkled and her nostrils flared, careful to allow only the slimmest line of sight to catch view of her body from behind the barrier wall between the kitchen and where she stood. Though cautious, he felt no fear. His pulse was regular, but his confidence soared. Even if she had spotted him—she had obviously detected the deep forest air he'd brought inside—he was now in the position to use brute force, if only earlier than he had planned to. Leaning back into the kitchen, he listened to the creaks from her steps up the stairs. Then his socked feet soundlessly moved him down the galley kitchen to the back side entrance, where he stepped out and into the sunroom, suddenly startled to see her still standing at the base of the staircase, head facing downward and away from him. He froze, unsure where to move, desperate to preserve the tension of his hunt. She appeared unmoved and lost in a daydream. Finally, she climbed the stairs.

* * *

Torches lit their way on the path from the mess to the bar. Only half a dozen men sat inside or stood around smoking in a small circle near the entrance. A semi-trailer had been converted into this watering hole; windows had been sawed out of its sides for a view and some air. Henny and Ant sat at the bar when the golden-skinned woman from the mess hall reappeared in front of them, wearing a pink hoodie, seeming much less engaged and engaging.

"That was a quick move," Ant said to her.

"I'm only overflow at the mess. This is my main gig," she said while pouring warm beer over ice for two other customers.

"Can't keep an underground freezer?" he teased.

"We can. We do. Last winter was a cold one, and they cut out blocks of ice from the pond and keep it under sawdust in the house barn. They just don't allow the beer in there. So, we use the ice."

"Waters it down more too," Henny added conspiratorially. "That's why there's not too many men here."

She shrugged and, in doing, sort of agreed with him but couldn't elaborate, couldn't say what she really thought about anything. Ant noticed that behind her eyes there was a lot of talking and believing and expressing, but her full pink lips were softly pressed shut.

"What's your name?" he asked gently.

"Lady," she said, smiling, placing the regulated beers before them, her eyes lingering. His groin surged with evolutionary lust.

"Nah, that's not it," he said.

"It's what *they* call me." Winking, she moved down to the other end of the bar to fill another order.

* * *

The house was completely secured from the inside, and Mina sat in the silence. The sun had finally inched its way down the back of the house, and darkness followed. A smaller lantern stood on a side table to the right of the bed, the side she slept on. The hall lantern she'd just extinguished, so only the soft little glow of candlelight filled the far ends of her bedroom. Stuffing the bed with pillows, she placed one of her grandfather's Special Ops wigs she'd found in the cellar at the top of the mound. It looked enough like a person to give her the time she would need to cock the gun and shoot him dead. Once the decoy was arranged to her liking, she slowly turned off the lantern, adjusted to the faint moonlight, and sat on the chair under a blanket among two towers of pillows and other bedroom junk she'd built at its sides. And waited.

An hour passed. Maybe two. There was nothing, not even the sound of the dog in the distance, not even the rustling of leaves by the wind. She began to hope he had moved on from her and toward someone else, imagining he'd heard her threats to kill and that they had worked to scare him off. The gun lay carefully in her lap, her finger on the trigger. Her eyelids grew heavy and drooped.

* * *

A couple of beers had turned into four, and though the alcohol levels were allegedly low and diluted by the ice, Ant had begun to feel a buzz, talking indiscreetly to other men in the bar, men he did not know nor would have intended to know. Henny laughed at his jokes and tried to keep an eye out for trouble. Ant gestured for Lady to come to his call. Henny pushed his arm down.

"Hey now, four's about all I got money for—"

"It's cool. Just one more."

"You doin' all right, skipper?" she asked.

"Skipper?"

"Yeah—*skipper*. If I'm the lady, you're the skipper. Another round?" She laughed in his face.

"Jus' one more." He leaned closer to her lips.

"I said I can't afford no more—" Henny repeated, trying to pull Ant back from getting too close to the lady.

"It's all right, Henny," she said. "He can owe me one." Henny raised his brow and went back to sipping his final beer.

* * *

Her snores filled the room, sounding deep into an inevitable but poorly timed slumber; something had reassured her of his absence. It was the silence. It was too quiet for a lumbering maniac to be lurking around outside. And the dog would have made some kind of noise. The comfort of the silence, of these seeming facts, had lulled her to sleep.

Pushing the closet door into the room, he stepped out and stared at her silly attempt to form a body under the duvet. He had been in the closet for some time, just waiting, having waited for longer in the sunroom downstairs until she made a final check around the perimeter of the house. He had then moved into position inside of the closet. The unlocked window in the front room had been his entry point, and it wasn't difficult for him to evade her movement around the house before he'd located the hiding spot in the bedroom. He had killed the dog the day before because of its potential to disrupt the necessary quiet of his predation, its dried blood still under his fingernails. The dull iron scent wafted to his nose in slight traces of the carnage as he waited for her to settle for the night. Now that she was asleep, he moved toward her, not knowing her left eye had opened into a slit.

* * *

The torches around the bar had been put out, and only the light of the moon shone on this half of the world. Ant and Henny weren't drunk, but what little alcohol they'd had to drink in the past year allowed what little alcohol they had just drunk to take effect more intensely. Not stumbling but meandering down the path, they discussed the future, as friends might do.

"I dunno, man," Henny said. "For so long, I didn't think about nothin' in the future but where am I gonna eat—*what* am I gonna eat. Where will I sleep—forget about sleeping with a woman. Things looked real bad before I found this place."

"You been here long?" Ant asked.

"Four months."

"I didn't realize that. Thought you were like me."

"Thought I was more of an itinerant kind of man too, but it's too good here, and by good, I mean stable, if not true good. No, life ain't good here. Can't have a relationship, can't get truly drunk, can't eat nothin' but what they serve, gotta sleep with at least a couple strangers in the room. No—it sure ain't good. But it's safe. It's clean. It's regular. I ain't some kind of maverick, you know?" He laughed at himself and nudged Ant, whose disinclination to comment turned Henny reflective. "Guess I should be. We all should be. Men, I mean. We all should be building towns and cities and industries. Having families. Raising kids to be strong and take over all the things we leave to them. But, nah. Most of us are scoundrels or too dumb to figure it all out, like me."

"You're not dumb, Henny. You're scared."

"I am, that's a certainty." He reviewed the heavens, careless of the stars. "You hear about Texas?"

"Have I heard about Texas? I am aware that a place called Texas exists," Ant replied.

"Yeah, I know, I know, but did you hear me when I told you about it?" Ant mimed confusion at the point. "It's s'posed to be the new place, like a renewed frontier. Another country. They got their own farms and industry. People are free. I hear it's best place to be."

Ant listened and nodded, looking up at the heavens too, careless of the stars, pondering their meager prospects. "Too far from here," he said, and Henny finally agreed.

They arrived at their bunkhouse and were kicking stones against its walls when a fair voice called out from behind. The lady was jogging toward them and carrying a cap.

"Hey!" she called before they went inside, because once inside, she wasn't allowed to knock and was surely prohibited from entering any of the men's houses.

"Now, *that's* trouble," Henny said and quickly opened the door and went beyond its forbidding threshold. Ant remained, slightly confused by the new surroundings, the new people and customs, the newness of the farm that was like learning the ways of a camp or a prison.

"This yours?" She stood before him and held up the cap.

"No, ma'am, it sure isn't."

"Oh—" Her eyes told him she didn't care about the cap or who it belonged to. "You're new here."

"I am."

"How do you like it?"

"Neither like it nor dislike it. It serves a purpose."

"I get it. I wouldn't stay too long here either, but I've no choice."

"Why's that?"

"You've seen it out there. Dangerous place this world is." She twirled her lusty hair, looking up from lowered eyes. Ant's body reacted against his better wishes, and she could tell. His mind became instantly hollowed out of better judgment.

"Let's go around back here," she suggested, moving behind the bunkhouse, and Ant dumbly followed. The hoodie was zipped but opened at the breast as she exposed herself to him. And like all magnetism insensible to reason, they embraced and skin against more skin, torso against torso, sweat against sweat, lips to lips, part into part, back and forth like a cradle of urging, higher and higher, sweeter and sweeter, then, "Fuck, fuck, fuck," he said and collapsed, both loving and hating having done this.

* * *

He lunged, and his grimy hands grabbed her shoulders, pulling her up from the chair. In a sudden terror, she had frozen. The stiffness of her body inhibited the attack, and they tumbled backward into the side of the mattress. The gun went flying under the bed to the far side. Adrenaline shocked her brain, provoking her body to action as she leapt across the bed to reach under it for the gun. His hand cupped the waistband of her pants, trying to pull her back, but the rubber gave, snapping at the tension as he tipped backward. Her left hand found the butt of the gun, drew it to the other, cocked the weapon, and without standing fired straight into the darkened foreground where he had begun to rise.

"Fuck. Fuck. Fuck," he said and collapsed onto the floor.

She stood and kicked his head as he groaned, bleeding out, hugging at his middle. The vacant, livid eyes of this assailant met hers, and, lifting the gun, she shot him point-blank in his head which smacked against the hardwood floor with a final clap.

Again, his head smacked each step as she dragged the body from upstairs to the front door, sweating like a mule from the work. Outside, she kicked his boots to the side of the porch as she continued to pull the corpse down the front steps toward the gravel drive. The body scraped against the dirt and rocks, making a long mark the length of the space she had dragged him. A small chair, an old schoolhouse chair, served as his perch. The body, propped up by its bulk, slumped into itself and sat on the chair at the top of her drive as a warning to any and all who might think to come to this house looking for trouble.

* * *

The men grabbed at his feet and his arms and his legs.

"Get outta that bed, you dirty lil *nigger!*" one of them yelled. Ant hadn't heard that word in a very long time, and it stunned him to stillness. They pushed him, half naked, out the door and into the bright morning sun. The other working men who slept in the bunk had already left, earlier than usual, including Henny. He was alone against this small militia that included the tractor driver and the man who had given him the layout and the rules the day before.

"Cut that language out *now*, Trip!" the elder, imposing one said, then turned on Ant, pointing and visibly angry. "We told ya: *no* funny business. You broke them rules. You're gone and not ever to come back on penalty of death. You hear? *You* know what you done. You got what I will call ten minutes to run off this property and then we start shootin'. Ten. Starting now. Go—"

Ant stared at the men with his clothes in his hands, unsure what to do at first. "No gun?" he asked mindlessly.

The man's face flushed bloody red. "No gun. Now that's the last thing I'm a say to you. Go. *Now!*" He shot his revolver into the air, and Ant went running, not bothering to put on his clothes but carrying them as he ran down the hill and over the creek, into the field, and clear off the property.

When it was dark, he returned to the periphery of the farm to retrieve the pound of coffee he'd left behind. Sneaking through the night once the light was no good, he kept to the edge of the boundary, on the lookout for sentinels, and when it seemed all clear, he rushed to the top of the hill behind the bunkhouse where he'd stayed, searching for the stump where he'd hidden the backpack, and tripped, having knocked into the stump as the front door smacked against its frame and a man came out for a piss. Ant briefly caught the outline of the man, recognizing the shape of his former mate.

"Henny," he whispered.

"Huh?"

"Henny, is that you?"

"Yer goddamned lucky it's me," Henny whispered back. "What the *fuck* you doing here?"

"Forgot something."

"You better get off this land. You'll get me killed too."

"I'm leaving."

"Good—you done fucked up."

"Hey—Henny."

"*What*—"

"See you in Texas."

"Yeah, right. I'll see ya in the hereafter first, I spect."

"Take care."

"Go fuck yourself and get on out of here."

* * *

Anxiously, Mina wound a strand of yarn around her finger, winding and unwinding it over and over, while she reviewed her more pressing plans and interests. Now and again struck blank and in shock from the instant willingness to kill a man, the doubtlessness of her instinct, the lack of remorse in her conscience left her unmoved, unfeeling, unable to think. The subtle energies that had powered the endless buzzing of her mind had been zapped to death. The wall at which she stared was painted Easter yellow, but the plaster had begun to crack over the decades, conducting blackish lines through the spring-like melody of the original color. She traced them with her eyes, back and forth, wondering how many fissures the wall would suffer in the years ahead, leading at some point to its collapse. It was already buckling at the bottom edge. Who might rebuild it or remove its rubble forever?

* * *

A sorrowful ache like a cancerous plague began to throb at the very base of Ant's lower left back, and he bent over as if a bigger man were pushing him into a hunched position. His right arm triangulated his side as if holding up the failing structure of bones. When he finally approached Mina's house, a great eagerness to rest rose from his toes to his dry lips. He needed water to lubricate the engine of his worn-out soul, rusting at its edges. A stink, a waft of corpse-scented air, floated past his nose seconds before he came upon the mound of inanimate flesh propped onto the elementary school chair holding it mostly upright. Dark streaks of dried blood stained the clothes, and a swarm of flies flew on and off the rotting man as the wind blew them. Perceiving a victory, Ant walked around the corpse and up the drive to the house.

The door was open. The quietude of the warming day touched each plain thing around him. Not the chirp of a bird was heard. No fly buzzed at his ear. The wood flooring creaked at each step, announcing his presence, but she remained still as he observed her at the table staring at the cracked yellow wall. He rested his whole body onto a nearby armchair.

"You all right?" he asked, pondering her ponderousness.

Shock kept her quiet. He removed the ground coffee from the backpack, leaned up and beside her, offering its aroma for her to smell. Her nose caught its scent as it sniffed at the air; her spirit revived, her hands clasped the bag, her head gently fell into his side, and she sobbed without shedding tears.

"I killed a man," she said.

"I know. But listen," he said, pausing to groan from another sudden outburst of dull pain. "We gotta go to Texas."

"*Texas?*"

CHAPTER TWO

Jenna killed the dog first. It dropped dead as it leaped at Nelson. Bursting out the back door, full of fire and fury, in a blaze of vigor like a wrath of death, Jenna unloaded the entire clip inside the horde of ominous men while Jeremy, having bludgeoned the one closest to him, stood behind her yelling and screaming at the top of his lungs, commanding her to kill them all. The few remaining vagrants ran away, escaping certain death, yelling to unseen others not to proceed with the attack. Jenna's chest heaved from the excitement that coursed throughout her body like an electric current. Jeremy walked the perimeter of the yard, checking the body count, congratulating Jenna on a job well done.

"Great *fucking* work," he said and kicked the torso of one of the bigger corpses, slipping into his military persona as if never abandoning it. Jenna nodded silently, her head barely moving, calming herself, breathing deeply to restore the sanity she'd temporarily denied. Jeremy pulled her forehead to his like a soldier, but gently, staring directly into her eyes. "Good stuff. You saved our lives. Shake it off." He patted her shoulder and then went inside.

Jenna stayed in place. An irony almost like a smile appeared on her lips. "Shake it off," she mumbled to herself and chuffed at the absurdity of the phrase. Killing had come more naturally than she would have imagined—hardly a spontaneous joy but a rush not unlike that feeling. This was the revelation that her mind zoned out on. Was there really any need to rationalize this?

Protecting the people she loved, cared for, survived with—whatever—removed any hesitation to act with an unmitigated intent to kill. And it was shocking how quickly it had appeared at the surface for action.

Inside, Jeremy, Nelson, and Pru sat around the kitchen table, laughing when they saw her see them, and it relaxed her conscience.

"What the heck is so funny?" she asked.

"Oh darlin,' you looked like Clint Eastwood out there," Pru said.

Nelson was more impressed than amused. "You didn't give a single fuck, just bang, bang. Bang, bang!" He gestured as if holding the rifle himself. Pru enhanced his mime with more laughter, however oddly premeditated or performed or something, pretending to find humor to stabilize her horror at the situation. A certain semblance of sanity had set itself between the couple, but it was a too-obvious front. An instant cope. Performing for others had been their specialty in normal times.

* * *

In the background, Jeremy's expressionless face contrasted with their fragility, knowing their reaction was more from disorientation at the genuine horror. His eyes resolved and widened when Jenna looked his way, confirming her own intuition to keep some psychological distance from the pair, giving them space to work through the catastrophic disruption to their version of reality, if at all possible.

Jeremy engaged Jenna quietly as Nelson and Pru removed themselves from the kitchen to sit in the living room, suddenly silent and embracing one another.

"We've got a lot on our hands here," he said.

"I know," she said gravely. "But there's no way we can abandon them now. We have to watch out for them."

"Goddammit," Jeremy mumbled.

106

"We'll just have to give them explicit direction."

"But *nicely*," Jeremy said, rolling his eyes.

"Yeah," she said flatly. "They're in a delicate state. It is what it is."

One of the corpses began to move outside in the backyard. Jeremy's eagle eye caught it through the window of the breakfast nook. Its arm was pulling its carcass across the lawn. He grabbed the rifle and went outside.

Jenna turned away, squeezing her eyes as the blast from the gun echoed throughout what felt like the diminished potential of the world.

* * *

Upstairs, Nelson held his face in his hands quietly sobbing into them. Jeremy stood in the hall and stared at the man, feeling some pity for the guy and not a little resentment. *Another burden*, he thought. Another person to have to tend to. Another who must be told what to do, and when, and probably how. Jeremy would not waste time with why.

"Hey," he said softly, frightening Nelson out from his private struggle. "You need to snap out of it. I know you lost a kid and all, and I'm sorry for it, but I need you to be strong, man. To be able to make decisions, and smart ones, the right ones. I can't have you simping out on me." Nelson sat expressionless, his mouth open in shock, his chin beginning to quiver, which made Jeremy feel like he'd wronged the guy but also that his interests wouldn't be met, and now he might catch some slack for having directly expressed them. "Jesus Christ" was all he could say in response to the pathetic heap of male flesh in front of him.

Nelson put his face back into his hands. The door to the ensuite bathroom opened, and Jeremy quickly bowed out of the room, sensing Pru's destructive influence on Nelson's remaining sanity.

"Leave them alone right now," Jenna said, leading Jeremy down the stairs. "They are a mess. We're going to have to leave this house and this area, now that we've been spotted, but we've bought some time by attacking them first. You need to focus."

"I'm thinking we take the car toward Atlanta and head west on 20 to Birmingham," he replied. "It's got a full tank. My family is that way. It's the best move."

"Could be," she said. "I'm just afraid we'll go as far as that one tank, not be able to refuel, and only have our feet to walk on."

He shrugged. "At some point, that might be where we're at. I just want to make sure it's near some resources when it does. Plus, Texas got to be pretty independent these last few years. That's the safest place to be with the most hope for the future." They looked up to a noise which came through the ceiling like something large had dropped onto the floor. "And I've got to think about what we're going to do with them." He pointed upward.

"Well, don't. They're coming with us whether you like it or not."

"I know," he said, disappointed.

"And get over it too. Get along. Look for his strengths. Help him out. Do something good here."

Jeremy understood but fought it still.

Like a relic, Jenna carefully unfurled an old AAA map of the southeastern United States. "I found this in the utility room."

"Haven't looked at one of those since middle school," Jeremy joked. "And even then, it was history class."

"Seriously," she said, studying the region generally, analyzing the scope of possibilities, while Jeremy ran his finger from Marietta to Atlanta down to I-20 going west to Alabama.

"Pretty much a straight shot. We've just got to hope Atlanta isn't wild with fire and fury."

Her eyes rolled up to his face. "It *absolutely* is," she affirmed. "We should expect that. We should expect every obstacle."

He shook his head and forcefully blew out the breath in a sigh, again realizing the extent of their problems. "It's like being back at Taiwan. Never thought I'd have to fight through a war zone here."

"It's going to be one puzzle after another; one problem after another for a long time."

"Fuck all this, man— Who knew this would've happened when we were kids? One minute, I'm with it. I'm here. I get it. The next—total disbelief."

"I know. We just have to keep our heads down and our feet underneath us."

"Our only option is to take the car, look for fuel wherever possible, and just keep pushing on."

"Agreed. Now, we need to decide what to bring."

"We've already got a ton of baggage with those two," he said.

"Sure do," she said, zoning out and into the growing worry within.

* * *

In the downpour, Charlie held out a discarded bucket he'd found along the shoulder of the road. The runoff was heavy, forming rivulets and pools around and through the grass on which they trekked toward Jacksonville. Roland lifted his head to wet his dirty face, collecting a small amount to swallow. Charlie stopped and brought the bucket to his lips, drinking gulps of the tangy water. He smoothed back his soaked hair.

"If only we had some soap," he said.

Before the cityscape came into view, three thick spouts of black smoke towered over the horizon like urban tornados or funnels to other dimensions where a simulated planetary species wavered between self-destruction and prosperity.

"Funny that the rain doesn't put them out."

"The rain probably made the smoke of whatever is burning there even thicker," Roland replied.

"Oh."

On they marched—Charlie, with a carelessness only years of privilege could produce; Roland, with a distrust only success in the world of business and politics could. Roland wondered if Charlie might eventually become a liability, one he might have to break off or abandon altogether. It pained him to imagine it, but the world in which they'd cohabitated was the safest in all of human history, and it was gone.

The city limits never quite materialized, as the northeastern corner of Florida ran like an endless strip mall. Slowly the city, greener and cleaner than expected, rose up around them. People of various colors, clothes, stripes, looks, and intensity began to appear to their left, right, front, and back, when suddenly the couple was surrounded by a ruddy band of survivors not much inclined to cooperation.

"If anyone asks, we're associates of Rathausen," Roland mumbled.

"Do you think it's Rat-hausen or Rath-ausen?" Charlie asked.

Roland ignored the question and kept walking. "Time to act straight again," he said instead.

"Yeah, I got it. I had a feeling."

"Butch it up, babe."

"I get it. I get it."

"But don't overdo it. That's even worse. It'll make you look like a fucking lunatic." Roland stepped ahead then turned back. "And obviously gay."

"Roland—I get it. I probably did this better than you ever did. I played football and rushed a frat, don't forget."

"Until you got caught scuffing your knees in the keg room."

They continued hiking up I-95 toward Southbank and the bridge connecting that neighborhood to the downtown, where a building like a monolith pulled the eye to its heights beneath thick Florida clouds, gleaming in the heat of the day.

"I bet he's either in there or nearby it."

"Near where?" Charlie looked around as Roland continued forward. Above Roland's head, he saw the monolith. "Oh," he said and followed dutifully behind.

The stares they got seemed more directed at Roland than at Charlie, who was the more physically attractive if not taller of the two, but whose expression commanded less attention than the impenetrable gaze of his partner strutting before him; his head cocked upward toward heaven; his aquiline nose pointing down toward hell. Knowing his limitations, Charlie decided to act the bodyguard and remain silent as if mute and let Roland do the talking.

The empire-black high-rise was guarded at the revolving door at its middle. Roland stood catty-corner to the entrance and observed who went in and who came out for half an hour, calculating the best move.

"See if you can go find some food. Barter with your bracelet or that necklace you insisted on buying, if you can. Steal if you must. If I'm not here when you get back, wait for me in this exact spot. I'm going to talk my way inside. I'm convinced this is where he is or where the city's business is done."

Charlie took the order and wandered off, removing the braided gold chain from around his neck and the golden links around his wrist and sliding them both into his pocket. His eyes roved for a John to help him out with a tip where best to sell the metal.

Roland toured the city block of the building's perimeter and its former corporate gardens now occupied by vagrants and bums, wondering how he would get past the guards until he realized he'd do it just like any other person and walk right through the door as if he'd been there a million times. That was an old trick he'd used as a teenager when going to the clubs in New York City many lifetimes in the past. At seventeen, he'd find a group of slightly older-looking guys, seamlessly blend into their mix, and flirt past the bouncer, who'd welcome him like a lover rejoining the fray.

It might work this time too, but before he'd rounded the last corner of the block, Roland noticed a man passed out drunk in a hidden door's vestibule, wearing a metallic but undoubtedly fake gold chain around his neck, the thickness of which would have rivaled the greatest rapper's bling, and he swiped it, hanging it around his own neck, putting it inside his unbuttoned shirt to conceal its inauthenticity. A cane on the ground parallel to the drunk's contorted body would complement the garish look. Two distractions: one a shiny object; one a point of sympathy, the combination of which might work to play on the younger guard's inexperience. Fitting in was a necessity, and every man going in and out of this place, regardless of color or style of dress, had some sort of gangster quality. This would serve for his.

As he approached, he chose boldness as a further device of the disguise, and instead of using the revolving door, he approached one of the guards, limping on the cane, scowling at the world, and asked that he open the hinged steel door behind him as a courtesy to an older man of the business. And as instantly as his character had formed, he nodded at the sentinel and went through the door like he was home.

At the desk in the center of the green marble lobby sat a grumpy but muscular middle-aged man with long blond hair falling down and around a receding hairline, looking bored. Two more sentinels at his sides were more impressively armed than the guards out front. Roland marveled at the electric lighting far overhead, jealous of the apparent powers of this mafia organization.

"Name?"

Roland paused and stared at the gatekeeper.

"I said what's your name, old man."

"Roland. Roland Woolf."

The guard skimmed the page in front of him, which curled up at its bottom corner from overuse.

"There's no name like that on here."

"Of course not," Roland said.

"Of course not," the blond man mocked. "What are you doing here?"

"I'd like to talk to the man."

"The man?"

"Your boss."

"*My* boss?"

Roland felt a systemic glitch threatening his once ironclad nerve. "Rathausen."

"You sure he's my boss?"

"Ultimately. Yes—he's everyone's boss." Roland nodded, affirming his confidence.

"You got that part right," the man said, seeming to ease himself against the charms of Roland's directness.

* * *

The sign read "fresh ground beef," but when the cow was brought out from the shed by a lead, Charlie had to exit the establishment, pushing his way through a horde of men and a few women cheering the execution. At the door, he heard the cow moo as if annoyed or terrified and then the sound of a splashing noise onto the butcher's back pavement. The raucous glee from the overstimulated crowd followed him into the street.

Outside the shop, he assessed the environs for clockable petty crime, its hustlers and gang-bangers, having found some confidence in being on his own. Forgetting the incessant demands of a years-long relationship, he somehow felt free in this burning, lazy city when a car pulled up along the curb, a black car like a limousine but not quite as long, the black-tinted rear window of which came down to convey the voice behind it.

"What's your name?" the mysterious man asked from the darkened frame of the window.

"Charlie," he said, undisturbed.

"What are you doing here, Charlie?"

"Here in this city or here at this corner?"

"Either."

"Looking for food."

"Is that all you need?"

"At the moment."

"I've got that and more if you'd like to get into the car. This is not exactly a safe spot for a single person to be."

"I'm not single, I mean, I'm waiting for someone."

"And who is that?"

"What do you want?"

"To help."

"I don't take help from strangers, bud."

"That's a shame. I'm the only cat in this rat race who can." The window shot up, and the car drove down toward the monolith.

"Wait!" Charlie yelled, chasing the most viable option he'd have, especially if Roland never reappeared from whatever risk he was busy taking. The window ran down when he approached. "What did you say?"

"I said that I'm the only person who can help you."

Charlie stood there deciding.

"Get in."

The stranger opened the door, moving across the center footwell of the car to sit on the other side facing Charlie, who had to subdue whatever surprise shot into his face. The man was entirely dressed in black, covered with it: black gloves, black sleeves, black pants, black socks, black boots—even a black mask, black sunglasses, and a black hat. Not an inch of skin was revealed.

* * *

Roland studied the ceiling from the bottom of the cell, having been immediately ushered to the makeshift jail when he'd entered the old corporate high-rise; the stolen chain necklace and cane were removed from his possession concurrent to being thrown onto the cold concrete floor.

"You don't think we know old Luther and don't recognize his cane? Who you trying to scam?" the blond man asked.

"I'm just trying to get to someone," Roland said calmly.

"I know. I've heard you say that the last ten times. But who the hell are you? On what authority do you think you can swish up to me and ask to see him?"

"I have a lot to offer him."

"Like what?"

"Like—forget it." Roland hung his head between his legs, rested his arms across his knees.

The blond head-of-security threw a water bottle at Roland's feet, taking internal pity on the sickly-looking man, refusing to beat him but leaving him to decide later what use might be made of him, if any. Once the door was locked, Roland took an old vitamin bottle out of his pocket and shook out one of his pills, swigging it down with the water, staring at the base of the cell door in front of him which had the appearance of a converted janitor's closet. A hum, deep and droning, like a melancholic moaning of all the damned souls in hell reverberated down from the hollow center of the tower and into the skeletal lockup.

* * *

The living room had been converted into a rationing headquarters. The last of the grocery store haul, among other presumably essential items, lay spread out before them. New and unused products had been neatly grouped and displayed. Jenna stood over the apportioned piles of clothes, foodstuffs, hygienic supplies, maps, a small stove, cutlery, a couple of tents, sleeping bags, and other camping items, trying to decide what might still be cut.

"Most of that will run out at some point. Is hand soap and body gel all that necessary?" Nelson asked.

Jenna flinched over her shoulder, unwilling to abandon decency. "It might be better to start off with some soap," she said.

"Yes—" Pru said. "We need soap for as long as we can have it."

"Seems extra to me," Nelson said.

"It is," Jeremy added. "We already stink, and we don't even notice it."

"I was thinking to take it more for cleaning cuts, wounds, the occasional hands-and-face wash," Jenna said. "We don't have to go full Neanderthal just yet."

Down the neighborhood road, along which was strewn furniture, bedsheets, and all types of domestic refuse, products, and general detritus like the remnant upset of a tornado's path through a small town, they began their journey, and out of the supposed comforts of suburban retreat, they had packed into the vehicle like stunned fish in a herring can, speaking of nothing. Jeremy at the wheel. Jenna reviewing the map. Nelson in the back, staring out the window. Pru with her head on a pillow in his lap.

Jeremy glanced at the couple in the rearview mirror—wondering—more like expecting the duo to cause more drama than he would like to permit. He'd married Jenna for a few reasons, the main of which was her calm persona, her distaste for melodrama. Other than men trying to kill him, nothing made Jeremy more enraged than the petty, self-centered dramas of unresolved people. Pru's constant complaints of pain, insomnia, and general unwellness, he'd doubted, but said nothing. Saying nothing or saying little was a way of controlling himself. If he had told anyone how he felt about the tiniest irritant, he would risk the implosion of the discipline. Hard as it would be, his complaints, unlike anyone else's, would have to remain mostly unexpressed, building pressure instead.

Mullet whined from the overwhelmed cargo space, unable to move into a more comfortable position.

"Shhh, it's okay, buddy," Jeremy said, to which the animal responded with a deep sigh rounded by a disgruntled little growl.

The map in her lap, Jenna wondered through the windshield. "Road is surprisingly empty."

"We've got about three-quarters of a tank left. That'll easily get us to Birmingham."

"What if roads are blocked?"

"We'll have to deal with that as it comes."

"Makes me nervous."

"We have no choice. Constant movement will be a daily part of life for a long time now."

"It's really amazing, isn't it?" Nelson began. "How everything seemed perfect. We were all doing well, right? Making money. Buying all the things. We had everything we could ever want. Vacations to foreign cities and exciting places. We partied in Europe every year. Can you imagine ever going there again?" he asked Pru rhetorically. Emotion dominated his voice and threatened to steal it forever. "And now—now everything is *fucked*!" he suddenly yelled. Pru shot up with the pillow and shifted her body to the other side of the vehicle and rested her head against the wall of survival supplies. "We never said no to *anything*!" he ranted. "Just let everything go. Just let everything become some bullshit thing it was never meant to be. Everyone had to be *right* or *superior* or some special piece of fragmented shit. Like—"

"Hey, Nelson, my man, calm down a little," Jeremy ordered, more with his tone than the language he'd chosen. "You're right. Everything is fucked. But we're doing our best to figure a way through it. You gotta keep your head with me."

As if taking Jeremy's suggestion, Nelson put his head into his hands, resuming his default position.

"Everything would be fine if that selfish, autocratic fool hadn't taken office," Pru said angrily, trying to vent the impossible despair she fought.

Jenna reached over and squeezed Jeremy's thigh to distract him from the inevitable provocation Pru's politics would produce, soundlessly begging him not to be antagonized. His own emotional fragility threatening to destabilize the otherwise disciplined soldier, Jeremy silently pleaded with Jenna, whose own face was a mixture of compassion for Nelson's helplessness and annoyance at having to deal with such a man. Pru's extravagances she more or less ignored.

The local gas station came into view.

"Pull in here," Jenna said.

"What for? You think they still take credit?"

"Just try. You never know."

The pump had been leaking from the rubber hose, and Jeremy's hand slipped down the handle from the slick film of gas coating it. When he squeezed the trigger away from the car, an incontinent stream dribbled out, so he inserted the nozzle into the fuel filler, figuring any amount would be worth it. The smell was abnormally strong; he could feel a headache coming. Looking down, he realized the puddles underneath were not water but gas from the long-leaking nozzle, and the 4Runner had splashed its way through them, the tires wet with gas, the undercarriage possibly dripping with it too.

"*Shit*," he mumbled.

Jenna opened the passenger door. "What's wrong?" she asked.

"Nothing," he said. Nelson stared through the window and at the ground near his feet. The distant sound of another vehicle speeding toward them distracted him from the problem. "Let's get out of here." He hung up the nozzle, hopped back into the truck, and calmly but quickly drove off.

Down I-75, they passed an assortment of cars, trucks, and SUVs either on the shoulder, in the grassy median, or abandoned in any one of the traffic lanes like obstacles. The truck swerved around a gameboard of empty cars, one after the other.

"Slow down!" Jenna implored. Pru gripped Nelson's arm who gripped the door's handlebar.

"All right, all right," Jeremy said, looking back through the rearview mirror. Nelson caught his eyes. "I've been watching them too," he said.

"Who?" Pru demanded, looking back through the rear window. "There's nobody there."

"They're back there, behind the cars. They've been following us for miles."

"The truck from the gas station?" Jenna quickly asked Jeremy.

"Yep. They're on our tail."

"Fuck," Jenna said. "Did you load the shotguns?" she asked impulsively.

"Yes, of course. But I'd rather not have to use them." Silence managed their concerns, as saying anything now would only irritate the problem. After a few minutes of clear road, the truck in question appeared behind the last abandoned car.

"There they are," Nelson said tensely.

"It's all right. It's okay," Jeremy said, trying to keep control of their collective coolness given the pressure.

"Oh no. Oh no. Oh *no*," Pru moaned repeatedly.

"It's all right, Pru," Jenna said. "We just have to keep calm. We all have to chill."

"Hey, Nelson," Jeremy said. "There are two loaded rifles behind you."

"Okay." Nelson's obvious worry inflected his voice.

"The safety should be on for both but be careful."

"You want me to touch them?"

Jeremy had to suppress instant frustration. "Yes," he said evenly. "Please hand them to Jenna."

Nelson reached behind, moving the long tent bags to the side, disturbing Mullet, who almost barked. "I see them," he announced importantly and too carefully picked one up by its butt, working his hands down the length of the weapon, pushing it into the front seat, averting his head from the mouth of the barrel. He repeated the process with the other until both were secured by Jenna's side.

"If they fuck with us, we're ready," Jenna said. "We'll continue to do what we have to do."

"I guess we will!" Jeremy yelled, looking into the rearview before hitting the gas and taking off, as the predatory truck accelerated after them.

* * *

Mina led the goats. Ant led the bull. The pregnant heifer followed untethered. The plan was to barter with Albert and Lucinda: the bull for a horse and an older wagon, if possible.

"Sure you want a wagon? There's some cars 'round, I might locate for ya," Albert said. "But good luck trackin' down some reserve fuel; the trade for that's gone steep at the marketplace anyhow." He looked the animals over, inspecting their under and backsides. "Nice 'n clean, for sure."

"Well fed and cared for," Mina added.

"I can see that. I can see that." Albert chewed on a piece of straw. "And you want my wagon and a pony in exchange, is that right?"

"A horse. Yes, sir," Ant said.

"All right, all right." Pondering the deal, he twirled the straw between his lips. "Let's go inside for a cup and talk it over, shall we?"

The delay provoked Mina's impatience but why, she could not and anyway would not have articulated. Ant only observed the slack in her body and altered facial expression.

Inside, Lucinda had made tea and laid out some homemade bread with preserves and butter.

Mina's eyes lit at the sight. "This is a special treat," she said before thanking the missus and forgetting her prior interest in making the trade.

"Pleasure's mine," Lucinda answered. "We don't get visitors much. Certainly, I don't see other women about, 'less I travel to the market, but I don't like it there."

"Why is that?"

Lucinda sighed, looking off. "Oh," she exclaimed. "I guess it's just too harried, too much of a frenzy at times."

"I see. Sounds interesting to me."

"I like it quiet. Not much need to talk, myself. If you're at all curious, I would recommend the outing once or twice. Least to see what's all there. Changes often. Closest thing to a treasure trove as you're likely to find, however. 'Member that store, *Save Rite*? Much like that. Little bit of everything. And it's as honest as it could be. Safe and well guarded. Best one around. I just don't much like crowds no more."

The men took their tea to the porch and sat smoking cigars. Mina almost marveled at the luxury.

"The strangest part of this new, old world is being wonder-struck by things before too easily ignored or dismissed," Mina offered politely.

Lucinda rocked in her chair as if agreeing, looking at the men. "Never gave men as high a value, but the notion is apt," she said, winking at Mina, whose wit caught up to her host's. Lucinda established a warm kind of sorority between them. The women took their tea to the living room to be farther from the men, where Mina retold the story of her survival, starting in New England and the early outages, to the exodus south and the authoritarian roadblocks she'd encountered on the way to her family's homestead.

"Berti knew your grandfather and brother," Lucinda said, welcoming Mina's surprise.

"I don't know why I didn't expect that," she said. "Of course, he did."

"It's a strange time, my dear, when even old neighbors seem like strangers."

"Indeed." Mina quieted, unsure whether to retell her brother's passing to this new, old neighbor. "Denny, my brother," she clarified. "He struggled at the end." Lucinda sat deep in her chair and nodded gently, not knowing but understanding. "He was all alone at the end. I tried to get here as quickly as I could, but by the time I'd settled at the cottage, he was long gone, in the bottle and in his head. One day I found him—" Emotion silenced the sad tale.

"It's all right. I understand. Heard it too many times, I'm sore to report," Lucinda said, trying to comfort her only female companion in months, maybe in a year. Mina covered her eyes with one hand and lightly sobbed. Her host inched forward to rub her back.

"It's a good cry when it tends to our griefs," Lucinda said softly.

Behind the house, Albert showed Ant how to loosen the wheels from the wagon's frame using a square nut wrench. "Fix it to the nut and pull clockwise, like the wagon was goin' backwards," he said while grunting and pulling at the lever until it popped loose. "And then, you slide off the wheel, like so. That there's your axle, now, and they can crack easy, dependin'. I only got one spare one for y'all to take." Ant followed Albert with his eyes while he listened, watching to match the man's verbal instructions to the procedure. "And the only replacement wheels I got for ya are shorter, which aren't as good for traveling in a long journey. They take up too much space in the back too." Ant looked to where Albert had pointed at the smaller, bulkier wheels, then at the tight, empty space in the bed of the wagon.

"I guess we'll have to make do."

"I reckon that. Here, take this wrench with you." Albert reviewed Ant, comparing him to the wagon, knowing he could replace most all of it but the young man himself. "You're gonna need the heifer and the bull," he said. "Let the bull pull the wagon and let the cow follow. You don't need a horse."

"But what about the trade?" Ant asked.

"I'm fine with the goats. That's enough for me. You'll need that milk when the calf comes, God allowing, and maybe the meat. Just keep 'em guarded."

"I lost my machete at the plantation and—" Ant looked down after he spoke. "I didn't get the gun at the end."

The older man became skeptical. "Why not?"

Ant hesitated. Albert shifted his stance away.

"I broke one of their rules."

Albert nodded in his disappointment. "They're allies of mine, ya know. And they know my wagons. Any enemy of theirs has to be one of mine, son. What did you do?"

"I got caught up with—"

"A gal, no doubt."

"Yes, sir."

"I see. They run you out?"

"Oh yeah."

"Lucky you got all your limbs."

"I know."

"It ain't the worst crime there is." Albert decided the argument, favoring Ant, and walked back to the barn, leaving the younger man to wonder; when the old man came back with two rifles, one double-barreled and one semi-automatic, Ant's eyes seized upon the prospect of a gift as his eyes welled in deepest gratitude. Albert handed him the double-barrel.

"Let's go behind the barn and take some practice shots. You never know who else might come after ya these days."

* * *

There was no sign of Roland. A colossus of a building, the tower occupied its city-block, but there seemed to be a small number of men inside. Charlie still hoped to see some trace of his partner. He'd imagined Roland had already taken over the urban fortress, but worried that Roland was becoming weak and getting weaker.

Escorting him across the cool marble of the entryway, the man in black moved with such feline simplicity that Charlie instantly interpreted it as the walk of a gay man, figuring he had been taken as some sort of sexual prisoner; and he may have been, Charlie understood, but his sexual wits, often dulled by the practical matters of living, in survival mode, had remained sharp at hand. The man in black, ignorant of Charlie's willingness to please him, assumed he'd snagged yet another desperate street whore whose sole devotion was to the extravagances of influence and power that hid within the willingness of being of service, putting Charlie in a more profitable position.

In the parking garage, Charlie had heard a deep, resounding hum that appeared to vibrate the walls. "What was that noise downstairs?" he asked the man in black.

"Generators. Big ones," the man in black answered honestly.

"How do you get the fuel to—"

"If I told you that part, I would actually have to kill you," the man in black said, snickering at the brutal truth of the cliché.

* * *

Meanwhile, Roland crouched in the cold cell, hungry and annoyed, formulating a new strategy to pitch to the blond when another guard opened the door, throwing a couple of water bottles at his feet.

"Hey!" Roland yelled. The guard paused beyond the door. "When do I get something to eat?"

"I've no orders for that," the guard said.

"When do *you* eat?" Roland asked.

There was a silence like a confusion. "When there's food."

"And *when* is there food?"

"When the boss provisions it."

"People don't typically use that as a verb," Roland complained. "The next time he *provisions* it, would you mind bringing me some?" Entitlement in his tone had worked like a cultural magic, even after all the deprivations and the suffering.

The guard gave no clear response but again paused and then walked away. Roland figured he'd broken down the first barrier to getting what he wanted. To Roland, manipulating people was a question of the repetition in one's demands and requests, not so much the *what* of the something that was said. But he had to think bigger for Rathausen. He had to have something to offer him that no one currently around him could.

A second guard appeared, more handsome than the first, with a handful of stale white bread.

"You'd think the lights in here would've gone out at least once by now," Roland said, casually lobbing the observation, knowing its energy source must be a secret.

"They're on all the time," the guard said reflexively.

"Why's that?" Roland asked as innocently as he could.

"Generators. That's what the noise is," the guard said without thinking.

"Where does the fuel come from?" Roland asked more directly this time, but without the demanding tone.

The guard assessed the haggard man sitting on his butt in front of him, like death warmed up, and he pitied him his weakness without realizing the trouble that pity would bring. But he told him the truth, more for the fun of it, for breaking the code, a code that included him in order to control him and his life. The man was obviously gay, incredibly fragile, a threat to no man in this organization, so he thought he'd humor him to make him a little happier.

Astonished at the honesty but unsurprised by a person's need to talk and share stories, especially secrets, Roland listened obsessively to the entire tale or as much of it as the guard had to offer, and he played along like a poor old beggar happy for a little attention.

"It's *unreal*," the guard whispered. "And the silly little dude in black does whatever he wants. But not to me. Don't get near to me or I'll knock his ass out. And he knows it. He knows better than to mess around. Most of these guys are easy targets, though. Desperate for a little attention."

"You're all easy targets," Roland reminded him.

"How's that, now, bud?"

"You don't seem to have gotten any better offers."

Annoyed, the guard said, "Look here, guy. I run your life right now. I decide if you eat or sleep."

"And I hold yours in my hand, I imagine."

"You imagine?" The guard laughed defensively.

"I imagine, well, I can also *assume*, that what you've told me—and in the quiet, secret way that you did—would get you in a lot of trouble if anyone found out."

The second guard's face dropped like the idiot neighborhood bully thinking he'd had the upper hand but losing it to an unexpected superior. "I got you," he said. "I got you."

"Good," Roland replied gently.

Cautiously, Roland filled in the gaps of locations and procedures, the *wheres* and *hows* of stealing and making the fuel that made the most sense. Using what he now knew of the black-market oil trade, its geography, its distance, he had to formulate an argument for his services which found a flaw in the system as it was. What did Rathausen want? What did the blond man want? Roland had to figure these things out or make a good guess.

The first guard returned, opening the door.

"Here," he said, throwing a bag of potato chips to the floor.

"Thank you," Roland humbly replied, observing the sell-by date, which was over a year past its due. "I'm very grateful."

"You're welcome," the guard answered, looking behind his back. He remained to observe Roland, on the brink of speaking, not knowing what more to do or what more to say, which amused his prisoner.

"You can go now," Roland said calmly like a father, perfectly timed. The guard slightly bowed his head as if to a superior, giving Roland the necessary confidence in his new enterprise. Eating the chips, he zoned out on the gray metal door as it was closed and locked in front of him—thinking, planning, formulating.

An inexplicable cheer came booming into the depths of the building; guns were fired into its walls and ceilings—Rathausen's men must be celebrating another successful raid, Roland surmised. A smaller group of them had peeled off from the main cluster and shuffled down the corridor toward the cell-room, speaking in low tones. Roland stood and peered through the face-sized window at the center of the door and spotted Charlie who followed a man dressed all in black and the musclebound blond. Two other, base-level guards trailed them. Roland's eyes widened as if angered at seeing his partner and the chance to get his attention, but he could not make a sound nor gesture, only hoping Charlie would turn to see his face in the window.

* * *

Albert had treated Ant like a son, taking the goats but giving him and Mina the wagon, the rifles, and a canvas canopy that could collapse around the back corners of the trunk like a convertible top. And however excruciating it was for Mina to leave her homestead, Ant's willingness to accompany her through the wilderness of *whoknowswhat* was a comfort and blessing she could not dismiss.

"It will always be here. The land at least. It's a place you can come back to."

"Oh yeah, *how?*" she asked, inexplicably annoyed by the statement. "I can't handle the platitudes right now. You're asking me to do something major here. My life was good. I was fine, getting by, doing well, in fact," she said, forgetting recent disruptions to this precedent, clinging to the past. She almost said, *And then you came along*, completely forgetting her own solicitations of him to join her at her home. The moment overwhelmed wisdom, and she fretted like a terrified child.

Ant sympathized as she wiped tears from her eyes to avoid a torrid outburst of suppressed trauma, not feeling how incompatible her resentments suddenly were, illustrating to Ant a deeper instability he hadn't before seen. "You can stay if you want—" He paused, gently touching her shoulder. "And maybe you should. I don't want to be responsible for taking you away, or for taking you from the security you've created for yourself. I don't want you to blame me," he said, sensing something weirder in her, like a morbid rage.

But she forced herself to calm the surge of these fears. "No, I know. I just—" The rush of panic subsiding in her chest, she sat on the front steps, wanting to sob. Ant sat beside her and rubbed her back. "What if there is nothing for me in Texas? What if we don't make it? I'm an older woman now."

"All the more reason not to be alone. You killed one guy, but can you kill them all? I think more will come, some friendlier than others, but all looking for something."

"What if that was a fluke? I mean, I'm well-hidden here, and I can't live in fear of men. I know about the marketplace now. And these people knew my family. I'd almost rather stay with them. I would have Berti and Lucinda for friendship and protection." Regaining whatever composure was left from her well of solitude, she dabbed her eyes with the bottom of her shirt, sat up straight as if a decision had been made. "I'm going to stay here," she said.

Ant could only submit to her will on this point. "I understand," he said.

"You can have the bull, but I need to keep the cow."

"Absolutely."

"I just can't abandon this place." She looked around the yard. "There's too much of me here, and I am too old to strip it away. If I was a young woman—" She smiled at him. He nodded down at the dirt to appease the compliment. "You've got your whole life ahead of you. I'm going to live the rest of mine right here."

Ant leaned in and hugged her. "Thank you," he said. "Thank you for being the first person to give me some hope. Thank you for trusting in me. Thank you for your friendship."

"And you me," she said, picking up and fitting on his head the rancher hat he'd worn when she first set eyes on him, stumbling into her life. They embraced one first and last time, and he went off toward the wagon, now stocked with some food and gear: a gallon of fuel to trade, a sleeping bag, a tent, and as many of the organic provisions she had stored in the basement as she could spare that wouldn't spoil or rot too soon, and one of the twenty-gallon vats of filtered rain water which had gone unused. Climbing into the driver's seat, he took the reins like a renewed pioneer ready to face challenges of unknown dimension.

"You be careful, now. You stay alive and prosper for me. Have some babies with a smart and wonderful woman. Carry on the legacy of this once-great country."

Before the tears in his eyes could fall, he tipped his hat, slapped the reins on the bull's hind, and the wagon carried him away.

* * *

Roland made it his mission to begin counseling various guards, building trust, massaging egos, asking for favors, requesting visitors on the sly. After several days of this, the door to his cell opened, and Charlie walked through, greeting his lifelong companion as if he'd barely known him a minute.

"Hello," Roland returned, extending the final vowel sound to signal his distance from and dominion over the man who had entered his space. Charlie placed the vitamin bottle on the pillow at the head of the bed, having refilled it with the remainder of Roland's medication.

"How are you feeling?" Charlie asked, but Roland did not respond. "No one is nearby. We can talk, if only briefly," he added.

"I want you to get me access to the man in black," Roland announced. "I want to question him. Think you can do that?"

"I don't know. I don't know who is who or who controls what."

"It's Rathausen. Figure out which one he is."

"I thought it was the blond."

"What's the blond's name?" Roland asked.

"I don't know."

"What does the man in black want with you?"

"I don't know."

"He's attracted to you."

"Yes."

"But he hasn't done anything yet?"

"No. I think I'm just another layer."

"Of what?"

"Of his position. His power. The more they see, but the less the other men know who or what or how, the better—I assume. They all want his approval."

Roland nodded as if understanding the strategy. "They're a bunch of meatheads with a lot of muscle but little mind. They're easy to charm with intelligence. Anyway, thank you for the pills," he said, dismissing his visitor by his tone.

Stunned by the bleak formality, Charlie understood only its necessity, realizing that he would once again play emissary to Roland's interests, and, walking back to attend to the man in black, to his place in the world as a trophy, as a useful idiot, as a man unworthy to follow his own pursuits, he grew sad by this eternal type of demoralization dictated by the fate of his character. The conversation with Roland felt more like a final rejection than a reunion or a meeting between loved ones to conspire an escape. He floated from one master to another as if he were a slight and breezy wind controlled by man-gods to do their bidding and forget the quality of his own worth. It was a role in a game he could play, but this would be his last tournament.

* * *

The executive suites on the 53rd floor served as Rathausen's lair, a man whose story had grown into mythology. Charlie had yet to see him. The center elevator doors opened onto the lobby of the floor where four guards stood, who had initially greeted him with guns drawn—even with the man in black as escort: All first-timers to this floor were targeted by their guns—barely acknowledging him this time. The man in black had approved of Charlie as a kind of servant, and to this moment, he had been free to roam wherever he chose. The blond man ignored him too, and Charlie suspected he was Rathausen, using the man in black as a kind of costumed decoy, but he didn't dare ask either man, nor the guards, about his suspicions. Like a fraternity house, there were unspoken rules established by unseen vibes, hierarchies formed by presence and not by reason.

He had been summoned to the man in black's private chamber shortly after he'd left Roland in his cell. The room was dimly lit by a pair of lamps whose bases were shaped like dragons made of green jade blowing fire toward the luminous bulbs.

"Sit down," a voice said from an unknown part of the room. Charlie did as he was told. "Who is the man in the cell?" the voice demanded.

"I don't know," Charlie answered.

"Why did you visit him?"

"He requested to speak with me."

"Who gave you this message?"

"One of the guards."

The silence that followed lasted long enough that Charlie had a sudden feeling he had been left alone. But the blond man came into the light and sat on the opposite couch.

"Do you know who I am?" he asked.

"I think I do, yes."

"Then you know how dangerous I am."

"I assume you are. Yes."

"Then you believe your life is in my hands."

"I do."

"Who is the man in the cell?"

"I don't know."

"Where does he come from?"

"Miami."

"How do you know this?"

Instantly caught by the rapidity of the questioning, he wavered. "That's what he said."

"The guards say he gives no information, only asks questions. Does he speak to you?"

"He did, yes."

"What does he want?"

"To speak to the man in black."

The blond man nodded. "He is speaking to him now."

The elevator door dinged in the lobby as the doors came apart. The man in black walked out and into the space with one of the guards from the cell block. They entered the darkened room where the blond man sat with Charlie.

"Stand up," the guard said to Charlie. "Turn around." Charlie, doing again what he was told, found his wrists being bound by rope; then he was escorted out of the room. In the elevator, Charlie said nothing. The man in black seemed to be staring at him boldly, however surreptitiously, behind the absurdly black-tinted glasses. The guard looked forward at the closed doors. On the prison floor, Charlie was escorted to Roland's cell, which was now empty.

"Where is he?" he couldn't help but yell out. "What happened to him?" Charlie panicked and then collapsed onto the bed where he could still smell traces of the man he thought he had loved as the door was locked behind him.

* * *

It took a week to make the trek from Weaverville to the outskirts of Atlanta. The water supply was one-third gone. The bull appeared run down.

"A few more miles and then we'll camp," Ant said to the bull, patting its hairy cheek while it lapped tepid water from a large mixing bowl. Squinting, he lost the moment to the distant and sinking light. Its yellow hues dulled by dusk, seeming to swirl as a great globe of fire among its rusted orange flares. The highlights blushed his brown cheek. His form and figure, beside the animal-engine of his craft, in relief to the twilight sky, impressed the scene like an old photograph imitating destiny. His hands shielded his eyes at their peripheries to focus on the future terrain of the journey enveloped by the dying bursts of the sun. The bull's tongue smacked at its gums for final drops as Ant stole back the bowl and said, "We'd better get goin' now." The bull groaned for more.

Instead of riding atop the cart, Ant exercised his legs, walking alongside the bull, tugging at its harness to keep it on point. The land became bulbous like broccoli humps, one mound grown into the next, not steep, but rolling. The wagon bounced from the impediments.

In the fading daylight, he spotted a thin trail of smoke winding its way upward. The country terrain between the Blue Ridge Mountains down to Atlanta had been so depopulated, he'd almost forgotten how desperate people had become. Now that he was near Atlanta, a city that had fallen to chaos even before collapse, he'd have to restoke his personal ire and keep his guard up. One of the two rifles Albert had given him lay beneath the front seat. Carefully, soundlessly as if being observed, Ant retrieved the weapon, checked the chamber, calmly held it slack at his dominant side, and advanced to a large hedge of bushes behind which he undoubtedly believed were people. He peered over the edge and observed two men—one large and fearsome; one smaller and meager—and two women—one alert and healthy; one sickly and pale. A chocolate lab sat by the larger man, sniffing at the air in Ant's direction. A foursome that seemed an unlikely grouping. A lack of uniformity to their appearance and behavior produced the intuition that they were good people thrown together by chance and not to be feared. Ant at least felt no fear. Stepping into view, he lowered his head and raised his left hand, saying, "Excuse me, folks."

The dog began to bark, and Jeremy exploded onto his feet. "What do you want," he said immediately and put his body between the visitor and his company. Jenna approached the man from another angle.

"I mean no threat to y'all. I spent the last couple weeks riding down in a wagon. I've got a bull with me. I'm looking for good people, some company is all."

"What do you need a bull for?" Pru asked abruptly like a curious child.

"Other than to move my wheels, I'm not sure," Ant answered calmly. "Please," he continued to speak more to Jeremy. "I'm looking for refuge for the night. I got a couple rifles, but that's all."

"Where's the other one?" Jenna asked, holding her rifle slack in her hands.

"In the wagon behind this hedge."

"Put that one on the ground," Jeremy ordered.

Ant obeyed, moving casually and calmly. "I mean no harm," he said, standing straight with both hands up, palms outward, facing Jeremy. "Would you like to see the wagon and the bull?"

* * *

Jeremy decided that the guy seemed all right. War had taught him to listen to his gut, giving no leeway to anyone who appeared anything less than honest. There were no other messages darting in this man's eyes, no layers of deceit. The dude seemed good. No hesitations in his speech, a fair speaker, evenness in the eyes, honest about his weapons. Two capable and good men recognizing the value of the other, perhaps.

"I'm Jeremy," he said, putting out his hand, locking his eyes into this new man's. Introductions, once a meaningless reflex, now conveyed the character of one's intentions. Ant's hand clapped cleanly into Jeremy's as a firm, warm, and even grip. "All right. Let's go see it," Jeremy said. The bull groaned as soon as they rounded the protective hedge. "That's a big guy."

"Stubborn as hell," Ant replied. "If he stops, everything stops."

"*Damn*, he's *huge*," Jeremy emphasized. "Never seen a beast like this before."

The men fraternized while Jenna carted heavy logs available on the forest floor, turning them over to check for wetness, gasping while heaving the larger pieces of the wood onto a pile. Jeremy came around the hedge.

"Everything all right?" he asked.

"Sure," she said between heaves. "Just doing some work." The comment and her expression were enough to communicate the need for help. Ant stepped farther into the campsite, but then turned and walked back quickly to his wagon.

"What's he doing? You sure about him?" Jenna asked while handing Jeremy a piece of wood. He simply responded to her with a look as if to say, *He's fine—back off.* But Ant came back with an axe, and Jenna, instantly oblivious to her doubts, almost shed a tear for joy, reaching out for the tool, though Jeremy grew instantly guarded like in an immediate exchange of their minds. Ant presented the axe to her. "I know this seems stupid, but," she wiped her sweat-drenched eyes, "we've been doing *literally* everything with our hands, and my skin's about to rub off. We haven't caught a break since—" She broke off, trying not to cry. Pru rose and stood beside Jenna, rubbing her back. "I'm fine. I'm okay, really. I'm just—tired."

"I get it, Miss," Ant replied. "Allow me to chop some wood for the night's fire."

Hushed by the chivalry, by being called Miss in such uncivilized circumstances and too tired to question the good nature of the act, Jenna was grateful to have a moment's rest: Pru was fairly helpless. Nelson seemed to be a man in perpetual shock, only capable of venting whatever pent-up anxieties he'd kept hidden in the old world that he'd attached himself to a brand of uselessness all its own. She and Jeremy had borne the weight of responsibility mostly without complaint. Even now, the guilt of breaking down, of showing the slightest crack of weakness was an unwelcome irritant to her persistent grit. Having another willing and able body to do work seemed too good to be true.

Ant began to chop but came back toward the circle of exhausted compatriots after making six more pieces for the fire and sat around the reinvigorated blaze, finding no reason to continue chopping. "I've got a few gallons of water left in the wagon, some stale bread, cured salami, if you're hungry." Jenna's eyes beamed at the prospect of meat. "There's some powder for hot chocolate too, if you'd take the lead from the—"

Like a schoolboy eager to plunder the school store, Jeremy jumped to guide the bull and the wagon into the hidden backside of the camp. The four suburbanites stood over the cooler as Jeremy handed out its contents like refugees in line for meager nourishment. Nelson grabbed a piece of the salami and a hunk of stale bread and fed chunks of each to Pru, who continued to behave like a rattled sprite. Jenna watched as Pru grew mesmerized by the glowing, rebuilt fire, perpetually dazed by the persistence of traumas she couldn't resolve. Ant observed both women, catching Jenna's eye, projecting and receiving an understanding about these other companions only communicable through silent exchange. Mullet roved among them, sniffing at the food. Jenna fed him a chunk of bread and a smaller piece of the meat.

The fire cracked and hissed, throwing off sparks past their shins and into the dirt of the circle they had created. They sipped too-hot chocolate from a couple of mugs Mina had given to Ant.

"If only we had some ice cubes to cool this down," Jenna said.

"Nothing's ever perfect, nothing just right when you're out in the world like this," Ant responded.

"Still—it'd be nice. Balance would be nice. Everything's so extreme out here."

"Only feels that way," Ant said, winking at her, which made her uncomfortable.

Talk among them hadn't flourished, but this was more an effect of survival, starvation, and thirst than disinterest or sudden animosity. Stomachs full from what small portion of bread and meat they could swallow, they sat until Jeremy began to tell the tale of their story.

"We've had a rough go of it," he began, speaking to the crackling fire, petting Mullet's side as the dog leaned against his leg. "We'd had an entire truck—an SUV—fully loaded with tents, sleeping bags, food, tools." He spoke to their guest, who kept his head down, staring at the illuminated dirt. "We got jacked. Carjacked." Nelson's eyes went teary, and he turned away. Jenna clenched her jaw to subdue the anger she'd been suppressing, not having heard, nor told the story yet, not even to herself. "A whole lot of them in one car, maybe four. Total scumbags. Psychos."

"All we managed to save was ourselves, our dog, Mullet, and these two rifles," Jenna added.

"What happened to the thieves?" Ant asked.

"I blew them up," Jeremy answered. There was a confused pause.

"What do you mean?"

"I shot at them as they drove off and hit the underside of my truck, and it blew."

"Jesus," Ant remarked.

"We'd gotten gas minutes before they started to chase us. The pump was leaking. We drove through, not knowing it wasn't water. Got all over the undercarriage of the truck," Jenna said.

"Blew the damn thing right up." Jeremy made the exploding gesture with his hands. "Caught fire first, but then—"

Jenna nodded as if seeing it again. "Yeah, the underside caught fire first, and they drove off not knowing it. And then—"

"Bang," Jeremy said, using his hands to mimic the explosion again.

"It was really bright," Nelson said. "Blinding."

"Yeah," Pru murmured, subdued by the memory.

"Jesus," Ant said again. "Lucky you're all alive."

"Lucky they didn't shoot us first," Jeremy said.

"I think we were too hyped up, too focused on getting back what we had to think about anything else. But we didn't," Nelson added.

"Well—they're dead now. Watched them burn. Watched them writhe around and burn until they stopped." Jeremy's eyes scanned the ground as he spoke.

"Damn," Ant whispered.

"That's not even the first of it. We've seen some major shit." Jenna slipped into a dark humor, smiling, suppressing a chuckle, which provoked Nelson to giggles. Pru cried out and cackled into the darkness beyond them. The four of them laughing with each other and entirely to themselves, sitting around the community of the fire as it cackled back, while Ant could only observe the tortured disconnection between their story and their laughter, but understanding how deeply satisfying it was to laugh, and cracked a smile at his own hardships in unison with theirs.

CHAPTER THREE

Beneath the reflective high-rise, the closest thing to a skyscraper in the Jacksonville skyline—formerly a corporate bank—existed an entire subterranean lair dedicated to what Central Power in DC would have branded treason, an illegal energy monopoly operation stretching from Texas moving east, matching the locations of federal stockpile facilities, with checkpoints guarded by armed goons every hundred miles: the Black Oil Slick. The street men who worked enforcement in the game had shortened the unofficial name to the more officious "BOS." Headquarters for the enterprise was this former corporate bank. Inside the imposing walls of its cavernous lower levels, a deep and reverberant hum from the large CAT emergency generators vibrated the floor.

The man in black led Roland down a corridor to the fuel stock room. "The generators run on diesel," he said.

"Is that what's in the tanks?" Roland asked.

"Has to be kept at seventy degrees; dehumidifier runs at all times." He flipped a line of switches, and the vast room like a warehouse illuminated one row at a time. The burst of electric light offended Roland's increasingly sensitive eyes. Hundreds of vats were arranged like excess pawns on a chessboard. "Those will last roughly six months without chemical stabilizer."

"Where do you keep that?"

"There's little left. It can be difficult to find."

"Surely, there are stashes at these fuel storage facilities—"

"It is quite a contentious resource," the man in black said rather too fastidiously for the toxic male environs of the upper floors. Only down there and in the penthouse executive suites would he dare speak with such a crisp sting of his tongue.

"Are there not generators that run on regular gasoline?" Roland knew nothing about the business he had suddenly entered.

"There are, but typically smaller. Insufficient. This building is the biggest in Jacksonville with the most generators, which is why the street gangs captured it at the beginning. And they run on diesel. It was meant to be what it is today: a power source in the event of severe blackouts. It is capable of powering a fifth of the downtown. And some of the immediate suburbs on occasion, which is typically when Rathausen needs the peons to regard him for his generosity."

Roland ignored the disclosure. "Are your men, your pirates, are they in order?"

"They are—" he wavered "difficult to control, I'll say, but we have our ways. I have mine, in particular."

"And what is that?" Roland asked, having an inkling. There were no women allowed in the building; the men often couldn't leave, and this was the most effeminate body for what might as well have been miles, fully disguised in black, though one only assumed it was a male body. But some gays, Roland knew, were notoriously delusional for seeing in themselves a degree of sexual appeal that even the straightest of men couldn't resist. Most were entirely repulsed. Danger spiced the essence of conquest.

The man in black studied Roland, whose regained confidence had begun to affect his posture, standing to his full height, sensing a kind of telepathic mockery in the awkward silence. "You mention-ed you had experience leading telenet campaigns, large staffs, powerful men," the man in black said as a compliment to Roland's reclaimed self-assurance.

"I do. I did."

"And you believe you can settle the divisions among the men."

"I might. And more. I'm sure your logistics are shit."

The man in black sighed. "Rathausen is impossible to work with. Next to the fuel, stabilizer is the most important resource we need. But as much as he doesn't mind killing people, he hates warring with the county gangs that stalk the slick."

"The slick?"

"The oil slick, we call it."

"I see," Roland said. "That's *clever*."

The man in black couldn't compute Roland's intended tone, somewhere between sardonic demon and benevolent father, and chose to view him both ways and be taken in by neither. "If we don't secure enough stabilizer, this fuel will oxidize and become useless. And you can imagine what might happen after that. Whatever order we do have will once again collapse, and the men will go wild."

Roland's expression, always sullen or drab, had the effect of wresting the full loyalty of the man in black; this man's powers of impartiality far outperformed his own. "It's already happened once, as you say. Part of the illusion of power is making sure the people, in this case these hostile brute-types, don't understand reality as it is but as we make it seem to them. We need to make everything *seem* secure for their futures and prospects. The feeling of superiority intoxicates them."

"The master has struggled with this."

Roland hid his lack surprise at the revelation. The admission by reference to a weakness in the man in charge was the only surprising part. "Rathausen?" Roland asked as if nudging the man in black: one would-be court usurper seeing in the other a loyal dog to pet and fawn over in private. "Does he make you call him *the master*?"

At first, the man in black said nothing but only very slightly bowed his head to affirm, a confirmation that doubled as newfound allegiance to Roland. "He has been brutal. And that has caused more anger than compliance. The men are restless and looking for a new hero-master, someone they can revere and obey; some others, fewer others, are looking for a chance at fame among their peers. None have it in them to take over."

"None?" Roland asked, almost chipper.

"*Well—*"

Roland sensed the urgency, however subdued, in his host's tone, as if he might like it if Roland made a bigger move on power.

"If we play it low key for a while, and we get to know one another—" The man in black nodded to conspiracy as he spoke. "Then we might figure a way to something else." They stood together in silence like a synergetic contemplation.

"And Charlie is very good at finding and getting whatever he wants, especially when it's something that I want," Roland added.

"The stabilizer," the man in black said.

"Yes," Roland replied. "We could call him that."

A noise, loud but muted, many floors higher, like industrial steel doors locking together, interrupted the intimacy of their chat. The man in black flicked his forefinger toward the exit and led the way out.

* * *

In the morning, the coolness of the dew refreshed the air and covered every surface with tiny droplets of the mystical vapor. Reflexively, Jenna wiped her face of the wetness and rolled to her side. They had slept in the open, behind their protective hedge. The previous night featured perfectly mild temperatures for human comfort beneath a cloudless, starry sky. Ant had regaled the group with his knowledge of the constellations, their names and relationships, remembering a phone application he'd had as a young boy that mapped the mythological heavens.

An odor like an upset stomach distorted the air, and soft retching sounds paired to light splashes matched to the smell. Around camp, everyone was either soundly sleeping or beginning to turn over. Pru was missing.

Near the bull by a large wild rose shrub shedding the last of its October petals, Pru held her hair back as her little stomach gushed forth.

"I gotchu," Jenna said, moving quickly toward her one female companion. Her left arm wrapped around Pru's midsection, and the other cradled her head. Jenna's right hand gently clasped Pru's hot and damp forehead, helping to brace and to comfort the wan, sickly woman.

"You're burning up," Jenna said. "When did you start to feel sick?"

Pru almost fully collapsed onto the ground without answering, but Jenna pulled Pru's body against her own, squatting together to assess Pru's condition.

"Just all of a sudden," she said with little force behind her words. "I feel horrible," she added. "Like I'm dying."

"Don't be silly. You're not dying."

Pru closed her eyes, almost instantly falling asleep once relieved by the final retch of her guts.

"Let's get you back to the group and see if Ant has a blanket in the wagon." Lifting Pru to her feet, Jenna staggered, and the slighter woman lost her feet beneath her, virtually passing out. "Oh *shit*," Jenna mumbled, concerned for the woman but doubting some of it for drama; her helplessness almost seemed ridiculous. Jenna knew Pru was psychologically weak, though she had pretended otherwise, played like they were equals, like they had the same thoughts and opinions—because it had comforted Pru, not because it emerged from an honest symbiosis of thought and feeling. In the old world, women had always done this but to what purpose, Jenna could never tell, and in this moment, a long-suppressed rage—not at Pru, nor at her weakness, but at the old world's insistence that each woman tell every other that she empathized, that she agreed, that she understood, that she felt bad and was sorry, that she knew, that she felt everything and all things exactly the same way—gave her the strength to lift Pru off the ground and carry her to a more comfortable spot under a shelter of branches.

"You'd better not be faking this," she suddenly blurted out, but Pru could hardly respond, practically hyperventilating from a fluttering rush of her heart rate. Ashamed by her outburst, Jenna instead focused on coaching Pru to breathe deeply to calm her cramping, angry body. And when Jenna could see Pru's hands shaking—her entire body quaking from the pain—shame further directed her attentions back to the woman as she sat to hold and rock her friend to try to foster some peace, some stillness, some compassion, some comfort. It was all that she was capable of doing.

* * *

Nelson had been awake, pretending to be asleep but watching the scene between the two women, horrified at Pru's sickness but not surprised at her vulnerability, a trait he had more successfully disguised in his own character prior to collapse. He shivered at his wife's morbid disposition; her arms and legs haphazardly dangling from Jenna's embrace when their eyes met: hers an icy, unaccented stare; his: strange, estranged, and terrified.

"She's dying," Jenna called over to him, seeing his widening eyes.

"I know," he coldly replied, quickly turning his body to face the other side.

The unemotional response from the only one of them who should have cared mirrored Jenna's own callousness just minutes before, and she could say nothing, could do nothing but turn back to Pru, who had fallen asleep in her arms.

* * *

Ant had been tending to the bull, giving it some water from the frothing rivulet—not a creek, nor a river—behind their camp from which a jet the thickness of a bathroom faucet protruding from a rocky formation was sufficient to fill the bull's drinking bowl. Observing the others from a few yards, he used the distance to reassess their characters. The one woman was obviously very ill.

The other was strong, undoubtedly, both mentally and physically. The two women weren't friends, but the strong one cared for the other like women did. Men would do no such thing. The one man was mousy, doubtful—someone to keep at an arm's length. And the other one, the Polynesian-looking man, Ant had decided to approach and test the depth of his manhood, but Jeremy was already approaching him to continue testing his.

"All the way down from the Weaverville area, yeah?"

"That town's somewhere nearby us, yes." Ant almost answered, "Yes, sir," a reflex he'd acquired around his grandfather whose presence could provoke such respect. This one had it in him to lead, but Ant still had to figure its depth and its quality—was it golden and true? Or fetid and rotting? He would have to wait and see.

Jeremy smiled as if surprised, as if maybe lied to, as if this guy hadn't been upfront with him. "Who's us?" he asked plainly but smiling.

Ant perceived Jeremy's immediate and irrational distrust, which reminded him of fellas growing up, of a different breed, if not exclusively white or black, something other than one of his kin and color who would throw up defenses offensively at the slightest seeming slight. Ant grew wary but resolved not to reveal the pounding in his heart and carefully, to say precisely, answered the question. The previous evening's trust and amity had bumped into the reality of a newborn alliance in this newly treacherous land.

"A friend named Mina. Stayed behind at her family's little cottage farm. She helped me. We helped each other, I spect. She's a good woman, and I wish she was here with us."

"Is she—" Jeremy couldn't finish the question. "Is she—"

"What? Black?"

"I'm just curious if—"

"Nah, she's a white lady. Greek, I think, actually." Distant and disappointed, Ant smiled at the sky.

"I didn't mean anything by that, just curious if you had any people left."

"I get you," Ant said. "You're a darker-skinned brother too." There was more mockery in the jest than he had intended.

Jeremy laughed. "Yeah—yup, I sure am. But my people are mostly over in Hawaii, and I talk like a redneck."

"We both do," Ant clarified.

"True, son. True that." They shared a common view of the world only an American could know.

"Hawaii, huh? Never been."

"And never will," Jeremy added, making them both wild with laughter.

"What's so funny, y'all?" Nelson asked, striding over to the two other men.

"Aww, nothing, Nelson," Jeremy said. "Just laughin'."

"I see," Nelson answered and scuffed his feet against the dirt as he walked away.

"Go help your wife, for Christ's sake," Jeremy yelled after him.

* * *

Jeremy grew confident as he and Ant talked. Adrenaline had become a long-term resident, as it wasn't Ant's persona which had bothered him initially, seeming good and firm; it was just another male, a stranger in his midst, none of whom of late had been worthy of trust. Especially Nelson. Ant's matter-of-fact peace of mind helped to assuage the uncertainty.

"All we can do is help each other. That's all we got," Jeremy said more quietly in Nelson's direction.

"She's not doing so well, is she?" Ant asked.

Jeremy glanced over his shoulder at Pru, who was warming her failing body by the morning fire Jenna had fixed beside her. "No, she's definitely not."

"What you think is wrong?"

"I've no idea—well, no. I take that back." Jeremy faltered, not used to being so honest with people he didn't know, straddling between liking this guy and being out of practice with candid conversation. "There was a bad pregnancy—a terminated one, you know, I can't think of the word—"

"A miscarriage?"

"Yeah, that."

"How long ago?"

"Can't be two weeks, maybe a little more. Time is another uncertain thing."

Ant turned his eyes to the ground. "I don't know a whole lot about that, but I do know that on a farm pregnant women have to stay away from the animals. Real vulnerable to infections. E. coli is common. She could be in a bad way."

"She's been complaining about feeling sick, but there's not much we can do. We're barely getting through the days, ourselves. All of our stuff we packed—just up in flames. We lost some medical supplies too."

"Better than losing your lives or seeing one or a couple of you shot."

"As bad as it was, I have to say it could have been worse, but this feels pretty much worse."

"I hear ya. I've got a long story to tell, myself, but it'll have to come out here and there."

Jeremy put his hand on Ant's shoulder, squeezing it. "I understand, man."

"I sense you don't trust me, but I'm not out for any bad thing."

"No, no." Jeremy, embarrassed, waved his hands in front of him. "It's not that I don't trust you. I just—we just—"

"Not to worry," Ant said. "We all got reasons not to trust anyone. I watched my whole family either die or run away, so I know all about being alone with no one to fall back on."

"Damn, I'm sorry," Jeremy said.

"Don't be too sorry. We're going to see a lot more death than we ever thought we would."

"I hear that. Though I'm a marine. Back in twenty-eight, my platoon fought at Taiwan. No massacre could compare to that."

"I see," Ant said, bobbing his bent head in respect.

"Saw a lot of shit there, a quarter of which I'd never expected to see here."

"Really? I saw it coming. I could feel it coming up through school, man. It was obvious no one knew what the hell was up about anything. Total ignorance. My grandfather pretty much raised and educated me."

Jenna wandered near them; her dirt-stained face couldn't suppress the vital womanly beauty which overcame it, having renounced any vanities for the new harshness of life. The men paused in their talk.

"Hey—do you, like, have any more food?" she asked Ant awkwardly, not wanting to demand it and start issuing people orders, though it would have come easily to her.

Ant was hesitant to reveal all, not knowing yet if he'd stay on with them or if they were compatible for the long haul. "Yeah," he said, giving in to whatever compassion was left to gild the contours of his darkened soul. "There's some beef jerky in the cooler under the middle row seat."

* * *

In the weeks since Ant's departure, Mina had frequented the marketplace, the biggest boon to her will to live. Not only was the variety of trade a pleasant distraction on a doubt-minded day, but it further secured her sense that continued survival in this familiar region was more than a possibility; it was her established reality. The fall air felt crisper, morphing into winter, and more fragrant as dough-baked scents filled the house from the pies she was now making from eggs traded for flour. As for the butter, she'd had some traded milk to churn which was more than enough for the pies and further trade. Life settled around her, even as the leaves colored like aged burgundy, and golden yellow trim bled inwardly to greener stems, on the early close of each sleepy day, soon falling to rest in the mud.

Albert and Lucinda had become touchstones and quick, comfortable friends, a place of society and one of spiritual solace when she'd needed an ear to hear her concerns or for them to use hers, listening on the floor as Albert wove a finer story of his days at the marketplace and the characters who took to the living stage there. In fact, it was rumored that a traveling pack of actors, of all superfluous activities, might be making its way for bread, and Albert, among others, had been asked to help construct the proscenium while those others managed the center, right, and left of the stage. His wood would be needed, but, ever the businessman, Albert had demanded a continuous supply of Montgomery's farm ale until he'd deemed it sufficient payback.

"They'd had the temeritee to say naw, sir, at first—well, I jus' packed up ma things and walked off when, a course, they had to have me in the mix and relented, giving me the deal." Albert raised his glass of room-temperature, good Montgomery's ale toward Mina, who smiled and sipped at her pint while he boasted in more affected accents. Lucinda drank her Barnyard Daisy tea, a country name for chamomile, the dainty white daisies for which she'd grown herself out back the last summer among other fragrant herbs: rosemary, mint, lavender, sage, and basil.

"It might be interesting to meet some of these actors," Lucinda commented. "Strange sort of thing to do these days, don't you think?"

Mina agreed.

"I certainly don't think they'll be worth any time spent on 'em. Actors are some of the very reason we're in this mess we're in. Them Hollywood folk never done us right," Albert declared.

Lucinda nodded into her cup. "Still," she said, "it's almost too out of the ordinary not to miss it. Who would settle on that kind of life in these kinds of times?"

"Thieves," Mina said to a burst of chuckling applause from both hosts.

"I don't for one nit-pickin' nano byte of a minute doubt that right there."

"Not everyone is as capable of building and operating farms, now, Berti. We can't be dragging to hell all assortment of souls just 'cause we don't understand their lives."

Albert looked sideways to his wife, her knowing his deep interest in storytelling, but his even deeper suspicion of those who told them. "Nah, ma'am," he said. "If you're cartwheelin' your way through the country at a time like this, you're up to no good. I'd bet my life on that."

"It's an oddity," Mina put forth. "Who would have thought a band of American troubadours would be circling these parts like medieval Il Capitanos? The bizarre world grows stranger by the day. It's like all the history we forbade our learning brains has come back to haunt us, the ghosts of each century reminding us of the whole of what we have lost."

"Yeah, well, I wouldn't trust a single one a them," Albert reiterated, not following her subtle thread. "I 'member once, not too while back, a man, but dressed as a lady—you know the type—started galloping like a horse around the market, had some kinda fascination with the school bus. Seemed more than odd. I know it was in the culture before the fall and all. I know it was a widespread kinda thing, but I was always far removed from it. This one man, he'd powder his face, red his cheeks, curtsy at the women, and wink at the men all while scratchin' the stubble on his jaw and the itch on his nuts. I 'bout lost my lunch from laughin'. Me and Old John. Didn't bother us none. I was entertained which I spect was the goal of it. But I don't know about some actors saying shit on a stage. What the hell they have to say now anyway? Let's all pretend that we're *not* in an apocalyptic mess? That everything is just fine, it's another time, another world? No thank you, sir and ma'am. *Good night.*"

"I still want to see what they'll do. That'll be worth the loaf of bread."

"Better bring a stale one then." Albert became suddenly morose. "Those types who get drawn to the theatrical have *unnatural* selves." He pointed at the women.

"Don't be silly," his wife chided. Mina looked on as if watching a performance herself. "You sound like a superstitious loon," Lucinda finished.

"You've been warned." He downed the rest of his ale. "You've *both* been warned." He stood up. "I'm going out back now to check on all the beasts."

Once he was gone, the women had the silence to fill for themselves.

"My god, is he a blusterer."

"A little," Mina admitted. "But a good and sturdy man."

Lucinda agreed. "I did get lucky, even if I have to endure the melodrama. He's only talkin' about himself just now."

"Aren't we all—"

"I spect so."

"I'll go with you if he doesn't. I'd love a bit of entertainment. Been a long time since we've been properly distracted. And if it sucks, we can leave."

* * *

The following Tuesday was the opening night of three nights of shows; no one was sure what was going to be performed, only that the troupe did many things. They'd been told it would be a "pastiche" of recitals: some comedy, some tragedy, a juggling act, a contortionist, and two hosts who'd gained a reputation, according to their charcoaled posters, for winning a crowd.

There were stage lights installed, and only the one, on far stage right, shone on the platform that evening of the opening Tuesday. An audience had gathered while the junior clowns, wigged and powdered in various styles, appeared to collect whatever foodstuffs were brought for this troupe of mangy vagabonds. And then silence fell among the watchers, a silence almost unfamiliar, almost civilized, a public one—the one which encompassed expectation, many dreams, a whim or two, and childlike exultation.

Out walked a ghoulish-looking clown dressed in a man's suit with bright hair of indeterminate florescence and hospital-white paint around his face but blackened in his deep raccoon eyes and overdrawn red on his lips. He posed. One arm raised, fingers tight, palm turned inwardly like a hackneyed poet to sing a ballad or to pronounce his lines in a withering manner: a pathos, incarnate. His other hand rested elegantly on his hip. A morose opera escaped from his depths as he sang Iago's "Credo in un Dio Crudel" from the composer, Verdi's, *Otello*, commanding an army of everyday fiends: the villain cursing the world, condemning it to the worst of God's renunciations. Iago, like the great Satan fallen to the lake of fire, now casting his gloom upon the blathering masses.

Lucinda leaned toward Mina and whispered, "He sounds like a madman. I'm *obsessed*." She laughed into the pillow of Mina's shoulder.

Mina regarded the girlishness with undetectable humor and mocked, but sweetly, her titillated companion, whose chest blushed at her passion for the music.

The final note announced triumph over conscience at the pith of the aria, conducting its way toward the dumbness of heaven as the man left the stage to slow but determined clapping until the whole audience seemed convinced of his genius and total commitment to the piece, culminating as maniacal applause. Lucinda stood to clap furiously with many others, either naturally affectionate to opera or educated to know how well it was done or so starved of the magic of talent and art that, spellbound, they praised its blessing. Some of them whistled and proclaimed *bravo*!

"That was *marvelous*," Lucinda said, entranced by the communal lust for something higher in life.

"It was good—yeah," Mina said.

Smaller curtains pulled open to reveal the incompleteness of backstage as a chorus of hums harmonized in an orchestral allegro rondo, and the smaller actors mimed an incoherent ballet like a crackhead *Nutcracker* until the hums turned to moans and discordant groans, and they all collapsed onto the floor of the stage to muffled, awkward laughter in the audience. The crowd seemed perplexed and didn't move or make a noise.

"*Ooooo*-kay," Mina intoned.

By the end, few of the audience remained, though an innocent young woman spoke a soliloquy from *As You Like It*—Rosalind in the woods, dressed as a young man, berating a desperate lover and his prideful woman; only this line, spoken to herself as both man and woman, remained in Mina's mind:

> 'tis such fools as you that make the world full of ill-favour'd children

Lucinda had pushed her way backstage while Mina stayed in her seat, lost in memory and terrible thoughts of the past, of the world that had been undone by the extravagances and limitless multiplicity of selves all clamoring for attention, money, and finally some power. This progression seemed to strike her as the most typical pattern of the human ego: At first, the child needs attention, then wants it; then the teenager desires money to do the things expected of them by peers, and for that, they may get some power, which distorts their self-sense (and any vision they might have), and they then carry this unholy burden into the world as adult players further maligning the nature of humanity, further destabilizing tradition, further progressing into collective idiocy: singular actors behaving impulsively according to strict rules of progressive derangements.

The performances that night had ushered in with them a contemplation, a provocation, once a hardy dream, one that Mina had either forgotten or resisted for the necessities involved with staying alive. Thoughts, images, art, philosophy had a tendency to preoccupy her mind during college days at Kenyon. She had been bright and hard-working, and her grandfather had directed her to apply to smaller but excellent liberal arts colleges that leaned toward the conservation of knowledge. As much as her mind naturally adhered to creative thinking, the collapse of Western civilization had spoiled her mood for it, and she resented the intrusion of art into this world, wishing she'd never gone to the show. Residual trauma from the attack precluded further musings on the why's and how's of life, as any thought indicative of more profound revelation might rekindle the memory of that horror and set her to rage. One foot in front of the other was all she had wanted to manage. *No more thoughts*, she thought. *No more artful thoughts.*

The following Sunday, Albert had invited her for dinner, a Sunday roast, only he would serve pork instead of beef, his pigs being more numerous than his cows. Walking up the stairs, she could hear talk in low baritones, like that vicious melody she'd renounced, and she froze in place, recognizing its onerousness but not knowing its owner.

The front door was open to allow the coolness of the chilly afternoon to invade the house, pushing out whatever hotter air had been baked inside by the loitering day. She recognized Albert in his standard position, seated in his favorite chair, with the look of a man trying to forbid a sour expression from commanding his face. Her heart sped; her body convulsed. Albert noticed her standing outside the room and cocked his head for her to enter. On the couch was a man whose voice she had heard before. Lucinda sat upright like a schoolgirl wishing to cling to the man's sides, swallow his every spoken word. The monologue ceased when she entered, and they all looked to her.

"Mina, please, sit," Lucinda said.

Albert shot Mina another irritated look as the tension relaxed into itself, and he felt free to express it more openly. The stranger stared with passive eyes when she remembered.

"You sang that song, didn't you?" she asked.

"I did, yes. Did you like it?" he asked pleasantly.

"Not particularly."

He frowned like a clown, looking like he cared but not caring. Lucinda giggled at his theatrical playfulness, passing around some tea to Mina, who grew as irritated and as wary as Albert. There was something off about the man, but Lucinda was thoroughly taken by whatever charms she had perceived. His features were bold, not quite too prominent to be ugly, but distinctive: attractive enough in person, better at a distance, likely best in a photograph if any could be taken.

"I am Pierrot." He placed his hand on his heart, lying about his name.

"Is that your real name?" she asked. He bowed his head in answer. "A medieval clown, then?"

The smirk across his face altered his expression, giving a glint of something deeper, a range of japes and jabberies, hidden from most but revealed as an infinity of contentious selves in that one instant. And yet, his aspect altered again, and he was soft, sweet, gentle, pulling Mina's attentions closer toward him. Mina's affect was also altered by his magic and seemed open to being delighted by the actor.

Albert, disgusted by a woman's moody infidelities, rose and left the room murmuring to himself about the inconstancies of affection.

Throughout the meeting, Pierrot mesmerized them with tales of life on the road, through forests and hostile territories, people and tribes disinterested in entertainments to the point of violence, feeling forever degraded by the disharmony between country life and the more urbane, however unpredictable, ways of the living arts. A more grounded, realistic tone offset her doubts yet again as he presented himself as an educated man, separate from the performer, who was also trying to survive the insecurities of the fallen world with what he had to give.

"There are some communities along the Eastern Seaboard that are ginned up for widespread war. Many pockets of sectarian conflict still run down the coast. It's during a ceasefire that we can sometimes play our parts and earn some food or other resources, but it is difficult. We have children too, most of whom perform, but they need to eat, and we, their guardians, are not much given to a routine kind of life except by mirror or mockery."

Lucinda nodded idiotically, drying a tear from the corner of an eye. Mina was more taken by the heroism of their survival regardless of their manner of style in doing it, ignoring whatever seductions that had clearly secured Lucinda's baser drives, her torso practically gyrating as he spoke.

"Have you traded much at the marketplace?" Mina asked.

"We trade what we can," he replied gently. "But we have little that others would want, only what they dream of. I find, if I can attract the children of the audience, I can win the affections of the parents and then some food, maybe some fuel. We had a bus, once."

"I understand," Mina said, more concerned about the children in his troupe as he described their living conditions. "I brought some fruit from my little arbor for Berti and Lucinda—fresh apples, canned pears, and frozen peaches from this summer's harvest. Please, take them back to the children."

"*Yes*, please do that," Lucinda said.

"We are very thankful," he said. "They will love it."

By the time Mina left for home, having acclimated to the stranger, playing along with the intrigues of an artist and his most unified persona, she'd decided that all was well. But as she took to the porch steps and walked down the path to the road, her initial impressions of the man, her sympathies with Albert's disinterest, even his apparent displeasure at receiving the player as a guest, returned. The closer she was to home, the more anxious she became, but wondering if her trauma, symbolized by the corpse, which no longer sat at the head of her drive but had fallen to pieces like an exhausted scarecrow, was the root of the encroaching fears about this man.

Once inside, she went for the newer handgun Albert had loaned her the day after Ant's departure, checked its chamber for bullets, and decided to return to their homestead, just in case. Relations had become more unreliable than the stability she'd regained by knowing and befriending the couple would have implied, and concern for self-delusion, of ignoring the intuitive pang that had called attention to the oddness of the man might be another mistake in a time when mistaking the intentions of a man—pretending to mistake them to reclaim a social normalcy long ago discarded—could allow any range of pathologies to prevail.

She shook it off and decided not to go: a paranoid thought; her feelings were inaccurate; her intuition was too troubled by her attack. Something else was going on, and this man, however different, was another walk of life she was not used to. It was prejudice, she thought. Everyone deserves a chance to prove themselves.

Before dusk, Mina threw on a winter coat, took the handgun, locked the front door, and started the hour walk back to Albert and Lucinda's, all the while more convinced of her wilder thoughts, walking faster, sweating inside the downy insulation of the coat.

The house was lit by candle but only in the front windows of that living room, and there was movement; shadows darted around in the glow. As she got closer, she cocked the gun and stepped up to the porch. Something was in fact very wrong. Through the window, she could see the man painting red letters on the wall, singing to himself like a lunatic. She opened the door, pointed the gun, and read what was written in blood on the walls:

Hooray for HOLLYWOOD!!!

The lyrics of the song he sang while writing these infernal words on the wall with a dripping rag.

"*Hey!*" she growled from her deepest point. He stopped, slowly turned his head, smiling like a fiend, his face painted stark white like a clown, his teeth bloody too and seeming sharp. And she shot him, blowing his brains out against the wall, obscuring the message with his blood.

Poor Lucinda was face-up, draped over the arm of the couch, throat sliced open. Albert was face down in front of his old chair, his beer mug dashed against the wall from an obvious struggle, likely too drunk by that point to subdue the killer. Blood traced the outline of his generous body.

Mina collapsed onto the floor.

On their front porch, she sat through the sleeping night, disbelief from shock and deeper demoralization keeping her body upright. The bodies of her friends lay behind her, inside the house she'd begun to know as a neighborly refuge. The intensity of her life the past weeks had finally become too much. The assault in her home and now this; she had never known violence before, both events too horrific to reconcile, even in the barbarous conditions of civilizational collapse. The region had gone bad, maybe because of the marketplace and the devious types that it could draw, or the migrant farm where Ant had worked, again attracting the most desperate of vagabond and psychopathic men.

The sun broke out above the horizon, thawing the night's long despair. A pair of cardinals, bright red and reddish brown, a couple, flitted onto the ground in front of her, looking for scraps before the flight farther south. The oblivion of nature, continuing in spite of the heinous corruptions of man, distracted her from the unease. When the birds flew off, she resolved to leave the area once and for all.

In the barn, there were three horses, a small horde of pigs, one cow, and her old goats. Opening the gates to all their pens, she freed them, not wanting to leave them locked up. The pigs and goats would be too difficult to shepherd, especially without a trained dog. Of the horses, she took the mare, the sturdiest of the three. The other two instantly trotted off and into the front yard to graze. Animals meandered out of their pens and into the corridor of the barn, moving toward the light at the opened end.

The horse whinnied, snorted, and then neighed as Mina tightened the saddle, the largest of which had side pockets big enough to carry bladders full of water.

"Sorry, girl," she said. The horse craned its head toward its new companion and nudged at her side. Mina patted its haunches. Once the bridle was on and the reins attached, she mounted the beast. "We gotta get out of here now." She tapped its sides with her heels as the horse jolted forward before easing into a steady walk.

Before noon, back at her homestead, she'd packed as much into the saddle as it could fit, tied a sleeping bag to its backside, and journeyed out toward the open road and the vaster wild, having abandoned her home and her grandfather's legacy, towing the cow on a rope like a leash. Too numb to process thoughts or feelings, Mina mindlessly rode the horse as it walked where it would in the direction she had pointed its head. In the direction that Ant had gone.

Far away and never to return, she might remember all the happy years she'd spent there as a child, before the world had rotted to its core, before humanity had turned on itself, wrecking the work done by tireless past generations, billions of people doing what they could so humanity would have a chance at a more permanent kind of peace, but it wasn't to be. Peace and prosperity had seeded fields of resentment, giving time and space enough for those who had grieved to remember and to take revenge. They coerced a dream of progress that had ignored its nightmarish shadow, its fetid underbelly, a set of darker motivations disinterested in truth, entranced by selfish vision and eager to fill each baser request, satisfy every passionate slur against them. Finally, one hope sustained Mina in her trek into the greatest American unknown: Would she reunite with Ant? Would it be possible to find him?

The horse plodded along its course. The cow followed, hoof by hoof, behind them.

* * *

Special permissions granted by the man in black kept suspicious players subdued. Charlie was released, and Roland was returned to the cell like a prisoner, but around him, men sniffed like hounds, sensing a change in the stressors and the stressed. One of them spotted the man in black escorting Roland around the pits, as they called it. Character, like gravity, but the timely punch of power, too, seemed to draw the men to Roland as they clustered outside his cell, chatting in low hums and silent nods; men pacing the corridor, eyes darting from one to another. They could feel the shift before they knew it had shifted.

The man in black didn't run the halls as much. The musclebound man with the long blond hair had disappeared. A new hulking sentry oversaw the guardianship of the lobby and its entrances. This one wore a ski mask and barely spoke. At the man in black's command, Charlie was posted on patrol to restrict movement near Roland's cell as the other men had begun to ask him desperate questions. The man in black visited regularly to consult Roland, slowly introducing the men to the new power player like a new dog adjusting to the pack. Eventually, the door to the cell would remain open during the day. Food and drink were brought to Roland at Charlie's command, whose power increased by association.

For the next move in their strategy to integrate Roland as newly crowned master and commander, the man in black ordered Charlie on an expedition with a band of the men to track down the location where the man in black believed a stash of stabilizer, octane boosters, and other chemical additives had been secreted away by military special forces. Charlie was meant to keep the men—who'd come to view him relative to the man in black—focused on the mission, if not to lead the piratical brigade: to provoke their bravery against the insult of Charlie's impotent authority.

Roland's cell had morphed into central intelligence for the operation, and in the afternoon of the same quiet day, Roland stepped out and into what had become his lobby.

"The refinery—" he announced.

The man in black followed his lead to the giant cement staircase which led up and into the parking garage, where a black-tinted SUV waited to carry them northeast to the old Marathon Petroleum Corporation site.

Inside the narrow, millennial building—so rusted at its corners, they were crumbling to dust, walls that had been entirely glass, long ago shattered, leaving jagged edges to frame the view—a man, perhaps in his sixties, shouldering an aspect of intellectual quirk, acted his days costumed in a light blue workman's suit like a onesie with a nametag displaying his character's name. Roland reached for the man's hand.

"Hauser?" Roland read the name out loud as they shook.

"Yes. And you are?"

"The new man in charge."

"I see." Hauser squared his body, engaging Roland's eyes with an expression twice as blank.

Agitated by the sudden entitlement of the man, Roland came close to losing his patience. "Are you the rat, then?" he asked boldly.

"By any other name I'd smell as sweet—"

Roland cocked both brows, expecting humor to reveal itself in the brazen keeper.

"I'm not the man you're looking for," Hauser said finally, waving off the inquiry and wiping his oil-black palms onto his pants. Roland noticed the residue on his own hand and held it out and away from himself as if slimed by a communal disease. The man in black handed him one of many gray towels resting in clumps around the office.

"In fact, you are," Roland said, wiping his hand partially clean. "You're to show me around the facility—if you please."

"Aye, aye, captain," Hauser quipped, saluting the odd and ornery fellow. As if possessed by habitual tic, the man mumbled to himself, taking a ring of a thousand keys off its hook, identifying the exact one without effort and exiting the office, leading into a hallway connecting the administrative brain to the guts of the processing plant. Hauser swiftly unlocked the massive metal door of its entrance. The main distillation tower stood like a queen bee at the center of her hive, towering above like a peculiar kind of judge.

"Crude goes in through a large pipe at the back, feeding it into the boiler, which then heats it up—"

"No kidding," Roland affirmed.

The man regarded Roland, unimpressed by the sarcasm, but continued without a change to his tone. "Then up into the tower it goes, colder molecules at the top to the very hot at bottom, here. That's your jet fuel, your diesel. Called fractional distillation. And once the vapor turns to liquid, it is culled out of the tower, sucked into its own pipe, channeling the product into a separate container where'd we then add the stabilizer and such. Runnin' low on all that, by the way."

"I'm aware." Roland paced the floor as if inspecting something he'd seen a million times, having never seen a single one. "What do you do with the jet fuel? Can cars go on that?"

The man shook his head decidedly. "No. No. Sure can't. Would ruin the catalytic converter, amongst other things."

"I see," Roland said, again pretending to follow, having recognized the terms but lacking the practical knowledge of their purpose. "And how do you ship it?"

The workman deferred to the man in black for an answer.

"We have a system for that," the man in black said.

Roland accepted the limitation for the moment, but, back in the car, he asked, "So, why is distribution top secret?"

"We rely on certain gangs, and they are not well liked by the community, and we try to keep them both happy." He paused, looking out the window at the empty highway as they zoomed down the road. "They do many different things."

"Nothing's illegal anymore, so what gives?"

"Perhaps there's no justice system, but there is still the means to justice."

"I see."

"They do good things for us, like transporting the oil for a cut. They operate the generator manufacturing plant. But they also do some very bad things."

"I get it."

"Charlie is with a few of them now, at the raid."

"He should be fine," Roland said, awkwardly blotting out the doubts in his concerns.

* * *

Charlie was not, in fact, fine, but terrified. The team of assassins or gang of pirates, whatever these men were who Roland had commanded, he attended like some kind of corporate scold, meant to oversee but lacking the gravitas to gain their respect. They ignored him, likely resented him as a strange addition, knowing he was put in place to surveil and not to defend or to procure. The warehouse they had located prior to Charlie's anointment as their nanny, one that housed many vats of the necessary stabilizer, was situated at the perimeter of a heavily fortified base. Whatever remnant of the U.S. military that still existed, some of it could be found guarding formerly official sites where excess fuel and its corollary products were stored. Fuel had not lost its value, and in the markets where it was still viable—where still powerful, still rich-enough cliques of elites in New York, D.C., LA, and the like purchased the resource—it was costing many hundred more times its cost before collapse.

"We're going in for a closer look," the action commander said. "You stay here and say nothin', ya hear? You keep your eye on that black door. When one of us comes out and waves, you drive the truck down to the door. If you fuck this up, I will kill you. I don't care who protects you now." The lead soldier, action commander, or whatever he was, continued to threaten Charlie, poking him in the chest while Charlie nodded like a schoolboy stunned by a bully, who smirked at the soft acquiescence of his target, as if proving the superiority of his manhood. "Good boy," he said mockingly. Watching from behind a barrier of indeterminate material, Charlie crouched down, uncertain what he would do if anything other than what was planned occurred. The action commander, ten yards into the siege, turned and hissed, "*Get back in the fucking truck!*"

"Shit, shit, shit!" Charlie chanted quietly, unable to go but bounced on his toes as he squatted. "I don't even know what the *fuck* we're supposed to be getting here," he said to himself, halving his height to scuttle back to the truck, where he stared at the black door and waited, repeating—out loud and in his head, "What the fuck, what the fuck, what the fuck!"

Mere minutes had passed, but his inexperienced nerves drew a lifetime from each one. His palms became clammy while his blood pressure rose, and his forehead sweated. His hands, blanched of blood, repeatedly gripped the steering wheel until gunshots began to pop in the distance, maybe twenty, maybe fifty, but as soon as they stopped, one of the men burst out the black door, waving his arms.

Charlie floored the gas, but the car only lurched forward. "Fuck!" he yelled, bringing the shift out of park and into drive. Then he floored it again, almost tipping the truck over as he swerved its backside toward the door, shocked by his facility at the wheel. As soon as the truck stopped shaking back and forth, the back door was heaved up and flew down its tracks on the ceiling. Barrels of chemicals were hoisted by grunting men into the cargo dock. Random shots were fired, whizzing backward. A boss pirate opened the driver's side door and hopped into the cab, pushing Charlie into the center, when another entered the passenger side, whose menacing appearance in the seat kept Charlie from running away, if the looks on their faces were any measure of the moment.

Pounding on the interior wall of the hold, the worker-pirates indicated their readiness to leave, and the sergeant captain pirate put the shift into gear and took off, whipping Charlie's head back against the metal divider between the front seats and the cargo behind him. The infantry boss pirate to his right disapproved of him from behind tinted glasses like a terminator, and then shifted his lifeless gaze straight ahead, toward the windshield, saying nothing.

"Did we get it?" Charlie asked.

And, after a pause, more confused than awkward, the driving soldier said, "Yes."

"That's good," Charlie replied, staying mute for the rest of the drive.

* * *

Back at the fortress, Roland continued to demonstrate his new position in ever-bolder moves, making it clear that he was taking over. The man in black had handed his will to the newly minted boss, mostly by the simplest method of performing personal admiration and administrative services. The man in black liked Roland, respected his authoritarian intelligence, and bowed to his logistical know-how without question, it seemed. There were, as there always are, men in the pack who recognized the coup for what it was and kept their disapproving comments to a whisper.

But generally, the men spoke suspiciously about Roland among themselves. This replacement was too tall, his eyes too sharp and knowing, his voice too worn and dark, his entire aspect too entitled to the position that verbal dissent of any meaningful kind had to be sidelined. An assessment of his skill to command would have to be made first. Cunning, if not smart, they'd wondered aloud if this wasn't Rathausen finally in the flesh.

Roland and select men who'd begun to form an inner circle like a council or a cabinet met the SUV as it came through the thirty-foot garage door, slashing harsh daylight across the cave as it opened. Marius, a lead crude scout, more like a captain than any foot soldier, jumped from the cargo hold of the truck and stood behind the new chief executive, who'd stood observing with his arms crossed. On the other side was the man in black, stoic and still. The back door of the truck was yanked open, and the men cheered as barrels of stabilizer were removed from its port. Twelve barrels in all.

"It's not enough," the man in black said to Roland.

"Added to what we've already got, how much? In terms of time, how much?"

"Six months, maybe."

Roland hid his satisfaction. "Another expedition is necessary then. And then another. And another. This is the way the world works now."

The man in black bowed his head and went off with the pirates to unlock for them the diesel room farther below to begin the process of finishing the fuel. The generators needed topping off. The trucks, SUVs and other vehicles were low too. The man in black was the perfect administrator whose job it was to ensure that all operations were properly serviced and running smoothly. *He is not Rathausen, is he?* Roland wondered. How could he be? Did it matter? Would he use Roland's expertise, his command over the men, only to have him killed once resentments built and better systems were in place? These were questions to be aware of when observing the behaviors of the other men, Roland decided. Retaining power required his constant vigilance, manipulation, and the presumption that anyone could make a play for it—and a little but constant meddling.

* * *

Charlie jumped from the truck, noting Roland's glory in newfound power, the king again at his court, knowing he would not be permitted to interact with his former partner, his once domestic companion—whatever they were—"lover" had died off a long while back—but to simply serve him and his unspoken needs, left to bank on his friend—His brother? His life? Hoping to be included in whatever exit plan might evolve behind Roland's inscrutable and expressionless face.

Half the men followed the barrels and the man in black; finally, Charlie's eyes rested on Marius, a freshly promoted recruit from the wasteland that had become Alabama, whose natural beauty astonished Charlie and threatened his composure. "*Jesus Christ,*" he mumbled for lust.

"What's that?" Roland quickly asked, having clearly heard him.

Taking the cue, Charlie replied, "Nothing. All good." But Marius—his wavy, thick brown hair, lush dark beard, the handsomeness of his manhood was a sight to behold, like a god, a warrior prince—approached the two, and Charlie had to look away, when suddenly, he spoke to Roland.

"My other crew has plans for a run on the stock. The West Hackberry depot. Intel from BOS says Bayou Choctaw is running low from lootings. Big Hill is heavily guarded, and Bryan Mound is too remote for now. Nowhere to regroup, nor safely spend the night if we had to."

"I see," Roland said, only partially understanding the information. Marius regarded Charlie, who stood like a do-nothing in front of the men as they talked. "Leave us—*now,*" Roland said angrily, but Charlie again complied, taking the abuse, walking off alone and back into the fortress, not sure where to go.

* * *

On the 53rd floor, the new master's silhouette, faint from the final blush of evening light, stood alone within the frame of a window, practically the height and length of the wall, looking out at the nighttime city and its flickering lights. The illuminated trails ran up three main avenues, branching into smaller clusters of homes and residential units. The rest was dark, but the movements of toiling men, like amorphous, blackened blobs, could be detected if he strained his eyes to see them. What light there was appeared meager, glowing like torches.

"Even in the worst of times, we can find a way," he said.

"Short of nuclear annihilation, sure," the man in black answered.

"These clusters of lights. *This* is the new kingdom."

"Just like the old one."

Roland demonstrated his approval by amusement. The man in black's recognizable sass grew as a comfort, and for a moment, Roland marveled at the many ways—by disguise, ingenuity, or rank duplicity—men like them had found a manner by which to survive.

"You know, Charlie and I—" Roland appeared to become vulnerable. Intimate.

"Yes?"

"We thought you were Rathausen, at first. I see now he doesn't exist."

"Don't be too sure of that," the man in black asserted.

Roland traced his new companion's flightiness as he darted into the shadows of the room. "Then where is he?" he asked. A shock of pain surged up Roland's left side, and he tried not to wince. The small scab on his forehead, once a mere discoloration, had morphed into a sickly mark, difficult to hide. And there was another beside it.

"He's here and there and everywhere," the man in black said, returning with drinks.

"Cut the drama. If he exists then where is he?"

"I don't know but—"

"Is he that man with the long blond hair?"

"There was a time I thought he was," the man in black said.

"Oh, so now we're playing games? *You* don't even know who Rathausen is, do you?"

"No." The man in black rejoined Roland closer to the window, speaking out toward the town. "Someone did this, and it wasn't me. Someone started this, maybe years ago, working on a plan—maniacal then, sensible now?—that would result in the reconstitution of this city, or whatever we'll call it. Someone decided to form a tribe to loot the government stockpiles of crude oil. Someone figured out how to restart the refinery, to locate a competent manager. All this was an undertaking."

"Not possible by one man."

"But started by one. Someone who called himself Rathausen. Maybe he still exists. Maybe he has spies. Maybe he's planning against you at this very moment."

Roland nodded. "I know. Someone always is, anyway, whatever they wish to be called. Seen or unseen."

"Or both," the man in black concluded.

* * *

For all humanity reborn into darkness and desperation, when the sun drops down and behind another day, danger is the most vocal torment of their unsettled minds. There was maybe an hour left of the light. Mina had proved worthy of the traumatic challenges she'd so far faced. She knew killing those men had altered her, in a way, obliterating her moral senses, or so she had assumed. Not quite guilt but shock had nudged her psyche the longest: She'd killed evil men, but she had killed them, and that designation would alter anyone's self-concept, certainly anyone whose character had previously intended to preserve the contours of a civilized personality.

Her body jostled side to side as the horse crept down a small but steep embankment. The cow stopped in its tracks, refusing to attempt the cliff. Mina lazily regarded the stubborn cow and marveled at the increase in size to its belly, gestating new life. Mina's bleary eyes and parched mind hallucinated the coming calf had run up behind its mother, curious why the parade had stopped, nudging its nose around the cow's haunches. It brayed a whiny baby sound, tripped down the cliff, but staggered to its feet and sort of shook its body like a wet dog. The horse whinnied and stomped its right-front hoof as if approving the example for the mother cow. But there was no calf, no sweet distraction of innocent life. Just a thousand-pound beast refusing to budge. Mina pulled on the rope, but the big girl pushed her font hooves into the dirt to resist. Mina kicked at the horse's sides. The animal sort of instinctively knew not to jump with a burst of energy but methodically heaved its weight forward, taking a step, pulling the cow forward a single one, and then it mooed in defiance.

"Come on, ya fat heifer," Mina chided, riled by the stubborn, terrified beast. She kicked the horse again, and it seemed to decide it was finished indulging its cousin's nonsense and lurched forward, bringing the cow to the ground, sledding down the soft dirt of the ridge by its knees. It slowly took to its four legs once more and mooed again. The horse brayed in its cousin's face, seemingly from joy.

"There we go, big lady," Mina said approvingly.

Shipped by a sudden windswept cold front, the coolness in the latter end of the day chilled her bones, so Mina decided upon a clearing she'd spied deeper into the woods, maybe fifty yards east. Maneuvering her tribe toward it, they arrived at a grassy patch of earth when the cow instantly heaved itself onto the softest tufts and laid its head down. The horse grazed but stood still against the natural entrance to the sacred little spot then rested its eyes.

The cow was sleeping now, the horse resting on its legs, and Mina hadn't the appetite for food, nor the energy for making a fire. She unfurled the sleeping bag, climbed into its length, inching her body like a worm next to the cow for warmth, and fell quickly asleep, feeling safe around such large animals.

The harmony of night sounds sang the trusty company to sleep, and the stars blinked through the mostly barren treetops, keeping watch; the wind danced around them, growing colder. A sound in the deeper woods of a sniffing and snorting type ascended the air unnoticed. The black beast smelled the freshness of different flesh and hunted toward the scent. Stalking quietly, it used whatever stealth it had been given by God to approach the scene. It saw the cow first, then sensed other large animals. Cautiously, it stepped into the circular encampment, sniffing at the sleeping bag, perceiving the helplessness of its captive. Around Mina's head it angled its jaws to get at the nakedness of her neck and perhaps pull her away and into the brush to devour. It leaned, quivering its lips as its maw reached for the uncovered skin when the horse awoke from the smell of the bear, perceived the trouble, and wickedly brayed, stomping its hooves. The alerted cow took to its legs, lowering its bulky head at the carnivore, watching what the bear might do, which had jumped a safer distance away at the horse's command. Mina quickly roused to the showdown, crawling backward toward the horse, frantically searching in the night for one of Albert's rifles. Grabbing the gun, she cocked open the chamber and felt for bullets—it was loaded. The bear swiped at the space in front of it.

"Get out of here!" Mina screamed, but the bear just growled, starving and determined. What light shone from the midnight moon and stars was her only aid, but she aimed. The bear lunged at the cow. She fired, hitting its exposed flank as it staggered backward with a horrible, high-pitched sound, like a crying and howling dog, and it barreled out of the encampment, back into the dark.

"God*dammit*!" she yelled, exhausted by the rush of danger. "I cannot get a fucking *break*!" Holding the last word at the top of her lungs, she vented the rage she'd held inside, and the horse stepped high and back from her, panicked itself by the intrusion. Mina brooded in the dark for a time to calm herself, listening to the deep woods for signs the wild animal had returned, but the cow resumed its mindless ease, relaxing its body on top of its legs, so Mina placed herself near the burgeoning mother, spoke calming phrases to the horse, and eased back into the sleeping bag.

In the morning, the cow sniffed around Mina's face and mouth, glazing her cheeks with its wet nose. The horse was alert and grazing, still guarding the entry point where they had walked into the space. Mina covered herself in two of the three wool sweaters she had brought. The temperature of the morning was shockingly colder than it had been the one before. Autumn was entering its final period, when darkness comes earlier, and any kind of warmth lasts but two to three hours in the higher day.

Back on the easy road, a rare flat mile relaxed any stress for the labor of travel, before the hilly terrain returned and thoughts like extremities swirled, dizzying her head, when she realized she hadn't eaten since noon the prior day. Her boots hit the dusty earth, then she drank from the bladder of water stashed in the saddle. The cow mooed for something to drink.

"I know, girl, but this is my water."

Mina knelt beside the warmth of its distended underbelly; its muddy animal scent and gentle nuzzling of her ear combined to comfort her. Though still months off, its teats would bare their fat-rich liquid, providing breakfast for its protector and the small wonder of life they would sustain. She ate a piece of the cured meat she'd packed.

Mina hugged the rear haunches of the beast and scratched its topside as Sally Baby's eyes drooped from the pleasure. A good smack at the end woke the animal back up.

In the warmth of the rising day, Mina shed her sweaters down to a tank top. The horse plodded along. The cow would lag behind, unseen until the rope on Sally Baby's leash tightened; then the parade would stop. Sally Baby would moo loudly, demandingly, and, after some head turning, some exploratory seeing and looking about, would regain her step in pace with the others.

Over hours, Sally Baby kept mooing to the annoyance of all. The horse increased its speed, now and then, in what seemed like punishment for the mooing. Mina kept tugging at the rope. The droning, tonal moo had so virtually merged with the background noises of nature that when they stopped to rest, and Mina could scan the landscape behind her for vagrants, she hadn't noticed the beastly moaning was no longer coming from the cow, but some other cattle; but this was the sound of an obdurate kind of beast, transcending mere stubbornness, like a rapacious brute hyped for a fight. Like a bull.

"Oh my god," she said, observing the muteness of her cow, as an emotion formed in her guts and surged throughout her body, tingling toward her fingertips and into her head, guided by a fateful tug toward the sound which had silenced Sally Baby.

Closer to it, Sally Baby mooed back in a call and response.

"That-a-girl. Keep talkin'. You know who that is."

Mina couldn't be sure, but she could at least hope; any jolt of better life hadn't felt so good. Instinct informed them both. Now closer to the excited bull, she could see smoke from a fire like a friendly sign but, knowing how wrong she could be, guarded herself against this hope, securing the rifle to her side, stopping her crew just beyond a hedge that served as a boundary.

"Hello?" she called out.

There was no response, but a noticeable silence persisted.

"Anybody there?" Mina said more loudly.

Inside, the company froze, unsure who was addressing them. Ant listened more carefully. "Mina?" Ant called back.

"Yes!" Mina cried.

Ant nearly tripped, bounding from behind the hedge. Mina dropped the horse's reins. They embraced and surprised themselves by the mutual surge of emotion, of pure joy. Jenna and Jeremy observed the happy reunion, relieved to have another known-person join their company, especially one who had two worthy animals and maybe more supplies.

The reunited friends calmed and began to chuckle at the demonstration.

"It's been a few weeks, maybe a month, feels longer," Mina said through happy tears. "Who knows at this point, but I thought I'd never see you again."

"What happened? Why'd you leave?" he asked.

"I'll save that for later. Horror upon horrors, but I'm alive."

"Oh shit, okay."

"What a beautiful cow," Jenna said, helping to nudge the conversation to a new subject.

"Thank you. Her name's Sally Baby."

"And who's this big guy," Jenna asked about the horse.

"You know," she paused at the realization, "I haven't given her a name."

Jenna sidled up against the tawny flank of the taller animal, which had carefully approached her as she rubbed its softer cheeks. "Okay, girl, we'll just have to come up with one, now, won't we?"

Behind the women, Ant was explaining to Jeremy how he'd known Mina and some of their recent history. In a lull, Jeremy spoke out while Ant and Jenna brought the animals around and into the camp. "That's quite a saga between you two, and I think I only heard a small part of it!"

"Hopefully, the fun part."

"For sure, for sure. We've had our share of the—what would you call it?—the madness, I guess."

"Certainly that. I cannot believe some of the things I've seen," she said casually, her eyes wandering the ground. "There are moments when I feel really shocked, and I can't think clearly, and I feel like I'm gonna break apart, and then there are times like these when I feel so happy that it overrides all the terrible things, and I feel normal again. More than normal." She kicked a loose rock at her feet. "But it doesn't last."

Jeremy escorted the new member of their survival pod inside the encampment; Mina's eyes foraged upon the scene, noticing a lump on the ground to the farther side that altered between convulsion and stillness.

"Is that a—person?"

"Yes," Jeremy answered gravely.

"Are they—"

"Not well," he said. "We don't know what's wrong with her, but—"

"Jesus—"

Jenna stepped closer to Mina. "I think she's dying," she whispered.

"What happened," Mina asked.

"She miscarried a few weeks ago, and—"

"Sepsis," Mina declared.

"What is that?" Jenna asked.

"Acute infection. From the miscarriage. If she wasn't properly cleaned up." Mina stopped, seeing Jenna's discomfort at her bluntness.

"I did my best." Her eyes began to tear.

"It's not your fault," Mina said.

"How do you know?" Jenna asked.

"I don't, but I worked for a medical journal when I graduated from college. It's more common in the Third World, where there's less sanitation, and now that we've rejoined their ranks, it'll be common here again."

"How long do you think—"

"I don't know, but if it is e. coli or some other bad bacteria thing, not long. This is going to be difficult. Who's that man over there watching us?"

"Her husband."

"I see."

"He's a mess. I would leave him alone," Jeremy suggested.

"Understood, but we're going to have to keep him in check. If it is sepsis, she'll die in pain and soon."

Jenna had already understood this, but her face dropped silently nonetheless. Mina rubbed her back and escorted her to the front side of the hedge so not to provoke Nelson, who stared more intently at them as they talked.

Jenna recounted their acquaintance and then faltered. "We don't even know each other that well, but Pru, Pru was—Pru is—"

"These are very tough times. I've been through hell, too. The horrors of the pre-industrial past were many, and they are coming back. We have to be strong like we've never had to be strong before."

"What's wrong with Pru?" Nelson asked, abruptly stepping into the space.

Mina exhaled. "She's in trouble."

"How bad?"

"It's likely bad, I'm afraid."

"Can't you see it?" Jenna asked through her dismay, ready to rip into him, but Nelson teared up.

"She's gonna die, isn't she?"

"I won't say either way because I can't know for sure. I'm not a doctor, but given her recent history and what I do know about infection, it is a possibility you have to prepare for. I'm sorry."

Nelson stood motionless but nodded gently, then walked off and away from the camp.

"Where you going?" Jenna called after him.

"Leave him be," Mina said. "Just let him process it all."

Jenna watched as he got smaller in the distance. "He's not coming back," she said instinctively.

Mina turned to see how far he'd gone, noticing the consistency of his pace that indicated Jenna might be right. She was about to contradict the statement firmly but hesitated. "No," she said, disbelieving it. "He's not, is he?"

Jenna shook her head in disbelief. "I don't know what to think or what to do anymore. We're totally helpless. There must be some way to do something, but then you try and see there's little to help make all this more tolerable, so ultimately it seems impossible."

"We have to relearn everything."

"Oh my god," Jenna whispered. "I mean, I know that, right? It's obvious, but when you start to really see it, to really know that's how it's gonna be, it's breathtaking. It's shocking. We were talking from holographs four months ago, or whatever, ordering whatever we wanted by speaking it out loud."

"There is nowhere to go but here," Mina said. "With people you trust and can cooperate with."

"We were planning on maybe going to Texas. Jeremy's family is there. We've heard it's one of the safest and most organized places at this point."

"Ant told me that too. Maybe it's true. Maybe it's not. Be careful about rumors. I learned that lesson coming down from New England. Every next city was supposed to be the one that was okay."

"We definitely don't know for sure, but what else is there to do? Teaming up with others seems too sketchy right now. And to have to do it randomly? That seems crazy. But we can't stay put. We have to keep moving. Not too far from here in Atlanta, the chaos and crime must be unreal. And it's sure to be pouring out in all directions at some point."

Pru began to groan.

"Let's get her some fresh water," Mina said. "I have some left."

Jenna crouched beside Pru, who was slurring her words and breathless.

"Where's Nels—" she tried to ask.

"He went for a walk. He'll be back soon." Jenna wiped the sweat from her forehead, wishing she could do more.

Mina returned with a cup of water. "Here, try to drink some of this."

Pru cocked her head as Mina tipped the cup against her lips, but she choked and spit it out.

"Feel her pulse," Mina directed Jenna, who gently placed two fingers onto the dying woman's wrist.

"It's racing like crazy," she said.

"Shit. What other symptoms have you seen?"

"She's been throwing up every morning. She can't talk, can barely lift her head."

"And there's nowhere to take her. Even if there were, we couldn't get there quickly enough."

Pru seized up in a stroke of sharp pain, trying to cry and not to cry, knowing her fate was secured, and that it was to die.

"I'm so sorry, Pru," Jenna said, caressing her head, fighting back tears.

Pru seemed to give up in that moment, and her spirit collapsed onto the ground where she lay, writhing in pain, barely getting enough oxygen. Mina gathered the other sleeping bags to make cushions under and against Pru's failing body.

Throughout the night, Jenna and Mina kept vigil beside Pru, whose life force slipped away further and further with each labored breath. Watching her suffer, Jenna almost couldn't take it, however strong and resilient her will otherwise could be. Seeing Pru suffer like this, the suffering of a woman who didn't deserve the brutal agony of this end, and the helplessness they faced in her demise was a tension almost irreconcilable. Fairness in the culture had died with the lockdowns, but the unfairness of collapse was unbearable for a generation of previously healthy, vibrant people, whose entire lives were predicated on the advancements of an imperious nation unprepared for systemic ruin.

Just past midnight, Pru's remaining stamina took the final turn. Her body calmed. Her breath irregular and shallow, she drifted off into the rest of eternal peace.

Mina leaned over, having stayed awake by her side. And in the silence of the departed soul, she prayed. "Dear Lord, take with you this innocent woman into heaven and keep her eternal in your happy kingdom and undisturbed peace, forever and ever. Amen."

"And please, reunite her with her child," Jenna added, having awoken where she lay, barely whispering the words as heavy, full tears dropped from her wearied eyes. Pru had passed. "What do we do now?" she asked.

"Let her be. We should get some rest."

The men were huddled into themselves, asleep by the dying fire. Jenna lay next to Jeremy's large and protective body, as Mina took a place opposite them.

In the morning, the fire crackled warmly, and Ant arranged a breakfast from the leftovers of his and Mina's stash of aging food: biscuits made of flour, water, and olive oil, the last of the cured salami, and the remaining but liquified butter. The cow and the bull grazed in the distance, while the horse calmly paced the forest's edge. A sorrowful peace pervaded the encampment as they woke to the day.

Pru's covered body was now stiff. Her lifeless form focused the thoughts of the remaining four.

"We've got no shovel to dig a proper grave," Ant said, trying to initiate the necessary conversation.

Mina stood beside him, looking down at the body. "I suppose we could carry her deeper into the woods, lay her to rest there, and cover her with gatherings from the forest floor."

"I don't know what else we *could* do," Jenna said. "Other than cremate her, but that seems like a lot—"

They zipped the body into one of the sleeping bags, pulling another one down from the top to cover her head.

"*Wait*," Jenna said suddenly. "We'll need these."

"I didn't want to say it," Mina added.

The men removed the body from the bags and carried Pru by the shoulders and ankles into the woods and laid her on a bed of moss beside a large live oak. The women collected leaves, dirt, and evergreen branches from fir trees, the embellishments of a loving nature, to create a mound to serve as a grave. They bowed their heads, but no one spoke, as the stillness among them was sacred enough.

It was time to move on. They would spend the rest of the morning packing what goods they had that weren't now spoiled and determining a new course to travel.

"Nelson's not coming back," Jeremy declared, however obvious it was to them all.

"No" was all Jenna could say.

"He'll die out there—all alone."

"He might," Mina said. "But we can't worry about that now."

"I know," Jeremy answered, struck by the kind of sudden disbelief for their circumstances that repeated with each beginning and end of a day.

"At daybreak, tomorrow, we should go," Ant announced.

* * *

Come daylight, they began the trek thirty miles west, toward the arc of the lowering sun, the advancing winter sun, which receded from the earth or the earth from it, while the northern top of the planet tilted away from its heat. Walking mostly in silence, but for a groan or a moo from the cattle, the weary group kept to a grassy lane that ran the side of Highway 280 south. When they reached the exit for Highway 20 west, Ant suggested they find a spot to make camp for the night. The likelihood of meeting more people, however dreadful, was higher at the crossroads. They needed to trade, and they wanted whatever information they could get. The ruin of an old building, perhaps once a rest area for truckers, the northeast corner of which remained, resolved within the picture of a half mile: a brick wall leading to what used to be the space for a large window or glass door, may have been its former entrance; its perpendicular wall ran progressively lower as time took revenge against it.

"Not a soul," Ant said.

"I know. It's eerie," Jenna added. "I don't like it."

"It's better than being surrounded by wandering strangers. I've had my fill of all that," Mina said.

Another fire was quickly arranged and lit. Now that the lighter fluid was out, Ant proved the one person capable of bringing it to life without the tools of the modern world. A consummate survivalist, he'd won the awe and admiration of his male counterpart.

"Years in the Marine Corps, and I never could pull that off," Jeremy said.

"Marine, huh? Country boy here," Ant affirmed.

"Yep. Fought at Taiwan."

"Damn."

"Yeah. Pretty rough stuff. Men here one day, gone the next. Snatched out of life."

"I can't imagine—well, sort of, I guess I can."

"But at least we had provisions—supplies. Food." He looked around. "We're almost out of water, and we're going to need to eat something soon."

"We should build a structure here too. Something steady and more permanent."

"We could. I'd like to spend a few nights and days to see what's around first, particularly water and meat sources," Jeremy concluded.

"I'd say it's time we went hunting then," Ant suggested.

"'Bout to say the same thing myself."

"In the morning, we'll go. I've been waking up before dawn, so I'll get the rifles ready."

"And don't hesitate to shake me awake. I'm not falling asleep until late, but by the early hours, I tend to conk out. I go in deep, so you gotta shake me a bit."

Ant laughed. "No problem, hoss."

"With that, I'm gonna turn in. The ladies appear to be down for the count already."

"Good thing. They deserve some rest. I'll be up a little while longer," Ant said.

"Night, friend."

"Good night."

The warmness in Jeremy's voice might have felt awkward for their race differences, their maleness and manhood, their relative ages, but these beings had been shucked of their casings, as raw and exposed humans to the elements of humankind; and, however riskier, men of goodwill were freer to be natural actors in the world. The insidious construct of American relations—promoted by a fascist spirit for power at any cost, strictly adhering to those tribal considerations that had finally broken the kinship among her people—had been crushed and condemned to hell, losing the luminous spot-lit favor of the gaslit masses in the collapse of the country, or so they hoped, and they behaved according to that hope.

At dawn, they armed themselves with the rifles and went searching for prey: squirrels, rabbits, a deer maybe—anything they could skin, cook, and eat; returning to the women, who had stoked a roaring fire, they boasted of future triumphs and sat sharpening flinty rocks into more blades, with two rabbits hanging one from each of their backs.

"Bravo, gentlemen," Mina said on their return.

"I wanna go next time," Jenna said, annoyed she'd had to stay camp-side at the hearth.

The men both nodded, neither one willing to say they'd prefer to keep the activity for themselves.

"See, we can get back to doing this right," Ant declared, flipping his rabbit carcass on top of a rock, readying it for the removal of its organs. "Ever skin a rabbit?" he asked Mina.

"I've seen it done, but I never have. Teach me."

Ant unhinged a pocketknife and locked into place the longest blade.

"*Now* you show us," Mina said. "We've been trying to make cutting utensils from rocks all morning."

Ant smirked. "That's all right. This little blade won't last long anyhow. I'm sure the rocks will come in handy."

"Yeah, right," she said, smirking at the lameness of the compliment, watching as he firmly sawed down the center of the carcass's underside, making quick work of scooping out the sloppy entrails.

Next, he removed the head and set it aside and began to cut underneath the fur to skin it. By the end, Jeremy had brought over a stick, the bark of which he had removed with one of the ladies' sharpened rocks.

"See," he said, holding up both tools. "They came in handy."

Carefully, Ant worked the stick up the length of the spine to set atop the Y-shaped stand Jenna had twisted into the dirt at each end of the fire. A spit-roast by which, in under thirty minutes, they had freshly cooked meat. Among the animals, the fatty-scented air only triggered Mullet's nose to attention, and he whimpered. Ant chopped off the cooked carcass's limbs with one of the sharpened rocks to portion out the meat. As they sat to eat what seemed like the greatest of all delicacies, Mina began to speak with her mouth full.

"I want to thank you all for including me so quickly and easily." She sucked on her greasy thumb and forefinger. "I left a home that had been in my family for decades, and I had turned it into a self-sufficient farm, but the area had become very suddenly *too* dangerous. Ant came into my life because I was searching for a bull to breed with my cow. And I hope to have a calf by summertime. She's pregnant, so you know."

"*Oh*—they're gonna be a little family," Jenna said, surprised, looking back at the bovines grazing on the grasses closest to the thicker part of the forest.

"Yes," Ant answered, also looking back at the livestock.

"And everything was great," Mina continued. "Ant and I were sympatico; things were looking fairly stable. But then he went for a hike to look for—"

"I wanted to find a marketplace or a trading post."

"And you did, and it was good. We met a nice couple named—" She paused as a rush of unexpected emotion jumped into her chest and eyes. "Named Berti and Lucinda."

"Are they all right?" Ant asked quickly, noticing the change.

Mina shook her head as a tear fell onto her cheek. "No. They were—" Her voice quivered. "They were killed." Her easy gab was hushed by the memory.

"Goddamn it," Ant said, shaking his head. "Berti treated me like a son. Brought me into his home. Guided me to a farm, like a plantation—"

Jeremy's eyes widened at the description. "A plantation?" he asked.

"Yeah, but it seemed all right. Heavily guarded and all, but that's to be expected. Was supposed to be there for three days to work for a gun and some bullets. That was the pay. That and the room and board. But I didn't make it the whole three days."

"What happened?" Jeremy asked cautiously.

"Save that for another time."

"Ant had kindly introduced me to Berti and Lucinda when he decided to leave. They were just under an hour away by foot, but it was nice to have friends who felt like neighbors. But—" Mina stopped, not from emotion this time but trauma, stunned to stillness at the memory of the crazed killer and his hideous, smiling face, fighting any destabilizing effects. "But a troupe of actors had come to town, advertised at the market where Berti and Lucinda were beloved fixtures. She was so excited to see them. I was indifferent, and Berti had no interest. But we went, she and I, and it was fine, I suppose. A little odd, but what would you expect from people who choose to be actors in a time like this? The next day, however, one of the main performers, a man of about thirty, had come to their house at Lucinda's invitation. I sat with them for tea, and his oddness sort of morphed into charm, but there was still something off about him I could not quite name. And once I had gotten home, my intuition was blaring, and I eventually returned to the road to head back, only to find him dressed as a clown with fully painted face, horribly white with dark eyes and red all around his mouth, writing in their blood on the wall." She had to catch her breath. "I stepped through the front door, seeing my friends in pools of blood on the floor, and I shot him in the head."

"Oh my god," Jenna said, cupping her mouth. The other two said nothing, but Ant shook his head and stared at the ground.

"It was a horror. Hard to believe. I practically ran the whole length back, knowing something was wrong, wanting to throw up along the way. I'd decided to take one of Berti's horses and get the hell out of the area. I don't know if it was the plantation or the market or the increase in population from both, but the region had soured. I'd been attacked in a break-in while Ant was gone. Killed him too."

"*Jesus*," Jeremy said, almost forgetting the recent violence in their own lives.

"Meeting you all, the luck of finding you, Ant. To have some company. Has been a literal lifesaver."

"I'm so grateful you were here when Pru passed," Jenna said. "You have comforted me."

"I forget just how terrible everything is at times. How ruined. And then the next day, I remember. The demoralization is overwhelming. I don't think I would have lasted much longer if I didn't find some good people. So, thank you too. We have to be grateful and continue to express it to each other. It helps."

"Of course. We've all seen some real bad stuff," Jeremy said.

"And there's sure to be more," Jenna added.

Ant moved to sit next to Mina and placed his arm around her shoulders. They rocked back and forth quietly while Jeremy and Jenna reflected.

The horse stood by the ruin's eastern wall with its head raised above its top, beginning to agitate the ground with its hooves.

"What's the matter, big mama?" Jenna asked, getting up to comfort the animal when a gravelly voice yelled out from beyond the wall of the camp.

"I know someone's back behind in there!"

"Oh *shit*," Jeremy mumbled, grabbing a rifle, throwing it to Ant, and picking up the other for himself. Mina and Jenna loitered behind the men. The horse's agitation increased the man's panic.

"I can hear ya's rustlin' about!" he yelled.

Jeremy stepped forward. "What do you want?"

"Don't get bossy with me," he said. "This here AR will take you all out before that measly single-shot you got gets a nut off."

Ant cocked back his weapon, aiming at the intruder, seeing through the viewfinder a large vehicle barreling down the highway toward them all. "Looks like he's got backup," Ant quietly informed Jeremy.

"*Fuck*—" Jeremy hissed.

The man raised his rifle, aiming at them. "Imma *fuck* you *all up*! I've had enough of this bullshit!" Spittle spurt from his frothing mouth.

The vehicle zoomed closer, moving wildly, careening side to side, spinning out cyclones of brown dirt as it ran off the road and toward the man. Another sedan had been racing behind it.

"You're all *dead*! You hear *me*!" He turned and looked behind him at the monstrous velocity of the truck. "You're *dea*—"

The SUV smacked against the raging man, flipping his mangled body, casting him instantly to the dark oblivion of death, then crashed into Ant's hardy wagon, smashing its backside to pieces and jamming its frontside against a tree.

CHAPTER FOUR

Roland leaned on a cane, trying not to drag his left leg, and stepped to his lookout from the executive suites, and through the picture window that had become like a sovereign balcony, he reviewed, like a dictator, the new kingdom he'd acquired. Scabs similar to the one on his forehead had emerged around his torso. Lesions, likely Kaposi's sarcoma, began to rash his entire body. One began to darken the pink in his gums. Full-blown AIDS, as it was originally called, had come for him. Though a miracle medication had saved their lives, a cure had never been developed. Funding went to more pressing interests.

Charlie lay on one of the large, plush couches, himself staring at the ceiling and into the blankness that was his own lack of destiny.

"They all ignore me. They move away from me in the corridors," he said.

"It's fine. Let them be," Roland replied.

"But it's not. They might respect you and your willingness to share the spoils, but they are suspicious of me, and that might come around to you, eventually. Especially when they see you're sick."

Roland waved the comment off like a pestering fly. "I've not long to live, it's true. The medication isn't working anymore. Hasn't worked for weeks, maybe months by now. I have deep pains in my bones. My death is going to be horrific and slow. You are going to have to tend to me. I had to get the upper hand here if we had any hope of leaving together. This is my last moment to revel in everything I've wanted to do in this life. But soon, we're going to have to plan a way out. We must escape."

"What am I supposed to do?"

"I want you to ready one of the less used SUVs, make sure it has water and fuel, and position it somewhere we can get to quickly and get out just as fast."

* * *

Many floors below, Marius had gathered the better men around him in a circle. One of them, Dominick, the primary berserker of the clan, paced the floor, scuffing his boots against it.

"We've got a problem," Marius calmly began.

"Yeah, no shit," Dominick exclaimed. "We've been deceived, swindled, cheated."

"Please relax," Marius implored. "We won't do this right, if—"

Dominick stomped up to Marius's face, inches away, and seethed. "I *am fucking relaxed.*"

"Fine. Great. Look—"

"We have to get rid of them."

"Where's Rathausen?" someone asked.

"I thought he was—"

"Enough of that," Marius interrupted, knowing Rathausen was an identity best kept secret for its power, but how much longer it had as a source of great mystery, he didn't know.

"I can't believe I thought he was real," Dominick said, shaking his head.

"He's not?" yet another asked.

Dominick rolled his eyes in the general direction of the question and said, "Shut the fuck up."

"What now?" a fifth voice asked.

"We have to get rid of them, as I said," Dominick reiterated.

"Yes," Marius capitulated. "We do. But we're gonna do it in a dignified way."

"Are we now? Who says?"

Marius erupted. "Do you want this barbaric shit to keep cycling in and out? I thought you told me you wanted to get back to civil order! I thought you had some dignity."

Dominick rushed him, actually grabbing him by the throat. "I'll tell ya what, pretty boy. You just proved your weakness. And my strength." He released his grip. Marius dropped to his knees. "I'll tell *all* of you something. The old world—it's never coming back. However much we used to talk about how it should be, and it would be, how it will be—it won't. You're now either with me and against him or against me and with him. You choose." He paused, objectifying Marius, still on his knees, unable to speak or to stand. "In fact," he said. "All of you. All of you right now. Get on one knee before me and pledge your allegiance to *me*. Be for what's going to happen!"

One by one, the men sank to a knee. Marius viewed his rival's twisted mouth as it scored its demands, disappointed by his own deceits but knowing he was powerless against this new barbarism.

"And say it after me! Be for what's to happen! Be for what's to happen!"

The men chanted louder and louder as the revolutionary bloodlust echoed up and into the lobby of the 52nd floor.

The man in black, late to the meeting with Roland and Charlie stopped cold, hearing the unwelcomed excitement in the sound.

PART THREE

CHAOS

CHAPTER ONE

Moving like a mystic on fire, the rubber toes of his sneakers softly tapping the concrete, Charlie made his way down a corner staircase to the garage, clutching the fob to the SUV in his sweaty palm. Most of the men were out in the town, harassing the locals, shaking them down, but some had remained and lurked around the labyrinthine twists of the corporate fortress. Any one of them might appear from a darkened spot. But instead of fear, he felt urgency. Escaping the pressures of this brutish fraternity was his only interest, so more quickly he moved to outmaneuver his fears and apprehensions. If he was caught, he'd surely seem as guilty as he felt.

The lock in the door when it sensed the advancing fob reverberated through the garage like the snap heard of a giant breaking an enemy's bones. He was sweating. The trunk had two vats. Prying off the lids with his fingertips, he could see one was full of water, and one was full of fuel, the funnel to administer which was lying on the floor to its side. Turning the engine was risky. The noise would betray him, but checking the placement of the fuel meter was essential.

Easing his stiffened body into the seat, he pressed the ignition and the truck sprang to life, the engine humming throughout the concrete cavern. The gas meter was close to empty.

"*Fuck*," he whispered.

Lugging out the vat and funneling fuel into the tank was an unavoidable task. Once the big tub was on the ground, he sucked at the tube to conjure the fuel, rushing up and into his mouth. As he gagged, he thrust the top end into the funnel to fill the tank and, wiping his soured mouth, he vomited as a voice spoke from behind.

"What are you doing?" Marius asked calmly, as if disappointed.

Charlie jumped from the spook.

"Relax," Marius continued as gas began to rush into the filler neck.

Charlie pushed the tube in deeper, catching his breath, but, too astonished by the handsomeness of his interlocuter, the pressure of being caught, the sentence that would be death if any of the others found out, he fumbled without responding.

"Are you leaving?" Marius asked and then paused. "You should be leaving. The men are agitated, and they don't like you."

"I know," Charlie said.

"Then are you leaving? Your life is in danger. Only Roland protects you, and even he is not long for his position. They know what you are, and they don't like it."

"I understand. And, yes, we are leaving. Can you help?"

"Yes."

"Roland is dying."

"So, you *are* familiar with him. You do know each other from before. Not surprised. I've been protecting you too. Roland doesn't look well. His increasing weakness has got them men sniffing at death in the air. And wouldn't mind making it happen faster." Marius removed the tube and screwed the top back into the fuel neck as he spoke. "The men have planned a feast to throw you off. They're out finding the beast for it now. I suggest you leave before it's over."

"I'm not going to any kind of dinner with those assholes."

"That would look suspicious. You have to be there and seem as flighty as you usually do."

"Got it," Charlie said, swallowing the insult without further protest.

A roar from above ended their conspiracy.

"They're back and coming down here to make the firepit out back. Go up. Tell Roland the plan. You come to the dinner, then return to your rooms before it is ended. They'll be wild, and they'll be coming for you both. I'll move the truck out back and leave the keys inside. Go out the front entrance, come around back, and go."

"This isn't a trap, is it?"

"No. I'm the only one you can trust. But, yes, I also want you gone."

At the sound of stomping down the stairs, Charlie jumped toward the elevator and hopped inside, full of doubt and demoralization, and, just as the door closed, he heard Marius addressed by the men.

"Make room for Milly!" the voice cried as the central garage door was raised and a lumbering, ornery beast was pushed into the cavern. The men called out above its moos.

"Anyone know how to kill this thing?"

Before the question could be asked twice, a round-faced newbie stuck the cow in the neck with a dagger, marveling at the blood pouring out of its neck as its groans eased to sighs, and its legs gave out, the animal slumping onto the floor.

"Goddamnit, now who's gonna clean this shit up?" Dominick yelled, stomping his boot into the muddy mess of blood, laughing. He moved to Marius. "Is the pit constructed?"

"Yes," Marius answered.

"Suppose we should take the head off first, then the hide. Never seen it done myself. And where's that vat of shine?" he yelled, commanding the room like a newly promoted general.

Two older men who brewed the alcohol slowly carried the large plastic barrel over to him, Dominick dunked a plastic cup inside, swigging so much it gushed out the sides of his mouth.

"Easy with that," one of the older men said. "Or your breath'll light the air on fire." They laughed at him.

Dominick threw away the cup and wiped his face with his arm. "Quiet, you old putz." He turned round the room, reveling in the men's bloody work on the carcass, chopping and hacking away at its limbs, pulling down the hide. The meaty red rump was exposed, the latticework of muscle fibers looking like some ghastly art exhibit in the false electric light. "There's an ass I wouldn't hump. Speaking of, where's that faggot at?" The other men laughed at the word as they hacked, relieved it had finally been said in a more official space.

Marius observed this madness quietly, but before Dominick could sling the word again into the air, he asked, "Who do you mean?"

"The one who walks around here like a sissing shadow, that little weasel dressed all in black," he said. "Is he upstairs with the other two pansies, having a little cock and tail party to themselves?" He sneered, spitting as he did.

"He's at the refinery but will be back for the dinner."

"I see—" Dominick said, reducing his spite, remembering he knew nothing of the processes in making the fuel, suddenly reminded of their need for the man in black. "I want to talk to him when he gets back."

Marius added nothing further, unimpressed by his cohort's belligerence, and continued to measure out the four-foot hole, to be dug as wide as the cow, that would be filled with wood and whatever other refuse needed discarding onto the pile, making a mound for the bonfire.

* * *

The man in black had already arrived from the refinery, making haste to the executive suites to speak with Roland, whom he'd found standing in what appeared to be a silent pause of an otherwise tense conversation. Annoyed by the interruption, Charlie, who had been doing most of the talking, did not finish his sentence but shifted the pressure of speech to the man in black.

"Sorry to interrupt."

"No worries," Roland blithely answered without turning.

"Are you not coming to the feast tonight?"

"And miss out on meat and moonshine?" Roland joked, mocking some of the other men's rougher accents.

"We'll be there," Charlie said in polite answer to the question.

The man in black seated himself across from Charlie and took off his sunglasses, his hat, and the black face covering, shocking his audience.

"Why'd you do that?" Charlie asked.

"Do what?" Roland asked back, turning around to see the man in black unmasked. "He's one of us," Roland informed Charlie.

"My name's Derek."

"It's nice to see your face, Derek," Charlie said. "How'd you end up in this motley crew of dropouts, killers, and ex-cons?"

"The first Rathausen was my stepdad. He'd gotten my mom pregnant and dragged us around, place to place, while he built his criminal empire. My half-brother was stillborn. My mother was banished, and I was forced to wear all black so he didn't have to see my face, but to serve as his assistant and general slave. Him being white and my mom being black, it had a certain pang of history, you could say, though it protected me for a bit." His warm and carefree laugh filled the room like an interruption to offset sadness. "I did all that was asked of me. It would have been hard to say no. He'd probably have killed me if I had. There's no other way to live a semi-decent life, and what I get from here, I share with my mom, who I keep tucked away a few miles near the outskirts in a cottage."

"Interesting," Charlie said. "Like a fairy tale."

"Not really," Derek replied, with the same warm laugh but louder, more awkward.

"I was about to escape the whole thing, but then you two showed up, and I sort of figured us three for like-types, so I stayed. And it's been better. More organized. The corporation, or whatever this all is, was about to fall apart under me and that blond, who's since disappeared. I was barely keeping the men from an uprising."

"What happened to your stepdad?" Roland asked as he used the cane to get to the couch and fall into its seat.

"Gone. No one knows. Been missing for something like ten months, not quite a year."

"Think he's coming back?" Roland asked.

"I don't think so. I think he was dying," he said bluntly but then stopped himself, realizing Roland's condition. "But who knows. I tend to sense things in my body first; then something unfurls in my mind, like a picture, almost like a little movie, and I can see things before they happen, kind of. Lately, I've had the feeling in my body but no picture yet."

"I see," Roland said dismissively.

"After the dinner tonight, or whatever this is, we're leaving," Charlie said.

"That's wise."

Roland nodded pensively.

"And you agree?" Derek asked.

Roland sat there still nodding, saying nothing. Derek looked to Charlie, who signaled his ignorance of Roland's mind.

"He doesn't really have a choice," Charlie said.

"I'm leaving too then. Half of them haven't seen my face in forever, and the other half never have. I'll be safe from them out in the streets. There's nothing for me to do here anymore, and I think Marius and Dominick are about to duke it out over who's the next Rathausen. I couldn't care less. Maybe I can hitch a ride with you all, drop me off at my mom's place? It's actually quite far by foot."

"Sure thing," Charlie said, trying to reassure the young man who had next to nothing in this world. They all had next to nothing in this world.

"I should put this stupid costume back on and head down for this feast thing."

Once Derek had left, Roland's face winced to show his pain. Charlie sat next to him and embraced his ailing lover for the first time since they'd left home.

"I'm dying," Roland said.

"I know."

* * *

Down at the feast, the men were already drunk by the moonshine, yelling and fighting or laughing and hollering at the fire, the unhallowed eve, and their beastly feast. Pieces of carcass were scattered across an old boardroom table from one of the upper floors. The flesh was black on the undersides from being lazily thrown into the pit. When Roland appeared with his cane, his scowling face, and Charlie behind him, the men fell silent at the power in the man's presence, a kind of imperial omniscience to which they had long aspired. The man in black was in a quiet corner with two other men. Some of the rest shuffled to the other side of the yard; some went inside. Dominick raised his plastic cup to the moon.

"A toast. To the best faggot I ever known." His eyes cut through the crowd and met the other eyes and regrouped to make a proper homage. "The best organizer. The best logistician. And the most sharing of the treasure." He stopped and took a deep swig. "May your death be quick!" He sneered, held up the cup once more, downed the remains, and joined others collecting near the pit as if preparing for Act II of the evening.

Roland had to sit. Marius pulled a chair to the head of the table and offered him some water, some meat. Instead, Roland said, "Bring me some of that moonshine, if you please."

Marius looked to Charlie, who nodded.

"Only painkiller I'll get from here on out."

When he returned with the drink, Roland downed the half-filled cup. Marius sat nearby to speak quietly but candidly.

"I think you should leave now, immediately," he said. "Now is the time. This is moving faster than I anticipated."

Roland stared at him blankly, signaling no inclination to move.

"You're in danger. I know they're planning to—"

"We are leaving," Charlie said decisively. "Now."

"Goodbye," Marius mumbled to Roland. "I've helped as much as I can. I cannot stop them from trying to kill you if you stay."

"*Goodbye,*" Roland answered absently.

Back in the suite above, Charlie threw some things into a duffel bag that had been stashed in the closet, filled with thicker, warmer clothes that Rathausen had pillaged from the local mall. Roland leaned against his cane, musing out the window. A mad clamor boomed up the elevator shaft. Running to the doors, Charlie watched the numbers light up, expecting the gang of executioners to burst into the suite, but the lights passed the 52nd floor, illuminating higher ones. He could hear them yelling like monsters. Charlie ran back to Roland.

"We have to leave. *Now!*" He grabbed Roland's arm.

Roland resisted, and then he spoke, "I don't think I'll ever see anything more beautiful than this view again in my life. I don't think—"

"Come *on*," Charlie urged, pulling on his arm. "We *have* to go."

"I just—what was I saying?" Roland turned away to regard the view once more as a body all in black dropped right in front of their eyes.

"Oh fuck—they've killed Derek." Charlie's stomach knotted; his mouth flooded with warm saliva.

Hoisting the duffel onto his shoulder, Charlie lifted Roland's body against his and ran as well as he could to the elevator, the door to which mercifully opened. Down they flew to the front lobby and rushed out the main entrance, seeing Derek's poor body smashed on the pavement in front of them.

"*Jesus—*" Charlie cried, on the verge of tears as he lurched down the broken sidewalk and around the city block, still holding Roland on his side. The SUV, as promised, was parked against the curb. Leaping out to open the passenger door for Roland's failing body, Marius completed his task. No words were spoken but a quick thank you, and off they tore down the street.

CHAPTER TWO

"**H**oly *fuck*!" Jeremy yelled, hurrying to the wrecked SUV, hands instinctively gripping the dislodged driver's-side doorframe, yanking it open wider. Bloodied and unconscious, Charlie fell out and into Jeremy's stronger arms. Dragging the man away from the wreck, he rushed back to the passenger side, which was bent into the shell of the vehicle, to rescue the other man who was still stuck inside.

Ant came up from behind. "Watch out," he said, hammering the door with a large rock, denting it more, trying to invert the deformation even further.

The groaning man jostled at each contact of the rock to the metal until the door gave way enough to open space around its edges, as Jeremy and Ant together pulled it off the vehicle to get him out. The deranged shooter's broken body lay ignored and mangled on the spot where the impact had thrown it.

All four of the survivors acted to help these newly arrived who had inadvertently saved them from another horror. Moving quickly, they propped the men up and catered water to their lips. Mullet sniffed around the edges of their bodies, smelling sickness and blood.

"Not now," Jenna said, gently pushing off the curious dog.

Mina checked their vitals while Ant and Jeremy, per Mina's instruction, inspected their bodies for obvious breaks or gushing wounds. There appeared to be no more than Charlie's nose, broken by the security inflation device. While he remained unconscious, Mina did her best to realign the break, to set it into better place, and held a T-shirt against the bleeding. While they worked, two figures appeared at the opening in the hedge, making Mullet growl.

"Everything all right back there?" one of the men asked. "There's a dead body out here."

Ant stood to meet the sudden appearance of yet more strangers who had followed too suddenly behind the raging gunman and the crash to be sensible, perhaps a factor of being close to the intersection of cardinal highways. "There's been a wreck," he said.

"We saw that," the stranger replied. "Bad one too. Looks like the third one didn't survive it. And that car chasing the truck whipped around and sped off."

Ant silently nodded, wary and defensive. "Where'd you two come from?" he asked.

"Been walking for a couple days," the younger one said. "Out of Atlanta, but that place was too much, man." He bent his head to look around the camp. "You got any water we might, uh, have, if you please? We're dyin' a thirst."

"Sure," Ant answered, looking to Mina, who rose from her spot, annoyed by these new burdens, and brought them two cups of water from their store.

"Here you are," she said.

The men gulped it down. "Got any more?" the older one asked abruptly.

Mina disregarded the insolence at the corners of the older man's mouth. "We're running low," she answered.

The younger one wiped the drips from his mouth after downing the second cup and gently handed it back to Mina. "Thanks a lot, Miss."

Mina just nodded, retaining the same blank wariness in her face as Ant held in his.

"I used ta be a paramedic up north," the younger one said. "Can I help here?"

"Yes," Mina said, as if she'd expected it. "You can start by moving that dead man over into the woods." Mina pointed to the far side of the new settlement. Wanting to appear helpful, the two men submitted to the morbid task, carrying the nomadic lunatic's corpse to the edge of the forest and dropping it onto the undergrowth then rejoining the group.

Calling to Mullet, Jenna went to Jeremy, and the dog followed. "I've got to go for a walk. I need a break from all this insanity." Jeremy nodded.

Roland revived first. "What happened?" he asked quietly. "Where's Charlie?"

"Been in some kinda wreck, sir," the younger man said. "Your friend is lyin' next to you."

Roland looked over at Charlie, who was breathing but unconscious.

"Likely concussed," he said. "You seem all right, though. Where's the pain?"

"Where do you think?" Roland asked sarcastically.

"Everywhere, I get it, yeah. You're pretty banged up. Don't see no broken bones or nothin'. Just a few contusions on your face and hands. A scratch up your right arm. This other guy has a broken nose."

"Is that all?"

"Other than probably a big-time concussion, looks like it, yeah."

"Thank you. What's your name?"

"I'm Tommy. My old man and I just came across you people."

"Who's you people?" Roland tried to look around and above him, but his eyesight was too blurry. "I can't see too well."

"There's a real nice group of people here who got you out of the wreck. Whatcha names?"

"Roland. And he's Charlie."

"Okay, Roland. You need some rest, now, fella."

Roland nodded, taking a deep, weary breath.

Tommy signaled Ant and Jeremy, who stood at a distance just watching. The older man leaned on a large rock for rest. Tommy reached out his hand.

"I'm Tommy. And that's my old man, Ronnie."

The men shook hands with the newcomer. Ronnie just held up his right one to greet them. Both were muscular, tough-looking men. Tommy's body had the tauter frame as Ronnie's skin had begun to sag over the fairly dense muscles that still protruded from his shirt. Not quite handsome, neither one was ugly, having robust features and a warm masculinity that any woman might feel safe to be around.

"You two been traveling far?" Ant asked. "Atlanta, you said?"

"Fuckin' circus, that place. Never seen so much violence in my life."

Ant listened carefully, trying to decipher any hidden meanings. Northerners were new to him, and the accent, thick and layered, contained seemingly important emphases. Like an alley cat's code, it sounded tricky. Its tone worked on many levels, but some sounded off, insincere. Ant began to train his ear to the various hints and indications within them.

"And, so ah, that's about it."

"That's about it?" Ronnie questioned from his seat on the rock. "Like hell it is, but anyways—" He swiped his hand across the space in front of him.

Tommy's greedy eyes scanned the camp. "Do ya mind if we stay the night here?" His palms opened to the sky within the space of the question.

Ant stared but kept his face free of doubtful tics, watching each twitch in Tommy's form and figure.

Jeremy wrinkled his nose. "We have these men to take care of now. Not sure—" he said.

"What kind of resources do you have?" Jenna asked abruptly, deciding against the walk, refusing to accommodate any game-playing.

Ronnie scuffed his boots in the dirt. Tommy projected a mixture of patriarchal disappointment and comic defeat.

"We have some," Roland said, speaking up after clearing his throat. They all turned to him. "If it's not all wasted by the crash."

* * *

Mina thanked Roland and inspected the wrecked SUV, the back of which was still largely intact. Closer, she could see two pairs of feet beneath the undercarriage on its opposite side. Cautiously, as if expecting some new weirdness among them, she rounded its backside. A woman was face-first in the unsealed barrel of water, sucking down as much as she could take in, and another man, tall and black as night in contrast to the red and white mismatch of the older woman's sun-damaged skin, previously so white it could have made the sun squint.

This towering man was glowering at her, chomping on a thick piece of what appeared to be beef jerky. He nodded as if to a passerby on a casual Sunday. The woman, retirement age and stout like a bakery muffin, lifted her head out of the vat and gulped for air. The crayon-red tips of her scraggly hair contrasted more strongly to the admixture of white and gray at its roots for being wet.

"Can we help you?" Mina asked, blurting it out from veritable rage at the piggishness of these two. The man paced away and back again, put off by her aggression.

The woman began to speak, a smile plastered to her face as her hair was plastered to her head. "I haven't had a drink of water since—"

"Yesterday," the tall man said.

"You shut up, D." A laugh, not so much forced but habitual, bellowed out of her. Devonte bounced his head in submission but added nothing.

"Those are not your resources," Mina said.

"They're ours," Jenna confirmed, now standing behind Mina with her arms folded.

"I know, I know. I'm sorry. Would you blame an old lady? We've been on the road since, Christ, I think, June, is it, D?" She yelled the question over her shoulder.

"Huh?" he yelled back from the smashed end of the useless hunk of metal.

"Never mind," she quietly replied, more for the women than for Devonte.

"Huh?" he repeated, trying to annoy her.

"I said never mind!" she yelled, then apologized. "We're not used to being around others, you can understand."

"Sure," Mina said.

* * *

"What's going on over here?" Ant asked as he scanned the additional travelers.

The woman raised her brow at Ant's handsome, young form. "Why, nothing, sheriff," she answered sweetly.

"Who are you?" he asked.

"I don't doubt you've already met the other two we're with," she said. "We like to call them Mr. Dead and Mr. Weight."

"*You* do," Devonte said. "I ain't got nothing to do with them. They weak ass bitch—" Interrupted, he stood in front of Ant, who stared back in equal silence, both unsure what to make of the other.

"Who's this bitch-ass nigga, here?" Devonte asked the ether, pointing at Ant like to an imposition.

Ant lunged at him, throwing Devonte's body against the side of the car, Ant's sharper teeth in his face. "Don't you ever refer to me in any kinda way like that again, you hear?"

"Whoa-whoa-whoa, man. Get your hands offa me."

Ant released and backed off. Devonte took a moment to process the explosion.

"You one of them country *ni*—country folk, then huh?"

"That's right. And we don't talk like that."

"We down tawk like that." Devonte mocked the slight twang in Ant's voice, laughing. "Yeah, right. Aww, *man*. It don't mean nothin'." He held out his arm and opened his palm to embrace Ant's, but Ant resisted.

"No," he said. "We'll get to know one another first."

"That mean we can stay?" the woman piped up to break the tension.

Ant evaluated her from the ragged tips of her Fifth Avenue shoes to the crayon-red tips in her hair. "Time will tell," he said.

"I'm Dolores. This is D."

"Devonte," he said angrily.

Dolores rolled her eyes and led the way back into the camp. "I see you two have made yourselves comfortable," she said, addressing Ronnie and Tommy. "D!" She hollered behind her. "Bring that water and food from the truck back here!"

The rest of them stood amazed by the woman's confidence, barking orders and settling into a stranger's camp with the simplicity of a child. Exchanging glances and worried looks, the original settlers stayed silent.

* * *

"Ant and I are off to hunt," Jeremy whispered into Jenna's ear who hadn't been quite able to go for her walk, distracted by the tumult of the newcomers.

"And leave me with these people? Absolutely not. I'm coming with you."

"You can't leave Mina here by herself."

"Then *I'll* go with Ant, and *you* stay here."

Jeremy relented, knowing she needed a break. "Fine."

"What are you two gabbin' about over there?" Dolores yelled.

"God help me, I don't murder this woman," Jenna mumbled, making Jeremy laugh.

Ant collected the guns and called Mullet over to him. "You ready?" he asked the dog and the man.

"Jenna's going with you this time. I'll stay here and watch over these quacks."

"I'm none too pleased they're here," Ant said.

"Me neither. But, you two, go and find some meat. I'll build a fire," Jeremy insisted.

"Why haven't you all built a shelter yet?" Dolores asked loudly.

Mina sat across from the newly arrived guests, ready to pounce. "And where are you all from?"

Dolores's face flattened. "New York."

"I thought I'd detected an accent," Mina said playfully.

"Ya did?" Tommy asked without interest in the answer.

"Yes. I did." Mina let her shortness rest in the air.

"I worked corporate in my time, so mine is more refined. We've had a hellava time," Dolores continued. "Lots of fightin' up there. Like a fuckin' war zone."

"Not like," Ronnie added. "It's a madhouse. What it's like is like a sectarian civil war in the Middle East! Never thought we'd find ourselves down here but—such is life." He shrugged like an apathetic schoolboy.

"Are you two married?" Mina asked.

"Yes," Ronnie answered.

"Lotta good it done me," Dolores said.

"Ah, stuff it," Ronnie answered. "I shoulda listened to ma when she told me not to marry an Irish broad."

"Ma, Papino. Please," Tommy interjected. "We don't want our hosts to think bad of us."

Devonte chuckled to himself.

Ignoring the family recital, Jeremy began collecting wood to perpetuate the daily fire, nudging Devonte in silent request for help. Devonte looked at him like at a confusing puzzle.

"*Hell* no," he said.

Without help, nor even the recognition of his labor, Jeremy continued to gather the driest, thickest logs of wood and smaller kindling, setting to work parsing out the sequence of the fire's build, tempted to mumble under his breath, tempted more so to verbally assault the lot of them, knowing in his gut that they might cause trouble.

Charlie rose from his flattened, comatose state just as Jeremy was harnessing his most unpredictable energies, and wiped his swollen face of whatever dirt and grime had accumulated there. "What happened?" he asked, confused, touching at the numb pain across the center of his face.

Roland rolled from his side to his back to see his partner. "You're alive then. I thought we were going to have to put you down."

"*Thanks.* Where's the truck?"

"Smashed into a wagon, a man first, but—"

"Holy shit, I think I remember that man. He have a gun?"

"Yes, he was pointing it at *us*," Mina chimed in.

"And we *killed* him?"

"Well. You did," Roland corrected. "We were being chased."

"Not on purpose. I don't think. Did I kill him on purpose? Weird."

"None of us would mind a bit if you had," Mina said, trying to brush off whatever guilt Charlie might be pretending. "Don't think twice about it. I've killed two already myself."

"My goodness," Roland said, chuckling. "A regular Annie Oakley."

"Yeah." She mimed his humor by crouching like she was aiming a rifle at some man's bulls-eye. "By necessity."

"I don't think Annie had much choice either," Roland added.

"The old Wild West," Charlie said, amazed by her admission.

"And we're about back there now," Jeremy added. "Any of you know how to light a fire without a match?"

"Back in my Eagle Scouts days, sure, but I'm a bit too feeble for all that at present," Roland said. "You ever do that in Boy Scouts, Charles?"

"Me? Oh gosh, no. I hated Scouts. Not really sure why, though. All I remember is getting into trouble for having dried paint from art class on my hands at inspection night. It was a Thursday, in like 2010, and my mother was ridiculous about it."

"My grandfather could. I've seen it done a thousand times. I could try," Mina offered.

"That's more than our new bossy guests are willing to do. Look at them over there. All in a huddle. I don't trust them," Jeremy offered.

"Neither do I," Mina answered. "Jenna said the same before she and Ant took off."

"And Ant and the big guy have already had a scuffle. I'll be glad when they go."

"*If* they go," Roland said.

In the opposite corner of the encampment, the New York crew was busy establishing their own court. Dolores stood in the middle of the three men, who toiled for her every wish and command, hauling wood and kindling, dropping it all near the spot where she stood. In the meantime, she had snuck back to the SUV to loot it of its goods. There was a tarp with some rope. The vat of water that had been tightly resealed, escaping damage in the crash with just a dent in its side. The rest of the foodstuffs that she'd stolen from the wagon, which was mostly a hidden box with dried meats and a rock-stale loaf of bread, she'd thrown into the center of the tarp with some of the warmer clothes, pinching the corners of which into a bag and slinging its weight onto her back.

"Hey D!" Dolores yelled over her shoulder toward the camp. "Get over here!"

Devonte peered from behind the wall, seeing her struggle to manage both the bag and the vat, amused by her frustration. "Don't just stand there. Make yourself useful and get that barrel to our side." Appreciating its value, he nodded quickly, jogged to the truck, and got to work stealing the filtered water.

Patiently, Jeremy watched as they tied the tarp to four branches in a cluster of trees. "Son of a bitch," he murmured, more at their brazenness than at the theft.

Though weak, Charlie was up and gathering kindling, the unnatural blue of the tarps catching his eye. "That's ours," he said. "From the truck. There's a bag of warmer, winter clothes in there too."

"We need to get all that's left in there *right now*. Whatever there is—grab it," Jeremy quietly ordered. "And whatever guns or weapons you have too. I don't want these creeps to take anything else."

Charlie circled the camp on the north side, so they wouldn't spot him, and retrieved the larger duffle of clothes, the other smaller tarp, and the one rifle Marius had hidden under the flooring near the spare tire. Jeremy met him out of view from the others and secured the rifle and the two boxes of ammunition, stuffing them into the duffle, which he hid in the underbrush. They returned to huddle near Roland.

"Damn, they've got the bigger tarp," he said. "Should've done this sooner."

"We were kinda out of it," Charlie said, sarcastically.

"Yeah, I know—I'm sorry. Not sayin' that to be a dick. But Jenna's gonna be pissed we didn't get to it before they did."

Roland studied Jeremy silently before speaking. "Are you Hawaiian?" he asked. "Or Polynesian of some extraction?"

Jeremy stared at the man, wondering why the hell that could matter. "Yeah, Hawaiian, so what?"

"I mean no offense," Roland said. "Did you grow up there?"

"No. Texas. But I went back a lot. What's your point?"

Roland calmed himself further to soothe the annoyance he'd provoked in Jeremy. "My point is a question: Have you ever constructed a hale?"

Jeremy acknowledged this silently, his face scrunched from sudden emotion, remembering his family, his traditions, and how easily it had all been forgotten. "Yeah. I did. I have."

"You know how to do it?" Roland asked to clarify his inquiry.

"Maybe. I think I could do it."

"I vote we start by making a list once Ant and Jenna return," Roland said, again assuming the director's position. "And then we can search the area for materials. I know the earth around here should have a healthy admixture of clay."

Jeremy understood. "That would be good, like cement," he said. "No palms here, but we could substitute that for fir branches, grass, and mud."

"Now you're thinkin'," Roland said, encouragingly tapping at his temple, trying not to sound patronizing. "We can do this. We'll have to build something anyway. And though I may know what is needed for its design, I'm afraid I'm not much practiced in the art of building anything."

"You're not much able to stand on your own two feet at this point," Charlie said while he adjusted the other tarp that served as Roland's pillow.

"How long you think this'll take?" Mina asked.

"Without their help? I don't think we'd want it anyway. I'd say about, I don't know, a couple weeks once we have all the materials," Jeremy answered.

"Are we even sure we want to stay in the area?" Mina asked.

"At this rate, here's as good as any place," Roland answered, not knowing how long he had left to live.

"I'll check the truck again to see if there's anything helpful remaining," Charlie said, although no one seemed to notice.

"The flattest point is here, around our fire," Mina offered.

Jeremy viewed the other camp. Devonte had been rubbing dry wood into the lighter bits of refuse from the forest floor, and he'd sparked it to life, handing a torch over to Tommy, who used it to ignite a well-built rectangular fire. "*Son* of a bitch wouldn't do it when *I* asked for help."

"Why are they even here? Like, who are they?" Charlie asked.

"Who's anyone these days, Charles?" Roland asked rhetorically.

"They're parasites," Mina answered. "Type of people who are helpless unless they're taking ideas or resources from others. Common thieves. Corporate hounds. They probably met in some Human Resources department. I bet she was its director."

"We'll have to steal their fire then," Charlie said, smirking like a clever imp. "And we can't let ours go out ever again." He snuck toward the others, adding action to their conspiracy.

"Fine," Jeremy said in a low voice. "You take wood collection as a daily chore," he said in euphemism as Charlie nodded back at Jeremy's assertion, flashing an affirmative grin as if flirting with the excitement of the plot against these invaders.

"Nice flame you got," Charlie said to the open air of what was now competing camps of survivors.

"Scram, pansy-boy," Dolores said, snickering.

"Aww, that's no way for a lady to talk," Charlie answered.

"That's right," Ronnie said. "You'd better be nice, Dolores."

"Or what?" she demanded, staring at her husband as he mumbled and turned his eyes to the ground. Devonte tee-heed into his fist.

Seeing the exchange fail as he'd predicted, Jeremy joined the circle. "Look, we helped you all out when you got here. Gave you water. Food," he said.

"Ha!" Dolores piped. "That beefy jerky from the wreck? That ain't yours." Mullet began sniffing at her legs around which she swatted. "Get away from me."

"Mullet!" Jeremy called and the dog came trotting toward him. "Don't you ever touch that dog, you hear me, lady?"

"Yeah, yeah," she said, now swatting at the air in Jeremy's direction.

Meanwhile, Charlie had placed a dry stick into the raging fire, carrying the flame-tipped wand back to the other camp.

"Hey, where you goin' with that?" Devonte called out.

"What are you gonna do about it?" Jeremy asked, challenging him.

Devonte mumbled to himself, "I'll kick your motherfuckin' ass is what I'll do."

"Try it, buddy. You're talkin' to a marine who fought at Taiwan."

"*Oooo*," Dolores said, mocking his service, her fingers tickling the air.

"Enough of this," Tommy interrupted, getting inside the space between the two larger men. "Take the fire, it's fine. We took from you."

Like a spoiled duchess, Dolores made a bratty face and continued with her work, using her feet like a broom to sweep out a line, a barrier to distinguish their side of the camp, when Jenna and Ant returned from the morning hunt.

"At least they have people in their group who do something worthwhile," Dolores said, more to Devonte and Tommy.

Jeremy turned his back to greet his wife and friend to distract himself from the New Yorkers' antisocial intensity, when Tommy touched his shoulder. "Do you think we could share the meat?" he asked.

Tommy's face appeared to soften; his eyes gleamed and a warmness not common in the others emanated from his better nature.

Seeing his earnestness but doubting his deeper character, Jeremy said, "We'll see."

"Great, we've got fire!" Jenna exclaimed.

"Yeah, thanks to us!" Dolores fired back with equal enthusiasm to mock Jenna's delight, but Jenna ignored her, and the two groups carried on building their settlements.

Ant spoke softly against Jeremy's side. "We found a pretty clear stream 'bout a half mile back. Might make us a little sick at first, I don't know, but it's better than drinkin' raindrops. Mina's water's almost out."

"That's good."

Roland groaned in pain. Charlie bent to him as he beckoned for a word and then messengered it to Jeremy. "There's some iodine in the truck if it didn't spill out in the crash."

Jeremy nodded, but his eyes grew steely as he watched Dolores round the hedge with the jug of iodine clasped between her chubby paws.

"What the hell is this stuff?" she asked, not caring, just wanting everything she could take.

"*Great*," Roland mumbled. "Tell her it's hair dye. She needs to do her roots."

Mina and Jenna laughed.

"I'd rather tell her it's Coca-Cola so she drinks it all and dies," Mina sniped.

"Mina and I are going to bring the animals to the stream for a drink," Jenna told Ant.

"Plus, I need to get the hell away from these people for a while," Mina said.

The women tended to the far end of the camp where the horse, bull, and cow were grazing. Mullet trotted behind.

"Where they goin'?" Ronnie asked his group.

Dolores looked up. "Who the hell knows."

"Should I follow them?" Devonte asked.

Overhearing, Ant said, "Don't you even think about that."

"Oh, okay, big man. You some kind of protector of white ladies now?"

"That's ours," Jeremy said, ignoring Devonte's comment, pointing to the tub of iodine.

"Is it—" Dolores said more than asked. "What you got in exchange?"

"How about some of that meat?" Ronnie asked. "What is it, rabbit?"

"Yuck," Dolores said.

"You certainly don't have to eat it," Ant told her.

"I'll eat what I want," she replied.

215

"And then some," Ronnie said under his breath while she waddled back to the crashed truck.

"We'd be willing to give you some meat for the tub," Ant said.

"What is it, anyway?" Tommy asked.

"Iodine, you morons," Roland called out.

"Who you callin' a moron, you skinny faggot," Devonte said.

"That's the last time you say that," Jeremy said.

"What you gonna do, brown boy?" Devonte challenged.

"He's dying, you fucking asshole!" Charlie yelled.

Devonte lunged at Charlie, but Jeremy sprang toward his charging body like a defensive lineman. The men brawled on the ground for supremacy. Devonte's street-fighting past landed a right hook to Jeremy's left jaw. But incensed by the pain, Jeremy rallied the full power and thrust of his massive legs to lift and dump Devonte onto his back, climbing on top of him to secure his opponent's more dangerous arms, screaming spit into Devonte's face about killing each other. Devonte submitted to the psychosis he'd provoked, in that moment, far more interested in his life than his pride. He flattened his palms in surrender. Jeremy got off him, wiping snot from his face.

Ant aimed the rifle at Devonte.

"There's no need for that," Tommy said nervously. "I don't know why anyone would need a weapon like that."

"Too bad we didn't take 'em all from you country pigs when we had the chance," Dolores hollered.

Blood rushed into Ant's head in a spasmodic rage. It was all he could do not to shoot her dead right there.

"Easy," Charlie said to him quietly, pumping his hand toward the ground. Ant cut his eyes toward the plea and back again to his target.

"We're too jacked up right now," Jeremy said. "You all stay on your side, and we'll stay on ours."

Disgruntled, angry, dissatisfied, they all took the advice, knowing how close they stood to true violence, the likes of which no one of them had previously anticipated—the escalation was vicious and quick. These were not compatriots but enemies, side by side.

* * *

Not one to be put off by dogs, but not one to indulge them either, Dolores nevertheless planned to kill Mullet. It was annoying enough. All dogs were a menace to her mind. Always sniffing around where they shouldn't. Shitting where they wanted. Whining and barking at any blurry streak in their periphery. Nothing would be a better shock to Jenna and her clan than the disbelief of that discovery. Disbelief was a traumatic space, the exploitation of which Dolores was a master.

The mists of the morning fog could be caught loitering among the lower greens becoming frosted browns in the creeping days of winter. Mullet sniffed at the hardening ground, trotting the perimeter of its people's settlement, seeking smells indicating food, death, or danger. Anyone accepted into its masters' domain, the animal obeyed, following any who moved away from camp. Dolores barely had to look back to assure its commitment to her lead. The switchblade her son had kept she squeezed in her right front pocket, her fingers mostly translucent from the pressure of her hate around the handy metal bulk. The dog continued sniffing at patches of ground in a trail of pauses, further incensing the petulant old woman, rather prone to stomping, but she had to stay quiet, pushing branches and dying vegetation slimed by morning dews and the declensions of seasonal shift out of her face and out of the way. The glow of rising day enlivened the white undergrowth on her head, its rusting tips faded and fading from the last time they had clung to chemical red.

The dog's innocent and meandering trot halted as she glared, waiting for it to catch up. But it had stopped, sensing the evil convection arising within her. Impatience could have thwarted her plans had the dog remained stubbornly unmoved behind her. Wanting to scream and yell and command—barking in her own way—she squeezed the knife instead, turned, and kept marching toward the edge of an advancing cliff, off of which she'd planned to throw the eviscerated corpse.

The cliff rose above a pool that collected at the base of the creek where she squatted, waiting for the animal to approach. As it came up behind her, innocently sniffing at her backside and greasy, tangled hair, it flinched.

"Get over here," she said, trying to sound sweet but failing to disguise her aggression. "I said get ovah here." Snapping her fingers with one hand, she grabbed the resistant dog by the excess skin around its neck and yanked it downward. Mullet collapsed and cried. "Oh, shut up," she growled and stabbed him in the neck in a single violent thrust of her entire arm, landing with a thud. Mullet's eyes widened as he absorbed the shock of the trauma. She ripped the knife downward and began to flay the animal alive amidst its shrill little cries.

* * *

"I'm going to get some water," Jenna said.

"Take both buckets and make sure Mullet hasn't run off again," Jeremy instructed.

Mumbling about the coldness in the air and "this lazy butthead" rolling around in the comfort of the sleeping bag, she crossed the camp and entered the woods on the trail, calling for Mullet. Farther into the trees she heard an odd sound, like laughter but also like moaning, like someone in sharp pain. Slowly through the branches, ducking dead limbs leaning against trunks, fusty brown and black leaves draping the canopy like a patchwork of quilted mud, she could begin to see a form resolve into a figure. Mullet's lanky brown legs stretched out from behind Dolores's hulking body crouched over him, working her hands into the open carcass.

Dolores raised blood-coated fingers, dripping across her clothing, weaving them through her whitened hair, turning it reddish in parts but gunky black in the main, making a sticky mess. Blood smears stained her face, and as her head tilted back into the light, she moaned. Jenna stood astonished, destroyed, disbelieving, silenced by an unbelievable despair. Mullet's half-empty corpse lay upon the ground before her. And she wanted to scream and to cry both to relieve her fright and to signal her intentions against this brutal old hag, who was laughing on her knees before an altar of satanic possession, mere feet from Jenna's coiled fingers, ready to strike, ready to twist off the old woman's head. But she remained frozen.

Dolores smirked, sensing the younger woman, as she helped herself up, one leg at a time, hoisting her body onto her stronger thigh. "You know," she said. "I just knew you were a coward underneath it all. I just knew it." She pretended the woods was an unseen crowd praising her omniscience and smiled. "No one ever believes me," she said, staring directly at Jenna's hunched and diminished spirit; then lowering her voice, she said, "But I'm always right."

With all her love for Mullet, Jenna sprang like a trap and shoved the mass of flesh before her. Too short in time to be shocked, Dolores's head flipped back as she tumbled, slipping off and over the cliff. Down through the shrubs and brambles that grew out of the rock of its face, her body tumbled and flopped, landing with a thud onto the boulders beneath.

Jenna crouched above her beloved Mullet, now a gruesome mess of flesh. She could barely allow herself to touch the flabby pelt of fur on its shank before rising up and turning away, walking back to the camp neither thinking what to say, nor knowing whom she should tell. Blank and unfeeling, she strode slowly as if wandering inside a perilous nightmare.

Things were turning there. Something in the air conveyed knowledge of the killing on a furious coil to the senses of the remaining men.

* * *

The vagrant man's dead body that Tommy and his father had dumped began to foul up the air, merging symbolically with the foulness of Dolores's deviant amusements. Terminated by the inadequacies of multiple bad fortunes, the body, alone, lay at peace with the natural world, laid to rest in the far corner of the lot they occupied.

"Damn, that shit stinks," Devonte said.

"We shoulda buried it," Tommy added.

"It's not too late, you know," Ronnie affirmed.

"It might fall apart in our hands if we tried now," Tommy answered.

"Don't be a sissy. He's not that far gone," Ronnie said. The three men moved like a unit to the corpse that was beginning to meld with the hues of the dirty earth beneath it. "See, them animals are already chompin' on him," he added.

"*Shit*," Devonte whispered.

"What?" Tommy asked.

"That's what I been hearin' at night? I heard dem cracks and shit from the animals eatin' him up."

Ronnie noticed Jenna walking out of the woods toward the other men huddled by the fire. "Look at that fright over there," Ronnie said. The others turned to see Jenna arriving slowly into the clearing like a floating ghost as if subverted by decompensated shock.

"Lookin' like a zombie or some shit," Devonte murmured.

"What's up her ass, you think?" Ronnie asked.

"Ma dick, pretty soon," Devonte joked.

Ronnie cut his eyes. "Eh, who knows, but I don't trust her none. I don't trust any one of them."

"Where's Ma?" Tommy asked.

"Fuck if I know," Ronnie rejoined curtly.

"Didn't she go down that same path earlier?"

Neither Ronnie nor Devonte responded but just watched the other survivors gather closely by the fire, seeming to console Jenna. Mina appeared to be instructing her in taking very deep breaths.

"We're gonna need one of those tarps we got for this," Devonte said standing over the corpse plastered in leaves just beyond the line between the woods and the clearing.

"Then go get it," Tommy commanded.

Ronnie smacked his son's face. "Don't you talk shit to him, you hear me, kid? We got to stay even with each other here, or we're fucked. Now, go get the tarp."

The smugness of Devonte's smile warmed his devilish face, and he folded his arms in triumph. Tommy's humiliation could be seen in his stride as he walked the hundred yards to their broken-down getaway truck to retrieve a most useless and frayed white tarp they'd stowed in its cab.

The dead man's body loaded onto the opened plastic, his arms unnaturally folded in front of his chest, his face gray and wan, completely out of life, nonetheless communicated a deeper emotion about its former suffering. Tommy had to look away from it. As the three ex-cons carried it off, two at the top end and Ronnie at the feet, Tommy noticed Jenna's unnatural disturbance, sitting on her legs next to Jeremy whose jaw clenched so hard it looked like the muscles might pop.

"What's up with them?" Tommy asked.

"You think either of us know, genius?" Ronnie answered. "We're right here. With you."

They continued carrying the contorted, putrid, mangled body into the woods, down the same path from which Jenna had emerged. The same path they'd been using for fresh water for going on two weeks since their truck broke down, farther upstream.

* * *

As the procession passed, Jenna said to Jeremy, "Don't stare."

"Can't help it," Jeremy answered. "They're gonna see it all. What are we gonna do? Should I get the gun? Should I stand ready to fight? Like—"

Jenna lifted her head to the sky but closed her eyes, and a single line of tears streamed out of their corners before regaining her composure. "I'll tell them what happened," she said, pausing to swallow some grief; she could barely talk. "And we'll go from there."

* * *

It was fifty yards to the clearing right before the cliff and its deadly drop. The iron odor of the dog's blood permeated the freshness of the cooler air.

"Damn, I know that smell," Devonte said. "That's blood. Fresh blood."

Ronnie soundlessly agreed, observing the two men walking backward in front of him, watching the way. The corpse jostled left and right to the beat of their steps like a rag doll. The wound in the left thigh oozed with new pus and black sludge, and it wafted up and into Ronnie's nose. "Jesus *fucking* Christ!" he yelled and dropped his end of the load, pushed his fingers into his shut eyes as they teared from the putrescence all around him. He retched like he might be sick, but it was dry heaves only.

"Aww, quit being a baby and let's unload this fool," Devonte said.

Ronnie nodded, wiping the corners of his mouth of the warm saliva the nausea had triggered and retook his position.

He was the first to see the dog.

"*Goddamn,*" he said.

"Don't drop it!" Devonte warned him, referring to the feet end of the tarp. "We are tossing this shit right *now*," he continued, moving sideways to swing it off the ledge. "One, two—" The tarp snapped and ripped as they swung. "Three!" Ronnie had held onto the tarp too long, so the body fell out and tumbled down the side of the cliff, finally breaking into a few large pieces. Devonte shook his head, almost laughing.

"The *fuck* is that?" Ronnie exclaimed.

"The dog," Tommy said.

"Who did that? The girl?" Ronnie desperately asked.

"Nah," Devonte said. "She'd kill whoever did do this though."

"She did," Tommy said, pointing down toward the bottom of the ravine.

"Oh *shit*," Devonte said, covering his smiling mouth.

"What? What is it?" Ronnie asked, a few too many steps behind for him to see. He pushed past Devonte to get the view of his wife, the mother of his child, the damned old dame he'd married, Dolores, her body seeming broken and set at an odd angle; her hands caked in dark, oxidized blood; her entire front drenched in the dog's innards. "Holy motherfucker," he whispered, both enraged and relieved. "That blonde little *bitch*."

The others waiting around the fire could hear Ronnie roaring down the path, calling for her head. And when he burst through the final branches at the grass's edge, Jeremy was already standing at attention with a rifle in his hands, pointed to the ground.

"What's the problem?" he asked calmly.

Devonte dramatized the silence by soundlessly miming alarm, making a too-expressive face at the confrontation, excited by the possibility of more violence. The wind picked up, like a tornado brewing more hate among them, between the raging old man at one end and the intensely protective younger one at the other. Jeremy broke the moment with the truth.

"Your wife killed our dog," he said firmly. Ant stood closely behind his ally and friend.

"So *fucking* what!" Ronnie raged at him.

Jenna appeared from the far side of the brick ruin. "She cut him open, Ronnie," she said calmly. "I reacted. I didn't think. I just pushed, and—"

"How *dare* you? Who do you think *you are*, you entitled fuckin' bitch! You stupid white bitch! I oughtta strangle that lily-white neck a yours. You fucked with the wrong Italian!" He grabbed the empty space in front of him, his crooked fingers stiff with wrath as he stepped toward her.

Jeremy lifted the rifle and aimed it at the old man. "Don't be stupid," he said. "I won't think twice about it. And care even less. You'll be dumped in the same spot."

Ronnie focused his eyes to the round black ends of the gun, knowing he wouldn't make it two more steps, dropping his head and his hands.

"Let's go," Tommy said, taking his father's arm by its sagging flesh under his once rock-like bicep.

"You too," Ant said to Devonte. "Get goin'."

"What?" Devonte asked, perturbed by the association. "I didn't do *nothin'!* All I did was dump that fuckin' corpse!"

Jeremy moved the rifle's sight onto him.

"All right. *Damn.* I'm going."

"Put your hands on your heads as you walk out," Jeremy demanded suddenly.

"What for?" Tommy yelled back.

"Do it!"

The three men slowly lifted their arms and placed their hands in the air as they left the camp. Tears streamed down Ronnie's face—from anger, despair, old age, and the loss of his wife of over fifty years. He could do nothing. His son could do nothing. At least, not for now.

"You brown-skin niggas all be the same. Always go for the white girls. An' always fuck us over. You ain't a worthy brother, you hear?" Devonte yelled and grew increasingly agitated as Ant and Jeremy began to follow them to assure their passage beyond the frontside of the ruin that hid the camp.

"I'm Hawaiian, you dumb ass."

"I don't give a fuck *what* you are, *bitch*! You ain't white."

"You care more about all that than anyone else here," Ant said. "You're the one stuck in the past, *brother*."

In the open, Jeremy addressed them. "If you come back inside this camp, you're gonna be food for the birds and whatever else wants a taste, you hear me?"

"Yeah, yeah," Devonte said.

"Don't try it. You got a marine right here. An' I killed way more men on the battlefield than you did in the ghetto—promise. So, if you wanna try your luck with your life, come back here."

"We're going," Tommy said.

"I want justice!" Ronnie suddenly yelled.

"You're entitled to try for it, old man," Jeremy said. "But I am entitled to defend my wife and our lives as well. Come if you must but be warned. At that point, I will not hesitate to strike out at you all. And kill you."

"Why not do it now, big man?" Devonte asked.

"'Cause that's what ghetto punks like you do. I've got honor that you couldn't see if it—" He stopped. "Go," he said. "Now." Jeremy remained watching until they were out of sight.

He and Ant convened on the public side of the ruin, near the road. The air smelled like oil and gravel from a leak in the SUV. Ant wondered how long they should stay before they, too, picked up and moved on and away from these fresh traumas, these unchecked crimes, these human behaviors no longer restricted by civility or the law.

It was dusk. Staying to herself, Jenna quietly made a fire. Mina was putting together a meal from the last of the squirrels they had shot.

Jeremy took a seat to warm himself. "One of us has to stay up all night."

"We can do shifts," Ant replied. "I figure we should head out tomorrow. Not stay here a minute longer than that. They're comin' back."

"They might," Jeremy said, biting his nails, imagining the possible scenarios of attack.

CHAPTER THREE

The left side of her body, her once good side, had begun to bruise; livid, purple-black coloration appeared like competing liquids in a strange chemical mixture, like poisoned mushroom clouds blooming up the length of her body from her calf, rising to her shoulder blade. The elastic band of her sweatpants snapped back into place at her waist to protect the darkening flesh from the sting of colder air, and she pressed her numb hand against the too-sore physique and groaned. Her right-side hip had been worn down from age, so she hobbled between the crippled sides of her complete biology and trolled through the woods like a haunting, an apparition, the caked skin of dried blood shading its contours. Her face wrinkled from painful wincing as she hovered about the sticks in search of vengeance.

Dolores had lived. Any mortal shock to the vital organs of her body had been absorbed by the generous layer of flesh that had concealed them; fattening by years of excess had saved her life. However many days had passed since the fall, she did not know, nor could she properly conceive the current hour to guess. Obviously, she had fallen, but the reason why also disguised its history from present memory. All she was certain of was her relative ability to walk, so she took one step at a time, climbing up the slope that followed the loud and healthy creek down to where she had lain. Many knobby sticks that would make suitable walking staffs to balance against her gait appeared like divine wands promising help from the justness of unseen forces, but her right hand was too weak and her left hand too bruised, so all she could do was continue as she'd begun, being careful not to sit anywhere she could not easily rise up from. Her brain concussed, she couldn't conceive of her circumstances beyond the two feet surrounding her circumference. A bear could tear her to shreds if it chose. A thief would steal her soul. A darker man could raid her humanity, adding abuse to many bruises. Like a piñata swaying mindlessly between hits of fate, she staggered around the forest. Where she was, who she was, when she was—all were inconceivable. How she was, was all. And she wasn't well. Her stomach had turned gassy by nausea, and her mouth dripped wet with excessive saliva. The colder air this morning continued to smart her exposed skin, fluttering a chill down her wobbly length, making this survivor more painfully aware of her injury, reminding her of all she had wished to forget. However undeterred by these inhibitions, she would keep walking until she found someone, anyone, to give ground to her confusions and accommodate an old and ailing woman.

And at once but slowly, the flame of core character began to revive her mind: the person she had played for decades, one who was hidden; one who had played an act upon the world; one whose interests preceded all other concerns, most of all the concerns of others. From the pith of this construction, her spirit arose like a mist around a monster, and she climbed the sullen incline toward the brighter clouds barely shielding the gleam of a boisterous sun while the hostilities of her heart nurtured her will to go on.

* * *

Tommy cautiously searched the skinnier woods, losing the weight of the last of their leaves in larger clumps by the day. Winter was here, and his tribe had almost nothing secured to survive its mortal kiss; even a forty-degree night would eventually cause hypothermia and death. Wondering at the many possibilities for his demise, he faced the brick ruin before walking back into the camp to plead for reconciliation, because between him and beyond the careless mass of bricks lay a better survival. For diplomacy, the kindnesses he'd kept hidden from his parents, from his peers, from the bulk of the ruthless world in which he'd been ensconced, he could reveal more completely to the survivors who had intended to help them; even with the death of Dolores, a woman and a mother he'd submitted to but never loved, he felt nervous about giving too much affection away to his supposed enemies, about listening to his intuition, or acting against vulnerabilities. Like any messenger who must also play the diplomat, he would measure the difference between kindness and neutrality and fit himself therein.

Reflexively, Tommy expected Mullet to greet him, to jump to kiss his face, in the false hope of diffusing the impulse to back out of this task, but then he remembered the cause of their exile, how bizarre it was to have forgotten and instead resort to pleasanter memories; maybe it was some neurological cope, to necessarily disguise the fraud in diplomatic friendship, to keep the mind set to the positive, enabling the negotiation of space and resources he was tasked with.

The other men wouldn't do this, not Ronnie nor Devonte. They couldn't do this. Their temperament was too volatile, a hostility resulting from general cowardice and lack of sophistication. Dolores would have sent him to do it with Devonte as a silent guard to express her hostility to any disinterest in her demands. Tommy wondered why they needed to do this at all when a cloud opened up seemingly by the sun and warmed his face, and he realized he'd rather join these strangers than spend another second with his kin.

* * *

The instant Ronnie sat his tired old rear on a rock, he lost no time in kissing his hand to the sky, blessing God for relieving him of his wife while excoriating the divine for the loss of the support and resources of the others.

"Think they'll let us back in?" Ronnie asked Devonte.

"Fuck if I know, Ronnie. White people don't make no sense to me."

Ronnie chortled. "They're not all white."

"They act like it," Devonte said. "An' I don't like that shit."

"I hear ya," Ronnie answered. "Neither do I—that holier-than-thou or whatever the fuck bullshit." Devonte laughed at Ronnie's ignorance. "Protest-ants, my nonno used ta call 'em. Bunch a superior assholes."

"I was raised Baptist, old man," Devonte said. "I don' know. Don't care none about it. But I can't wait no more. I need a place to rest my head and a group to hunt some meat with, Ronnie. Don't be a fuckin' idiot here thinkin' you can make it without these people." Devonte became agitated, pacing back and forth. "And Tommy might fuck this up," he added, beginning to wander in the direction Tommy had walked.

"Don't get stupid!" Ronnie called after him before Devonte disappeared into a cluster of pine trees. Ronnie moped in the pacific warmth of the morning sun while his thoughts turned to the relief he felt on being left alone. "Fuckin' moron," he said.

"Watch ya mouth an' how you talk about him—" a hoarse old voice said bluntly behind him.

Ronnie flipped around to look. "*Holy* fuck," he said to the occupied space in front of him.

* * *

Boyish inhibition weakened Tommy's nerve, as he first spotted the big brown dude slicing large pieces of wood into quarters with an axe like a champion outdoorsman slicing a stick of butter. The women appeared to be both packing up and making breakfast. The healthy gay guy was tending to the dying gay guy's side. The black one or the mixed one was missing. The Italian-looking lady saw him first and simply stared and shook her head, not happy to see him return.

"Seriously, what do you want now?" she asked before the others even noticed.

He could barely speak, not knowing which part of himself to project. "I—"

"Yeah?" Mina asked without hesitation, annoyed. "Look," she said. "Some crazy shit happens all the time these days. Your mom lost her shit and killed Jenna's dog, so Jenna reacted. What happened, happened. There are no laws, no courts, no juries anymore. It is what it is."

"I know. I just—"

"What?"

"I want to make amends."

"So soon?" She almost laughed, pulling him to the side so Jenna could carry on working without having to listen to the nonsense.

"I never liked my mother," he said. "I'm not all that sad she's gone. Not sad at all, actually, and definitely not angry at anyone for it. It's just me and my pop and . . . and the other guy."

"The angry black guy? Yeah, I remember him," Mina said sarcastically. "We don't need any angry people around us."

"I hear ya. I would've left him at the nearest work camp if I coulda done it without my mother noticing."

"Here he comes," Mina said, spotting Devonte coming through the trees on the north side. "We'd really like you all to leave us alone."

Jeremy stopped hacking the wood and stood to face Devonte; his hands clutched the neck of the axe. "What are you doing here?" he asked abruptly.

Devonte put his hands up. "Look, man, I just want to survive, you know what I mean? I just want to get along with people, and—"

"You're gonna have to prove that," Jenna said.

Devonte cocked his head toward his chest and smiled to absorb the blow to his ego. "I get it, man. I get it. I'm tired of movin' around like we do. Tired of it. I'll get on my knees if I have to," he finished without moving, just staring at them for an answer.

"You're about as trustworthy as a shark around seals," Jeremy said. Neither one moved. Just stared, and Jeremy wondered what he might have to do next to end this strange encounter. "Maybe, yeah, get on your knees. Both of you," he said.

Tommy was the quicker one to the ground, nodding in obeyance of the order. Devonte rolled his eyes as he slowly went down, one knee at a time.

"And keep your hands up," Jeremy commanded. "Repeat after me." He stood between the two men. "I."

"I—" they echoed.

An argumentative rumbling came through the trees. "Get your dumb asses up," the mature and vengeful voice commanded back. Dolores stood seething at the sight of her son and lover on their knees before her rivals.

Devonte looked back and fell to his side on seeing Dolores, muddy and bloodied, heaving in great agitation with Ronnie at her side. "Oh *shit!*"

"The dragon-lady lives," Mina whispered. Jenna braced herself behind Mina.

Ant emerged from the southside woods, and Charlie jogged up to him, taking the dead rabbit from his shoulder to busy himself by the campfire. "They're back," he said.

"She's alive?" Ant asked, disbelieving what he saw.

"And angry as hell."

"Oh, fuck no," Ant said and walked to Jeremy's side.

"And here's the other one," Dolores said, as if interrupted.

"It's really about time you all left," Ant said, wiping his hands of the blood from his kill.

Jeremy noticed. "What'd you get?"

"Rabbit. About five-pounder, I think."

"Nice."

"Hey!" Dolores yelled, irritated at their disinterest in her. "I'm talking. *I'm* talking!"

"What do you want?" Mina asked.

"I want some *justice*," she seethed. "That bitch tried to kill me." She pointed to Jenna, who stepped out and in front of them all.

"And you gutted Mullet. You killed my dog," Jenna said. "You cut him in half and played with his guts. I saw you, *you*—"

Mina placed her hand onto Jenna's arm as her voice gained volume, needing her to stay guarded and controlled.

Dolores smirked, brought her still-stained hand to her face and sniffed at the dried entrails remaining on her skin.

Devonte shot up from his knees. "Whoa, whoa, *whoa*—that's some sick shit, woman," he said to Dolores who batted him away with the backside of her hand.

"Welcome to dystopia," she said, opening her arms, losing control and beginning to laugh, which tickled Ronnie who joined the laughter, the harmonies of which pleased Devonte, who also chuckled at the malignant absurdity of their predicament. Only Tommy was silent and stone-faced, and he looked over to Mina and Jenna, shaking his head at his family's inscrutable conduct.

"Whatever you lunatics want, you'd better say it now and then be on your way," Ant said, losing his patience with the histrionics.

Ronnie gently pushed Dolores aside and said, "Listen, she's in rough shape. We all are. But we're older people, all right? We can't tolerate none of this stuff as much as the rest of ya. Have a tiny bit of compassion, will ya?"

No one made a sound.

"I see. Well, we're not going anywhere. We can't survive on our own, all right? Do you want me ta admit that? We need you all."

"You have nothing to offer us."

"We can support you in whatever ways you need." Ronnie turned to Devonte. "He's young and strong. My son is too. My wife is a pretty good craftswoman, if we had the supplies is what I'm sayin'. Anyway, we can help. And we'll be good this time. My wife, she, ah, she's a bit—" He wavered his outspread hand in front of his face. "She used ta be on meds, ya know. And, uh, they're all gone." While the men chatted, Dolores wandered over to Charlie, laughing and talking sweetly to him.

Ant deferred to Mina and Jenna. "What do you think?"

"Do you *really* have to ask? I can't believe I have to deal with this evil woman," Jenna said, shaking her head, walking off to attend the fire and the morning's kill.

"Fine," Mina said, after waiting for Jenna to be farther away. "But she does anything crazy again, and—" She nodded her head quickly and widened her eyes madly.

"I know. I know. I understand," Ronnie said.

"Is there anything we can do to help this morning?" Tommy asked.

Jeremy spoke up. "Yeah, as a matter of fact, yes. If we're all going to stay here for a minute, then we're going to need a shelter, and I know how to build one. But I need the supplies. Why don't you take Devonte and your father to gather as many fallen branches —not twigs but substantial branches—and make a pile over on the north side where the animals are. Walk straight back into those woods," he said, pointing with his whole arm to the west.

* * *

The three tired men walked off like a chain gang, heads down as if repentant but more like a trio of various confusions, all trying to calculate how they'd come under Dolores's spell and why now they were at the mercy of Jeremy or whoever else. It almost didn't matter, these men of the kind who do best in reaction to another, more dominant voice, a more insistent mind. All three had been raised to cower at the feet of a heftier mother whose rages may or may not have ended with a beating just because she could throw her larger arm across the backside of a smaller, confused little boy, doing nothing for him except ensuring interminable obedience to her. Jeremy was a man they could never be, only Devonte saw and knew this, recognizing the potential in himself to break free of the chains. In Jeremy, he saw a man in the peak glaze of the sun, standing proud with a righteous glare moving about the earth to protect or correct the lesser beings, every one wavering for approval and love. But this was idol-worship of a kind Jeremy would never abide, doubling Devonte's increasing admiration of him.

Devonte looked back before being enveloped by the brambles of the woods to regard the man at the top of a chop, slamming the wooden block with mightiest wrath, and then followed with his eyes, as quickly, the chips that clipped off the edges and flicked about at lightning speed into the discrediting light.

* * *

A sudden coughing fit interrupted Roland's attempt to call to Jeremy when the younger man perceived the beckoning, placed the axe against the stump he used as a platform, and went to the dying man.

"Where are *they* going?" Roland asked.

"To get branches for the hale."

"What about the rocks?"

"I need to scout for those first. Can't have everyone wandering like lost crows looking for the sizes we'll need."

"That's sensible," Roland whispered, his voice retreating with each labored breath.

"How are you?" Jeremy asked, more from the silence than from not knowing.

Roland smiled, though it was a smile that bloomed as slowly as a rose might, death encroaching upon his every gesture. But after it lay fully across his happy face, he said, "*Dying*," as his chest punched skywards like a laugh transmuting a cough. Jeremy had no words but nodded as respectfully as he could. "No need," Roland said, belaboring each sentiment as if it were his last. "To stand here," he continued, "and watch." He finished and then that smile began again to push farther to its outmost reaches. Jeremy mimicked the expression, humored by the dying man's levity.

"Thank you for reminding me of what I know and what I can do," he said earnestly. Roland nodded slightly but more than once. "I don't think I would have thought to do this without your suggestion and support."

Fading at these last words, Roland gently shut his eyes. Charlie squatted by his side and wiped the spittle from his beloved friend's mouth, trying to preserve life's dignity, though each exhalation was siphoned by every inhalation of the deathless void.

Jeremy turned away, peering into the silent hum of this side of life, and when he turned back, Roland was gone. Charlie rested his head on his partner's inanimate chest, heaving and sobbing as quietly as he could.

"We're gonna have to dump his body somewhere soon," Jeremy said, not meaning to sound harsh or careless when Jenna pulled at his arm to bring him away from the scene, having heard the brief exchange. Bewildered by his lack of tact in the moment, Jeremy shook his head as if out of a daze and went with his wife to the campfire to eat some breakfast.

"Just—don't talk," she said.

Breakfast was meager but nourishing enough. Jenna sucked the bone of whatever fat dripped from her portion of the rabbit while Charlie dragged the sleeping bag swaddling Roland's mottled corpse across the foreground of her view. His left arm had fallen out and bounced with every step Charlie took in the direction of the woods. The rubbery gray aspect of the lifeless limb instantly stole her appetite.

"Go get the sleeping bag from him," Jeremy said urgently.

"Just wait. Let him finish what he needs to do, and then *you* can go get it—discreetly—and bring it back," she answered.

"Should we go join him? Like, support him?" he asked.

"No, just leave him alone. He had a hard enough time trying not to cry in front of us."

As she said this, the other men broke through the wooded barrier, dragging with them an impressive start to the collection of boughs and the many branches needed for the hale.

"Oh shit," Jeremy said, jumping up to help them deliver the materials in the area he'd mentally zoned for the structure. "Where's Ant?" he yelled back.

"Went hunting again," Mina called out.

Facing his laborers, he stood taller. "We're making a shelter. In Hawaii, we call it a hale."

Devonte nodded. Tommy looked to Devonte. Ronnie stared glumly.

"I'm too old for physical labor. My bones ache," Ronnie said.

"No, you ain't, nigga," Devonte said. "If a boss asked you to unload a ton of swag for a thirty cut, you'd have no problem with your fuckin' bones."

"Screw me, I like to be rewarded," Ronnie exclaimed, throwing his hands into the air.

Instead of a violent rage, Devonte burst forth in a deluge of words. "Old man, the next time it rains and the wind be blowin' a wind tunnel up yo muthafuckin' asshole, makin' it whistle the Sicilian *national-fucking-anthem*, and we in here chillin'? I will *make sure* you are sitting out in the open air. If you don't help. Is what *I'm* saying—"

Devonte drew his face three inches to Ronnie's expressionless one, and Ronnie agreed to be a part of the effort to build the homestead after all. They split up according to Jeremy's instruction. Two were to find trunks with thicker bases for columns; two were to construct handheld shovels from the crashed SUV's scrap metal and any rocks with appropriately tapered edges for digging.

"You took it like a man," Tommy said, patting his father on the back.

"Fuck you, kid, you hear?" Ronnie answered to the rounded amusement of the younger men.

* * *

While the men toiled in the hope of rediscovering their ancient skills and purposes, the women, excepting Dolores, sat in political contemplation of the group, measuring the character traits they'd so far observed.

"She's not mentally ill," Mina said to break the silence, the two of them tracking as Dolores attempted to console Charlie over Roland's passing. "She's a conniving bitch."

"Worse than that," Jenna said to Mina's silent agreement. "I hate having to even tolerate her."

"I know. But there's no other way at this point. Just pretend she's crazy and keep an eye on her."

"Tommy seems like a decent guy."

"His father is an asshole, though."

"Devonte is—I don't really know what."

"Unpredictable. He has the potential to play both sides."

"Yes."

"We have to be careful with all four of them."

Ant threw three squirrel carcasses down in front of the fire.

"That's a decent take," Mina said.

"Prefer the rabbits, but these will do. Found some blackberries about a quarter mile west of the creek. Got the last of those. Nettles too. We can cook the leaves down like spinach. But they're about to go dormant." He held up the bottom of his shirt even higher to reveal the pouch he'd made to hold a few handfuls of the berries and a dozen stalks of the nettles.

Mina snatched a couple and popped them into her mouth. "They're mulberries.

We should go for more," she said, and Jenna agreed with the plan. "Grab the spear," she said, "see if we can't also get some meat, ourselves."

"Walk due west, you'll see a cluster of the bushes 'bout a quarter mile in," Ant said. "Not much left, though. First frost is due very soon."

"But we're farther south, remember. Milder winters down here," Mina corrected. Ant just nodded, disbelieving her.

At the creek, the women paused as if in need to hear the rush of water moving from higher to lower ground. Like a welcome oblivion. Like being drunk on sound. Jenna closed her eyes, searching for peace, mourning her beloved Mullet, seeking to neutralize her hate for Dolores and the horrors they'd all endured. Mina clutched Jenna's hand, somehow reading the thoughts that raced inside of her mind and the tidal feelings cresting the top of her heart. Farther into the woods, they spotted a mother deer and her maturing fawn, months old from the summer birthing season, nosing the ground. The pebbles of their excrement spotted the forest floor, and Jenna pointed to them.

"Are those the berries?" she asked innocently.

Mina chuckled and said, "Definitely not. Those are deer droppings. But we should follow them if we can. See if they don't lead us to the shrubs."

Carefully, the women stalked the woods near the fawn, which trotted toward its mother whose ears rotated backward at their approach, not yet alarmed enough to run. The fawn reflexively ducked under its mother's belly to shield itself from the intruding creatures, but it had grown just beyond its height for true shelter. Mina delighted at being so close to the mother, she could pet its flank.

"I really should kill her," she said, squeezing the spear.

"Oh my god, no," Jenna said. "The baby will die."

"I know," Mina answered. "I can't do it, but Ant would. And we'd have meat for weeks." Her hand moved halfway down its smooth pelt when it flinched, spooked, and hopped away, the fawn doing its best to dash after its mother. The women continued forward, moving on and deeper into the woods.

"Look out there." Jenna pointed to the ground. "That looks like a huge dropping. Is that from a deer?"

Mina stepped around and in front of her friend to squat above the specimen. She picked it up.

"Ew, gross, put that down," Jenna pleaded, watching her friend pry the thing apart with her bare hands. "What are you doing?" Mina pulled out the meat from the shell and popped it into her mouth. "What in *actual* hell are you doing?"

Covering her mouth to keep from laughing out the nutmeat as she chewed, careful not to choke on the dryness in her throat, she finally swallowed. "Pecans," she said, releasing the humor she'd repressed. "There must be a tree around here."

"Pecans? On a tree?" Jenna appeared dumbfounded.

"That's where they come from!"

"Thank *god*. I literally thought you were eating deer shit right in front of me." They shared a hearty laugh, freeing some good endorphins that had been dammed like a vast lake since the introduction of new stressors by the latest arrivals to camp.

"Come on," Mina said, handing Jenna the other half of the nut. "There's more over there. I bet the tree is close by."

* * *

At home base, the men, through mind and mutual labor, had bonded their talents to action, a first step in Jeremy's plan to convert the energies of past hates into a kind of beneficial communion, but he could not expect to control their progress, merely to guide them and give the rest to posterity. Ant had joined the fray, working in sweaty tandem with Devonte to dig out deep holes for the stakes of the coming structure, a house made of the mountains' wares, the reinvented past, their once and future home. Slowly, it came into shape, one stake at a time: a stake of human toil, a stake of shared interest, a stake in the hope for a better day: a notion of collective effort stripped of its excesses, lifted of its cynical weights. The hale would serve as their capitol, their domain, their unification, their home. The first roof had collapsed from poor testing of the load-bearing columns. Jeremy had escaped being crushed by a hair of a second in the space, and Jenna spent a day keeping him from exploding in a rage at Devonte and Tommy, whom he'd entrusted with the task of ensuring the security of the structure's base.

"They said they worked construction!" he had yelled into the air, the only thing he'd said for them to hear as they cowered in a kind of shame, which served enough as an apology for Jeremy to regain his composure and get back to work.

But civility requires vigilance, and none of the men would allow any other to rest too long on his tail. They continuously urged one another to work; the more the vision became a three-dimensional thing, the more the men sank to their knees and prayed, stunning former selves into a deepening renewal of interest in their lives and future potential.

In a surprise gesture of goodwill, Dolores had taught the other women and Charlie how to strip skinnier branches down to youthful green straps and weave them into bowls, large and small, inside of which they'd stored pecans from the orchard Mina and Jenna had discovered, winter apples that Ant had found, and a smattering of scavenged fruits: leftover crabapples, persimmons, and pears. Being early winter, it was the last time to gather what they might conserve of the remaining resources for deep season rations.

Ant had become a fairly expert hunter of the small game in the area, teaching Mina and Jenna how best to stalk the critters and get close enough to spear them through. Jenna had proved a natural, while Mina, naturally competitive, struggled to get it exactly right. Pelts from the rabbits, squirrels, and deer had been cut from their carcasses and hung to dry out by the fire, which had grown into a four-by-four-foot pit of flame and embers, constantly in use. With each passing day, more and more of their natural skills and insights came to the fore, bringing with them a confidence and a sense of purpose no one of them had ever fully known. Mina was the closest to a proper homesteader though her survival skills amounted to maintaining the compound her grandfather had more or less already devised and a very twentieth-century sort of sustenance. This was different; this was pure survival, harkening back to their earliest human roots.

And it worked. Animosities remained but were tempered by new associations. Personalities clashed, but they lived together as a community would, one that didn't shy from conflict but understood it as a normal part of a group of strangers coming together to live. Jeremy had become a kind of chief; Ant had become a sort of warrior general, and a hierarchy of associations followed these truths. Only Dolores kept her distance, too embittered at the loss of her powers over the other men; too unmasked for the women to accept her entirely.

But she was useful, hoarding her talents for occasions to reveal them when her ego deemed it necessary. Mina and Jenna remained wary, long since come to terms with the woman's inability to appreciate in others their unique gifts or contributions, her incapacity to feel and convey empathy that she could otherwise pretend in shallow words and cliched phrases, so dead and decomposed that only vapors of that zombified, corporate language would affect Dolores's mind, producing incoherent mumblings about diversity, equity, and inclusion and their essential status in the core beliefs of any powerful corporation. Reciting these spells that had lent bigger thrust to her once indomitable career, they worked to captivate her wonder in the power that had once been hers, now lost to the barbarian ravages of time. Sometimes, she shook her head while she babbled. Lately, she had begun to rock and back and forth, fully embodying the traumatized individual she used to prey upon.

Ant had figured it must be Christmas or thereabouts. Temperatures during the day stayed comfortably above freezing, perhaps sixty degrees. At night, it was growing cold and colder with a breeze. The hale stood proudly, even if leaning a few degrees north off center, even with its twigs and random branches sticking out at the top, even as it vented grayish-white smoke from below; but it was sturdy and had proved its resilience to higher gusts of wind. Underneath, it was dry, as a fire burned all the day and through the night, simply needing to be refed kindling and a larger log in the early hours before breakfast.

From the edge of each side of its canopied roof, Jenna and Mina had hung dried deer hides to serve as barriers to the outdoors, two sewn together by a needle made of shrapnel from the crash and repurposed wool from one of the sweaters in the pile of clothes. The hides could not completely cover the openings, but they worked well enough to provide further shelter from sideways rain or crisper winds. They'd also managed a way to make moccasins like slippers and cozy mittens from the squirrel hides to warm hands and feet through the night.

It was Mina's idea to engineer a wall leading from the ruin around what had become the property of the camp. During the day, a chain gang of sorts was made among them: Jeremy, Ant, Devonte, Tommy, Ronnie, Mina, Jenna—everyone but Dolores and Charlie, whose sudden disinterest in the group disturbed its original members. He would wander off on long walks away from camp, returning without much explanation or narrative expositions of the days-long absences.

"We need you at the wall," Jeremy told him.

Charlie seemed plucked out of a trauma funk he hadn't wanted to leave. "What do you mean?" he asked, as if he were excluded from participation in the labors of the camp. Once he realized the request, he laughed, saying, "I don't do physical labor."

"The hell you don't," Jeremy said fairly calmly, given the provocation.

"What do you mean?" Charlie asked helplessly.

"I mean, get off your ass right now and come to the wall. We need your help adding twigs to the clay bricks." Jeremy lifted Charlie onto his feet. His face strained at the dead weight of the man; Charlie almost fell back onto the ground. "Get on your feet right now," Jeremy said. "Or you're out."

"Out?"

"Out of the camp. Like, no shelter or food for you. Like *goodbye*. Like, you will not be welcomed here. Got it?"

Charlie nodded weakly and trailed Jeremy to the northeast corner, where all but Dolores and Jenna were busy building some part of the wall: slapping the pliable clay bricks into place or axing slim tree trunks into pikes to hammer into place between sections of the mud. The wall was meant to designate their location, to notify any passersby of their presence, and to keep out wind shear. Charlie reluctantly bent down to his knees to help break twigs into smaller pieces to be mixed into the looser clay.

Jenna shouldered a carrying-staff like a milkmaid's yoke, bringing two vats filled with water from the frothy waters of their stream. It was meant to keep the clay from drying too quickly or to mix into Ant's attempt at a kind of cement, combining gravel, dirt, clay, and whatever else he could churn into it.

Mina leaned over him, watching him play with the concoction.

"There's bound to be some limestone around here, seeing we're near the coastal plain," he said. "We can heat big chunks of it and then grind the baked rocks into a powder to add to the mix. That will make it more like actual cement."

"Good luck extracting limestone," Mina said cynically. "Or even finding it."

Their work continued until they had completed enough wall to obstruct open passage into their space, leaving space at each end, finishing at the start of the forest on both northern and southern fronts: a wall like a backward letter "C" that encompassed the old brick ruin and the grassy field leading up to the woods where the animals were paddocked. In the hale, they had a dry shelter large enough to house everyone and a wall to protect from inclement weather and any too-curious souls who might wander into what the survivors now viewed as their territory. Fueled by the engine of basic human ingenuity, and like the colonial campgrounds of centuries' past, the enclave was becoming a bit of a permanent settlement.

While no one else was looking, Devonte took Dolores by the arm and led her into the southern woods where none of them usually explored. Being so close to the highway, the path eventually led to it and the possible exposure to unsavory types, eventually to be confronted by literal highwaymen or wanderers with absolutely nothing to lose. Ant nudged Jeremy once he saw them disappear behind some brush.

"What's goin' on there, you think?"

"Probably the thing it looks like."

"You think he's—"

"No," Ronnie said, interrupting them. "They been doing that since he came into the picture."

Surprised at the candor, Ant continued. "And you don't care?"

"Not so much, no." Ronnie managed his discomfort by acknowledging his disinterest to these men. "At first, it was her way of controlling him." His leathery hands dovetailed and made a scooping gesture from the left side of his body to the right side, as if shoveling information into more appropriate boxes.

Ant searched the hale for Tommy, but he had disappeared until he reemerged from the darkness on the east side. His eyes shifted nervously like he had no idea why Ant would be looking at him. "I see," Ant said. "All of you know about this and don't care."

"Why should we?" Ronnie asked.

"I suppose I don't need to answer that question," Ant finished.

Jenna tried ignoring the discussion, sipping on some hot water to warm herself. The cow stood close by, growing larger by the day, expanding by motherly vastness in creation, shifting to the grass to graze, and Jenna dreamed of the day she would milk Sally Baby by hand to keep its udders full of the rich source of protein the animal would produce. "That's a girl," she called toward the placid beast.

The larger animals were becoming restless in the protected enclave; once, the horse wandered off, but no one considered going after it, too tired to calculate its value; then miraculously, it reappeared. The bull was ornery and dangerous, roving all around the space but never too far, always circling back to his cow. Sally Baby's udders would fill up soon after the calf's birth, and Mina imagined breeding the cow again to the bull, perhaps to attempt a small herd with the ultimate benefit of slaughtering the animals for beef. Since the horse, bull, and cow were eating up the pasture of the campground, and the horse was beginning to grow thin, someone needed to take them to find another grazing field. Tommy had volunteered but emphasized his having no experience with livestock, so Ant agreed to go with him.

The horse had a bridle; the bull had the harness with the rope lead. They'd have to take the cow separately. Armed with one of the rifles, the two set off for a trek afield, down the country highway that deviated from the interstate road, going north. Two miles past ruined, old storefronts and fueling sites, there was a larger grove with a small-scale orchard of peach trees, probably a domestic farm with a side-street produce market, the trees now in seasonal dormancy. Grasses around and between the lanes of the orchard were overgrown and browning in the weaker light and colder air.

"Drop the lead," Ant instructed Tommy, as the horse trotted off, sniffing at the ground, nudging its muzzle around, snorting at the dead grasses to uncover fresher patches of green. The bull was more stubborn, sniffing at the air blowing down from the north, refusing to budge when Ant pushed and even punched at its hind. Its head whirled around so its gelatinous eyeballs could regard the pest at its rear. Waiting a minute longer as if in perpetual power struggle with all creation, the full rotundity of the most irritable thing that ever stood on four legs finally decided it was time to fill its maw with food.

Ant swung the rifle to his side and picked a longer blade of grass that had gone to seed and chewed it while watching the road for vagrants. Tommy paced the far side of the animals for fear of losing them to the wild.

A figure resolved in the blurry background of the distant road. Ant kept quiet but continued to measure its approach as it became clearer. A man walking at a quickened pace seemed to be the subject of the coming minutes of his life. A long trench coat flapped against the man's legs with each lunging step he took; a black baseball cap sat on his head, and modish, clear-framed prescription glasses perched on his nose. Having seen Ant resting against the trunk of a barren tree, the direction to which the stranger committed his energies led directly into the space before him, a man who appeared to the stranger more relaxed than was typical for the men he had seen on the long journey away from what had been the peak of urban civilization and his lifelong home. Gaunt, tired, thirsty, he gestured his arm, extending his hand like a summons to the man quietly eating a piece of grass against a tree. But Ant didn't move until he finally arrived; then Ant stood straight to greet him.

"How can I help you?" he asked skeptically.

Hurriedly, the man said, "Whatcha got for me?"

"I'm sorry?"

"Whatcha got? I mean, look here—you've got two large and healthy animals. I mean they look healthy. And is he your man or are you his man?"

"What do you mean *man*?"

The stranger instantly gestured for Tommy in the same hurried manner.

"Nah, nah, nah," Ant said. "You are talking to me, not to him." Ant put up his hand with the palm facing Tommy, signaling not to approach. Tommy nodded and continued to tend to the animals. The bull snorted loudly. The horse whinnied. "Who are you?" Ant asked, less politely.

"I'm Gerry, born Gerard. I'm from farther north. Do you know what's happened up there? Do you know?" Impatience twitched every nerve in his body.

Ant shook his head slightly, as if not as interested as Gerard seemed to be. "What's got you in such a panic?"

"Accident. Many dead. I just got up and started walking. And kept walking. I'm probably dying. We're all dying. I just need some bread and some water and oh *no!*" His face scrunched into a mass of wrinkles, and his voice turned into a groan from the worst kind of despair, the kind that perpetuates life and thrives on resentment. "Oh *no!*" he kept wailing. "What are we going to do? Everything is lost. There's no point to living!"

"Hold up, friend," Ant said abruptly. "Slow down and talk to me. What happened?"

"I was in a caravan of people, maybe a dozen of us, a baker's dozen, maybe, and we had escaped what was once the great city of New York." He paused to catch his breath, though his head shifted back and forth as if searching the past for the story; his right hand's lax fingers typed at the air beneath them as if counting syllables. "We crashed, somehow. I can't recall how. But we escaped. New York is on fire! All day. Every day. Fires everywhere. Buildings crashing down to the earth. The tallest buildings falling apart. Bombs exploding. Dead bodies everywhere. *Everywhere!* I couldn't take it. My wife—she hanged herself. My kid left years ago, and we never heard from him again. All is lost. All is forever lost!"

Ant couldn't decide what purpose this man could possibly serve the camp. The nervous energy, the basic incoherence of his speech, recanting, recalling unusual scenes. Fire and brimstone. The end of the world. Apocalypse. Calamity. His sanity had been permanently rearranged. "Do you need a place to rest for the night?" Ant asked, offering the man the only solace he could.

"Yes. Yes, I do," Gerry replied.

Everything stopped, even birds swallowed their chirps, when Gerry walked into the opening at the unfinished end of the wall. His trench coat, hat, and glasses made him look foreign, somewhat futuristic, not like the others, whose dirty faces and stinky underarms blended into the fragrances natural to the land. As he raised his hands to the sides of his waist, assessing the quality of their survival, estimating their worth, his face seemed to sour while prepared to judge the accommodation unworthy of his superior bones. Ant placed his hand gently on Gerry's back to move him forward so that he and Tommy could lead the animals around the westerly front of the wall, five feet open before the forest claimed the ground for wilderness.

"*Oh,*" Gerry said. "Excuse you. Excuse me; excuse you." He bowed playfully at the bull, especially, which jerked its head upward and snorted as it passed this latest intruder. The horse high-stepped cautiously around the wall, jerking its head away from Gerry, who stood too closely to it.

"Who's *this* creep?" Jenna asked Mina, who stared and shrugged.

"Lord knows," she said. "But I'm not giving any more ground to newcomers."

"He doesn't look the type to take any."

"Don't be so easily fooled."

Under the thatched roof of the hale, near the nighttime glow of a crackling fire, some finished off the remnants of a recent hunt while others sipped hot water with a shot of fermented crabapples, listening to this ever-talking man telling troubling but informative tales about the waging of the great sectarian wars up north.

"Makes it feel like an antebellum cemetery down here by comparison," Ant said.

"It is. Truly, it is. The silence is deafening." Gerry paused to trace his steps back into his story. "Anyway—there we were. Confronted by this army, the likes of which we'd never seen before. Men and, I guess, women too, all dressed in black with very intimidating weapons in their hands. Rifles, I'd guess. Big, scary guns anyway. Never been my thing, but—" Gerry flopped his hands in the space in front of him and leaned back onto the log set there for support.

"And what about the people? Do they get involved with the politics of it all, or what?" Jenna asked.

"*Politics?*" Gerry exclaimed before she could finish. "No, no. No such thing anymore, darling. Nope. No politics." His arms, crisscrossed, swiping out like an umpire. "That hasn't been a thing for months, if not going on a year. It's just one incorporated army and many groups, parties, affiliates, rebels—whatever they are—and one constant war."

"Are you hungry?" Jeremy asked, feeling sleepy but wanting to be a decent host.

"No. No food for me. Thank you. I don't need much."

"Where are you heading?" Mina inquired.

"I'm kind of a wanderer," Gerry said. "But I have some good connects. We, I, you know, whoever, heard there was a group of people around here trying to make a settlement." He looked around, trying not to seem unimpressed with their progress, knowing how hard it was to do.

"What do you mean, whoever?" Ant asked, deeply wary of the man's interests and sudden appearance into their lives.

"You know, people, around and about. Here, there, everywhere. That was an old nursery rhyme, wasn't it?" He smiled at Ant. "Where are all of you people from anyway?"

Too proud of personal history, Mina couldn't help herself being the first to answer. "New England for years. Boston— summered in New Hampshire. Raised in Greenwich. But before everything went to shit, I was homesteading at my grandfather's retreat just north of here in old Carolina. He was a CIA man. Had the place decked in the latest survivalist tech from roughly fifty or sixty years ago, I guess." Unconsciously, she mimicked his speech to signal her likeness, her smarts and northern exposure. "But then I joined this group." Mina became lost in the visuals of her memory, seeing her grandfather in yellowed photos and what felt like real-life images her brain had copied. The house. The animals. The backyard, the creek, the pool of water. And, as entranced as she was by the remembrances, she couldn't track the past few months and why she had to leave, and grew silent.

The bull groaned. The horse brayed. As if warning everyone.

Jenna placed her arm around Mina, who smiled into the embrace, embarrassed by her need to say it all so completely, suddenly remembering the futility of social prestige. Her head bent and relaxed into Jenna's side while Jenna addressed Gerry directly. "It's been a rough time. I don't even think we know how long this has been going on for. Some of us remember; some of us don't. We're from here now, in any event."

"Yes, yes," Gerry said. "We are now in the era when we all exist in the nameless place that we find ourselves; existence become more of a psychological event, I should think. Who's the strongest? Who's the fittest?"

"Are you staying the night with us, or what are your plans?" Ant asked.

"I should be going soon," Gerry said.

"To where, though?" Mina asked. "I thought you needed a place to stay?"

"To rest. Here and there," Gerry said absently, more closely observing Devonte, Dolores, and Ronnie huddled away from the group. "Who's that guy, there?" Gerry asked, pointing at Charlie, who was sitting by himself, half in the firelight, half in the dark.

"That's Charlie," Jenna said gently.

"And those people over there?" he asked.

"That's my mother and father," Tommy answered.

"And the black one?"

"His name is Devonte," Ant said plainly.

"A relation of yours?" Gerry asked, implying the racial similarity.

Ant glared at the man's impetuous face. "No," he said.

"Devonte was a part of *our* group that came down from New York too," Tommy said.

"I see, I see," Gerry mumbled. "I meant no offense, no offense."

Increasingly suspicious of the man who had now managed to center himself as inquisitor among the group of natives who'd held sovereignty over the encampment, Ant glared at his gesticulations, hoping to make him nervous.

"You sure are a curious fella, ain't ya?" Ant said with deliberate country twang. As if indicating to Gerry knowledge of his notions of them as people, coming near to mocking it, Ant stared at Gerry with a kind of dumb look, smiling as if stupidly omniscient.

Gerry smirked, as if caught, somehow found out. "I do have a few questions, yes."

"And how is it that you have been surviving around here? It's no easy feat. You some kind of magician?"

Again, Gerry smirked like he appreciated the comment as a compliment of his self-assured ability to survive in any set of conditions. "How I live is my business," he said. "I survive, that's enough to say about it." There was a pause in the subtle confrontation. A space for reason opened between them. Some truth could be told. "I am here, I will say, to warn you."

The seriousness of his tone and his face as it changed too quickly from jovial irony to earnest deployment of his message had further destabilized Gerry's image in Ant's mind. He looked around the hale for Jeremy, who leaned against one of the sturdier columns, holding the small fortress up against the sky, but, seeing Ant's need for support, Jeremy nodded while continuing to pick at his fingernails.

"What about?" Ant asked, as if the answer would affect nothing.

"There are factions," Gerry said. His audience remained silent, listening for more. "Groups of people each comprised of its own interests." He paused for comments, but there was only silence, fear, and skepticism. "One in particular that's coming near you all, and it has its interests."

"In us?" Mina asked, interfering with the coolness of the unmoved men. Charlie paced behind her, beginning to mumble. Jenna attempted to console him to quiet him.

"Potentially," Gerry answered.

"And why would you know this?" Ant interjected.

Seeming hesitant, Gerry simply nodded, trying to formulate a response.

"What's the answer?" Ant demanded.

Gerry patted the air in front of him like he was trying to calm Ant's building discontent. "The answer is," he said, stopping to search the air for exactly the correct response if not the correct answer, "I hear things where I go. And I've heard something about people of your general location and description."

"So, you went for a little stroll to try and find us?" Jeremy asked, now more engaged in the conversation.

Without answer, Gerry said, "It's a violent group. Mostly men. One woman. A mixed-race woman," he said, looking over at Ant, whose face instantly registered the shock and deep confoundment Gerry anticipated, and he staggered, dropping one knee to the ground, then collapsing on all fours.

"Ant—" Jenna exclaimed, lunging to help him back to his feet.

"And she's with child," Gerry said then paused again. "And they're looking for you," he finished, pointing at Ant.

"Why him?" Mina asked quickly.

"That I do not know."

"Did they ask you to do this or contract you or something?" Jeremy inquired further, knowing messengers in warzones don't do things for nothing. He took a step too close into the odd man's space. Gerry appeared reluctant to divulge any more truth about himself.

"I overheard them talking, and—and—"

"And what?" Jenna demanded.

"And I offered my services, yes."

"They're rewarding you somehow for finding us and telling us that they are tracking us to locate Ant? Is that right?" Jeremy asked, confirming the dismal situation.

* * *

Gerry stood to leave, trying not to say more, as he had not been instructed to say as much as he had, though he figured honesty would give him the upper hand with the hearts and minds of these hunted folks. Omitting the core reason for which they were being hunted—that they were to be trafficked as slaves—he figured would give him the upper hand with the continual negotiations. Lying to the trackers, saying he'd told the band of survivors little to nothing, would give him the upper hand with them. As long as everyone was partially in the dark, he'd have control. The risk not only outweighed the reward but could get him killed, and this, he found exhilarating. As it was in this moment, the electric vibe of their elevated concerns, his power in making them feel some extreme elemental fear, energized his will to live, a will that otherwise flagged and atrophied in the mire of dull and repetitive survival.

"I must go now," he said, moving quickly away, batting at the air to indicate his need to leave and his core disinterest in violence of any kind, a simpering but ambiguous plea not to maim the messenger. His stilt-like legs further stretched their gait to increase the pace of their man's desire to get away. A mist had rolled in, shielding the actual direction into which he disappeared.

* * *

"What the hell just happened?" Jeremy asked, turning away from the villain's exit toward his companions.

Ant spoke from his position on the ground. "It's my child," he said. "She's carrying my child."

"What?" Jeremy exclaimed.

"That's why they're here," Ant said, becoming emotional. "They want to kill me for it."

"What kind of nonsense are you talking about?" Mina asked while Devonte, Ronnie, and Dolores had snuck into the circle of the conversation, just listening.

Ant sat on his rear, crossed his legs, and hung his head, recalling his short but frenzied time on the plantation. "And there she was—this gorgeous girl watching me, seeing how I moved, how I navigated the world, and it didn't make me nervous; it didn't make me self-conscious, but it was like being watched by a mother and a sister and a lover all at once. I felt protected by her. Loved before I loved with her," he said, rather awkwardly, trying to measure his phrasing around the women. "And then she followed me back to my shack, to my room where I slept, and it was later at night, and then she seduced me, and I was ready to be seduced, and it happened under the moonlight behind the shack where I slept." He paused. "I can still smell the sweetness in the pine wood that made the walls." Gathering himself together, he stood. "I'm sorry," he said to his friends.

"No problemo, paisano," Tommy offered from behind, clapping his hand onto Ant's shoulder. "We're a unit, here. They'll have to come through us to get to you."

"Easy on the boss talk, kid," Dolores suddenly said, rolling her eyes at her son. "I'm nobody's goon, ya hear me? I am for myself, and that's it." She swiped her hands toward the ground. "The rest a youse can eat dirt," she continued and mumbled her way back to the hale, where she'd sit on a stump late into the night, tearing raw, greenish strings of sapwood from living branches she'd twisted off of younger trees, complaining of back pain and lashing out at anyone who dared to care.

"It's time for us to get some sleep, I think," Jeremy said to Jenna, who approved. "We will deal with this in the morning. No one is coming now."

Ant bent his mind deeper into his shame, while the others took to the various spots on the campsite they'd taken for fair-weather sleeping grounds. Instead of retreating to his, Ant walked into the night. The mists had dissipated, and only the moonlight called attention to itself, bright as it was, illuminating the things around him, the strange place, the dystopic circumstances, the tragic loss of a more perfect world where peace could prevail and security was the product of a network of successful propositions, the ultimate will of a people, who had agreed to stand watch for, to keep and promote the quiet civility of a neighborhood. That was what he had known in the old and increasingly threadbare memory of the small town he'd once thrived in, that was once thriving. All that he knew. All that he had wanted to know. And now this reckoning. Was the plantation gang coming for him? Was she really with them? Only fantasy could remake the fear he'd initially felt. If she was there or coming near, he could rescue her, and they could be off on their own, away from these confusions and intrusions, rid of the insidious infractions of other men, to produce and to raise the future race in their grateful and gracious image, sober beneath the twinkling lights of heaven, awash in the storied past, willing to be retold within the omniscient, omnipotent, omni-passionate consciousness of the one and true and ultimate soul of the universe under which they would sleep without a sound to disturb them nor even a moldy fruit to blight their delights.

* * *

Morning came, and the usual rustling of the two pots and their lids, which Jenna had salvaged from Charlie and Roland's truck, worked like a blunted chime to welcome the rising sun. Ant opened his eyes upon the dewy wood, somehow re-spirited by the Lord, knowing what needed to be done.

Jeremy squatted near him. "You good, my dude?"

Ant smirked. "Yeah," he said. "I'm good."

"Devonte and I are taking the cow and the horse to graze in the field up the road."

Ant raised a brow. "You sure you wanna go off alone with that one?"

"Yeah, it's fine. He's come around. Plus, it's a chance to pull him more over to us and away from her and her bullshit."

"True."

"You wanna join?"

"Nah, I'm still gonna keep my distance. One of us should."

"Good point," Jeremy replied when a faraway look captured his expression, a double and triple thought, a trove of repressed emotions that had lain dormant by the excessive demands of survival. The depth of its possession removed him from the moment. Keeping distance from danger. Keeping distance. Staying away.

"Are *you* good?" Ant asked, but Jeremy didn't answer. "Hey, buddy—" Ant prodded Jeremy's arm.

"What? Yeah, I'm good."

"Don't get looney on me."

"Nah, I won't. Don't worry."

But the blur he faced was made of his past, rising like a clawing feeling, as though he'd never lived it, returning to remind the father of what he'd abandoned, and the guilt that overrode all other considerations for the day, and it began to occupy a quarter of each minute that he lived.

Devonte trampled the grasses in front of him, leading the shorter animal, though the cow was becoming rounder by the day; its midsection suggested a future when it would match the animal's overall width. The mare followed Jeremy, not needing the lead but perhaps remembering where they were going, anxious to fill her muscular cheeks with pounds and pounds of whatever greens could be found.

In the openness of the field, the one farther down from the first, grass grew past their knees but was mostly brown, which wasn't good for the animals.

"Look there," Devonte said, pointing to shorter but greener grasses a hundred yards off from the longer, hay-like patches.

"Good spot," Jeremy said, trying to encourage Devonte's better attitude without sounding like a patronizing father of the new law that was no law at all, only men in direct competition with other men. Casual, unmitigated violence was never in their lifetimes more of an option for the settlement of personal grievances.

The animals slunk toward the middle of the healthier patch and bent their heads to pull at the food with their thick, dexterous lips, like fingers and thumbs grabbing and pulling up weeds in a garden.

"What's with you?" Devonte asked. The calmness, almost like a sweetness, like one brother to another, filled the tone of his voice and brokered a peace between them.

But feeling caught, Jeremy blew off the inquiry. "Nothin', man. Just, you know, bewildered by it all."

Devonte chuckled quietly.

"What's so funny?"

"Ah, man, you know, it's just *bewildered*." He laughed. "It's such a—" His eyes cut to Jeremy, who appeared like a classroom dunce, threatening Devonte's more complete control over himself. He had to look away to keep from cackling like a maniac. "Ah, you know. It's just the word—" He fanned his hands up against the royal blue of the sky. "*Bewildered*." He looked again at Jeremy, who did not follow the humor, and he lost its comic spirit shortly then too. "Never mind, man."

"It's a gay word, yeah," Jeremy said.

Devonte regained the joke, having a further little laugh.

But then the quiet took over once again. Natural sounds filled the space in the air where voices would travel, passing one another like missives on unseen currents, better unread for better seafaring. But inside, Jeremy's mind wrestled with the possibility of relieving the pressures in his heart, and who better than Devonte? Likely not interested in his personal drama; likely not going to care about the pangs of patrician guilt in another wilding man of an unmoored place in time. Devonte leaned against a boulder, probably older than civilization itself, chucked off the ridge of a receding glacier that had tumbled down the Appalachian slope to land by its lonesome in a lower plain of the continent, at one time called Georgia, renewed as a land of the lost. What did he have to lose?

Jeremy's anxiety appeared to embolden Devonte, who remained silent, but in a look, in a sideways glance, in a naughty smile, by a quick cock of his head toward the man, he proved open and receptive to whatever it was that Jeremy needed to say.

He kindly said, "Whatever it is, man, I can handle it. I seen a lot of shit in my day."

The silence persisted as Jeremy looked to the distant clouds and scraped his boot against the dry dirt beneath them.

"I got somethin' on my mind, yeah," Jeremy said, returning the side-eye to Devonte, demonstrating his need to talk but his reluctance too. "But—"

"But you ain't too sure about me, I know. It's good, man. I don't need to hear nothin' then."

"I'm married."

"You and Jenna? Yeah, I know."

"No."

"Who you talkin' about then?"

"A woman in Europe, when I was in the Marines. I was stationed there before we were deployed to Taiwan."

"Oh shit, yeah? You fought in Taiwan? *Damn*," he said.

"Yes."

"I heard that was some fucked-up shit. Like real trench war fightin' an' shit."

"Yes."

"You seen men die?"

"Many." Devonte was on the brink of asking more questions, genuinely curious. "I killed many too, yes," Jeremy finished.

"I don't know if I could do that, man. I mean, hood fightin' is one thing. Most of those niggas don't know shit about how to properly fire a fuckin' gun. They kill, but it's, like, random a lot of the time. Bitches be wavin' a piece in the air, tryna be bad and look tough and start firin' 'cause if they didn't, they'd be lower than a bitch the next morning." He stopped to think. "But there's cold-blooded assassins there too."

Again, silence dragged them down.

"I—I don't know what—" Jeremy stammered. Devonte almost stood on his toes to hear it. "I have children with her, a girl and a boy."

"That's all? That's your big secret? *Man*, that's nothing," he said, disappointed. "I got like a dozen kids, probably. Don't know half of them."

"I mean—Jenna doesn't know."

If Devonte's mouth had been full of water, he would have spit it out. "*What?*" he asked incredulously. "She don't know you got *kids*? She don't know you're married? Now, that's some *shit*."

Instantly, Jeremy regretted telling him, knowing he'd spoken to the wrong man, somehow perversely needing this wrong man to break the news for him and take responsibility for the drama of it all; at least, Jeremy could and would place it on him.

"I need you to keep this between us," he said.

Wide-eyed, Devonte answered, "Are you serious? Of course, I will, man! This is too much, too, too much."

Walking back, taking the lead for the young cow, Jeremy resented his plan to drop the news on Devonte and use him to drop the bomb on Jenna, instead of being an honorable man and doing it himself. The truth of his private life had proved a continuous struggle, a vault of turbulent feelings that he'd trapped. Like Aeolus, minor god of the winds, who had trapped the noble air, and in keeping those cardinal forces oppressed, when unleashed, they'd make more of a mess of the world for its men than intended, losing their value in gentler purposes. Jeremy had no gentle purpose; there was no easy way to tell her this difficult news. He'd always prided himself on having no secrets with her, but this one, or these many he'd viewed as one, so deep, so dark in his negligence, Jeremy could not bear to imagine the betrayal Jenna would feel from the hit to the security that they had built between them.

At dinner, around the firepit, while the earth exchanged the sun for the stars, Jeremy monitored Devonte as he whispered conspiratorially to Ronnie and Dolores, the last two people he had wanted to revel in his troubles. Their looks, their sly and witchy looks, their laughter like that of a squad of adolescent girls—the femininity of the men delighting in gossip, transforming ideals into weapons of infamy, sent Jeremy's mind afield of friendliness. He smashed a log onto the fire, spraying embers into the surroundings, stinging the arms or legs of the conspirators. This was not how he'd wanted it to go.

"Watch it!" Dolores yelled.

"What the fuck?" Ronnie said as an echo.

Devonte stared provocatively into Jeremy's raging eyes, which shifted inside the light of the flickering fire, not softening but rounding out their wrath, resolving into the vacancy of a bitter grudge.

Charlie came into the circle. "You shouldn't do that, you know," he said to Jeremy. "You shouldn't throw things like that. You shouldn't hurt people like that. You shouldn't—"

Mina pulled at Charlie's arm to come away; clearly, his mind was fracturing, becoming unhealthier by the day. "Come on now, Charlie. Leave those guys alone."

"But he shouldn't do that. You know it's dangerous and could cause a fire and hurt people, and he—"

"We know, Charlie. We know." Mina spoke to him like to a dog who'd not understand any of it but the tone, trying to soothe and to quiet him.

* * *

Jenna observed the mayhem from the vantage of the hale, having portioned out her share of the evening's food, two or three bites of fatty venison, and removed herself from the main of the group. Ant had slain and slaughtered the doe before the first chill, not quite a frost, but that was on its way, creeping ever closer down the country. She thought how easy it would be for her and Jeremy to abandon this mess now that they had an inkling about true survival. Wherever this crew might be by the spring and whomever it might then comprise wasn't a gamble she was interested in taking. Try to convince Mina to join her and Jeremy as she would, Mina might prefer to go with Ant or with some other person who had yet to appear in their untethered lives, aimless like unmanned ships on an open sound, drifting out to sea one by one.

The log's explosive contact with the Vulcan embers, the violence by which her unconquered husband had hurled it, made no particular mark upon her concept of him. She'd witnessed it before, and he had never harmed her, nor anything sensitive or slight in means or stature so no bit of worry could overwhelm the fact of this violence, however much it had disturbed the others. *Perhaps they needed disturbing*, she thought. The reasons for those bursts of night fire would not visit the darker nooks of her cooling heart until the next day, when she and Mina agreed to manage the husbandry of their makeshift little farm, if they could call it that, by taking the bull and Sally Baby down the road to the first of the grazing fields.

"He's gonna rear up higher than you'd expect," Mina said. Jenna nodded like an eager pupil, happy to learn the processes of any activity that would contribute to a more plentiful life. Mina pulled the bull toward the cow. "We might have to bring him around more than once," she said. "Won't take but a few minutes, but you'll be out of breath."

"The stress alone," Jenna claimed, shaking her hands to rid them of sweat and twitches.

"Don't stress; it's just practice so you'll know how to do it in the future."

The bull easily strode to the cow's rear, then quickly lifted itself onto its mate and inserted its tubular penis; its hindquarters shook ferociously, radiating the scene with a static might, like Zeus at the center of Poseidon's quake. Jenna braced herself against the forward thrusts of the cow as it groaned. And then it was done.

Jenna waited for more. "That's it?" she asked, wiping her forehead of instant sweatiness.

"That would be round one," Mina said. "But you always have to look for signs she's ready for it."

"Like, if she wasn't—"

"Standing still is usually a good sign of her readiness, but she's already pregnant and probably too tired to move. The bull would be sniffing around her, becoming more agitated. Making groaning noises."

"Just like a man. Hopefully, you'll be with us, so I won't have to do this alone," Jenna remarked, looking off to the farther side of the road following some disinterested wanderers toward the old interstate highway until her sightline met Devonte's figure hulking toward the field where they stood; but he passed the spot, snickering to himself, losing his mind to the distance before him as he walked. "Where do you think he's going?"

"Who knows," Mina answered. "Who cares?"

Overhearing, he yelled, "None a yo biz-ness!"

"I'll never trust him, or any of them," Jenna said.

"And you ought to keep it that way."

"Except for maybe Tommy. He doesn't seem so bad," Jenna restated.

"Well," Mina added as she bent to rub the bull's neck, hoping to coax him to leave the field sooner. The cow stepped farther into the grasses to graze. "Don't be too sure of anything, I'm afraid. We should consult Jeremy and Ant to see about a plan for what's next, but for now, let's get these two back into the enclosure. Too many vagrants around."

The cow's stubbornness and not the bull's delayed them. Two suspicious gents came slouching and bopping toward them.

"Come on, cow," Jenna urged, pushing its backside. It raised its head, chewing. Jenna slapped its ass, and it mooed at her. The men advanced within the open space. Mina was twenty yards ahead with the bull. Jenna abandoned the cow to keep a safer distance between her and the hustling comrades. Mina lodged her thumb and forefinger into the sides of her mouth to whistle.

A high-pitched tweet came shooting out the center of her mouth, snagging Sally Baby's attention, and the beast began to saunter back like a gloomy child. The men started jogging behind Jenna, and she ran faster.

"Get the *fuck* out of here!" Mina yelled at the men.

They broke into a run and reached out within an arm's length of Jenna's long blonde hair, which bounced in a tail before their greedy, bloodshot eyes. She could hear their sniveling and their snorting, like pigs by a sullied trough impatient to satiate their lusts.

Jenna screamed. The cow ran suddenly northward, away from the camp. In an instant, a rifle fired two shots, and the emaciated men fell onto the dirt, both dead. Jenna screamed again as their extended fingertips dropped closely behind her feet.

"Who *did that?*" Mina called out as she, too, had fallen to the ground, ducking the violence.

"Don't worry," he said. "You're both all right."

"Tommy?" Jenna asked, looking up into his happy face.

"I heard both a you yelling, so I grabbed the closest gun."

"Thank you. They came up fast."

"Have to be a little more cautious, I think," he enjoined, like a western hero of a film that none of them had ever seen: Evoked like an instinct, aroused by the distress of a community's women, the toughness of a regular Joe could emerge like a mountain over a good man and loom like a darkness over worse ones. "Anyway, they're dead."

Mina chuffed, somewhere between a laugh and the expression of a deeper impression. "They sure are," she said. Sally Baby mooed, demonstrating her distance from the camp. "Oh *Christ*," Mina complained. "Now we have to go get *her* again."

Tommy joined Mina in stepping over the bodies to retrieve their most prized resource, more precious than the horse and the bull combined.

"Whatcha doin', honey?" Dolores asked from behind Jenna's back, shocking her out of the moment. "These men pesterin' ya?"

She laughed as she kicked the closest corpse. "There's no man who's worth a pound of his bullshit," she said, holding a bowl of fermented apples in her hands, pinching each one she could catch in the fruity slop and slurping it into her mouth.

"Your son is a good man," Jenna said, knowingly provoking her.

"You think he's worth a shit?" She scoffed. "He's been a do-nothing since the first!" She almost lost her balance for drunkenness that had combined with malnutrition and dehydration to make inscrutable her once tactical personal composure.

"He just saved us from these two," Jenna continued. "Did you miss that? Or are you too spiteful to see it. Or too drunk," she said, moving around the hefty old woman.

"*Hey*! You stupid bitch. Watch it, who you're talkin' to."

Jenna fought a rather murderous impulse to strangle the old wretch to death and leave her rump of a carcass wasted on the ground next to the other dead pigs, but the woman's giggling stopped her cold, like something beyond witchery had arrived. Something to be pitied and ignored. Something like madness.

"You know, honey. You're all alone in this world. Your man isn't who he says he is."

Jenna turned around to face her again. "What did you say?"

Dolores's wickedness spread across her face like a smile. "You heard me, little girl. Your man is a fraud. He's a liar and a cheat."

"Shut the fuck up."

"He's married, you know."

"Shut up!" Jenna yelled.

"Two kids."

Jenna tore from her tormentor, trying to control the sobs erupting from her heart. Somehow, she knew what Dolores said was true, and all the unfamiliar shades in Jeremy's face, all of his rage, his violence against the world at times, now made perfect sense. Feeling more like a placeholder than a spouse, like some sort of crutch, she wanted to flee the campsite for good but ran into

265

the woods toward the stream, to the site where Mullet was murdered by that beastly woman, to where the last thing she had loved truly and with untainted innocence was stolen from her life.

* * *

Jeremy followed Jenna with his eyes across the camp as she fled. Abruptly, he strode after her, knowing she had been told his secret.

"I'm sorry," he said, embracing her from behind.

"How could you?" she asked without turning around. "How could you lie to me all these years?"

"I didn't—I didn't think I was lying."

She turned to face him so he could see her disgust.

"My wife is not a sane person," he said.

"What do you mean *your wife?*"

His face wrenched further and became a mass of wrinkles. "I love you," he said through the tight clench of his throat, losing his voice before he could repeat it.

"What are you telling me, that our marriage isn't legal? That you never divorced her?"

All he could do was shrug. "None of it was exactly official."

"And your children—" she added before being silenced by her own grief.

Jeremy dropped onto the ground when she said it, and she squatted beside him and embraced him in his pain.

"You are too good for me," he said, still weeping, wiping spit that had accumulated at the sides of his mouth. "I would be dead right now if it wasn't for you," he said, rounding his sentiment, having regained his unimpeded voice.

"No," she said, trying to massage a tragic humor. "You would be alive; you just would have killed a lot more people."

Self-pity morphed into some in-between thing, and Jeremy looked to the brightening sky, creasing his brow, souring his mouth, thinking. "Yep. That's likely right," he said.

"What about your kids, though?" she asked, genuinely concerned for their well-being, as if being married to their father was enough for her to feel responsible for them.

"I'm honestly not sure they're both mine, but the girl definitely is. The boy might be another man's, but I had been raising Max like he was mine, and then I left the military and Europe for good, and I came back here, and I met you, and you were decisive about not wanting children at first, and I didn't know if I'd ever see mine again, and I just kept it all quiet."

"Max and—? What's her name?"

"Leilani. Lani for short."

"That's beautiful."

"I insisted on my mother's name." Tears returned to wet his eyes. "She looks like me."

"How do you know Max isn't yours?"

"Timing, I guess. I was there and gone a lot when he was conceived, so it's more difficult to say—" He stopped.

"What?" Jenna asked.

"He's also—he's much lighter skinned. I hate to say it, but Lani is more my color and—"

"Max looks more European."

"Yes, but I love him too. He's a sweet boy. Always so impressed by me, so happy to see me." Jeremy struggled to keep composed, remembering the boy. He wiped his eyes again, making his fingers wet, and then his eyes retreated to the sky for shame. "I will never forgive myself for leaving them."

"What about her?"

"My ex?"

Jenna nodded.

"She's why I left. It was a nightmare. *She* is a nightmare, and that is why I will feel horrible for the rest of my life. I left my kids with a horrible woman."

"There's nothing you can do about it now," Jenna said, a tad punishingly. "Why did you lie to me all this time, or not tell me?"

"Sometimes a man's guilt is all he's got to drive him forward. To make things better. To be a better man."

"And doubt is all a woman's got to stay safe," Jenna answered to the vacant space in front of her. An emotional gap had opened between them, previously an unpartable union, and whatever renewed doubt had informed her view of all things was now partially directed at him.

"I'm sorry," he said.

"It doesn't matter now," she replied. "All that matters in this is those two kids." With that, she rose to leave him to whatever thoughts might work within him and toward making him the better man he allegedly wished to be.

* * *

Devonte went missing. He'd not returned from his hike, a routine the other campers had begun to rely on to tell the time of day, usually mid-morning, an hour after a paltry breakfast from the dinner's leftovers. When there was nothing to eat, the timing of his walk was more obvious to them all. But on the day when he had disappeared, enough venison had remained for people to get a few good bites of meat to start, so his departure was less noticed.

But Mina remembered because he'd heard her and Jenna discussing his wanderings when he flicked back his head with a salty phrase.

"This was—what—two days ago, Jenna?"

"When Tommy shot those creeps running after me?"

"That was three days ago, I think," Tommy said.

"Was it?"

"Right," Ant said, having decided something. "Tommy, Mina, and I will head out tomorrow to look for him."

Chapter Four

"And we're sure this is worth it?" Mina asked Ant indirectly as she, Tommy, and he began a dubious search for Devonte. "We're sure we want to stray far from camp for this guy?"

"No, he's really not worth it, but I don't trust him, and I want to get a handle on his whereabouts before we move on with our lives. If he's nowhere to be found or injured in a ditch somewhere, fine. But if he's mingling with others, gangs of rovers or some bullshit, then I want to send him a message to stay clear of our camp."

Tommy lifted the rifle in his hands.

"That's right, Tommy," Ant said.

"Just don't feel too obliged to do anything violent with me around," Mina implored. "Otherwise, I'll head back to camp right now. Too many men. I'll be assaulted or kidnapped."

"I need you for just that reason. I need you to be the voice of reason with him, and to soften our intent."

"Thanks for letting me know."

"Now you know."

"Yeah, thanks." The silence among them began to fill, each adding their own type of worry to it. "And why are we leaving so late in the day? Not more than an hour left of the sun. How will we find the way?"

"We stick to the road. Gangs are more active at night."

A single hour passed as they hiked down the same meandering pavement, seeing and hearing nothing but the dead crinkle of brown leaves rustling as they scraped across the ground.

"There's nothin'," Tommy said. "Nothing but the road and the silence. And it's fuckin' cold."

Ant stopped to retrieve something from the one remaining backpack. "Here," he said, handing Tommy a sweater he'd taken for the hike.

"I'm good," Tommy said. "Give it to Mina."

"There's people around, trust me, I can feel it," Mina said, pulling the sweater over her head. "They're lurking. We're probably being followed or at least watched."

"But not for long," Ant said.

"What's that mean?" Tommy asked.

"I've spotted groups here and there along the way, inside the edge of the woods. They follow for a couple hundred yards at most but probably give up because of the rifles." Ant held his up. "Just keep walking. I've got a feeling he's nearby."

"That's totally absurd," Mina said. "I'm not taking another step based on that. We don't know what the hell we're doing or where we're going, and we're at least an hour's walk back to camp and, given the sun's position, not likely to get there before dark. We'll have to sleep out here in this god-forsaken wasteland."

"Mina—"

"I'm serious. What the hell are we doing?" Her anger grew more searing as she spoke as if finally taking the lid off a boiling pot.

"Over there," Tommy said, interrupting Mina's rant, pointing to a line of wobbling light climbing into the darkening sky, growing brighter and then dimming.

"That's the sign. Devonte's with whoever that is," Ant said, restarting the pace toward the launch site of the flare.

"And we just know this somehow?" Mina asked, exchanging her worry with Tommy, hoping for support in heading back or finding a place to settle for the night.

Ant turned away. "You two stay here," he said. "Make a camp on the other side of the road, just beyond where that bent road sign is. Go under those pines. There'll be soft needles on the ground. I'll scout out the scene and come back."

"Fine," Mina said, satisfied and dissatisfied.

Ant had already jogged fifty yards away. "How will you know where we are?" she called into the distance, trying to keep it quiet. Ant made a loud caw sound like an ancient Native American coordinating a hunt. Mina rolled her eyes before Tommy answered back with a caw of his own. Ant gave a thumbs-up and continued toward the unknown settlement deeper into the woods.

* * *

Smoke from the company's fire drifted through the lower branches of the thickening fir trees. Ant could almost taste the meat's drippings that fell into the ash beneath the spit, or so he imagined, and it made his mouth water. Combined with the sweet menthol of the evergreens, a warm and festive feeling aroused his aching soul, and he suddenly remembered the past, his family, his mother and grandfather and their many worries about him and his future. Out from this memory, he could hear the hearty sounds of men laughing, the gruff and tough camaraderie of robust men. He could sense their race in their fireside tones. They sounded jovial, perhaps celebratory, but what they might be celebrating was yet to be confirmed. Ant scuttled closer but kept his posture at half its height, hiding behind the bulk of the trees. Finally, he had a view of the scene. All white men milled about their camp: talking, drinking, cursing, smacking ass, roasting their meat like a platoon on leave.

"Did all those assholes get back on that flare?" one of the cooks called out, but no one answered. "Sons-a-bitches, no one ever hears shit 'round here. I *said*, did all those fucktards get back by that last flare?"

"*Yes*, dickhead!" two of the men near the smallest of three tents called back, laughing. "Why d'you care so much, you fat faggot?" The laughing increased by the continued taunting.

"Because I'm cookin' for all a them, you dumb cunts," the rotund chef mumbled to himself while he turned the spit, pushing his finger into the meat and sucking off the fat, totally at ease and unaffected by the language thrown at him. The vulgarity was jarring to Ant, but that was because he hadn't been exclusively bunked with men since he'd left the plantation, and then that simple thought shocked him as stiff as a frozen pole: *This* was the plantation gang? If it was, then she was here. His heart beat like an electrified drum.

More men stalked the roasting meat, some talking more seriously as if planning, others moving from station to station around the grounds. Ant could deduce at least one, maybe two, large wagons covered by tarps, underneath of which were likely stored all manner of goods and necessary items: tools, bedding, weapons. He could only fantasize about what lay beneath it.

Devonte's ingratiating snicker climbed above the din of the other men and danced its way atop those other voices, shimmying into Ant's ears. *What is he laughing at?* He was angling for something. *Is he not in danger?* Ant couldn't spot the man within the limited field he had to view the camp, but he heard him, and he sounded happy, like he was partying and having a good time. This was not the scenario Ant had hoped for; he'd have preferred to have found him injured in a ditch. Devonte was forming new alliances, it seemed, and one with a questionable cohort of men whose greed and interest in human bodies maintained infernal openness to a range of demoralizing possibilities.

"Heads up!" someone yelled, and the curtness of the shout almost provoked a shout back from Ant. "Comin' through," the husky voice added before appearing in center of his view. The man was holding a leash, leading another man with a sack on his head and his wrists tied behind his back. It was a skinnier white man, very much not Devonte, whose deep ebony skin was as rich as the black wood itself. This one was being led to the largest of the three canvas tents. Before the entrance flap was pulled back, the burlap sack was removed from the man's head, and Ant could see a bewildered, handsome-looking individual whose eyes darted around, from man to man, from object to object, seemingly in an attempt to understand where he was. Then Ant noticed him more closely, felt distracted by his expression, and a sudden concern almost lifted him from his feet to rescue the poor soul.

"*Charlie?*" he whispered, surprised and ashamed no one had noticed he was also missing. "*Jesus Christ.*" Something about the nature of the danger before him—the raging fire and its heat, blistering the skin on the carcass, the barbarian aspect of the night itself, the moment of seeing a man who'd become more like a family member than a friend, bound and restrained— eliminated whatever faith remained in his heart, and so he prayed to feel it again. Until it was too quiet, and he opened his eyes. All of the men had withdrawn into the smaller and middle-sized tents. Devonte was neither seen nor heard, and without warning, Ant imagined he was being watched; fearful tingles crawled up his back, raising his skin and the tiny hairs that grew out of it, so he retreated, hustling back the way he'd come to rejoin Mina and Tommy and make some progress down the road and away from this place.

"I just want to get down the road a bit, farther away," he told them, a hint of frantic impulse within the phrase.

"That bad, huh?" Tommy asked.

Ant repeated nothing but kept his eyes fixed on the ground, waiting for them to rouse to their feet.

"What did you see?" Mina asked, stunned by Ant's disturbance. "Is Devonte there?"

"Yeah, yeah, he's there."

"Wow," Tommy said.

"Charlie's there too."

"*What?*" Mina asked incredulously.

"Let's get moving before I say more."

The waxing moon, three-quarters full, brightly illuminated the trio as they traveled, somewhat hurriedly at Ant's quickening pace. Every object in sight was glazed by the pale sheen of moonlight, the kind of nighttime brightness that would last until dawn and convince a man of the devil and all assortment of supernatural wights.

"I can't believe we didn't notice that he was gone," Mina said sadly. "Ever since Roland died, he's been strange."

"Always seemed crazy to me," Tommy said.

"He wasn't when those two first arrived. But after Roland's death, he spiraled. Anyway, I feel terrible. What do you think they want with him?"

"Who knows," Ant said wanting to change the pace to a jog but not wanting to startle his companions. "Some kind of slavery. To sell to other groups. Any kind a thing is possible, I imagine, as long as someone is paying or trading or whatever it is they want in exchange for a man."

"Why are we walking so fast?" Mina asked.

"Because we're being followed."

"Oh fuck," she said and matched the increased speed until all three of them were running down the road, but within a few minutes of the exertion, all three slowed to catch their breath.

"I can't run all the way back," Tommy pleaded.

Breathing heavily, Ant stood facing the way they'd run from, looking for any sign of movement in the short distance, like someone hurrying to catch up with them. Their chests heaved. Their breath was foggy and white for the colder air. Tommy reinstated the pace.

"Wait—" Ant quietly insisted.

"What?"

"There's something back there."

"You're just freaked out," Mina said. "If they wanted us, they would have gotten to us by now."

He continued to wait in what felt like the silent death of advancing night.

"There's nothing there. Let's go. I'm tired, and we've some miles to cover," she said, now holding Tommy's hand.

Ant agreed, knowing they needed to keep moving, but something was there; someone was following them. They were being tracked by a shadow, and he would soon meet whoever it was in the light of the day.

* * *

The old hermetic lamp guided these seekers of something better back to their divinely protected enclosure. Once arrived, they plunged into their separate sleeping quarters and fell quickly into a deep sleep. Even Ant, in the disturbance of what he had witnessed, had found enough left in himself to prioritize the most basic needs and let it all go for rest. The necessity of not deluding himself that he was or could be in total control of all things had been a lesson at the beginning of this arduous journey into manhood. But whatever his mind had known, his body ticked like a clock and a presumption of fate invaded the hue of all things.

Come dawn, the sun began as a mere suggestion, like ambience from a screen viewer's wavefront, illuminating the rambling foothills, falling out from the exhausted landscape. Few moved about, but Devonte sat by the fire, slicing pieces of mushroom to boil in some water for a morning tea. Ant opened a single eye to the day and caught the man smiling toward the stump he used for a cutting board as he diced the colorful fungi, and Ant shot up in shock. Devonte amused himself with the sounds of surprise he had elicited.

Ant quickly confronted him. "What the fuck?" he asked almost as a whisper. "I thought you were with that plantation gang?"

The hulking ranger squished his brow with powerful facial muscles. "Nah," he simply said.

"I saw you. I fucking *saw* you," Ant insisted.

Devonte only nodded as if it might be true, but he couldn't say for sure. Charlie stepped out of a nearby bush and sat next to his keeper.

"Okay, now this is some crazy shit."

Subservient to his new master, Charlie stayed mute but took one of two new mugs from Devonte and returned to his little piece of land on the grounds.

"Where've *you* been?" Jenna asked as pleasantly as she could. "And where'd you get those mugs?"

Devonte ignored her at first, angry to have to explain himself, seeming not to have realized he might be pressured to, and stumbled when Jenna didn't look away. "I had these."

"Oh, *right*," she said, affirming his lie and walking back to her nest, flicking open her sleeping bag, which was becoming more worn by the day. The sleeping bags would need replacing soon, and none of the lot had been thinking about the full range of materials they would need beyond food and the most basic shelter. Was it trauma? Too-complete shock that kept them from seeing the truth that reimagining the world in the ways of the old was essential and not enough time was being devoted to seeing it?

"What's going on?" Jeremy asked the men, addressing his eyes to the fire to showcase the seriousness of his question.

Again, Devonte was still, until the pressure in the silence from the imposing Hawaiian broke his will to keep quiet. "What you mean, son?" He sucked his teeth. "I'm nothing *but* good," he said, sneering.

"Clearly, something is off here," Ant declared.

Over the wall, in the distance, someone ca-cawed just as Ant had done the previous night after spying on the horde of traders, the gang of barbarians, the more successfully organized group of men.

"What was that?" Jeremy asked. "That was a person," he said, answering himself.

"Yeah," Ant affirmed, staring so hard at Devonte he might have killed him if he hadn't looked away. Abruptly, Ant left camp to confront whoever it was calling him from the other side of the wall.

"Where are you going?" Jeremy asked, somewhat needfully. "Don't get crazy!" he yelled, but Ant was already beyond the barrier.

The more adrenaline pumped into his muscles, the more erratic and angrier he became. He hadn't actually thought they would have followed them all the way back to their camp. "Who's there!" he demanded and then waited.

Ca-caw, ca-caw—the volume proved the sound was closer. "Show yourself!"

A man in a dark gray trench coat pushed through the denser woods making the sound with his hands cupped around his mouth.

"Gerry? What are you doing here?"

"Antonio, how are you?"

"How did you know—"

"Just figured, as we do. Sometimes we figure, and we are correct. It's good to figure and to listen to figures and follow them."

Ant nodded at the mystery of it. "All right, fine," he said. "What's going on here?"

Gerry did not answer but wiped some dirt from his dress shoes, which appeared brand-new. "Can we have a serious talk?"

"I'm trying my best to cut to the quick of this, yes."

"So, I can be blunt?"

"Go on then."

Gerry mimed disturbance from Ant's impatience, like it wasn't aligned with his ways of gaining control of a conversation, cleared his throat, and started again. "I'll put it to you straight, Antonio." He thrust his arms out and framed the distant sky with his hands as if some abstracted goal he wished them both to imagine were hidden there. "Life is a set of conquests," he began, dropping his hands, pausing. "Especially these days." He walked away and urged Ant to accompany him. "Loyalty is a baron's wish and a king's command. The first is the longing of a weakling; the second is the duty of a powerful man. The first has no means to enforce his wish, so he continually fails to attract a following. The second enforces it with gold and steel."

"All right, so loyalty ain't real, is what you're saying."

"I'm saying it is *rarely* real. Everything a man does is for himself first."

"I know that—"

"He does nothing to intentionally jeopardize his assets, his territory."

"What's the point here?"

"In short, Antonio, you have a choice to make. The woman with whom you engaged in intercourse while working on Tidal Ridge Farm, some five months ago—"

"Are you their lawyer or something?"

"*Yes*," Gerry said definitively, "but I don't practice."

"That makes no sense."

Exasperated by his own humor, Gerry continued. "Your woman, the mother of your unborn child, her name is Luna, and she is roughly four months pregnant. She is owned by the Tidal Ridge Farm Company, where a Mr. Harlan Butcher presides as chief executive officer, founder, and sole owner."

"Is he here?"

Gerry interrupted his recital, its points of interest, and cocked one eye toward Ant. "Yes," he said. "The company is prepared to exchange her in full health for two of your men."

"My men?"

"Yes." Gerry turned to regard Ant directly. "You have been followed and watched for two weeks now, and they have concluded you lead this group of eight, six of whom are up for the negotiation, and that includes the three women."

"What? Up for negotiation. Like—"

"Yes, like that."

"No way in hell," Ant said.

"Then she dies, I'm afraid, and your unborn child."

The silence between them shook the world to its core as Ant processed the hideous choice. "I can't—" he whispered.

"That fella over there has already visited the camp, and he is prepared to sell the man called Charlie."

"But they were here this morning and—" Ant's confusion pushed him into a misery he'd not known before, a misery of experience and decision his grandfather had only ever tried to warn him about: the decision whether to treat men as moveable things.

"Apparently, Charlie is willing to be sold, which is atypical." Gerry emphasized the last word.

"He's lost his mind. He can't decide for himself. He's been troubled ever since Roland died."

Gerry simply nodded as if feeling empathy, but it was merely another gesture in the process of negotiation. "He's already signed the agreement."

"And what is Devonte getting for it?"

"A horse. Some food and water, supplies. Enough to get him to Clearwater Ways. A gun."

"Clearwater Ways?"

"A trading post, large, like a small city. The northern army is making its way south and clearing out any they deem disloyal or unworthy. So, many are leaving the far hinterlands for the towns to show solidarity with them."

"Like a cleansing—" Ant began to say.

"Yes. But different this time. A new hierarchy. A kind of reversal of the old. Led by all the surviving corporations that unified after collapse. And if you resist them—" Gerry made a slashing gesture with his forefinger across his neck.

"Corpo-fascist genocide," Ant said. "I read about this once." Gerry nodded, knowing the parallels from the deeper past but adding nothing. "Why do you work for these men? You don't seem like one of them."

"You are correct. I am not. All I can say is the northern army, while all-powerful and fearsome—they are rebuilding civilization better than anyone—but it is too dangerous. The treachery is terrible. These men, while they might disparage me, I disparage them in my mind—they are more consistent in their respect for what I can offer them."

"They're loyal."

"Yes," Gerry admitted. "But, beyond that, they have interests. Self-interest rules the world, my friend. And I am just trying to get back to my family."

"Where are they?"

Gerry had already begun to wag his finger abruptly. "I never discuss them," he said and looked over Ant's shoulder, seeing one of the women. "Who is she? I recognize her," he said, for the first and only time appearing confused and distraught.

Ant turned to see Dolores spying on them. "She's a part of our camp, but she's trouble. Crazy woman. Killed my friends' dog."

"Get rid of her then," Gerry said matter-of-factly; Ant simply looked at him, rejecting the notion more from natural disposition than purpose. "Think about it."

"Think about what?" Ant asked incredulously. "The choice between the mother of my child and that child versus the lives of the people I've been surviving with?"

"Think about it," Gerry said finally, merging with the woods, the lower branches of which baffled Ant's view of the legs and hoofs of their horses stepping up and down in restless repositioning of the weight they carried. Mina saw Gerry's backside as he entered the brush and snuck off after the man to question him herself.

* * *

"What does *he* want?" Dolores demanded as Ant crossed the threshold of the opening in the wall.

"Nothing."

"Bullshit!" she yelled, getting everyone's immediate attention. "I heard there were white men somewhere near here? Nazis? We have *Nazis* surrounding us? You ever hear about the *Nazis*? And what they do?" Ant regarded the older woman like an immediate threat. "What are you talking to them for?" she demanded.

"I said *nothing*," Ant replied firmly, waving off her madness and away from him.

Stunned, she went mute, to be comforted only by the insufficient mumblings of her husband; a shell of a man, clinging to the barest notion of his existence, he pulled her toward the hale to her seat there, hoping she would resolve her disturbance with what he prayed would be a bout of dementia, though she said, "Don't think for a second you can quarantine me or some shit, motherfucker. I own you. And I always will." Ronnie just nodded like he always had and patted her shoulder until her seething relaxed into simmering hatred.

* * *

After calming his wife, Ronnie confronted the situation. "What the hell is going on?" he asked, charging toward Ant.

Jeremy and Jenna stood closely behind him, not wanting to seem as desperate to know. Tommy sat stoking the fire, listening patiently.

"I need a minute," Ant said, feeling light-headed and nauseous.

"Sit here," Tommy said, standing to give Ant a fireside stump.

Ant waved that off too. "Thank you, but I'm all right. I'll be all right."

"We need to know what that was all about. Is what Dolores said true?" Mina asked.

Ant observed Ronnie's face, the pathetic expressions of which altered within each second and awaited some conclusion to the performance. "Sort of," he said. "Not really. But maybe. I don't know."

"That's just fucking great!" Ronnie exclaimed as if it was someone's fault.

Tommy bent his head as if burdening himself with the shame of the world, "Just—just relax," he said to his father.

"What else did he say?" Jenna asked gently, honoring the distress in Ant's face.

"There's a place," he said confusedly, trying to filter the information about Luna and his child. "It's called—" His mind stuttered through thoughts, trying to find the words. "Clear-something," he said. "Clearwater. Ways. That's what he said. Clearwater Ways. Said it was a trading post that got popular and became a big small town of sorts."

"Really?" Jeremy asked, suddenly reignited by the prospects of real life. "How far'd he say it was?"

"Don't quite remember, but I got the impression it was better to do it on horseback."

"Don't you even *think* about teamin' up with some white devil men," Dolores called out to Jeremy as if warning him. "You know what those evil bastards have done throughout history and all time. They should be castrated. Every last one of them."

"*Dolores*—" Ronnie implored, trying to seem like he cared.

"We don't need this right now," Jenna said to the older woman, which was enough to startle Dolores and silence her rant but not enough to keep her from mumbling angrily back into her seat.

"I hope they kill you all! 'Cause that's what they do," she called back to them.

Ronnie smiled and shrugged, genuinely embarrassed at this point.

"Ma—*Enough!*" Tommy yelled, fuming at his mother's aggression.

"The town sounds promising," Jenna said, returning the conversation to the important issues. "Is there something else?" she asked, sensing the deeper disturbance in Ant. "You look lost."

"I'm—I'm a little overwhelmed."

"What did he say, Ant?" Jeremy asked, equally concerned, not knowing if everyone was in danger or what.

"There's an army," he said. "Like a northern army coming down from New York and D.C. And they're killing everyone who doesn't fall in line with their new hierarchies." His four companions looked confused. "That's what Gerry said, but he didn't say what that meant exactly."

"That's no good," Jeremy said, alarmed by the news. "A genocidal army on American territory? What the fuck—"

"I don't know what's true and what's not."

"None of us do," Mina interjected, exasperated by the extremities.

"But he also said—" Ant faded out again.

"Yeah? What did he say?" Jenna asked.

Ant's eyes filled with tears, one large drop falling from each side. "A woman I had a romance with on their farm many months ago is with them. And she's carrying my child."

The group nodded quietly, knowing this. "That's what you said before. So, it's true?" Jeremy asked.

"I guess so. I don't know. I didn't see her there last night." He looked over at Devonte sitting near the fire, laughing next to Charlie, who was stone-faced. "I saw both of *them* there, though." Ant eyes were wide, red, and wary.

"Devonte and Charlie?" Jenna asked, surprised.

"Yeah," Mina affirmed. "That's what Ant told us last night. I didn't want to say anything. Something, uh, *weird* is going on with them."

"I heard Devonte's laugh inside their camp. That same laugh. Like he was chillin' with his boys." Ant gestured to the man who was holding his stomach from laughter, seeming to taunt Charlie. "And Charlie was led out of a tent wearing a hood over his head with his hands tied behind his back," he finished, not able to say what else he'd learned about it.

"What the fuck—" Jenna exclaimed, but the diabolical nature of what she'd heard prevented her from action.

Every soulful heart in the camp froze at the revelation, inhibiting further inquiry. The evil it would take for both Devonte and Charlie to behave in these ways was too dark and too deep to excavate, as if to neutralize concerns. If both men were agreed to the arrangement, how could any of them criticize it? The moral relativism from the prior age had yet to die out. None could take a clear-minded position on the issue. *Live and let live* had prevailed for even the most perverse propositions, like a voluntary slave and his spiteful vendor being free to demoralize one another.

* * *

The southern placement of the winter sun and its lowered arc across the spectacle of the skies made it more difficult to identify the time as noon, as peak day, but Devonte's inner clockwork proved more efficient to the task and told him to move his body out of the camp.

"Let's do it, bitch. Let's *go*," he murmured to Charlie, aroused by every inch of power he now held over the man.

They slunk out of the camp; the one hulking and menacing, filled by the vigor of spite, the kind needed to dehumanize another; the other slight, wan, full of self-pity and resignation.

* * *

The rest of the survivors noticed them walk off but reserved their fears for Charlie, unsure how to approach the issue or how to reason with either, especially Charlie.

Mina spoke once they'd passed the barrier of the wall: "A great writer once said: To be given dominion over another is a *hard* thing; to take dominion over another is a *wrong* thing; to give dominion of oneself to another is an *evil* thing."

No one else spoke but understood the message—meaning, what they witnessed was a form of evil, and taking it on was a huge responsibility, and none of them wished to do so but rather wished to focus on the salvation of their own lives, instead.

"Couple of fags," Dolores squawked from her perch.

Jeremy couldn't help but laugh. Jenna gave him the *stop it* look that all wives sometimes give to their husbands, and he tried to relent, but that seasoned more tension into the matter. Devonte and Charlie's leaving on such an impudent venture, Dolores's vulgar ad hominem, and everyone's suspicions about the truth of it all infected the group with sorrowful laughter, revealing how limply remained the veil between sanity and madness.

"Oh my god, we're the evil ones," Tommy said, wiping the wetted sides of his mouth.

"The whole thing is terrible," Mina added.

"What whole thing?" Jenna asked.

"The whole *goddamned* thing!" Jeremy yelled above himself.

"We don't even know what's what anymore," Tommy said.

"How could we? When's the last time you read the news somewhere?" Jeremy asked him.

Tommy thought but shrugged. "No clue."

"Half the world could have imploded by now, if not the whole damn thing," Mina added.

"Serves us right," Jenna said in the ponderous silence that followed.

* * *

In the remaining afternoon, most milled about, working the camp's daily routines to keep alive its subsistent, life-saving purposes. Dolores worked a pile of dogbane that Ronnie had collected to make rope. Half a hammock fell from her lap to the ground, as she wove the rope Ronnie had rolled in his hands by the method Jeremy had taught him. Mina and Tommy whispered to one another as if conspiring a plot against the rest.

Jeremy and Jenna consulted Ant about how he would like to proceed against the threat.

"We want to help you, Ant, but we have been talking, and we've decided that we'd like to move on to Texas," Jeremy said. "We got stuck trying to survive here and forgot about the prospects that lay ahead in other parts."

Ant nodded, understanding, but disappointed.

Jeremy saw the slack in his friend's face. "We're *sorry*." He became emotional. "I'm not one to wimp out, you know that, but . . . but Jenna and I—we can't, we don't want to risk our lives anymore. We need to go—" He began to ramble from guilt. "I've got some family in Dallas, at least I used to. It's better than staying here, pawing at the ground, trying to get through another day. For what?" He stopped talking, observing Ant's silent resolve. "You all right?"

"I'm fine. I'm alone again, you know, man? I just now got the deepest feeling of my whole life of how completely alone I am."

"That's not true. You have her and your child," Jenna offered.

"Luna?" Ant tried not to be offended by these two whose move against him felt like the deepest betrayal.

"Yes," Jenna said, pleased to hear her name. "Luna."

"*They* have her. I'm stuck on the other side of the nightmare."

"True, but we are going to help you."

"*How*? You said you're leaving!" Ant said, more inflamed. His friends remained silent, as if acknowledging the platitude as a lie. "What if they only want to kill me? To see me dead for their entertainment? All because I broke one of their damned rules!"

Jenna and Jeremy could say nothing to ease that fear; all they could do was stand by his side in this single, trifling moment. But secretly, even that was a failing promise against the future prospect of a family. Their continued survival won out overall.

"But they want me to trade you all for *her*—" he said, hesitating after having said it out loud, revealing his own temptation to treachery.

"I see," Jeremy said, understanding the depth of their own duplicity, feeling it himself. "Well, we could go along with it, pretend like we are willing—like Charlie—"

"But he *is* willing," Jenna insisted, worried Jeremy might renounce their plans to escape.

Before Jeremy could finish imagining a way out of the puzzle, the sun had set, and a flare shot high into the air. It silenced him as they followed the bright zigzag of the lit smoke.

"They're here," Ant said. "That's gotta be less than a quarter mile away."

"Shhh," Mina called out and cocked her head. "I can hear them. They're closer than that. They're shouting. I can hear the hoofs of their horses."

The noise increased seemingly by the thrum of Ant's beating heart. A pounding drum preceded the horde. The horse grew agitated and stomped around the yard. The cow huddled by the corner. The bull stood in front of it, alert and at the ready. Like a battering ram, a twenty-foot wagon like a prairie schooner broke through the crusted mud holding the center of the wall. Crowned by a large bonnet, spiked staves as thick and long as a man protruded from its undercarriage.

The horse bolted into the forest.

"No!" Mina yelled, seeing the horse take off.

The bull groaned.

Weathered men on horseback galloped around the wall's farther ends and into the camp, flanking the wagon in single rows on both sides. A dark-eyed man who sunk in recess beneath the stiff rim of a black cowboy hat stole their attention, and when he stood to his full and fearsome height, the starkness of his skin and the blackness of his eyes hushed his men, who grew silent in deference to the icy control with which he'd won them over. The onyx-black eyes told no stories; his hands, blanched white but bloodstained to the wrists, conveyed no courtesies. Like a great shark, his head moved side to side, surveying the handmade baskets of goods and supplies, the dug and glowing firepit, the sturdy and still-standing hale, the meat on the spit and dried hides on sticks, the competence he could perceive in the campground home of this exhausted group of people. Capable human beings who would fetch high marks at trade.

"I'm impressed," he bellowed, his voice deep and coarse, scowling at the broken world. Harlan Butcher's blood-tinted hands were big enough to strangle a titan, and he took pleasure in the awed faces of the few who were privileged to see them displayed without losing their lives. The men on horseback arranged themselves more tightly on Harlan's two sides as if his arms outstretched like a calvary ready to embrace the world in a death grip.

"Thank you," Ant replied, instantly receiving the man's full attention.

"You must be the one we are looking for," he said. "The mixed one."

"Yes, sir."

"But that blonde one sure looks good to me. I'd like to take her behind a tree an' abuse her little backside till it's as red as your face, little man," one of the rowdier rangers said, directing his lewdness at Jeremy.

Harlan scowled at the transgression, and the man shut his mouth.

Jeremy's face dropped, expressionless, and his eyes grew dark with murder.

"That big brown one don't look too happy about that, Daryl," another one said.

They all smirked or chuffed in their superior posture. Jeremy had to take it. Jenna stared at the ground, suppressing the urge to grab one of the rifles.

"Fuckin' Nazis!" Dolores suddenly yelled from the hale. "Kill the fuckin' Nazis! Damn you! Damn you *all!*"

Unimpressed, the men exchanged irritations and curled lips and twisted brows. "Who the fuck is that?" one of them asked.

"She's one of us," Ant said defiantly.

Harlan cocked his head at Ant like at a bug he could smash with his fists. "Do you know who I am?" he asked him directly.

"Sort of—yes," he answered.

"Who am I?" Harlan asked.

"You're a Nazi devil! Racist!" Dolores yelled back. Harlan laughed at her.

"You're from that plantation where I worked that one time," Ant said.

Harlan nodded as if disappointed by the answer. "The orchard still smokes black, brown, and gray. We lost that farm," he said. "The Great Satan's northern army passed through and burned it to the ground." His tone waxed nostalgic. "Every tree. Every bush that bore fruit. Every cow. Every dog. Every pig. Every barn. And almost every man but us." He gestured to the men who surrounded him. "Mostly innocent men," he said firmly. "So now, who am I?" he asked rhetorically. "What have I become?" He paused to smell for traces of death in the airstream. "I am an eater of men. I am the consumer of towns. I am the vacuum into which everything will go. I will finish by devouring the air." He paused. "I have been provoked." A deep, ungodly laugh improved the finale of his speech until his men joined in, snickering and chuffing, disturbing the effortless simplicity of its message. Harlan rendered one swift motion of his right hand, and the man that side of the master unsheathed a machete and calmly trotted toward Dolores, who stood to face him, fearful and moaning.

"Ronnie, *get* him," she yelled and pointed. "Stop him!" She pushed her husband in front of her. Ronnie's head came off in one swipe of the sharp metal. Jenna shrieked but covered her mouth. Dolores stood like a block of arctic ice. And in another instant, her headless body flopped onto the ground.

"*No!*" Tommy yelled.

"*Quiet* or you're next," another man said from his horse.

Mina squeezed Tommy's hand as a plea to remain silent, so they could live and have a chance at a life together. He relented, bowed his head, and squeezed his eyes shut.

"Bring her out!" Harlan commanded.

Luna emerged from behind the curtain of the bonnet behind him. Humiliated, disgraced by the objectification, she kept her eyes down, trying to find the feet likeliest to be Ant's to find the courage to lift her head. Gold-complected, rosy lipped, a natural purple rouged her cheek; smokiness gathered on the lids of her fathomless eyes: a beauty incomparable to all but time. The entirety of the crowd gazed upon the milkiness of her breasts, the womanhood of her distended womb: motherly nature poised to bring forth newness to a surrendered world.

"Ain't she a show unto herself," one of the rangers said.

Ant stared in anguish and swelled with a love he could not have sensed before seeing her, and she carried his child. Pride, fear, hate filled his mind and coiled round his bursting heart.

"You can have her back," Harlan announced, "on the conditions you been instructed upon."

Ant nodded.

"Then you know what I ask. Put her back," he ordered abruptly, and Luna was quickly pulled behind the curtain and back into the bonnet. Ant kept silent but wanted to howl in the pressure to preserve their three precious lives. "Come to my camp," Harlan continued. "Be there before sundown tomorrow, the same place where you hid in the trees the other night." Then he gave a roar like a gallant hurrah, and all the men jolted awake, kicking their horses into action. The driver of the wagon slapped the reins on the rumps of his team, and the lawless gang disappeared around the ends of the wall with a speed that appeared faster than their arrival.

"What the *hell*?" Tommy asked, virtually traumatized.

"Tommy," Jeremy said. "You and Mina should go for a walk while we—"

"It's fine," he said, resolved to the grief. "I will help."

Ant, Jeremy, and Tommy then examined the two corpses of Tommy's parents, drenched in blood and unrecognizable, both heads missing. Tommy squatted in front of Dolores's body and grabbed her ankles, reflexively lifting her legs as he stood to drag the corpse into the woods where she would rest. The other two men carried Ronnie by his hands and ankles, following Tommy.

Where there was a natural gulf between a fallen fir, its trunk, the diameter of which was the length of a small man, and a muddy cliff, they placed the bodies, one on top of the other, and as gently as possible for Tommy's sake when a large, dark figure passed within Jeremy's periphery. He cast his head quickly to catch it, but it had disappeared. The other two men, oblivious to the motion, had begun to hike back to the camp. But Jeremy was drawn toward this thing, this shadow in the woods like a pulsating spot, dark with promise and potential, and a private future hope, when it moved again. It was the horse. Cautiously, he approached the skittish being. Carefully, he stepped closer, inching into its periphery. It whinnied, sensing him, and stomped its front hooves, sending a message as if revealed as a divine spirit guide given the duty of the couple's conveyance. Jeremy's fingers quaked as he reached out to soothe the noble beast as it bowed its head to receive his touch, and a fated dynamic sealed itself between them. Once he'd secured the mare and returned to camp, he would tell Jenna of his plans for them to escape that night.

At the edge of the woods, Tommy and Ant searched the ground near where the bodies had lain. The heads were missing, maybe carried off by some hungry coyotes now licking and snarling as they licked the bloodied messes. A mediocre effort, they gave up the morbid search to return to the reduced group, as if shrugging at the blight of the constant death they'd endured. But they turned back, feeling Mina come up behind them, having carried the heads away herself to save Tommy any further trauma.

"What do we do now?" she asked the men.

"We go to them," Tommy said, totally dedicated to ultimate destinies. "And we bring the bull and the pregnant cow as offerings in exchange for Luna and the dignity of our lives."

* * *

In the morning, they rose with the mists steaming off the pores of the heaving earth. Jeremy and Jenna were gone.

"It's like they never even existed," Mina said, acquiring further disbelief the more she searched the area for the two survivors.

"Strange," Tommy added. "I thought they were different. Like they'd be with us to the end."

Ant examined the rim above, where the leafless treetops touched the sky, not cursing his friends but begging the blessings of God that they would make it, not minding that they'd left, and so he prayed for their safety and good health. "God, bless them in their journey," he said, hushing his other companions' complaints.

"What are we going to do with all of our stuff? We just leave it here? Abandon everything?" Mina asked, suddenly worried about their fates, sensing the worst.

"Yes, we must," Ant said. "If we end up somewhere worse, we can do it again."

"It's a lot of work," she said.

"It is," he answered. "You don't have to come with me."

"No, we're coming," Mina said, defiant of her own hesitations, anxious to take her own next steps. "Let's put the harness on the bull and go."

The remaining three citizens, the ones who'd held out to fight the longest, wearily strode down the northward road to Harlan Butcher's realm, primarily discussing their strategy—how might they trick these ruthless men?

"I say we offer the animals. That should surprise them. And then freely give ourselves over to their service. It might be the only way," Tommy offered again.

Mina felt distant from the other two, wishing she had stayed at her grandfather's compound and lived out a quiet life. "What if we just walk away from the whole thing?" she asked absently.

Tommy regarded her like she might not vocalize her doubts. "We can't leave Ant all alone to face this."

Ant suddenly stopped. The bull finished three paces and nuzzled its snout against his lower back. "I will do this by myself if I must. I don't want either of you to risk your lives for me.

Mina, you seem confident one minute but then talk about escaping the next. I do not want either of you to feel obligated to me. You are free to go. *Please.*"

Mina couldn't answer, as if considering the version of herself with which she most identified: the fighter or the loner?

They began walking again. After a mile of listening to the ends of barren branches—beginning to sprout tiny buds in the longer days and shorter nights—tap against one another in the wind, their feet scuffing at the dirt on the ground, Tommy made the decision for everyone. "We do as I suggested. They get the animals. We save our lives for the moment. We enter their world, do what they ask. We're obedient. We are polite. We ingratiate ourselves. I lived all my life surrounded by brutal mafiosos. You knew my mother. But not just her. Men, mostly. Wouldn't think twice to cut your eyes out of your head. Smooth politicians otherwise. Always knew how to say the right thing. Meanwhile, they were conducting weekly murders of their enemies and antagonists. I know these men. Just follow my lead."

* * *

Whatever meat the pirates were roasting on their iron spit, the three suitors smelled the hair from off its hide before they saw the blackened carcass. Someone among them had the skills of a smithy, one of many crafts and trades this group had diligently cultivated on their farm. Formerly respectable tradesmen who had rebirthed the fundaments of a working society had been defamed, demoralized, removed from the heritage they'd given their lives to create, and now behaved like skillful beasts ready to kill, ready to deny, ready to give their lives to destroy the existing world.

Like three kings from foreign lands combining gifts with otherworldly power, the three suitors appeared in an attitude of prostrate beggars in the midst of the chaos of working men and stood with their heads lowered, awaiting notice. Ant had to suppress the urge to search for where Luna rested.

Two sentinels approached, both armed with machetes, daggers, and rifles. "Come with us," the bigger one said in a gentleman's tone of voice, striking Mina as uncommon, as if a man with a civil tone should've known better.

"I'd be surprised if any of these men could say the alphabet," she said under her breath, trying to insult him.

Having heard her, the sentinel turned an evil eye, raising his hand like he might slap her hard across the face, demonstrating his hate. Tommy shook his head at Mina, motioning for her to keep quiet. They neared the medium-sized tent, and just before the marching sentinel reached the entrance, the flaps pulled open allowing for a smooth transition from outside the tent to inside of it.

Harlan held court, seated on a kind of chair made of tree stumps in the center of the space where a rectangular table ran perfectly lengthwise from him, hewn from a large tree trunk by the master carpenters in the company. Tommy noted the level of ability in the furniture. Harlan consulted a rudimentary map with an advisor, trying to figure the hottest area of threat from the northern army.

"Excuse us, sir," the gentleman sentinel said.

Harlan dismissed the strategist and smiled warmly. "Welcome," he said. "We appreciate the cows and the bull and take it as a signal of your submission to us." His ingratiating tone mismatched the sadistic reality of his words.

"Where is she?" Ant blurted.

Harlan shook his head. "No, no, no. That's not the appropriate way, son."

"Son?" the consultant, like a general, blurted out, questioning the good nature of the language. "That's just another dirty nigger, like her."

"That's *enough!*" Harlan yelled, incensed and enraged. Red-faced, he said, "You say that word again, Weyland Jones, and I'll have your head on a pike by dinnertime."

Weyland finished rolling his maps and punched his way out through the tent's flap.

Inside of Ant, frustration swelled beyond tolerance, but he oppressed its more complete expression. Confused by the mix of messages, Ant could barely decide what to do, say, or even what to think next. Mina showed a similar distress. Tommy tried to keep his cool.

"Bind their hands. Take them to the big tent," Harlan said finally, after centering himself. "We will deal with this later."

Ant struggled to free himself from the grip of the sentinels' clutches. Anger restrained his better judgment, and he squirmed out of the hold and punched the man trying to bind him more tightly. Another tackled him to the rough dirt, rubbing his face against the rocky ground.

"Get the fuck *off* of me!" Ant yelled, inhaling dirt afterward, coughing as they tried pulling him to his feet, but he remained on the ground, exhausted.

Harlan waited until Ant could look up to see him standing above. "That's enough. Take them away."

As Ant, Mina, and Tommy were shoved into the largest tent, many heads turned to face the newly acquired chattel, some covered with burlap bags, some not. All three were forced onto their butts, hands bound behind their backs, their heads uncovered, leaning forward to keep a more comfortable position, feeling thoroughly abused by their own hope.

"I keep going around in my head," Mina said to Tommy. "If we ran away like Jenna and Jeremy, I couldn't forgive myself. If we hadn't come here, they would have tracked us to kill us; so, we came with an offering, hoping for better minds to win the day, but surely, we knew we'd end up like this, waiting like pigs to be slaughtered?"

"Keeping calm and cooling our heads is going to be the most important thing," he replied. "Keep your eyes peeled for Gerry like you told me before," he finished, more quietly. "We have an out there if we can make it happen. I'm close enough to him in kind that—" As too many heads were cocked in his direction, Tommy ceased speaking. Anything could be used against them for any kind of benefit. Prisoners would likely tell on them for planning, just to get another bite of food or a second sip of water.

"Why'd you do it? Why'd you give yourself away?" Ant asked the man to his right.

"I don't know," he said. "I guess I feel like I have nothing left in the world and nothing to do. No point, no purpose, so I might as well give myself over to service."

"This isn't service, Charlie," Ant said. "This is slavery. Trafficking."

"Same old, same old then, I guess," Charlie said. "How'd you end up here? I didn't think you'd let yourself be caught."

"They have something very important to me, and I have no choice but to play their rotten games."

"I see, though I can't imagine what that could be. These men don't keep anything worth a hero's valor. They trade it, sell it, kill it—whatever. Whether it's a human being or gold or what have you. You know the big irony here? Their greatest threat is the northern army, but the northern army is also their biggest client. By proxy, of course. But—whatever."

"Not surprised," Ant said.

"Shocked me, though. But foolish innocence has always been one of my greatest weaknesses."

"Now *that* surprises *me*," Ant said boldly, giving them both a reason to crack a merciful smile, but it was wiped clear by the obvious deprivations of hope. Ant's face reverted to its typical, worried look as his eyes darted around, less seeing or searching for anything and more frantic at the lack of vision to escape. "They have the woman I am meant to marry who carries my unborn child," he said frankly.

"You know," Charlie said. "There's, I think, a pregnant woman down at the other end of the tent." Ant instantly focused and scanned each body leading to the back. "It might be your person."

Animated by her closeness but enraged by his lack of power, every muscle, each tendon—all manner of strength in his body—conspired with the hellish gall in his guts to pull apart the rope that bound his wrists, and he lurched up to his feet, stumbling over a few bodies, one of whom was unmasked by the commotion and, alarmed by the action, began to scream for one of the guards. Ant tripped before he reached her, though she sensed him and turned her covered head in his direction. But before he could get to his feet, a guard had intervened and bashed Ant's head with his fists, knocking him cold onto the ground.

* * *

In the passing weeks, Ant floundered in and out of consciousness at Harlan's orders. Having his cargo of human capital sweat it out inside the tent was a form of suffering almost worse than the turpitude of slavery they would eventually face. Mina had become a babbling mess, mostly dehydrated and starving, curled into a fetal ball many feet from where she'd initially sat. Charlie hadn't moved. Tommy had shuffled his body closer to Mina's and tried to soothe her with his voice alone. They languished in the fiendish torment of life before the final boundary of death.

Until one night. A body lurched around the camp, one that never stayed longer than the duration of its intended appointments. A somebody whose cooperation was multivarious, multi-dimensional, in flux. A man whose mantra was minimal action until action was the bare minimum of survival. A man whose family had finally been secured inside an armed federation and word had come to him, conveyed by the swiftest shadows, that it was time for him to return home. Pulling back his hood, he handed Tommy a jug of fresh, cold water.

"Give this to her too," he said, pointing at Mina. He handed Tommy a fresh baguette with two slices of ham and cheese folded inside of it. Gerry put his finger to his mouth, keeping Tommy from asking any questions. "Dissolve it with the water in your mouth before you swallow." Then he pointed to Ant. "Tell him it's gonna be three nights from tomorrow in the middle of the night. I will tell the guards Butcher has ordered to lay off the beatings so he can revive. We will only have a small window until the men figure this out. Even then, huge risk. *Huge*." He stopped as another prisoner shifted in his sleep. "The dogs don't react to me because they know me. But as soon as we are up and moving, they will bark like crazy." Gerry cupped Tommy's ear to avoid waking any of the prisoners. "I will bring three pocketknives: one for me, one for you, and one for him." He wagged his finger toward Ant again. "We will cut as many free as we can to distract the soldiers. I know where the horses are kept. You and Mina together, Ant and Luna together, and I will get one: three in all. And then we take the northern path through the woods and gallop off like the dickens." He nodded furiously, waved frantically as he backed away to signal his departure, recovered his head with the hood, and disappeared into the darkness.

"That man will sell you out the first chance he gets," Ant said later in defiance of Tommy's speech about the plan. Luna sat at his side, holding her stomach but mute.

"He's trying to save our lives," Mina said, having revived from the brink. "He's brought us food and water two nights in a row. Tomorrow is the day."

"He works for the northern army, I know it," Ant insisted.

"What proof do you have?" Tommy asked, almost hissing. "It doesn't matter anyhow. He's all we got. And Mina and I are going with him to Clearwater Ways."

"We'll take the horse, but we are going our own way," Ant said. "I'm not trusting a single man anymore."

Tommy nodded. "But you will help us to escape, help with the plan?"

Ant was silent, not wanting to stay, not having a plan of his own. "Yes," he said. "We have no choice but to trust him for now." In the silence, Tommy nodded, relieved that Ant had relented. "But we are going our own way once it happens."

"That's fine," Tommy said. "You will be free to do what you want."

* * *

Night climbed the walls in opposition to the setting sun, and they waited. Mina bounced her knees Indian style. Tommy regulated his breathing. Ant sat stock-still, holding Luna against his warmer body. She had inched her way back to his side now that darkness would prevent detection if the guards were to inspect the tent, which they hardly did past midnight, needing sleep themselves.

Within hours of nightfall, Tommy grew increasingly despondent, unconvinced that Gerry would follow through with his word. Ant's skepticism of the man had wormed inside Tommy's thoughts and nibbled at the buds of hope he'd desperately protected. But then he heard him and then he felt him at his wrists, cutting off the rope, and his heart fluttered by the adrenalized infusion that pumped from there, filling him with inexpressible joy.

"You go cut Ant's and Luna's. Give this one to him and tell him to start cutting the other prisoners' bindings. Help him until all are freed and then move to the back and follow me to the horses. Mina, you bring Luna and follow me."

Ant was ready and quick-acting. Mina took Luna by the arm and led her to Gerry. The men slashed at the ropes and nudged people awake, whispering, "You're free. *Go!*" Many of the fifty-odd prisoners had been released from the bindings and began to leave the tent to roam the campground. A few ran off immediately. Some wandered as if hallucinating. A couple began to moan. One began to scream hysterically.

"All men up!" one of the primary guards commanded. The entire company of rangers jolted awake, grabbing their knives and guns to meet the invader or whatever challenge advanced before them. "Prisoners are escaped! Prisoners escaped!" he yelled repeatedly, rousing Harlan to his feet.

"No one escapes or no one lives!" he shouted.

"It's the Jew!" one of the men shouted back. "The Jew is behind it!"

Enraged, a bloodlust shot to Harlan's face as he searched in the dark for the perpetrator. "Give me some light! Give me *light!*" he raged.

Horses' hooves stomped at seemingly every angle. Torches were lit. One man doused the central bonfire with fuel, and it erupted as a massive fireball, reflecting the many frantic faces—soldiers, guards, prisoners alike—running in chaotic disunity of interest.

Tommy and Mina on one horse had galloped away while Ant took longer helping Luna onto theirs, being spotted by guards. "I will slice you open like a pig!" Ant growled at them, finally getting Luna seated atop the animal. Then he nearly yanked the hair out of the horse's mane and willed every muscle in his body to pull himself behind her while slashing his knife at the faces of the men who'd accosted them.

Harlan spotted Gerry fumbling with the lead of his horse, not realizing the help he needed to mount his steed. Harlan grabbed the man by the back of the hair on his graying head, and Gerry let out a pulverizing groan.

"Caught you, *Jew*," Harlan hissed. "And now you die for lack of honor!"

"No, no. *No!*" Gerry implored, begging, frantically grabbing at the space in front of him.

"*Die!*" Harlan screamed finally as he plunged his knife into Gerry's chest, relentlessly stabbing and destroying his heart, making minced meat of the flesh and bone arranged there until the body folded into itself, and Harlan dropped it like a needless husk to the ground, howling from the hellish pit of his hate.

Ant and Luna galloped toward the west, deeper into the darker night.

* * *

At daybreak, the fatigued couple slept soundly near the warmth of the horse, who had lain its body among hearty brown grasses speckled by greener sprouts of the earliest flowers. But Ant shot awake, knowing their trail would soon be tracked and pursued by a small brigade of frothing killers. Luna slept peacefully, finally nested in the love and security of that love Ant provided. Her eyes blinked open, feeling the baby kicking her inside. Placing her hand gently on his thigh, she reached for his and guided it to her womb, where the baby pushed its foot against his flat palm. Ant smiled and then dropped a tear in the first joy of fatherhood.

In the distance, a horn blared, a nineteenth-century reveille famous at racetracks and summer camps for boys, now, and again, a sound to spring young men to war. Ant's confusion stalled his better thinking, horrified by the image of two groups in constant pursuit of their lives.

"We have to get moving," he said, and she nodded, understanding that the endless threats required endless movement. She stepped into his cupped hands and climbed onto the horse's back. Using the mane, Ant swung his body behind hers. The horse grunted in its displeasure but regained its composure shortly, stomping around the grasses to adjust itself to the weight. Instead of simple tooting horns, they now heard war sounds, deep and guttural reverberations either from an army of men or a kind of otherworldly horn they'd never heard before.

The horse began to trot at Ant's command. Luna bounced, trying to hold her child in place.

"I'm sorry, but we have to gallop again," he said. She clenched her eyes shut and nodded as he delivered the call to the horse to get moving, and they took off even faster.

Out in the open field they rode. Newly along the path to freedom. Close between the world of forgotten lore and the unknown potential in a future realm. They ran. And ran. And ran, as the horse galloped onward. The wind blew sorrow from off their faces, though they were unsure of the likelihood of their survival. But they flew. And kept flying.

Like an infinite line of soldiers storming onto an endless battlefield, the northern army appeared half a mile in the distance. Line by line, row by row, like an oceanic wave of militaristic might they came in pursuit of all things, trampling and disquieting the world at their feet.

From the local south, Harlan and his band of bastards broke through the forest and galloped mercilessly toward the solitary horse, set to collide with the rows of militant men but obsessed by their sights on the young couple.

"He-*ya*!" Ant called to the horse to gallop ever faster. Luna clung fiercely to the mane of the beast, wrenching her face, streaming tears, crunching the terror coming up from her guts with gritted teeth, when they approached another wooded zone that appeared like a mirage behind a hill. The horse slowed to a quickened trot.

"Stop!" Luna cried out. "*Stop*! Stop the horse!"

"What? We can't!" Ant implored her to persevere.

"I can't," she said. "I just *can't* anymore!" The horse did stop, and she slid off its side and waddled into the woods to find a stump to rest her broken soul. "I *can't*!" she yelled at everything, her voice breaking into sobs, infinitely deep.

Ant's fear and urging transformed to protect his love as he comforted her. "We don't have to run anymore," he said.

"I can't," she repeated. He nodded. "It hurts too much, and the baby—" She gestured to the horse and the intensity of the ride.

Ant surveilled what soon would be the stage entrance of their demise. He could hear both groups raging, clanging, charging. Perhaps, they had begun to fight, he thought, he hoped, since it would buy them time. "Come on," he said, and he took her hand and led her into the trees, feeling drawn within its budding arms. Not knowing what they'd do or how they'd end up, they continued in good faith to walk toward a shred of shared destiny.

But within less than an hour, the angry men's voices, the vengeance of time, encroached upon all the goodness in the world, and their hearts sank. Luna sat. "It's no good," she said. "They're coming for us. They're going to get us."

"No," Ant said, refusing to give in. "We can't give up. We can't—" He buried his face into his arm, fighting the shame of warm tears. She bent her head, defeated when he looked up.

Deeper into the woods a chimera. Surrounding its fancy, a glimmering. Then she saw it too. And like children drawn to a secret, they were pulled toward a blaze of divine light. Approaching it, they saw a tiny black center, swirling, growing ever bigger around until a large black disc had materialized in the thickening air, white and yellowing flames flaring off its rim. A deafness, a muteness filled their ears, and they could hear nothing. Silence pervaded the uncanny drama unfurling before them.

And then, like a film, it began to play, or suddenly, the black became a mirror, and they saw themselves, the woods around them, the armies of men slowly gaining ground against all hope on Earth with weapons drawn and bloody. The mirror became an image, a home, a comfortable and welcoming room, like a family room, and Jenna appeared in its light and noticed them looking in. She quickly gestured to Jeremy, who entered the frame. Ecstatic, they smiled, waving the two old friends inside and into the safety of their home, welcoming them to the new world. Jenna took up their newborn child into her arms and pivoted to show them her face. All smiling. Waving them in. Ant and Luna sweetened each other's eyes by eyes, not a trace of disbelief, not a morsel of doubt, no need to question hope, and Ant took Luna by the hand, raising her up to step inside and through the circle as it began to shrink. One of the soldiers began to scream and to rage, beating his chest. The lot of them pulsing by defiance behind them. Within the threat, Ant could discern Devonte's haughty and horrible laugh. Harlan's murderous howl. The relentless stomp of the marching northern army. And suddenly Ant could hear the whole of human history, of suffering and blight, of wrath and pain and death bearing down upon him until he, too, stepped across the threshold of the closing disc, looking out and into our eyes, winking, and stepping out of sight.

THE END